MW01538248

Freedom Challenged

by

Karl Manke

Author of

Unintended Consequences

The Prodigal Father

Secret, Lies and Dreams

Age of Shame

The Scourge of Captain Seavey

Gone to Pot

The Adventures of Railcar Rogues

Harsens Island Revenge

Re-wired

Hope from Heaven

(Also known under movie title "Best Years Gone")

All of Karl's books and ebooks are available at: karlmanke.com

Curwood Publishing, LLC

Publisher: Curwood Publishing

Cover Design: Kirsten Pappas

Copyright ©2021 Karl Manke/ Curwood Publishing

All rights reserved.

Reproduction and translation of any part of this work beyond that permitted by Sections 107 and 108 of the United States Copyright Act without the permission of the copyright owners is unlawful.

ISBN 978-1-7338029-5-6

The author and publisher have made every effort in the preparation of this book to ensure the accuracy of the information. However, the information in this book is sold without warranty, either express or implied. Neither of the author nor Curwood Publishing will be liable for any damages caused or alleged to be caused directly, indirectly, incidentally, or consequentially by the author in this book.

The opinions expressed in this book are solely those of the author and are not necessarily those of Curwood Publishing.

Trademarks: Names of products mentioned in this book known to be or suspected of being trademarks or service marks are capitalized. The usage of a trademark or service mark in this book should not be regarded as affecting the validity of any trademark or service mark of Curwood Publishing.

All of Karl's books are available at karlmanke.com

Remember your

Freedom!

[signature]

Preface

It may be noted at this time that for every person born, there is never a time when a person is free. The womb is the first prison to hold a person captive. As in all instances, a case is made that this tradeoff is necessary for the well-being of the fetus. It can also be said with more certainty, the only time we people are of the same mindset is on the day we are born—we all come out of the womb free for a brief second, all being created in the image of God. From that moment on, in various ways, each of our minds, bodies, and souls becomes the property of others to corrupt with their well-meaning ways.

In the next phase of childhood is when the family begins to train a child to accept the norms and mores of their particular brand of culture, social structure, and religion—American, Chinese, Russian, German, Dutch, or African Fante. Following this training comes capitalism, socialism, communism, fascism, and so on. Then comes the question of the family's degree of religious fervor under the denominational umbrella of its choice, whether Catholicism, Lutheranism, Methodism, and thirty-nine thousand other Christian "isms" around the world, all vying for the souls of God's children.

In the African Fantes' case the likely religious choice is spiritism or Vodun, a form of Voodoo. In each case, this is seemingly done under God's direction for the well-being of the individual's mind and soul. Every child born of man has come in kicking and screaming against this training in one way or another, but usually succumbs under the penalty of a physical or mental spanking. In each instance a child is taught that to resist this training is a sign of the child's inherent evilness and must be dealt with in various ways depending on the culture and its brand of religion.

Chapter 1

Uprooted

It's 1814 in Ghana, Africa. A young Ghanaian man and his younger sister are busy tending a garden plot outside their village. A strange sound has brought their work to a halt. His eyes hold an unusual blank, unblinking expression unique with intense listening. The disturbing sounds of panic, mixed with screams of torment, are distant but distinct. In this moment, the only physical sensation this young man is aware of is the trickle of sweat making its way from his underarms to his waist. Even the normal sounds of the jungle have ceased in deference to this intrusive milieu, resulting in a singular, uninterrupted cacophony of human distress. There is no doubt the chaotic sound is emanating from the direction of the village. The young man's mind races for a probable cause. He recalls hearing his uncle discussing a problem with the village elders as a possible foundation for the disturbance. Charges had been brought forward by a neighboring village made up of Ashanti people toward his village consisting of Fante people accusing the latter of harboring two Ashanti men suspected of burglarizing graves. The accompanying gunshots tell him this is more than likely the case since the Ashanti are much more powerful than the Fante and possess firearms.

The young man senses the sound of the fearful sobbing of his younger sister. The gunshots have her terrified. It is without question that the endgame resulting from this attack is well known among the Fante. As has been true throughout history, a reprisal for nearly any infraction is for the victor to enjoy the spoils. In these African cases, this means the conqueror will seek retribution by selling the conquered to the slave traders for guns and ammunition. Supplying European slave traders with able men and women has become a

6

common practice over the years by nearly all tribes. The immediate benefit of increased power and wealth through a payoff of the latest in weaponry at the expense of the vanquished, continues to feed the practice. The Ashanti Kingdom is more than likely going to be on the receiving end in this case.

The young man's immediate realization of danger quickly turns into an urgency. "My mother and my brothers and sister must be undergoing this attack," is his first thought. The overwhelming need to save them from harm replaces any thoughts of hiding or running away. With both hands on his younger sister, he pushes her away, ordering her to stay put.

"You stay hidden in the forest and don't follow me. I'll come back and find you," he instructs.

Ignoring the certainty of the outcome, the young Fante man charges down the well-worn path from their garden plot to the village. What he meets is inexplicable. An overpowering force of Ashanti militia armed with European weapons powered by black powder are clearly in command. This superior firepower is hardly a match against the spears and clubs of the Fante. Many of the village huts are already burning as the Ashanti warriors continue to burn, loot, plunder, and rape. Spotting his family hut as one of these shooting up flames, the young man rushes forward only to be met by two Ashanti militiamen. They throw him to the ground and immediately bind him with cords. Surrounding him is a sea of tangled bodies of men, women, and children, bound with ropes and helplessly sitting or lying on the ground. His eyes are rapidly scanning for his family. He spots them only twenty feet away. His mother is being dragged off to the side by two Ashanti warriors. There is no question what the end result of this will be. Rape of nearly any female—regardless of age—is a recompense awarded to the conquering warriors. This practice is a given regardless of any protestation.

With all of the other chaos, his concern quickly turns to the welfare of his younger siblings. They have been left alone since their mother's fate. He spots them with an uncle who is also being bound with cords. As though this is not disturbing enough, in a reflexive turnaround he spots the sister he had ordered to hide. Having disobeyed his orders, she has followed him back to the village only to find herself forced by an Ashanti warrior into a hut that has not yet been destroyed. The young man is certain that his young sister is about to meet the same fate as their mother. With his mind in whirl, he is unable to complete or react to these thoughts before he's slammed with another atrocity to struggle to try and process. His younger brother's, two and four years of age are left crying and defenseless.

With everything moving so fast, he discovers he is being jerked to his feet and a wooden apparatus being fitted around his neck. It turns out to be a double wooden yoke with his neck through one portal and a fellow villager's neck through its twin. The two portals are connected by a two-foot-long shaft. The purpose of this design is to dissuade the wearers from attempting an escape. Unable to determine the further fate of his family before he is herded into the center of the village along with at least half of the village men and a handful of the younger women, he succumbs to his seeming destiny.

With his neck squarely set in its trap and barely an opportunity to take a last-minute search for his mother and siblings, he casts a last gaze across the carnage left by the warring Ashanti. All he can do is stare. It saddens him. A sick feeling of powerlessness is overtaking him. Lost in the moment and before he can process anything more, he feels his tethered partner begin to jerk him forward. The order has been given to begin a trek that can only lead to more despair.

Chapter 2

The First Trek

The young Fante man's name is Kumi Ackah. He is nearly twenty years old. His father is expected to provide food and living quarters in his mother's village but because of him having other wives and families, he is not expected to raise his own children. In the tradition of many African tribes, his mother's oldest brother has provided the male role model for Kumi. It is this uncle who Kumi caught sight of as he was being dragged off by the Ashanti. It is giving him some comfort that he will be in the company of his uncle but at the same time it saddens Kumi that his mother and his younger brothers and sisters will be left to fend for themselves.

Considering the history of this region, slavery is very often the endgame for any young man caught unawares. As a young man has grown from puberty to near adulthood, so grows the price on his head. At Kumi's age, he is in high demand by plantation owners both in Africa and America. To the Ashanti captors trading with the Dutch slave traders, he will easily bring at a minimum a musket, an ample supply of black powder, and a hundred musket balls. Many African kingdoms have grown wealthy by their involvement in African slave trading. Some kingdoms have reported the slave trade is the "Ruling principle" of their people and "The source and glory of their wealth," and most of them would be hard put to give it up. The African king of Bonny in the Nigerian delta proclaimed slavery to be "ordained by God."

9

Getting back to the plight of these captives, the first leg of this forced march is familiar as it is still in their home territory. As evening arrives, they are moving out of familiar terrain. For at least six hours of their trek, they have been given no water or food. Sweating and the lack of sufficient water ensures their captors that there would be no stops to relieve full bladders. With darkness making its way, each captive is given a handful of maize and beans and allowed to drink from a stream. The wooden halters are left on purposely to discourage any attempt to escape. Kumi and his partner, tethered together within this apparatus, are forced to learn how to eat, sleep, and relieve themselves as a team. This inconvenience compels each of them to use their time to concentrate on the simple comforts of life rather than plotting an escape.

With Kumi's mind preoccupied with this ill-fitting collar rubbing against the tender skin around his neck, the slaver's time proven program of placing just enough physical distress on their captives is proving to be successful. There doesn't appear to be any chance of relief with the collar's removal appearing anytime soon. Kumi is doing the best he can to grab a handful of leaves here and there to stuff between his neck and the rough halter. After a restless night, at the crack of dawn they are given an opportunity to relieve themselves and fill their bellies with water, but no rations.

Regardless of the destiny of these men, the jungle has also come alive. With all the waking sounds of its inhabitants, it's as though these fellow creatures are impervious to the fate of their jungle colleagues. The weak are not considered as being any great loss; they seem to have accepted the law of the jungle where only the strong and smart survive, all the rest are dross to be eliminated as soon as possible.

The captives are quickly ordered to huddle in a wad in the center of a nervous group of Ashanti warriors, all armed with muskets, ordered to guard them. This gives each of these captives an opportunity to get a better idea of who is in their group.

Kumi immediately sets his eyes on a village girl named Abina. Their eyes do not meet as she is crouched with her forehead resting on her knees. She is the daughter of his village chief. His heart has been hers since they were children. Abina is a few years younger than Kumi, and the fact that she was has been groomed by her father to be married to a royal from another village has made her unattainable. As he looks at her saddened demeanor of defeat and dejection, Kumi's heart grows even wearier. His gaze leaves Abina for the moment, drifting around with his mind to others in their group. In particular, he spots his uncle. He looks so small and lost in this setting compared to the strong mentor Kumi has come to know. Kumi has grown up with them all. Some, he has fought against; others, he has been friends with, but like any community, they all belong to each other. In this setting, they are all consumed with their own thoughts. Given that their fate is not specific, rather it's unfolding for each of them with each experience.

The Ashanti leader of this band of warriors is busying himself with a party of returning guerrilla scouts. (This top dog is also a slave himself. He's under the command of the chief of the Ashanti. He had been a military leader in another conquered tribe and is now assigned to perform the same task.) It's obvious they have information to share. Within a few minutes it becomes obvious where all this edginess is coming from. Suddenly there appears at least a dozen white men—and white they are—bearded, blue eyed, and blond haired. Their movements are particularly cautious and guarded. This group soon proves to be a band of Dutch slave traders. They have been doing business in this part of Africa among warring tribes long enough to know not to let their guard down for a minute. Survival is all about being in a state of awareness. What these merchants of misery don't immediately perceive is often the most dangerous. What has happened in the past is a troupe of a vanquished tribe has staged a sneak attack against them in an effort to free relatives and fellow tribesmen. There have not been enough successes to have this become a common practice but the attempt has happened often enough to bring an extra sense of caution.

11

In Kumi's short life, he has only seen a handful of white men. To add to their mystic, his tribe's Okomfo (shaman) has depicted the devil with a white face. As a result of this portrayal, Kumi has been leery of white men. This group of white men's suspicious actions bring even more fear to him. This can be attributed to the belief system of the Fante. Much of the time, the Fante's spirit world influences their sensory world to a greater extent than their sensory world influences their spirit world. In other words, their interaction with jungle spirits determines who they are as a people and as individuals. Kumi has a very bad feeling about this crew of light-skinned, light-haired men dressed in clothing made of materials his tribe would never be able to replicate. They are so strange that he is having a difficult time determining if they are really human beings. He is very much aware that he does not live anywhere near their world of understanding.

It's equally as puzzling on the side of the Dutch traders in dealing with a possible subhuman people they consider as godless heathen. (The irony of this recent mindset is the original purpose of the Europeans coming to Africa was to introduce Christianity to the Africans in order to ensure salvation for the African peoples' immortal souls—now the Africans are considered as soulless.) There is nothing they understand about these tribal people—nor do they care to understand—except they bring big profits in the new world as laborers, and they have given little or no resistance to make that happen.

With the negotiations over, the price settled on an ample cache of muskets, musket balls, and black powder, the Ahanti and the Dutchmen begin the process of exchange. The wooden neck halters and rope tethers are replaced with the Dutch's preference, chain collars, each connected to another by an additional four-foot length of chain. The finished design has produced a serpentine weave of hapless humans on a forced march to their final demise. For most of this drive, these men have been silent, buried in their own thoughts.

Kumi is not an exception. When he had first seen his uncle among the captives, it had lightened his heart to realize he had not been abandoned and was not alone, but now the realization that his mother and siblings will be at the mercy of all that's bad and dangerous without his uncle there to protect them, Kumi has become sick with worry. The division of responsibilities between his father and uncle have been traditionally well-defined. His father provided a hut and some support, but the uncle provides the day-to-day protection of the family. Now, they are at the mercy of all those who would do them harm. He prays silently to the spirits to guard his family.

Abina is also troubled. She had been preparing for her wedding when this startling interruption made everything other than her survival insignificant. Her fate had been in the hands of her father, the village chief. He is a typical African male who is quick to let it be known he comes from royalty as his father and mother had been slaves to the king in a now defeated kingdom. (It has been traditional for a family that had been in service to the king to become a part of the royal house.) None of this means anything to a slaver; Abina will sell no better or worse despite her royal Ghanaian rank.

There are eight females in this group of captives. The only thing that has protected these women from the inevitability of being raped is the stern commanding postures the warrior in charge of this unit has ordered. He has let it be known that they will be delivering healthy captives. He knows if any of these men in his charge damages even one among this chattel, the Dutch will find reasons to cheat them out of their asking price. He is also well aware what would await him from his own chief if he should return shortchanged.

Nonetheless, Abina remains wary of any unusual moves by these warriors in an effort to single her out. As a young woman, she is coming into her own. She is a bit taller than the other females and is capable of carrying herself with more self-assurance than the others. This confidence has come from her ranking among her village. Both her mother and her father hold high positions.

13

This alone sets her apart immediately as desirable. Having had a night without an assault, she nonetheless has no reason to believe these pale European men aren't just as lustful as their darker counterparts. Not accustomed to this kind of powerlessness, Abina rails against her fears. She realizes if she demonstrates fear or weakness, she could be viewed as an easy prey. For a young woman, this reality is disquieting. Other than a concern for food and water, the mounting worry of a sexual assault places an extra burden on her whole situation.

The same chains are placed on these eight females as the males. They are placed in the rear as the men are led out in front. Within an hour the water they drank earlier has made its way to their bladder. Rather than consider that they will be given an opportunity to stop to relieve themselves, one by one, they begin urinating while walking. If it doesn't make them unmarketable, their Dutch captors are indifferent to any of their personal needs. They have a job to do. Transferring this faceless commodity to the Atlantic coast is just another aspect of their slave trading operation. As most people of this era, they give in to the idea that at different times in everyone's life, there are either winners or losers—in this instance, it's their turn to be the winners.

It's been pointed out already that Kumi and Abina are well acquainted with the understanding that power is freedom; it's been verified in their tribal pecking order. They are also aware that few people possess that kind of power. They have resolved themselves to a life of limited power in one form or another.

To a large extent, the Dutch capturers have also been programed by well-meaning teachers to think similarly. They have been instructed to be at the disposal of their king, who is believed to have been appointed by God, to do whatever they are commanded to do without reservations. This includes trading in slaves. After all, people in communities throughout the world rely on their religious and secular leaders rather than their own experience to set a moral tone for life. Besides, slaves bring a high price on the American market and this fills the coffers of the Dutch kingdom guaranteeing economic power much as it does the African kings. In these cases, leaders believe the end justifies the means. Therefore, human trafficking remains an economic reality in all cultures of this period.

Within each culture are built-in penalties for those who may attempt to remember themselves back to that long-ago moment of freedom where their souls remained unencumbered with the fears of the world—where their souls still retained the pure image of God. Those who sense this loss and try and reclaim it are often given labels like rebellious, noncompliant, insubordinate, eccentric, possessed, or blasphemer, . . . In any case, they are dangerous to the norms and mores of their predominate culture and are generally dealt with harshly—often through such means as banishment, imprisonment, excommunication, shunning, ridiculing, and in some extreme cases being put to death. Freedom of thought is squashed by their religious as well as their secular teachers who are all worried about the disruptive effect freethinking behavior will have on the common people.

The concept of enslaving Africans by Africans is understood and accepted, resulting in the African culture absorbing the practice. The consequence of submitting to this practice for Kumi and Abina and the other Africans results not so much on being slaves as much as from their concern with the unknown aspects of their captivity or how uncomfortable it could become with the Dutch in charge. African to African slavery is more like an indentured servitude where freedom is restored at some point. This kind of relationship, as they have understood it throughout their lives, is now bringing with it a strange new chapter—beginning with the fact that people who have been caught up in it are never heard from again.

15

Chapter 3

Elmina

With a two-day march under the Dutch coming to a completion, Kumi and the rest are in sight of the sea. It's a phenomenon that they have only heard about but never witnessed. Even more absorbing, and at the same time foreboding, is a huge white structure looming before them. It's larger than any manmade building they have ever seen or could ever imagine. It's the legendary castle built several centuries before by the Portuguese to facilitate the exporting of African gold. They named it Elmina ("The mine"). Now days, it's controlled by the Dutch government. It's used to house and export slaves to America.

These jungle captives are demonstrating fears where they are reluctant to enter into such a foreboding building. At this point, the Dutch captors show an impatience toward the reluctance of their newly ensnared chattel to readily be herded into the prison's interior. The Dutch guards begin to kick, shove, and drag the Fante captives by their neck chains. What Kumi and the rest meet here is unprecedented anywhere in their African lives. African to African enslavement doesn't require the brutality the white slavers are employing. There is a beginning and an end with African enslavement. This does not seem to be something that is held out with this brand. One by one, the Fante captives are placed in the center court on what appear to be several platforms. The area is filled with white men with their attention directed at each of these black men personally. Kumi can't help but feel severely intimidated by all of these strange happenings. He suddenly is aware of the chain connecting him to his fellow being released. His group of males are herded into a cluster on one end of the

16

courtyard with their hands still manacled. They are met by some other blacks (castle slaves) who have been instructed to clean them. The first thing they do is strip newcomers or cut off their clothing. Supplied with a barrel of water, they begin the process. Potential buyers don't care for the smell of urine and crusted feces hanging on their potential property. Among the men, Kumi has been randomly selected to be placed on one of these blocks first. With the neck collar still attached to the chain, he is led to one of these platforms. He is next met by another white man who inspects him for cleanliness. Several other white men follow. Satisfied, they begin to probe his body, examining his arms, hands, and legs—even his feet. One grabs Kuni's hair, pulling his head back to position his head in a way to insert an appliance that forces his mouth open. He then finds several of these men examining his teeth. They're speaking in languages he doesn't understand and understands even less what is about to happen to him. He is taken aside where he is forced to his knees under the powerful grip of a very large white man. By now, Kumi has become aware he is totally powerless to prevent his captors from determining his fate. Regardless of how confused he is, he doesn't wish to give the impression of the slightest reluctance to follow their next command. The directive is soon indicated by a tug on his leash that he's to kneel. In his ensuing encounter, he experiences himself being held down by two large castle slaves. His head is shaved and without warning, he feels the excruciating pain of a severe burn followed by a shriek of agony. He is being branded on the back of his right shoulder with the stamp of his new owner. This is all happening faster than he can process it. He is jerked to his feet concluded with jamming a wooden bowl into his hands. With barely a shuffle, he is led along a stone-paved passageway to a large wooden door. There he is quickly unchained by a silent white man and the cords binding his hands are quickly cut. Without a word, the man unlocks the door, swinging it open; he pushes Kumi in quickly slamming the door behind him. What immediately hits Kumi's nostrils is the smell of human excrement. Unable to see in the dark room, within one step, he stumbles over something.

"Aarrugg!" exclaims the something as a male voice lets out a yell cursing Kumi in a language Kumi understands. Something proves to be the body of a fellow captive jammed nearly to the door. Following this eruption, there follows an uncanny silence to the room. It's not exactly silent; it's the sound humans make when there is a struggle to get air enough to breath. Kumi's eyes soon adjust to the dimness. The only light feeding the room is coming from two halfmoon slits carved into an outside wall stingily limiting the amount of brightness as if not to overindulge the room's captives. It is also the only source of fresh air supplying the entire chamber crammed with more bodies than it was ever intended to serve. Kumi's mind is racing. He cannot resolve these conditions. There is hardly enough room for the existing people to do more than sit with their heads resting on drawn up knees. For, at least the next hour Kumi remains standing, leaning against the wall next to the door. The searing pain of the fresh brand lacing his right shoulder is taking all of his endurance just to withstand the pain, much less worry about a place to sit down. All of these concerns soon change with the door opening once again only to have several more bodies shoved in. Kumi notices his hand went to his eyes to shield them from the brightness from the open door. In doing so he stumbles and finds himself wedged between two other captives. They are seemingly impervious to the new level of discomfort forced on them by Kumi's body hurling in-between them. The concern he may have had with what he may be sitting in may have given him pause under more normal circumstance. He's certain from the smell that it's human waste. As if this is not enough, he feels his raw wound grating against another body. He lets out a controlled gasp as the pain seems to offer no limit. Along with this struggle, he too finds himself joining the rest in struggling to get enough air to fill his lungs. This difficulty is only adding to his discomfort. What is slowly happening with his mind beginning to quiet is his brain is switching from a panic mode to a calculated sense of surviving.

"This is not the time for irrational thinking; I've got to slow my mind. I'm still breathing, I'm still alive. I've got to stay ahead of myself if I want to survive this." These thoughts dominate his mind.

The rest of the day continues to drag on with the monotony broken only by the occasional door opening to cram in fresh bodies. Kumi is amazed at how quickly he is adjusting himself to this abhorrent behavior. With no idea what his future may bring, he is willing to grasp on to whatever fragment of life is still in the offering. The night passes with his restless body finding support against another immovable body crammed next to him, with that one in turn finding the same support against another neighboring body finding support against another, and so on. With exhaustion brought on by the forced march over several days, along with the ordeal of never knowing what plans these Dutch handlers were prepared to conjure, Kumi finds himself suddenly awakening at the movement of the bodies next to himself. It seems the doors have been thrown open and a filing out of the survivors are filling the courtyard. Kumi is aware of the sound of what sounds like wood being clunked on stone. It's the sound these wooden bowls make as they are being retrieved from a resting place around, under, between them. They are not free of whatever debris they may have come in contact with over the last day. It hardly seems to matter as the naked men line up to receive their quota of beans and water. Since they are at the expense of the castle and are not under a work order, their caloric ration is cut back to one meal a day. It's in the best interest of the Dutch to keep as many of these captives healthy enough to make the next leg of their journey known as the "middle journey." While these hundred or so males are in the courtyard, forbidden to speak, but nonetheless, getting a break for as long as it takes for castle slaves to bring out those who are too weak and sick to make it on their own and also to dispose of those who have died. Often, the sick are disposed of in the same manner as the dead: by dumping their hapless bodies into the sea.

Chapter 4

Abina

It's the early 1800s in rural Africa, and Abina's royal position permits her special privileges aside from those of common birth. This rank has allowed Abina an avoidance of many of the hardships experienced by ordinary villagers. Unfortunately, this experience has relegated her value to being no better than the next captive; her royal status means zero to a Dutch slave trader. Now devalued, Abina has become only one among equals; they shave her head and strip her of her clothing as quickly as any of the rest of the female slaves. The only quality the slaver is concerned with is how Abina will appeal to a buyer because of her looks and sexual appeal.

Abina's concern is singular. Survival. Along with experiencing this new situation, she feels a growing sense of powerlessness. As fast as things are changing, her mind and eyes are on a continual search toward what is transpiring around her; she is careful to dodge all avoidable pitfalls.

The women are categorically separated from the men. The reason given is to protect the women from unwanted sexual advances from these male captives. The irony of this is that the Dutch soldiers, all sent here with no wives or available women, abuse these female captives at will. Oftentimes, these women become pregnant and are sent to special housing in the nearby village until they give birth. These mixed-race children are sent back to the castle to be raised as slaves and educated to serve as liaisons between Europeans and Africans while their mothers are then sold to the highest bidder.

From his quarters, it is the custom of the governor to stand on his balcony overlooking the courtyard below and observe the influx of new captives. His interest is to calculate the cost of housing these captives among other things. Often, it's up to three months he needs to feed them and keep as many alive as is possible until a ship arrives to transport them to the new world. This holding period also provides him with an opportunity to catch a glimpse of all the new females. His interest is soon focused on the remarkable angular beauty of Abina. In spite of her disheveled appearance, the way she carries herself causes her to catch his attention—along with that of every other male in the compound.

With a signal to an officer in charge, the governor has Abina separated from the rest of the women. Her reaction is one of deep suspicion, especially after she is being scrubbed from head to toe, getting her hair done by a female castle slave, and provided with a fancy European dress. Her second thought is that her royal position may at last be recognized. With this thought her apprehensions begin to lessen. She is then led to a staircase with instructions to ascend. She is met at the top of the stairs by an older woman speaking her language. The woman has a matter of fact air about her. It's apparent she has performed this task many times. If it has ever had a conflicting effect on her, she has normalized it.

In an abrupt tone she declares, "If you cry, he'll beat you, so don't cry no matter what he asks you to do."

Abina is shaken at this cautionary injunction. Her father and bothers have always been her protectors; now, she is left with an admonition that she needs to hide her vulnerability, not to show any apprehension over what jeopardy may be in store for her. With this warning leaving her to ponder a future event with no options other than "don't cry" leaves her more frightened than ever. With nothing left to do, the woman silently leads Abina down a hall to a closed door. Standing before it, she lightly knocks. In a moment her knock is answered by a portly looking middle-aged white man. His face, other than bearing a red flushed appearance, has a mix of part smirk, part smile. It apparent he's pleased with what he sees.

Taking her hand, he delicately leads her to a table sumptuously supplied with meats and several choices of wines. Abina has never eaten at a table and has no idea what is expected of her; nor has she in her young life been in the presence of an important white man before, much less finding herself sitting at his table. He seats her after which he has a glass of wine poured for her. The closest she has come to drinking alcohol was a taste from a cup of palm wine left out by her father.

"Nsanom ('drink'),"compels the governor in her native tongue from his seat across the table.

Abina is much more interested in the food than she is the wine. "I have never in my life seen food like this," is her prevailing thought. The long trek has left Abina famished to the bone. The sight of all this food and the aroma is almost more than she can withstand without scooping a handful. Nonetheless, looking across the table at her benefactor, she gingerly tastes the wine as she has been commanded to do. The tartness gives her a little shiver. But withstanding all of this, her entire body is screaming for the food she is callously compelled to look at. It's all she can do to prevent herself from grabbing a piece of bread and begin to sop up all she can stuff into her mouth. To encourage her to drink more of the alcohol, the governor lifts his glass toward her with his continuing smile and a nod toward her glass to do the same. Abina, not wanting to offend this luminary who has seemingly requested her presence, awkwardly lifts her glass to his and follows suit in consuming the rest of the contents. The governor sets the next part of this venture by having a light-skinned male castle slave prepare their plates. Abina is beginning to feel the effects of the wine. It's only adding another component to her burgeoning hunger. Not aware of any European dining protocol, along with the effects of the wine dulling her sensibilities, she ignores the metal utensils and begins to eat with her hands as she always has—in the Ghanaian culture food is meant to be felt as well as smelled and tasted. Her Dutch champion is quite at ease with this habit of his new vassal. He in turn refills her glass once again. His face has lost its smile and has been replaced by a more intense demeanor as he watches Abina. Within five minutes, Abina has consumed more food than she has eaten in the last three days. Looking up from her eating, she is faced with the young male castle slave looking down at her with a look of distain. In his hand is a bowl of water and a towel. Abina obliges herself by washing her hands and wiping them dry on the towel. With her inhibitions evacuated by the wine, she downs the second glass the governor has poured for her in a moment.

A numbness and a foggy mind are the primary awareness Abina has as she is led to another room. Here she is thrown on a bed, feeling the heavy hands of her Dutch captor removing her clothing. The alcohol is doing the job the governor has envisioned. There is nothing better than a willing partner in his estimation—or at least one too drunk to fight back.

Abina awakens in a dark room on a cold, wet floor and the overwhelming stench of human waste. Since her use is of no further value, she has been unceremoniously returned to the level below, where life takes on a whole different prospect. Unlike the others, the opulence she had observed just one floor above exaggerate the appalling conditions of this lower hellhole. Two hundred females are packed into a room that may hold fifty comfortably. Abina also notices that the better kente skirt she'd arrived wearing, depicting her royal status, has been replaced by a skirt of near primitive value. Making her way around as best she can, she locates the buckets designated for relieving bodily waste only to discover they are overflowing. Left with no other option, Abina relieves herself where she is as best that she can.

Chapter 5

Willie

The year is 1807, near the Baltic Sea sits a small, German village named Pumlo. The people are close to the land in this region. To own land in this province gives honor and prestige. As the generations move forward, the family farms have become smaller due to the tradition of splitting the land among the male offspring. Finding it no longer viable to continue to split the already diminished plots among all the male offspring, a new tradition has taken hold where the land has been set aside for the eldest son. The other brothers are obliged to find other skills.

A prominent family in this region is the family of Heinrich Beinecke. This family name has occupied this farm for more generations than one cares to count. At this time, Heinrich, is about to turn the farm over to his eldest son who has just gotten married. Along with this, Heinrich has another decision to make. He has another son. He's fourteen-year-old, Wilhelm—now called Willie for short. He has finished his education and has no place on the farm to begin his working career. A decision has to be made. After a tough time with his wife, who doesn't want her youngest son to leave, Heinrich has made the ruling that he is prepared to indenture this boy to a blacksmith. The normal period of this indenture is for seven years. The upside of this pronouncement will result in Willie leaving home and learning the blacksmith trade. The downside will result in Willie being enslaved by law to a master blacksmith.

The Beinecke family live in the northern part of Germany where Martin Luther's movement for the reformation of the Catholic Church has taken root—referred to as "Evangelische." Willie has spent his education years in a parochial school rooted in Luther's reformation beliefs. He is above normal in academics and has always envisaged himself doing some sort of church work as a career choice. To fulfill this dream, a university education is required. All of that thought has been put to rest by his father, who has no discretionary money to send his son to a university.

Nonetheless, when Willie's confirmation in the Lutheran Church is finished as well as his schooling—and at fourteen years of age—it's time for him to move out of the world of children and enter the adult phase of his life. Taking his obligation as the family patriarch seriously, Heinrich begins his search for a career for his Willie. A friendly neighbor has a brother living near Austria who is a blacksmith. He has more than once made a suggestion to Heinrich to write his brother about taking on Willie on as an apprentice. Under German tradition, this will require Heinrich to indenture his son. With the responsibility to bring this task to fruition, Heinrich writes a letter to the blacksmith. The blacksmith's response is encouraging and indicates that he would like to meet the boy along with Heinrich. Once a suitable meeting time is agreed upon, it's quickly arranged between Heinrich and the blacksmith to meet and work out the details. Willie, on the other hand, has not been informed of these negotiations until the meeting time has been agreed on.

Heretofore, Willie has been the apple of his mother's eye. He's her youngest, and she has no problem catering to his every need. Since this new set of circumstances comes with no other contrasting life experiences, Willie reasonably assumes that this will be nothing other than an extension of his present life.

The journey turns out to be a two-day trek by horse and wagon. All in all, in Willie's fourteen years of life, this is the furthest he has traveled outside his village. Although the horse does most of the work, it is nonetheless, an exhausting trip. It requires an overnight stay at an inn and rest stops for the horse for water and hay. It's unusual for one to travel from village to village without arousing the local suspicions. Most people are content to remain in their respective villages, where life is safe and predictable. Many spend their entire lives without stepping outside their community. This leaves them with a fundamental suspicion of travelers. Willie and his father are not exceptions. It's fine if outsiders are only passing through, but to set up residence without the permission of the village is out of the question.

After an exhausting two-day journey. Willie and his father finally arrive. After the introductions, the blacksmith looks Willie over. He explains what will be expected of him, after which he goes into some detail concerning the amount of payment that he is willing to make to Heinrich for the use of his son for the next seven years. The expected result is Willie becoming a master blacksmith. The legal papers for indenturing are available at the office of the Schulze (supervisor). The papers are signed by Heinrich and the blacksmith and are witnessed by members of the Gerichet (the board of commissioners).

Nothing about all this has noticeably changed the life for fourteen-year-old Willie until he watches his father leave. Suddenly, Willie senses a separation anxiety. It hits him in such a way that it is all he can do to keep from running after his father's wagon. He feels alone and abandoned. Observing nothing but the remaining dust from the disappearing wagon, Willie chokes back an anxious tear. With great apprehension, he turns around only to face the hardened demeanor of his new master glowering at him. This man is named August Yunk. He is to be Willie's master until he reaches the age of twenty-one.

"Well, boy you might as well get started. We got a lot of work to do. From here on you will refer to me as Herr Meister. You will obey my orders without question, is that understood?"

"Yes, Herr Yunk," says Willie with a deep sense of respect.

No sooner were the words out of his mouth when the hard, calloused hand of this new master shoots out striking Willie alongside of his head, rolling him in the dirt.

"NICHT HERR YUNK, DUMBKOFF! ICH BIN HERR MEISTER!" Shouts Yunk. "Not Herr Yunk, idiot! I am lord and master."

Grabbing Willie by the scruff of his shirt, Yunk yanks him to his feet and, to add a bit more clarification as to who is the master, he plants a foot in his behind sending Willie stumbling back to the dirt.

"Steh auf, du fauler lumpfh! Du arbeiten mus!" ("Get up, you lazy bum! Get to work!"), shouts Yunk as he grabs Willie once again by the scruff of his shirt.

Willie struggles to stay afoot as he's dragged into the building that houses the forge. The smell of burning coke and hot iron permeate the enclosed space. Yunk, still grasping Willie by the collar, is dragging him from one station to another telling him how important it is that he keep all the rust off the tools, where they are to be kept, what they are called, how important it is to preserve the place of unnecessary debris, and how he is to never, never, never let the fire in the forge go out. Confused and intimidated, Willie is finally shown his sleeping quarters. It turns out to have been an overflow horse stall that had been reserved for horses that have been shoed but hadn't been retrieved by their owners. It was a small area, but large enough for a bed-like structure with a straw mattress and a rough horse blanket for warmth. This was far different from the room Willie had at home, where his ever-attentive mother made certain he was always comfortable.

At this point, Willie feels entirely victimized. First by his mother for letting his father have his way, then by his father for turning him over to such a hellish life, and now to Yunk for surfacing as his overbearing tormentor.

At fourteen, Willie's education has been halted. Only the privileged go on for formal schooling. It seems prescribed education has never been meant for farm children. Laying in his straw bed on this first night, Willie reviews his life up until now. At the moment, he sees all his outward suffering ending in the inner bleakness of his present life. It's easy for him to lament over his circumstances with a victimized attitude.

The fire in the forge has been banked for the night, and Willie has been forewarned not to let it go out. Come rain or shine from this day forward, he will be held exclusively responsible for the health of the fire in the forge.

"Listen to me, boy, we can't afford to get behind in our work because you have been careless with your time. This forge has become your child, its health is totally in your hands, it comes before you eat, shit, or sleep—do you understand?"

Willie is overwhelmed with fear. He has never been in such a situation before. "Yes, Herr Meister." There is a slight quiver to his voice. To say that he slept well is an understatement. Every hour, he awoke to check the fire, always adding a slight amount of charcoal to the embers. By the crack of dawn, he is up and preparing the fire for Yunk's arrival. He's also been charged to make certain the livestock gets fed and watered. In this case, he feeds the two horses sharing stalls. They are uneasy with his displacing their usual manager. In this work, their normal attendant happens to be Frau Yunk. She has taken advantage of this bound servant to replace her in her livestock feeding.

Soon, Herr Yunk makes an entrance. He's as disheveled today as he was yesterday. His shock of red hair is uncombed and his hands hold a permanent grime from years of exposing them to the varying conditions it takes to accomplish his trade. Frau Yunk follows behind carrying a basket. She's a stout woman. She's been so gifted to meet the physical needs to maintain not only farm animals, but a garden, and the day-to-day household responsibilities. The basket she's carrying is provided with a cloth covering the top. She says nothing as she arranges the container on a bench in front of Willie. She next removes the covering exposing a small loaf of fresh bread and a piece of boiled pork. Willie couldn't be more pleased if the devil himself had prepared it. He has had little to eat while traveling and less since he arrived. He looks at this benefactor as one would a savior. She smiles and nods to indicate that he must eat. He doesn't need a second invitation.

In the meantime, without a word, Yunk pokes a rod into the fire.

"How much charcoal you waste, boy?!" Yunk barks.

This explosive reaction causes Willie to drop the basket and jump to his feet nearly choking on a piece of pork.

With unchewed portions of his breakfast preventing him from answering, and unwilling to wait for Willie's response, Herr Yunk drags him by the arm to the forge.

"You used this morning's share of charcoal through the night. You may as well get started making more, with the work we have to do this week, we're going to need it." Raising his voice to another level, Yunk adds the imperative, Schnell ("quickly"), just for emphasis.

Willie's reaction is one of panic. He has watched his father make charcoal for the fuel they needed around the farm but, like most children, if he wasn't compelled to be a part of its manufacture, he wasn't paying that close attention.

Surreptitiously, standing in the doorway is a young girl about the same age as Willie. She's been watching at a distance. She is well aware of her father's temperament when things don't go smoothly. Her name is Magdalena. She is the fifteen-year-old daughter of the Yunk's. She is the youngest of four sister siblings. The others are grown and have households of their own. Because of her birth order, Magdalena has enjoyed much of her life as an only child. Having finished her church confirmation, her parents have kept her in school. Her desire is to someday become a teacher. Her father, on the other hand, expects she will become a household manager like her mother, which includes not only the day-to-day household baking and cleaning routine, but also managing servants and bookkeeping for the family business.

After observing Willie, Magdalena is not satisfied in the least that this new boy has any skills at all. At this point, Magdalena seizes the opportunity to practice her managerial talents. It has been her task since she was nine years old to make the charcoal. With Willie as her replacement, things have changed, she is given a reprieve. Even though this task is laborious and time consuming, causing her to complain, nonetheless she takes a certain amount of satisfaction in performing the task well. With this new interloper assuming a responsibility that had been exclusively hers, she isn't prepared to turn it over haphazardly without a close inspection of his charcoal making capability.

Willie, on the other hand, is attempting to overcome his trembling enough to begin this task. His mind is desperately reaching back to any fragment of remembrance as to what his father had done to begin the process. Unfortunately, nothing is coming to him and fear flaunts itself through the stress lines forming on his young face. Even though Magdalena remains hidden, she is positioning herself to oversee his every movement. Not able to withstand his obvious ineptness for another minute, she intervenes.

With hands on her hips, Magdalena watches with disgust as Willie fumbles with each measure. "You don't know a thing about making charcoal, do you?" she derides.

Caught completely off guard, Willie's head snaps around to confront this encounter. He suddenly finds himself face-to-face with a blond-haired, blue-eyed girl he surmises to be his age. She's actually one year older. She's also taller by several inches. He is certainly finding something attractive about her fresh looks. He immediately is aware of something else compelling about her that defies his vocabulary; some may see it as haughtiness, where others see confidence. Whatever it is, Willie's attracted to it. Not willing to spend anymore thought about it, another part tells him not to be intimidated by a girl. Finally settling on a singular response, he gives a disapproving scowl.

"Ya, I know how to make charcoal. I've done it a million times," snaps Willie.

"Yah, but you don't know how my father wants it done," counters Magdalena.

This answer stops Willie in his tracks. It takes him a second longer to process what has just been said. Even though this is a girl, and girls shouldn't know anything, his second thought is effortlessly piling in. He is quickly recalling the rough treatment his master is capable of imposing. His swirling thoughts suddenly settle down. A suggestion quickly comes to mind. "Maybe, for your own good, you better take heed as to what she is willing to share with you."

"Okay, tell me what you think your father will want," grants Willie with an acquiescent shrug.

Magdalena spends the next hour carefully leading Willie through the process, all the while aware of her father's wary eye taking careful note of each of their behaviors.

"My father says you are Evangelische, Lutheran, is that so?" She probes with an investigative tone.

"Yes," is Willie's simple reply not knowing where this aggressive girl is taking him.

"That's good, because my father hates Catholics," informs Magdalena. Her demeanor suggests she is in agreement with her father.

This makes Willie wonder how much more unpleasant his master could be if he were a Catholic.

When this charcoal making task has concluded, Herr Yunk orders him back into the shop. Amongst a lot of hollering, cussing, and impatient actions, Yunk manages to keep Willie on his toes. Here, there is no such thing as person's teenage years becoming a separate part of life where one is ascribed to a distinctive class called teenager. In this nineteenth century German world, if a boy Willie's age doesn't aspire to become a man as prescribed by his culture, and quickly take on the responsibilities of a man of this tradition, he will soon find himself on the fringe of the community, ostracized, and written off as a criminal.

Herr Yunk, himself is such a product of this same hardnosed system that he is imposing on Willie and his own family. When one considers he had learned the blacksmith trade through the same methods, it explains his attitude. He too had been indentured and had been treated harshly. As a man true to his beliefs, he is making certain that he continues the tradition.

Chapter 6

The Middle Passage Begins

Thousands of miles to the south, the middle passage is described where a slave ship comes from Europe to the coast of Africa secures a boatload of slaves, sails to America where the slaves are sold, then returns back to Europe and repeats the entire offense all over again.

Kumi and Abina have been held in the dungeons of Elmina for nearly two months awaiting the ship that will transport them on this middle passage to the United States. They both bear the same brand of the same buyer. To say the least, this has been a disorienting experience for all the captives. They have been torn from their families and given numbers to replace their names. At this point, they are hardly aware of anything other than survival. There have been to date at least forty, maybe fifty captives who have succumbed to the harsh rigors of dungeon life and died. There is no funeral, merely casting the lifeless carcass into the sea. The phenomenon of need for community is quickly developing among the survivors. Kumi has taken what little comfort can be afforded in having conversations with those sharing the same fate as himself. There is an agreement that if an opportunity to escape was available—no matter how small—they would take it. There are also conversations regarding suicide if an escape was not forthcoming. Kumi is not among these. He has a strong desire to live regardless of conditions. But make no mistake, if that remote opportunity to escape avails itself, he will go for it. There is continual talk among the captives as to the wrongness of their destiny and how savage their white captors are. A few of these Elmina captives had become slaves as a result of warring tribes losing a war. The difference between the kinds of slavery among Africans and the Europeans is as wide as the sea. The accounts shared from African slaves tells how their African masters allowed them to have families, and their workload was no larger than that of free men. The only noticeable difference was they were not allowed to eat with freemen.

For Kumi and the rest of the captives, their lives have changed. Not subject to reliable information, the rumors abounding among them run rampant. Much like Kumi, many of these inner continental Africans had never seen white men before. The thought by many is that white men are cannibals and are taking them somewhere to be eaten.

The truth is, several times a month a different cargo ship appears in the harbor prepared to load its cargo of human freight. These ships were originally designed to carry cargos of sugar, gold, tobacco, and other nonliving items, now their holds have been retrofitted with shelves or platforms to carry as many human captives as they are able to cram in for a two to six-month voyage to America. This is wholly organized to answer the need for slave labor to work the American plantations.

Today, a ship appears anchored offshore bearing the name HMS Brooks. Kumi's jailers have learned enough pidgin language to make their intentions known. Today is the day he will be leaving the confines of his dungeon to be loaded onto a ship for a reason he will fully not comprehend. He has witnessed others being singled out never to be seen again—now it's his turn. A jailer stands by motioning each person's turn. Still naked and chained in twos, the captives are led out to a narrow door and motioned to pass through. The door leads to the outside. This is the first breath of fresh air, minus the odor of human waste, Kumi has breathed in months. Despite being chained, this breath of fresh air and sunlight lifts his spirits more than anything has for some time. They are next forced to march to a waiting long canoe, much like his own back in his village. He and eight more are motioned to get aboard. One captive makes a point to refuse to board. His mind is rapidly changed when a white man with a cat-o'-nine-tails makes several lashes across his back. It soon becomes obvious to all that they are being transferred to the waiting ship. The closer they get, the more ominous this giant wooden behemoth appears to become. Kumi, along with his tethered brother in chains, are next struggling to get up a rope ladder draped over the side of this floating prison. Once on board, they are quickly pushed down into a dark chamber below the deck. After the last half-hour of fresh air, the first thing that hits his nostrils is the putrid odor of human debasement. Once here, they are forced along a narrow alley lined with a platform no more than three feet high and ordered to crawl in. Kumi is quickly aware of what is expected of him. He is not the same twenty-year-old young man who was captured by slave traders two months ago. Along with his tethered partner, he is expected to crawl into a space no more than eighteen inches wide and maybe three-feet high. As young a man as he is, his body, mind, and soul have aged more in the last couple months than it would take to accomplish in ten years of normal maturing. It is in enduring things like this that this young man is becoming very acquainted with himself. "I can either see myself as a victim and probably die or I can withstand this for the hope of a brighter day. Today, I'll choose life." These sole thoughts have become powerful enough for Kumi to allow himself to be placed on this shelf as one would store a lifeless item.

The day drags on as all his days have since his capture. He can hear the sounds on the deck just above him. Sometimes it's the jangle of defiance from an unwilling captive, other times it's the sound of a gruff voice in a language he doesn't understand but can discern by its tone that its losing patience with a bewildered captive.

After considering these past months of a miserable and often violent incarceration, Kumi is not surprised by anything his captors can dream up to be more savage, though this particular situation is one that will reach beyond brutal. His captors are well aware that to transport this many men without taking extreme security measures would most likely be foolhardy. What this captain fears most is a slave resistance at sea with an overwhelming number of slaves compared to his minimal amount of crew to quell it. In every population there is a mix of personalities. This group is not to be the exception. There are leaders and there are followers. There is no time nor desire on the part of the ship's crew to sort them out. Considering these risks, security becomes the ultimate concern to this sea captain—even if it means restraining as much of their movement as possible. Packing them in as tight as possible reduces a resistance threat and makes life so miserable for its recipients that it reduces their fighting inclinations inasmuch as they are totally preoccupied with their own survival.

Out of need for some kind of a forbearance against the extreme confinement both now and at Elmina, Kumi has developed a way of staying in touch with his soul. It's a very confusing and frustrating time for anyone caught up in this dragnet of slave traders. But to allow one's self to become a victim is to choose death. For a young man like Kumi to harness his thoughts may be easier than one might think. It's a matter of what he is committed to. If he is committed to negative thoughts, he will consciously or unconsciously attempt to end his life. Either way, he will be dead long before his body dies. If on the other hand, if he's committed to thoughts that choose life, he will never become a victim. Lying in his eighteen-inch by three-foot shelf, he is currently deciding either to rest or stress. In Kumi's case, he is determining that if he dies, it will be by some bad spirit he allowed into his body. He begins to pray to the spirits of his past ancestors to protect his family. Consequently, he wishes himself to choose life instead of death. He is discovering that his first reaction to his tormentors is to relinquish his person to them and become their victim. His second thought is to listen to the urges of his soul rather than his mind. In this case he lives another day.

Chapter 7

Begin the Passage

The women's quarters are as filthy as the men's quarters. The kind of filth they are expected to endure is not a condition that is ever acceptable or gotten used to. After all, these women have been the harbingers of order and cleanliness in their communities. Now, to be living day to day with floor coverings of menses and excrement as their constant companions is difficult to adapt to.

They become aware when they are about to be used for sexual purposes because they undergo a bath. This bathing is always done in the courtyard where everyone can watch. Stripping these women of their God-given dignity, forcing them to live in fear and filth, and misusing them sexually are having a variety of effects on them. For some it is a defeating effect; for others it is unspeakable embarrassment; still, with others it brings a very hostile reaction; and yet others welcome it as a relief from their drudgery. Many of these women would gladly trade a day without this oppressive filth for a seeming lighter oppression of gratifying a tyrannical white man.

One outstanding characteristic among these women in these uncertain times is their propensity to create a nurturing community among themselves. They have a tendency to verbally communicate more than the men and have developed bonds among themselves. One feature of this phenomenon is those who have become ill are tended to by those who are well.

38

Over the past two months, Abina has been summoned by the governor several times. Each time she is given the privilege of a bath and some clean clothing. She is aware of how this seeming privilege is viewed by others; it creates envy. Nonetheless, when one is demonstrating a caring attitude for each in their community, it is necessary to include oneself. In this case Abina has to decide what is best for her in this particular situation. She definitely needs a break from the rigors of dungeon living. In this situation, having to put up with the governor's sexual comportments is a small price to pay. What she is looking forward to in these encounters more than anything is the food. The volume of dignity Abina may have held prior to this situation has long ago been compromised by the extreme severities of her living conditions.

Her time with the governor has been cut short as a castle soldier has sent word that she is scheduled to board a ship that is set to sail to the United States of America. Well-fed, Abina is ushered down the familiar flight of stairs from the governor's quarters for the last time. Still wearing the clothes supplied to her, she is quickly stripped naked and led to the "door of no return." Here she is matched with her brand and her slave number and sent with the last of the females to the water's edge where she is loaded into a long canoe prepared to make its way to the waiting vessel HMS Brooks.

Abina is positioned in the canoe in such a way that she can watch her homeland grow more distant with every stroke of the canoe's paddle. She realizes for the first time the enormity of her capture. Her heart is broken as tears begin to stream down her face.

Arriving at the waiting vessel, with tears still streaking her face and no one to care or know the cause of her grief, she is prodded with a canoe paddle to get herself up the ladder along with the rest of the women. Once on board, the women are given space on the deck. They are not chained as they are considered a much lower risk than the men.

Suddenly there comes to them sounds they have never heard before. It's the groans a sailing ship makes as it struggles to move forward; iron anchor chains meeting wooden decking and the "floop" sound a sail makes as the wind swells it to its fullest potential. The breeze that is accompanying the movement of the ship should be a welcome relief from the soggy heat created in the dungeons, but in this case it's a dreaded reminder that everything they know and hold dear—family, friends, community, customs, their family name—all are now left behind forever.

Another sound suddenly comes to them over the dominating sounds of the ocean water separating itself as it slips by the hull's wooden planking—it's the gruff sound of a man's voice speaking in yet another language they are unaccustomed to hearing. The man is bearded and dirtier than the men at Elmina. He's the ship's cook. His next move is to slam a wooden pail down on the deck. It's filled with beans. A burlap bag is also produced. It's filled with yams. A container filled with water is next brought forward. The women are each given a hand full of beans, a yam, and a liter of water. Accustomed to this feeding, they realize this will be all the nourishment they will receive for the entire day.

Another man appears. He is a giant of a man. His hair long and neatly brushed back under a strange looking hat with the brim forming a point both in the front as well as the back. He's wearing a frocked coat. There is no doubt in anyone's mind that he commands an important position. He has situated himself on the elevated aft deck which gives him an authoritative advantage. He is quietly surveying what is below him. The women know exactly what he is doing. Each, in her own way attempt to divert her eyes. They've experienced the same attention from white men at Elmina. It's clear to them that he's making his selection among them to grace his bed throughout the voyage. Little has changed for these female chattels. They are seeing firsthand what their lives are going to be.

40

Chapter 8

A New Decision

Thousands of miles to the north life is also having its way with Germany's inhabitants. Days have turned into weeks; weeks into months for Willie. He's passed from fourteen to fifteen years of age. There is no doubt his world has changed drastically. He has gone from a boy to a young man. His approach to life has become much more focused. He's developing a sense of community with the forge. Its complexities have taken on an order that has been hard learned. Not once since his arrival, has he set foot in the living quarters of his master, nor has he eaten a meal with anyone other than himself. The strict protocol involving indentured servants is strictly adhered to in Herr Yunk's realm. There is no doubt in Herr Yunk's mind that he would never be entitled enough to go against such a long-held regulation to personally bring about a reform. As far as he is concerned, "The boy's place is in the forge."

On Sunday, Willie is given the morning off. As an adherent to the teachings of his church, it's his obligation to prepare himself for Holy Communion. How better to reflect on his sins than a ride on the back of the family wagon to St. Paul's Evangelische Lutheran church. On arrival, he sits in pews placed in a small balcony intended to house the church's organ along with other servants. Since its sound emanates from bellows powered by a hand crank, and because of his experience with bellows, he has been volunteered by Herr Yunk to make certain the crank never stops.

At this point, Willie is very assuredly learning his sole purpose in life is to follow, without question, every instruction his master stipulates; during six days of the week, he is to mind the forge, on Sundays it's to crank the church organ—all this without query. If one expects to survive, then this is the kind of discipline required of each male in nineteenth century Germany.

Magdalena, has channeled her highhandedness into her schooling once again. As disciplined as her parents are with every item in their lives, they admittedly have thrown up their hands with Magdalena. They would like nothing better than to have had a carbon copy of themselves in this daughter. By all accounts this has not happened. Magdalena is developing into the kind of young woman who in some ways her mother had always hoped she could have realized. Germany is undergoing the pains of emerging from a strictly agricultural state to a pre-industrialized country; everything in the country is undergoing a useful scrutiny. Magdalena has lived under the tutelage of her parents, her church, her government, all expressing to her the ways she is to place herself in submission to each of them. Her school has joined the others in guaranteeing a smooth transition from her education to applying what has been taught for the good of family, village, and state. This would be in perfect harmony with the German tradition, all but for a school class she took exposing her to a bigger life outside Germany. It was here that she learned how a famous American president's wife Abigail Adams declared she would "never consent to have our sex considered in an inferior point of light." Even at her young age, and for reasons she feels she doesn't have to explain, this statement is as true a fact to her soul as the sun is coming over the horizon. There is something bigger about this feeling concerning her identity other than the criticism she is finding at nearly every corner. At her age, it remains difficult to put these feelings into words although her soul has no problem recognizing them as normal endowments. Many of her schoolmates view her as an undisciplined radical and shun her as much as possible.

When she is home from school, Magdalena has found an unforeseen listener in Willie. It's not so much that he is interested in her opinions as much as he is interested in her. There is something about her determination, or maybe her tenacity, or maybe it's everything about her he finds captivating. Knowing how protective Herr Yunk is of his daughter, he keeps a wary eye open for anything that can get him a whipping. Magdalena has also been warned to be aware of her status and not to engage with her father's servant. Her father has given her countless lectures on the protocol concerning the appropriate conduct in handling an indentured servant. Magdalena has politely listened to her father but also finds herself uncannily drawn to the person of Willie. She finds his seeming sympathetic ear an attractive characteristic. All the males in her school see her as a highhanded female who needs to find her traditional place in German life and stop being a troublemaker. By attempting to make disciples of other girls her age, she makes school authorities nervous; she refuses to subject herself to the rules and controls that circumscribe the behavior of German women.

Willie, on the other hand, is not involved with her politics; he's simply happy to have the attention of such an attractive girl. He misses his home and is more than ready to have any kind of tender interaction with another human. His father had been harsh but not nearly as harsh as Herr Yunk. His relations with his mother had frequently been where she functioned as his advocate maneuvering against the unforgiving directives of his father. More than once she was able to soften her husband's temper against his seeming unacceptable behavior. This advocacy is found in Magdalena.

No trade in Germany equals that of the village blacksmith. Herr Yunk is the backbone of this community. There isn't business or farm whose livelihood in this district doesn't at one time or another depend on the skills within this forge. All the tools used are handmade, even the anvil is Herr Yunk's personal design, as are the hammers, dozens of various tongs ranging in sizes that depend on only one hand up to those requiring two men to manipulate.

The most important tool in the blacksmith's shop is the forge. "Watch the wind boy, watch the wind" are the most frequent heard admonitions in the shop. Willie is much like the surgeon's assistant as he assists Herr Yunk in nearly every function of the trade. In this instance, it's his responsibility to maintain just the right amount of wind created by just the right amount of pressure on the goatskin bellows. It's just one of the many assignments Willie is beginning to learn. Little by little he is gaining in his ability to foresee the next needed procedure and is readying the next tool to effectively and efficiently move forward. Although, he's catching on fast, the only praise he receives for doing a satisfactory job is in not being scolded.

The seasons are changing. The cooler fall weather is a welcome addendum against the blistering heat created in the forge during the summer months. But as with all things pleasant, they have their season and move on to something not so pleasant. The winters in this area can be fierce. Temperatures can remain below freezing for weeks on end. On this particular November morning Herr Yunk is rousting Willie out of his bed. This is totally unusual as Willie is always way ahead of Herr Yunk in getting the forge prepared for the day's work. On this morning his young body had finally given in to the gruesome workload he's expected to maintain. He has overslept. Yunk is behind in his work and now to find this indentured delinquent lying in bed and the forge nowhere near the capacity needed to begin the workday, he grabs Willie out of a deep slumber, jerking him to his feet. His first move is to start to beat him with his hands. The only conscious awareness Willie has is the blows that are encompassing his head as Yunk batters him on one side of his head and then the other. The primordial reaction imbedded in Willie is to yelp like a wounded animal and throw his own hands back as a defense. In doing so he strikes his master square in the face. Herr Yunk reels back from the blow from this good-for-nothing servant/slave. It is only adding to his fury as he grabs a nearby horse whip. His arm is raised and ready to strike when a hand stops the whip poised above Willie's already faltering body. A voice accompanies the hand.

45

"No, father don't do this!" It's the pleading voice of Magdalena. "Please, not another blow!"

This is the first time in Magdalena's life that she has defied her father in a physical way. The moment stuns both herself and her father. In the face of this blatant incident Yunk has set Willie aside as he stares into the face of an emerging young woman he doesn't know. Realizing she has suddenly stepped into a realm she has never been in before, out of fear, she steps back. Her face reveals a look foretelling that she is in over her head.

Yunk's mind is in a turmoil. He has also discovered that he is on new ground. Determined to hold his superior position, he verbally lashes out at Magdalena. "Get out of my forge and go to the house! I'll deal with you later." Frustrated, she turns and runs to the house.

This interruption has been enough to take a break and regroup with, hopefully, a different line of consciousness. Yunk is assessing his role as master to one of these seeming belligerents and father to another. Feeling he has made his point and still has protected his untouchable role, without a further word, he leaves the whip where it lays and begins his workday.

Still smarting from his master's blows, Willie takes advantage of the pause by quickly busying himself with the forge. He has repeated this task to a point that it comes with no thought. This allows his mind to be elsewhere. And elsewhere it is. He has decided at his first opportunity that he is going to run away and make his way back home. Physically he's recovered—it's his spirit that's smarting. For the first time in his young life it's near broken.

Chapter 9

The Getaway

As the morning progresses, Yunk begins to review the earlier episode. As he recalls how his daughter had dared to interfere with his disciplining of Willie, his resentment continues to grow. It finally reaches the point he feels compelled to revisit Magdalena's interference. Leaving his shop, he makes his way to the house. He finds Magdalena and her mother working on a household project. Taking liberties with his position as the head of his

family, Yunk confronts his daughter.

"What did you think to accomplish this morning with your interference?" he asks.

The question has left Magdalena with the realization in spite of all her highhandedness, her father is still capable of a full force intimidation. With a noticeable amount of reservation, her natural inclination to not let a wrong go unanswered, she addresses the question.

"I think what you did to Willie was wrong."

Yunk is measuring his daughter's viewpoints as she answers his question. He and his village have lived through innovative ideas that brought them into periods of near starvation and ruin because of their failure. He has watched Magdalena's belligerence grow as her education has distanced her from the time proven values this district has set as a standard. Without a hesitation, he gives her opinion his response.

"I think it's time you left school and begin to reevaluate your thinking. This is not the way you have been raised. I'm not going to spend hard earned money for you to defy your father and your church. You are drifting to far from the values we hold as good God-fearing Germans. Therefore, you will leave school, return home, and assist your mother with the matters at home."

Magdalena stands shocked. She can't believe her father would do this to her. She has come to believe her education was a respectable German tradition. Behind it, she has surreptitiously hoped that it would be her ticket out of Germany. She has had an ardent desire to go to America—specifically the United States. Now she feels her prospects are all but gone. She is hoping by hanging on to what is left of her chances, she'll find another way.

For Willie, the day is progressing like every other day since his indenture. He begins his workday before the sun comes up and doesn't finish until it's too dark to see. The day has ended as usual with Herr Yunk leaving him to clean up the shop. Frau Yunk has brought him his supper of a potato and a helping of pickled herring and a pint of her home-brewed beer. When there is a disturbance in the family, her way of dealing with it is to remain silent. Willie never questions her behavior. He is well aware of his part in the fray and doesn't wish to bring any of it back to his door again. Just as silently Willie eats his meal alone as he always has all the while gazing at the house, he continues his watch until he sees the lantern turn off. His eyes quickly turns to the potato cellar—although up until tonight, he has had little reason to pay attention to it.

This is Frau Yunk's domain. She can account for every potato in its enclosure. But tonight, is different. Willie has made up his mind to leave. He misses his mother and father and wishes to return home. His mind tells him he can find his solace there. Stealthily, he makes his way to the potato cellar. It's

48

darker inside than it is outside. Feeling around with his hands he feels the familiar texture of a potato. He crams as many down the front of his shirt as it will hold. He clearly distinguishes his heart beating against the weight of his ill-gotten supplies. He quietly closes the cellar door and stealthily makes his way back to the forge. After putting together a few of his belongings, he rolls them up in his horse blanket, ties the corner together and hastily rams a broken hoe handle through the binding serving as a handle to rest across his shoulder.

Stepping outside, he realizes it's beginning to snow. Feeling the warmth of his coat against his back, he boldly makes his first step into an unknown. What he does know is that he doesn't want to remain here. For him there is no turning back. The fear motivating him is his master's intent on breaking him. He is afraid of losing himself in the process. Willie has no words for this fear but he is willing to run from its consequences. What drives him on is a hatred that he has built against one man—Herr Yunk.

The night is dark. The sky has covered itself with snow clouds. The wind moans as it forces its way through swaying, leafless tree branches. Like a thousand needles, the squall carries bits of sleet, biting the bare flesh around Willie's face and neck. He stands stiff against the cold wind with only his eyes making movement. The one direction he recalls to begin his escape is the direction which he and his father arrived by several months ago. He gazes up at the sky hoping to find a moon. No moon is to be seen. His eyes return to face the darkness and the dim road ahead. The snow is thickening to where the wind has shaped it into an elegant white sheet streaming across the road. Not able to see a dozen steps ahead, Willie shifts his shoulders against the warmth of his coat. Its warmness along with his blood running hot with hatred gives him the reassurance he needs to move forward. It's not merely the physical things that occupy his thoughts but also the mental vision of his predicament. Recalling all the years in his father's house, he has never felt this kind of oppression. Without looking back, he brazenly begins his trek.

49

It's dawn before Willie's energy is depleted. He's near exhaustion. Each of his thousands of breaths have passed through the wool fibers of his scarf creating a thick coating of ice clinging to its strands. Breathing a sigh of relief that he has safely made it this far, he begins to look for a suitable place to build a fire, roast one of his potatoes and get some sleep. A nearby stand of low hanging pines grabs his attention. For a short time, Willie stands on its edge alert and watchful. He feels nothing other than exhaustion from fighting the force of the blizzard, and the press of an unrelenting hunger.

Within a few minutes he has penetrated the denseness of the pine enclosure. It promises to conceal him from anyone happening along the road. To his advantage, the thick boughs have prevented the storm from penetrating its underside leaving only a thin layer of snow. Gathering up enough dry materials to assure an adequate cooking fire, he sparks a flame from a small piece of steel struck against a chunk of flint into his bundle of dry thatch. It immediately begins to smoke. By gently blowing into it, Willie soon bursts the bundle into a flame. Within minutes, he is roasting a potato.

With his hunger soon satisfied, Willie turns his actions toward putting a warm bed together. He manages to collect a big pile of fallen pine needles to assure that along with his horse blanket he can sufficiently ward off the cold. Shortly after burrowing into his insulating cover of pine needles and his warm wool horse blanket, he drifts into a long-needed sleep.

Chapter 10

Middle Passage Certainties

Kumi is chained not only to his shelf but to another young man from a different part of Africa who doesn't speak his language. Their shelf barely allows for spoonlike laying much less sitting up without banging their heads on the floor of the shelf above them—rolling over is out of the question. This design serves two major purposes. One is the ratio of Africans to crew is ten to one. The rightful fear by the ship's master is a resistance by these captives. It's been known to happen when captured Africans are being brought out of the interior to the coast their relatives will attempt a raid to set them free. It's also been a reality in the castles. And one in ten ships carrying slaves has been known to deal with various resistances—most have been failures, but it remains true that humans will fight for their right to be free. The other reason is, by using this method, the ship can carry its maximum cargo of captives. The shipping companies are enriching themselves with this human freight more than any other payload including gold. This is not to exclude many of the kingdoms in Africa, which are also enriching themselves by trading their own people for weapons that give them wealth and power.

The wails of the discontent compete through the night with the creaking sounds a ship makes as it forces its way through rough seas. By morning, sea sickness has caused the lower deck to be slick with vomit. In groups they are brought to the upper deck still manacled to a partner. There are no toilet facilities—at least not for the captives. They have been forced to relieve themselves where they lay. Once on deck, the crew toss buckets of sea water

51

on them. This an attempt to clean everything from feces to vomit stuck to their naked bodies. They also get their heads shaved in the hopes of limiting lice. In the past, this captain has experienced the loss of half his slave cargo and a good share of his crew to the diseases that can fester aboard these ships. At the advice of his ship's physician, he is attempting to keep ahead of the killing diseases. There is also an attempt to mop out the shelves housing the slaves below the deck, but because of the heat and overwhelming odor this remains a halfhearted effort.

The men are kept on the deck throughout the day if it's not storming. Here, under the penalty of the cat-o'-nine-tails, they are forced to exercise by jumping or being given an option to dance. Dancing in their cultures is performed for the sake of a celebration. There are no known dances created for being in chains. Nonetheless, rather than feel the sting of the lash and the crews' well known desire to demonstrate their prowess with it, they comply.

Kumi is no exception. Along with his chained partner, he begins to utter a well-known song. As if on cue, his partner joins in with a slightly different tune in his own language. They begin a counterclockwise dance with very small steps. Unbeknown to the crew, it's a dance calling upon the spirits to protect them. Soon another pair join in. It's enough to entertain the crew and prevent any retribution toward them. There are a few of these male captives who are incensed at the spectacle and have become reluctant to comply. This prompts the ship's master to have them brought forward, tethered and spread eagled between the rigging, and whipped. Their backs lay stripped with open gashes as they are sent below deck to lay with their wounds unattended in some feted shelf.

With this activity completed, the ship's cook comes on deck assisted by several assistants laboring with two large wooden tubs with what appears to be one filled with boiled rice and one with boiled yams. The males are lined up and are each given a liter of water. This is expected to be consumed on the spot.

From here, they are pushed toward the tubs and formed into another line. They are allowed one yam and a handful of boiled rice. This is the singular meal and ration of water for the day. Being rushed they are forced into another line and pushed back below deck, with their ankle manacles locked to the ship until the next day.

Although, Kumi's body is slowed with all of these new confinements, his mind is still racing. Laying manacled to the ship and to another with whom he can't communicate, he listens to the creaking planks of the ship's hull straining under the weight of its cargo. This gives him pause. Without an understanding of ship construction, he's left with only a lively imagination. Living in the jungle his entire life has promoted a way of life that questions anything that appears to threaten survival. In this situation, not able to see because of the lack of light and feeling the snugness of the iron restraints against the baroness of his bare ankles cause his mind to reel in terror of drowning. What has kept him alive thus far is the tenacious gift God has given him to seek life under every rock of discouragement. With each body giving off heat and no ventilation, the temperature is rising to a near stifling level. Being left with the anxiety of drowning, all these other antagonisms are out of mind.

Suddenly, Kumi's mind shifts to a new thought. "Am I ever going to see my family again? What has happened to them?" With this last thought unfulfilled, he awakes, realizing that he has slept for some time. What wakes him is the feeling of moisture pouring onto his chest. It's obviously coming from the platform above him. He realizes that it's urine from its occupant pouring through the loosely fit boards. Also having the urge to relieve himself, he holds it as long as he can realizing there is only one solution—to relieve himself where he lay.

The days begin to linger on. All of these captives come from villages depending on agriculture and hunting, where they spent their days in nature. Now, to find themselves confined in the belly of a ship without enough room to sit up or roll over is taking its toll on their mental stability. They find themselves combating this ailment by singing to communicate with others speaking their language. When someone answers, it carries with it a profound settling by reminding them they are not alone. It also allows them to team up between themselves without their captives knowing they are communicating with one another.

The children of these slaves are allowed to run free on the ship. They often wander down into the hold where the male captives are held. They scamper up and down the center aisle separating the tiers of platformed prisoners playing their chasing games. In this particular incident, two boys are chasing one another arguing over possession of a length of wood. With instincts sharpened by near blindness, there is just enough light pouring in from the open entrance to the lower deck to allow a prisoner to see well enough to grab the piece of wood from the boy's hand. Quick as a cat, he conceals it in the back of his compartment behind his head leaving the boys to run off frightened and empty handed. It becomes obvious this episode went undetected as there is no member of the crew investigating the incident.

It has become routine in nice weather for a crew member to make his way to the lower deck with a key to unlock the padlock and release the manacles holding each prisoner to their shelf. His normal way is to release two at a time, always waiting until those two have made their way to into the hands of those on the upper deck. After he had released the first two, he turns back to release the second pair. As soon as the manacles are freed allowing the men to slide out from their platform, the prisoner with the piece of wood catches the crew member off guard, striking him squarely across his forehead. The crew member goes down like a poleaxed steer. In a flurry of panic, the prisoner continues to beat the man until he is certain he's no longer a threat. His next move is to extract the set of keys from the disabled jailer and remove the manacle connecting him to his bunk mate. In a flash, the prisoner is up the stairs to the upper deck. His nimble un-manacled presence catches this upper deck team unaware. Stunned by the unexpected breakout, the crew member watches with

54

no response as the prisoner hurls himself over the side of the ship only to have his effort thwarted by a suicide prevention net draped along the sides of the ship. This netting has been employed several times in preventing distraught prisoners from throwing themselves overboard. As this determined prisoner clumsily attempts to right himself, his feet awkwardly catch in the mesh further preventing him from continuing his suicide attempt. This delay has given the crew members the needed time to retrieve him from his failed efforts. They have him pinned to the deck as the ship's master is alerted to the fracas. Making his appearance as he always does from the upper aft deck, he gives the executive order to have the man lashed to a mast. The struggling prisoner is quickly restrained. The next order is to bring every prisoner from the hold topside. Under careful and close scrutiny, each pair of manacled prisoners is brought to the deck. There is much more effort on the part of the crew to push them into a formation allowing them to view the prisoner shackled to the mast. This whole procedure is orchestrated under the utmost vigilence. When the first mate is satisfied things are assembled the way the ship's master has ordered, he reports his achievement. In a short time, the ship's master makes a grand appearance from his stately position on the aft deck. He slowly raises his hand and brings it down in a chopping movement. In the next moment a crew member appears to confront the prisoner shackled to the mast. In his hand he carries an ax. In one swift movement he delivers the ax directly into the prisoner's ankle severing his foot from his leg. Along with the prisoners' look of terror a loud spontaneous gasp is sucked up by the crowd as if to alert every deity they have ever called upon. This visual exhibition is to serve as a warning that conveys a message that is designed to specifically override all language barriers. "Try and escape and this fate will be yours."

Kumi is dumbstruck by this demonstration. Even more so, he is traumatized. He is beginning to realize to a much fuller extent the inescapable threat these white men hold over him. He has seen war in his village but never anything as brutally calculated as this event; never has he seen anything as barbaric as this display.

The deadly reality of this voyage comes to life for anyone who has survived disease and death by witnessing the corpses carried out of the hold each day. They are callously disposed of over the side without ritual. It's come to where the sharks follow in the ship's wake, like persistent dogs waiting below the master's table for scraps—certain of another meal.

Chapter 11

Accosted Yet Again

The women on deck are sequestered on the opposite end of the ship away from the men. They have not had to go through nearly the number of rough rigors the men have had to endure—other than they too, along with the men, have had their heads shaved and have undergone a branding.

Unceremoniously jerked out of their villages, most of these women are fulfilling their longing to fight isolation by seeking out those who speak the same language and share the same traditions. Taking advantage of every opportunity, they sort each other out and quickly develop a bond. They spend a portion of their time singing. Included in these lyrics are messages to the segregated men who have been brought to the upper deck and are separated by a barrier. This performance is staged in the hopes of finding missing brothers and sisters.

In their village, Abina's mother shouldered a very important responsibility. The Vodun religion is a matriarchal religion; she is considered the "Queen Mother" and the protector of its priesthood. She organizes prayer, leads in ritual ceremonies, such as baptisms, weddings, and funerals. Songs and dances specific to an occasion are also prescribed by this elder. She also is instrumental in organizing the marketplace. Abina's role was to support her mother in overseeing all of the marketplace venders as well as assisting her in her religious duties. Others remember this "Queen Mother" organizing them when their men went off to war. Still more recall how they brought their produce and pigs to trade at this very market. Considering the loss of their close relatives—and this loss is irrevocable, to be forever transforming—provides these women with enough reason to consider themselves nearly as close as kin in sharing similar memories and a common religion. With these connections, they begin to form a community much as they did in their villages, and during their imprisonment in Elmina.

What these slave traders are inadvertently doing by wrenching these women out of their rightful places in their communities is to plunder more than a physical body—they have disintegrated the very fabric of knowledge within these communities. Previously, when African captives reached American shores, try as they may to attempt to reconstruct any links to their past, they remain fragmented at best. One can only appreciate these fragments that survive and are being used to construct a new African American culture.

The women spend much of their idle hours looking after the number of children that have also been taken, and talking among themselves—but always with a wary eye. Not only are they prisoners, they are also women in the company of men jailers. Being women places them in a different category than the men prisoners. In spite of being viewed as chattel, these African women have taught themselves how to navigate their enslavement differently than the men in that they can use their sexuality to bargain for what is best for themselves. These crewmen are often able to supply their paramour with an extra yam or another handful of rice. On the evolutionary scale, these crewmen have not evolved much beyond their base needs. They are at best opportunists, overdrinking, overeating, lying, and cheating as it pleases them. To pass up an opportunity to gratify themselves at the expense of a woman slave—especially when her owner is absent—is beyond the mindset of these men. They are rude, ill-mannered opportunists at every level.

When it comes to slave women, the ship's master is no better. The only difference between himself and his crew is he sets the rules. These rules have left the crew with rules prohibiting them from consorting with the females while he decides for himself who will squire his bed. Of course, many of these crewmen will take the risk and disobey the order. With the ship's master not able to be everywhere and with the many places on a ship to remain undetected, it's not unusual for a woman to be dragged off for five minutes or less of undetected buggery.

"Months at sea without the sound of a woman's voice, without a glimpse of her anatomy, with only dreams to live on make me a little demented," bemoans the ship's master to his first mate as he orders him to, "Bring me that tall black with the angular back."

The first mate knows exactly who his commander is speaking of. It's Abina. Because of her fine features and stately physique, she catches the attention of all males—black or white. If she were a free white woman, these same men would think twice before taking the liberties they do with a black defenseless slave woman. Be that as it may, Abina is summoned, given a pail of sea water and ordered to "clean up."

Being allowed to self-bathe is a luxury never afforded these captives. With the men, buckets of sea water are poured on them to clean them up enough to attempt to hold disease down. As for the women, the crew will surround them and toss buckets of sea water into the crowd. Dragging this simple luxury out as long as she dares, meticulously scrubbing every crevasse on her body, Abina relishes the bath more than she can express.

This is not the first time, Abina has been summoned by this ship's master. There is always an agony of uncertainty accompanying any of these summonses. To consider them as anything other than a rape would be to dismiss her offender. Her concern is how to be prepared as best she can if encountered by a violent perpetrator. She was surprised the first time she was solicited by this particular accoster to find him much shorter than he appears on his upper deck and less assured with his sexuality. Another surprising feature

59

turns out to be—unlike the Elmina governor who liked to have her well-dressed as a dining guest—this man is only willing to have her available long enough to get his business done and send her back with her companions. This encounter is not to be an exception. Within fifteen minutes, she is back on the deck finding her place.

The consequence following these sexual encounters only leads to more mental and spiritual isolation. There is a slow awareness overcoming Abina that she is property to be used and discarded at will. Alone in the night, seemingly lost at sea with her own increasing misgivings, she mourns her capture and fears for her future.

Chapter 12

Insurgency

For centuries, slavery has configured into the African society. In the African arrangement, it seldom forced the individual to lose his or her personhood. This European innovation brought with it a cruel twist. Its design from its inception is to degrade the slave to the level of an animal. Not accustomed to this humiliation, these men and women are finding it loathsome to adjust to this dehumanizing circumstance.

To combat this inclination toward despair among the women, out of a need to address her own spiritual vacuum, Abina has taken it upon herself to assume the role of her mother in absentia. She begins to take special interest in her fellow captives often leading them in song and dance.

"We will not dwell on this sad time, rather we will sing and dance in the anticipations of better times. We will let these barbarians know that we exist not only to have our bodies abused by them, but that we have a soul they can't touch," declares Abina. "We must always look forward. So, we shall shout and dance to the spirits of our ancestors and feel their presence as we look to tomorrow."

Of course, as usual their European slavers interpreted this seeming joyful behavior as proof of their captive's contentment with their squalid conditions. Even the ship's master has relaxed in seeing all this contentment believing that the apparent acceptance of their status stifles any inclination among the captives toward rebelliousness.

Six weeks pass before land is seen. As usual, the crew is elated. On completion of their delivery, they will enjoy some long anticipated free time. After becoming accustomed—as much as is possible—with the dreadfulness of their crossing, the captives are suffering anxiousness at new levels. They see land— but they aren't certain whether it's their homeland.

The ship has anchored, a hundred yards off shore to assure they won't be grounded on the shoals nearer to the coast. Carrying a brief-case securely under his arm, the ship's master orders a jon boat and a crew member to row him ashore. He has business to attend to before he is willing to bring one slave ashore. There is the matter of settling the expenses of carrying this cargo of slaves nearly five thousand miles and to arrange the long boats needed to ferry hundreds of slaves to shore.

The crewmen left on board begin the arduous process of disembarking the several hundred slaves. It's taking all hands on deck to begin this enormous task. The male captives are regarded the most problematic. The ship's master had cut rations halfway through the voyage to weaken the risk of having a resistance with any muscle. While he believed this formula to be necessary, it came at a cost—it has increased the death toll among those who were near failing. Kumi is aware of more deaths than he could count—including several crew members. He discovered a week ago his own shelf mate had died while still manacled to him.

The first mate is in charge of the entire procedure. It's his chore to assure an efficient, orderly, expeditious trip ashore. Kumi has been brought on deck with several others. They are to remain naked as they have for the past five months of their incarceration. The ship's master has ordered all surviving slaves to be cleaned, watered, and fed before any attempt to put them on the auction block. As buckets of sea water are thrown on them, each slave hand washes all the fecal material and filth off from himself and herself as best as they can. With no thought from the crew to clean their racks below deck, the ship's hold has developed into a fetid mass of uncleaned secretions. This has been left for any number of captives to lay in resulting in many of them suffering with flux (a condition where blood has mixed with a discharge of fecal matter).

As soon as one group has been washed, they are moved to a place on deck where they are fed. To their surprise, today they're given full rations. They're aware of being on the shores of land and having their normal routine disrupted. It's signaling something different is about to occur—but, the captive Africans are not at all certain as to its breadth and depth. Kumi has just finished his liter of water, been given his handful of boiled rice, and a boiled yam when the loud voices of men in a fracas comes rolling back across the deck. From the sounds of the language it's having something to do with the Nigerians. They have been prone to resist even where they know they have no chance of succeeding. They have had their people thrown overboard while still alive, they've been whipped and starved, but to no avail. They seem hell-bent on never yielding to slavery. With the voices becoming more intent, the crewmen in charge of Kumi's group are abandoning their post, running toward the fray. Even though he's left unguarded, Kumi is not inclined to rush into a ruckus he knows nothing about, nor are any of the members in his group. Without realizing it, Kumi has abandoned his earlier zest for freedom and resigned himself to captivity.

The noise continues with screams and cries of terror cutting sharply through the air like the final heaves of a dying men. Shortly, the mystery comes to a head. Kumi is taken aback to see several Nigerians running free of their manacles. They are from a tribe that has produced a taller and more muscular variety of people than most. The sweat in these men, is manifesting itself in shining ripples of skin stretched over tense muscle. Some of them are stained with blood. It's difficult to differentiate its source but each male is in possession

63

of a weapon. Whatever crew are left alive are jumping overboard. One of the Nigerians with a wild eye tosses a ring of keys into the Kumi's midst. Not certain as to what has just transpired, no one touches the keys.

It soon becomes apparent that the Nigerians have captured the ship. No one in Kumi's group is clear what this means except there is no white man left on board to determine this sudden change of events for them. They are all faced with the possibility of freedom, even if it's for a brief time. Kumi is frozen along with everyone else. This is what everyone has been waiting for—now it's laying before them and they're frozen with fear. Not fear of retribution, but fear of freedom. After months of oppression, and traumatization, they're so disconnected, they find themselves more conditioned to their status as chattel than to their hopes as men.

In view of the aftermath, the insurgence has captured the attention of everyone aboard the ship. At the same time, it has caught these remaining captives off guard—including Kumi. No one knows what course these angry Nigerians are charting or where the rest are to find themselves. As for these remaining, they are anxious to weigh any option that won't cost them their lives.

Kumi is fully engrossed but remains paradoxically pensive—it's leaving him conflicted. His eyes are moving from one point to another. His heart is pounding, his mind is racing, all that's left is something within his soul that tells him this is his opportunity. He finds himself unconsciously looking for some solid leadership that suggests there is a plan going forward. As much as he is looking, nothing is coming forward with the exception of the Nigerians clumsily attempting to raise the sails. Kumi's thought is "These men know nothing about sailing." His thoughts are telling him "This is not the time for me to get involved."

Simultaneously, the disturbance on board has not gone without notice. People on shore couldn't help but see and hear the vociferous cries of men being thrown overboard. Some of these injured crewmen, in spite of their wounds, have made it to shore. They spend little time informing these onlookers of the facts surrounding the incident.

Back on the ship, the Nigerians are still frantically attempting to put up a sail. The fact they have no prior knowledge in sailing doesn't seem to dampen their fervor. They have come to the conclusion that to risk their own lives rather than succumb to being a white man's chattel is worth the price—even to the point of death. For the present they are trying to take advantage every option laying before them to achieve their ends. Miraculously, they have managed to get a sail up. This, in turn, has caused the ship to twist into the wind, which is causing the ship to drag its gigantic anchor. The expressions on these men's faces reflect their willingness to do whatever it takes to make their escape. Unfortunately, the sail they've managed to get in place is not the mainsail; rather a small jib that is doing little to move the huge wooden behemoth, especially while dragging an anchor. Their next step is to attempt to reel up the anchor. The tension caused by the weight of the ship pulling on the anchor line is too much for even several of the men to lurch it loose.

Enough time has lapsed for others to decide if they are joining the rebellion. A few are making their way to the ring of keys still laying at Kumi's feet, unlocking their manacles, and joining with the determinations of the Nigerians.

What hasn't been noticed, is how an onshore militia has loaded themselves into a series of long boats and has made their way to the sides of the ship. They are armed with every kind of firearm available. Before any meaningful reaction by the insurgents can form, this militia, using rope ladders has scaled both the port and starboard sides of the ship. With muskets in hand along with several blunder busses loaded with nails and broken glass; this group of anti-abolitionists are prepared for a full-on confrontation. The first group over the rail indiscriminately fires at everyone regardless of their activities. Seeing the inevitable as at least thirty or forty armed men come pouring in over the rails, the Nigerian freedom fighters quickly assess their disadvantage. One by one, they abandon their weapons and run to the sides of the ship. As if rehearsed, they hurl themselves overboard. As each hits the water and resurfaces, they make themselves easy targets. The air on the deck is grey with clouds of gun smoke as man after man empties his weapon into the hapless captives below. Within a short time, the gunfire has ceased. With no one willing to retrieve the bodies, the dying rebels are left to the mercy of the sea. Each insurgent has left a small ring of blood spreading on the surface of the water surrounding his body, slowly spreading with the hope of the sea carrying his spirit back to Africa as a free man.

Abina and the women are quartered on the aft section of the ship. They were also in the process of bathing when their crewmen abandoned them to investigate the disruption on the men's end. Because they are out of sight of the men, they have no way of measuring the danger this fracas is causing. It has them terrified. Since they cannot see, they can only hear and surmise from the sounds that things have gone awry. The only thing Abina is certain of is when the volley of gunfire has subsided, she is still alive.

Chapter 13

Frostbite

Willie shoots up from his nest of pine needles like a scalded cat, eyes wide open, startled, he thinks, "Damn! Did I over sleep again?" His heart is pounding with fear. His mind has taken him back to the forge. He's expecting to see Herr Yunk standing by with a whip. Willie's terror of his master is greater than that of death. It takes another second for him to process his thoughts. He quickly gathers he is no longer at the forge, rather he's in a pine thicket. The full brunt of his rash actions hit him squarely, leaving his face an ashen white. Taking a deep breath and letting it out slowly, Willie calms himself—at least for the moment. The sudden realization of the magnitude of his decision, under a cooler mind, is giving him pause. At fifteen, he is full of the Geist ("spirit") of an emerging young man. His emotions can fly like the wind carrying him in a storm—never knowing where they may land him and to what consequence.

The days are short this time of year. Willie has slept most of the daylight away. Peering out of his forested camp, the sky and the earth touch, melding together in a grey ghostly gloom. He quickly builds a fire and roasts a potato and melts several hands full of snow along with it to rehydrate himself. He can hear the wind making a louder whisper as it forces its way through the swaying pine boughs overhead. It's the kind of wind that gives a warning of impending bad weather. Realizing he is going to face falling temperatures, Willie hugs his scarf up around his face a bit further.

67

Making his way back onto the road, he notices the wind and additional snow have obliterated his earlier tracks. The snow has grown heavier and, with the increasing darkness, it grows more difficult to differentiate the road from the rest of the terrain. The mounting strength of the wind strikes Willie so hard that it compels him to forge headlong bent forward. He can feel the might of the wind against his struggling legs as he continues his unrelenting fight against Mother Nature's merciless fury. His breathe is coming in short pants. Little by little, his strength is beginning to wane. Two potatoes in twenty-four hours under normal circumstances would hardly be enough to sustain life, much less enough to put his body through this test.

It seems an incessant time walking through the snow before Willie passes a distant tree he'd set as a goal. Then another, and another, and another with each becoming dimmer and dimmer as the coming night slowly squeezes out any remaining light from the day. Willie's concentration no longer hears the wail of the wind. The task is consuming his thoughts. He has battled the blizzard yard by yard most of the night. He feels the growing pain behind his eyes. It's from the penetrating cold headwind. Little by little, his legs are not heeding the commands from his mind.

"Maybe if I just stop and rest for a minute, I'll be okay to go on till dawn." With a rest break settled in his mind, Willie drops to the snow-covered ground. Lying prone with his body totally at rest for the first time all night, he feels no cold, hears no wind, only comfort. His mind is suddenly taking him home to his mother's hearth. It's a vision of warmth and well-being that seems to be carried by the wind. Soon, the vision fades. It's followed by a feeling of sleepiness. He can feel the cold beginning to creep in on him ever so slowly. The earlier plan he had of a quick rest and then resuming his trudge once again is becoming less and less a willful thought. Sleep is beckoning. Fighting to open his eyes, he catches a glimpse of the morning light. The storm has lessened and the redness of a rising sun is striking its colors on the horizon. He feels more chill as the sweat from his slog is beginning to cool along with a deep bite of cold against his exhausted body. Despite the chill, and no fire, and lying in the snow drenched road, he is not uncomfortable. More and more an overwhelming desire to sleep has engulfed his will. He is no longer fighting the drifts. He is captivated by the contentment his longing to sleep is offering him. Giving in to the bliss is no longer a fight as he drifts into a fast sleep. While the rising sun begins to take on a warm glow, Willie's body temperature begins to fall lower as the cold begins to demand more and more of his warmth.

The morning sun silently glistening against the crest of the new fallen snow announces the end of the blizzard. A sudden disruption breaking the silence is the approaching sound of man and beast in the form of a horse-drawn sleigh.

"Look, Father!" cries a voice from an oncoming sleigh. "There, in the road. It must be him."

It's the voice of a young girl leaping from the sleigh, rushing headlong into a foot of snow prepared to confront her. She stumbles against its depth. Regaining her footing, she continues her trudge toward the dark form lying still in the white snow.

"It is him, Father!" echoes the voice once again. It's the voice of Magdalena. She has accompanied her father in his quest to retrieve his servant.

Herr Yunk remains seated on the sleigh. The reins are still in his hands as though he is torn between running the sleigh over the seeming lifeless body in front of him or doing what needs to be done to sustain Willie's life. Still conflicted, he finds himself reacting more to Magdalena reaction than to the helpless form of his servant lying in the road.

"Don't do a thing until I see his condition," shouts Herr Yunk climbing down from his lofty seat.

Not heeding her father's imperative, Magdalena is already making a rapid diagnosis of Willie's condition. By the time her father arrives, she is on her knees beside his seeming lifeless body. Willie's skin has taken on the blue/gray color of the dead. His body is rigid and he has no responsive movements. The only clue that there may still be some life left in him is the gasp his lungs make as Magdalena attempts to sit him up right.

By now, Herr Yunk is positioned to assess Willie's lifeless repose. Quickly removing a glove, one after the other, Yunk pulls Willie's closed eyelids open to examine his eye movements. Something tells him, this servant still has some remaining life—not much—but enough to retrieve his sprawling body from the road and heave it up onto the back of his wagon. Magdalena follows her father's wordless actions—not certain as to how her father may end Willie's willful defiance. She's mentally preparing herself for the worst. She is aware that, by law, her father owns Willie, having nearly the power of life and death over him. Indentured servants possess some rights but nearly all of these are compromised in the event of an attempted escape. She'd insisted she accompany her father in his pursuit of his headstrong servant. She not only possesses a strain of patience where her father demonstrates none, she has also begun to develop some feelings for Willie. This latter part she would deny if it meant cutting her tongue out rather than admit it.

If things go well, the journey back home should be a little over an hour. Willie had only managed a mere seven miles. The team of horses are well-fed and strong. They will make short time of this distance. Herr Yunk is just as silent on the return leg of the journey as he was with the beginning. He could give the impression he's intrenched in a knowing conviction that he has a handle on exactly what the outcome this disruption is going to produce. Unfortunately, this is not the case. The only example he has had to guide him with Willie is his own experience when he too had been indentured to a master blacksmith many years ago. Since he had never tried to escape and he holds much of his dealings with Willie by reflecting back on his own experiences, he is at a loss as to how

70

to effectively deal with this ordeal. Yunk holds to the idea that a blacksmith holds an honorable position, that he is considered one of the most essential, if not in many circumstances, the most essential member of his community. He is heavily depended upon. He's the tool maker. Only he can supply the necessary tools for his village to thrive. There isn't a horse or a mule in a day's distance that he has not trimmed and reshod several times. Farm tools, farm wagons, which are the chief mode of transportation, all need the skilled hands of the blacksmith to repair. Furthermore, even housewives depend on his talents at maintaining their supply of pans and kettles. Now, he is responsible for continuing the next generation of this essential trade. These are the thoughts that force him to remain silent. He knows he has to deal with this disturbance in a traditional fashion. The reason he has been voted as an outsider to become a member of this village is because of his readiness to adapt to the traditions of its citizens. Punishment, in this case, is a must. Designing it to fit the circumstance is going to take a discernment he must develop.

The return trip is uneventful. There are places in the road that are drifted over with snow that would have prevented a hiker such as Willie to navigate, but Herr Yunk's huge draft horses make light work of them.

Magdalena has taken a position in the back of the sleigh tending to Willie. She is vigorously rubbing his hands and face. His breathing remains shallow and slow.

"Don't die Willie, please don't die." She whispers to prevent her father from overhearing her sentiments. She has grown quite fond of Willie. If her father knew of her feelings, he would have her shipped off to his sisters in Stralsund rather than deal with it. In Yunk's world, an indentured servant has to be kept in their place. It doesn't include joining in with his family members.

For the rest of the morning, Herr Yunk urges the team on. The snapping sound of the horses' traces is all that is heard as the sleigh slips silently across the glittering snow. Magdalena remains at her posting attending to Willie as he slips in and out of consciousness. She has his horse blanket wrapped around him with his head in her lap warming him with as much of her body she dares while avoiding the surveillance of her father.

The horses are picking up speed as they sense they are close to the end of their journey. The smoke from a well-kept hearth can be seen gathering in a white haze above the trees. It's always a welcome sight to Herr Yunk; not so much can be said for Willie. He remains in a near coma as a result of his brush with death. As soon as her father has stopped the team, he will busy himself taking care of his animals before his attention will turn to his recalcitrant bondservant. Knowing this, and waiting until her father has busied himself with the horses, Magdalena slips from the sleigh speeding in the direction of the house.

"Mother, Mother, we found him. He's half dead. Please hurry and help," cries Magdalena.

Sensing the urgency in her daughter's voice, Frau Yunk throws a shawl over her shoulders and follows her frantic daughter out to the back of the sleigh. Willie, still more dead than alive, is still breathing but noticeably unconscious.

With the same anxiousness in her voice, Magdalena queries, "Do you think he's going to live?"

Frau Yunk is looking hard at the frostbite on Willie's hands and face. "I honestly don't know until we get him inside and see how bad he's frozen."

In a position to overhear the conversation, Herr Yunk makes his position upon his wife's last statement known. Holding true to his conviction a bondservant is never to enter his master's house, he snaps, "Put him to bed in the barn. Tend to him there."

From the tone of his voice both wife and daughter know better than to question this decision. The barn temperature is warmer than the freezing temperature outside but not as warm as it would have been behind the hearth in the house. Between the two of them, they carry Willie to his cot in the rear of the forge. Leaving him fully dressed, Frau Yunk removes his leather boots to examine his feet for frostbite. His socks are frozen to his boot tops. This is not a good sign. Once his feet are exposed, it's apparent his injuries are recoverable. Frau Yunk notices he has some frostbite around the skin on the end of his toes. She remembers seeing this condition one other time. Her brother lost all his toes on his left foot at a time he had gotten drunk and passed out outside on a cold winter's night. "The doctor had to remove them before he died from the poison in his blood," she recalls. Upon further examination of Willie's toes, she goes on to say, "This looks a lot better than I suspected. At least we don't have to alert Doctor Franz for an amputation."

Magdalena feels a heartfelt reassurance at her mother's positive prognosis. Relieved, she prepares to heat some bricks to pack around Willie's recovering body. Herr Yunk is busying himself with feeding the horses in a neighboring stall. In spite of the cold temperature, they have worked up a lather. They need to be wiped down, watered, and fed.

Watching all the fuss over his bondservant, Herr Yunk feels compelled to comment, "Don't make him too damn comfortable, he doesn't deserve it." With that said, he returns to the meticulous care he renders his horses.

73

Chapter 14

The Sale

Several thousand miles south of Willie is another happening with another young man who is no longer in charge of his own life. He is a Ghanaian named Kumi. His plight is similar to Willie's in that he is also suffering. He has suffered being caught up in the dragnet of Africans selling Africans to slavers, being held in subhuman conditions in the slave dungeons at Elmina, forced on board a disease-ridden slave bearing ship headed to the United States of America. Now his suffering is about to take another twist. The agricultural boom in the new world is demanding more labor than the country is able to provide. This has fueled a quick solution to revert to a slave based labor system.

There has been an insurrection on board the slavers' ship that has brought Kumi to the coast of the United States. This was brought to a quick end. The next step was to bring the slaves by long boats to the shore.

Still chained together, the captives are lined up waiting on the beach until the entire boat is emptied. Crew members who survived the insurrection are armed with every weapon from muskets to swords and axes. They are rightfully nervous. As much as they would like to consider these captives as animals, they know each of them, if given the opportunity, have a calculating intelligence that can defeat them. The more their captors fear these beings, the more determined they are to subjugate them to animal status. In their minds,

74

their own safety demands each of these beings must be broken in mind, body, and spirit. The preferred method is to create fear. To do this, the use of the whip is the most common weapon believed to produce the needed suppression.

"You can get a nigger outta the jungle, but ya gotta beat the jungle outta 'im." This very statement suggests every slave owner fears he is sitting on a powder keg of repressed anger of his own creation.

Kumi has not the slightest idea where he may be. The trees are different than his home in Ghana. And there are many more white people than he has ever seen before. The beach is wet. There is a simple delight in the feeling of clean, wet sand beneath his feet. He can feel it forcing itself between his toes. This simple sensation is enough to give him a sense of pleasure he has not felt since his capture. For that moment, his heart is filed with joy, he is one with the universe. The feeling is suddenly interrupted by the shouts of the white guards. They are ordering a group of chained Nigerians to halt. Ignoring the order, the chained captives have backed themselves into the ocean. The guards are truly in a panic as these problematic captives continue to back themselves into the sea. Soon, the Nigerians are up to their waists in the welcoming waters of the ocean. This group of a dozen men have taken their fate into their own hands. Rather than surrender their lives to the white slavers for a life of servitude, they have made the decision to drown themselves. Undaunted by their guards' shouts and the musket fire striking some of them, they continue their backward trek deeper and deeper until their heavy chains pull them one-by-one into the deep, where they are no longer visible.

Kumi and the rest of the remaining captives have no other choice as to their own fate. There is still a strong will to live among the young. They have not had a sufficient amount life to have suffered enough defeats to give up at this time. They are still willing to endure what it takes to sustain life with the hope things will get better.

With the Nigerians' suicide pacts behind them, the remaining captives are led from the beach to a slave pen. It's an enclosed area that is filthy but a palace compared to what they've survived so far. Here they are rubbed down with some kind of oil. In spite of being nearly starved to death, this is to make them shine with a healthy appearance for their next buyer. They are also examined for any kind of wounds. If some are discovered they are filled in with tar. They are also shaved once again from head to toe. Lastly, each captive is given a loose-fitting shirt and a pair of trousers. Despite the torturous four months they've survived, their broker/owner want them to appear as healthy and strong as possible. They are separated by brand marks and taken to an elevated stage, where they are to be bid on by buyers who need labor.

The time finally arrives for Kumi. He is led out with several others with the same brand. Not understanding English, they are pushed and prodded like cattle to the stage where they are expected to be reviewed and examined by potential buyers.

Stumbling up the steps in his chains, Kumi tops the stage. His eyes suddenly set on a familiar sight—it's Abina. She bears the same brand and has been placed on the auction block along with himself. The broker expects to auction them as a breeding pair. Neither Kumi or Abina are certain what is happening with them but are certain that it's not in their best interest. White men with strange looking clothing, with foul smelling breath, smoking cigars crowd up on the platform and begin to prod each of them. They examine their arms and legs, force their mouths open to examine their teeth. Abina has had enough experience with white men to know better than to resist any kind of fondling. She has been granted at least a one-piece gingham dress to cover herself. Nonetheless, at the request of a portly white man chomping on a cigar, she is undressed once again. He begins to look her up and down, turning her around, with his cigar between his fingers and a suspicious calculating look, he lifts her heavy breasts.

76

Turning to the broker while poking Abina in her abdomen, the white man says, "This here nigger looks tah be pregnant. I don't believe I'm gonna pay yer price tah risk gettin' a pregnant nigger back ta Georgia 'fore she has a kid, 'side that she ain't nothin' but skin an' bones with a tanned hide pull o'er her skeleton, gonna take a lot ah nursin 'fore this'n get back tah work."

The broker listens to his potential buyer trying to bargain his asking price down. This longtime broker's been at this business too long to be beaten down by the likes of this buyer. Instead, his rebuff brings out another detail. "Yer damn lucky I ain't askin' ya'all ta pay extra fer the spare nigger ya'all gettin' fer the price ah one."

"Yer point is taken, but I ain't gonna be gettin' no work out'n this wench 'till after she lays-in," rejects the buyer. "Tell ya what I'll do. I'll give ya, yer askin' price fer the buck, an' you give me ten percent discount on the wench, an' we got a deal."

Hands are shaken. The deal's been made. The new owner is a cotton grower from Georgia named Col. Winslow Kilbourn, although he mainly goes by "The Colonel." He orders another slave to take possession of this fresh batch of new slaves, including Kumi and Abina. They're each given the brand of their new owner and abruptly led to a crude wagon with a barred cage fitted into it. It's a bare wagon with no benches. The only amenity is a pail chained to a corner. The slave in charge doesn't speak any African language, as he was born here, but with the tone of his voice and a few hand gestures pointing at his rear end, he makes one thing clear.

"De Colonel don' wan' none you niggers shitin' on da wagon flo,' he wan ya'all use dis here slop bucket."

They're each given a bowl of boiled corn, a liter of water and ordered inside. Seven slaves to each side, all hunched down on the floor. The slave that is instructing and feeding them is also their driver.

77

The Colonel, given to an ostentatious twist, is in the lead, comfortably situated inside a horse-drawn Hackney. His driver is a "house slave" outfitted in a uniform usually reserved for staff attending England's royalty.

Kumi and Abina share a moment of joy with seeing each other again. They are the only two in the wagon able to communicate using the same language.

Abina is the first to speak. "I saw you a few times on the boat. I always watched for you after they would throw someone overboard."

In her village she never would have initiated a conversation first. Her status separated them, but her forced community break up with her shipmates presents an opportunity to renew her past life once again. For the present, it's enough to be pleased with Kumi's company.

"My uncle was one of those. He became sick to death. They threw him overboard while he was still alive," replies Kumi.

Abina processes Kumi's account of his uncle's fate. "We lost a lot too. Some were from our village; I had grown close to many of them."

Kumi misses his uncle and, not wanting to dwell on his loss, he chooses to change the subject.

"I hate to say it, but this part of this horrid journey is the best so far. We're outside. I had a difficult time keeping my spirit alive those many days buried in that stinking dungeon in Elmina and then in the rotten ship's hold they made us dwell in. Sometimes the air was so bad, I didn't want to take another breath."

Taking in another deep breath, Kumi says, "This air is good for my soul."

78

Soon, both become weary and retire to their own thoughts. Kumi can't help but look around at the other companions in their wagon. Like himself, in just four months, they have all been uprooted from very familiar surroundings to a complete culture shock. All are mere shadows of their former selves. All, not unlike himself, are skin and bones.

It isn't just their bodies that are undergoing malnourishment—their very souls are suffering. Nowadays their thoughts have little to do with being of home and with relatives. Most feelings are fraught with fear and tension. More of their concerns have to do with being in a strange place with so many white people with whom they share very little in common, especially since they are treated more like animals than as humans. Some of their more immediate concerns have to do with a fear of their immediate fate, like "Where am I going; what's going to happen to me?" Fear of the unknown is a real human concern. These white men are more dangerous than any jungle beast they've had to contend with. Each, in their own way is beginning to suspect they are going to have to remain much more alert than they had in the jungle.

Chapter 15

Initiation

The contained slave wagon continues to ramble along the dusty roads of the southern state of Georgia. It's been a three-day journey thus far with the expectation of a half-a-day left before concluding at the Kilbourn Plantation. It's a sprawling area of the state with much of it either wooded or in agriculture. Kumi is taken by how many Africans, both men and women, are to be seen along the way. He is also aware that they seem to be busy doing something in the fields with plants that have white balls of something growing from their branches. "I wonder if we are still in Africa?" is a sudden thought. He doesn't recognize any of the vegetation as being of the same varieties found in his home district; nor does the air smell like the air he was accustomed to. "But where did all these Africans come from?" The question continues to haunt him, "And why are they all wearing white man's clothing?"

By afternoon the small caravan has reached the outskirts of the plantation. Kumi is agonized by all the listless black African faces. They are everywhere, tired with hollow death eyes. His spirit has hoped it had left its deepest abyss behind, now discovers it can go even deeper. It's as if the bright white of The Colonel's plantation house is designed to contrast his darkened spirit even more. This is the first time this surmounting cloud of hopelessness has managed to enshroud Kumi in this way. A sick feeling in his stomach has seemingly cloaked his soul in its bile. He has survived being kidnapped, the foul dungeons of Elmina, and the disease-ridden ship's hold because he had always lived with the hope of a better day—now he is seeing the culmination of all his hope dissolved in the tribulation of these souls.

The lead coach carrying The Colonel veers to the right leading to the plantation house while Kumi's caged conveyance veers to the left leading to a row of ram shackled buildings in various stages of ruination. The same distraught faces are on display here as has been noted for days. Kumi has never felt as empty in his life. His mind drifts back to his life in his village and how the ways of his people were substantially more rewarding than this existence. Many times, as young men often do, he felt a stifling in his village surroundings—so confining—as though he knew there was more than what was there. But now, looking at the immensity of open fields that seem to go to the edge of the world, his village surroundings all seems so barren and bleak. At this moment, for the first time since his capture, Kumi is feeling the emptiness of his person. Knowing he can never go home again, "but neither can I live in this white man's world. There is no place in this white man's world I belong," becomes his weighty conclusion. He has never felt so lost and confused. There are plenty of places for sympathy to be considered in this place, but no time is made for it.

Their driver's name is Tom. It turns out he is also in charge of earmarking them into an empty shack. Kumi and Abina are placed together. Other male and female parings are also made. This is all at the design of The Colonel. Importing slaves from Africa has been illegal for a number of years. (The law is rarely enforced, Kumi and Abina are examples of this.) Since all children born to a slave mother are considered property of the plantation owners, these owners have found ways of placing males and females together as breeding pairs to ensure another generation of laborers.

Not certain what lies beyond the opening, the two gingerly enter the cabin. Kumi looks up at the ceiling to determine its ability to prevent rain while Abina is concerned with what kind household items may be about and their use. The floor is dirt, the bed is structured from a small tree cut to make four posts

81

sunk in the earthen floor with a simple frame around it with some planking across the frame. In some places the planks are missing. When these shacks become vacant through death or the slave being sold, others will scavenge as much of its contents as they can without being caught. There is a hearth, but no pot or wood. There is also the proverbial slop bucket resting in the corner.

Still contemplating the details surrounding what is to be her shelter, an African woman appears carrying an armload of items along with what appears to be a ten-year-old boy toting an iron pot and some wooden spoons and bowls.

Not realizing neither Abina nor Kumi understand a word in English, she begins to explain, "Dis her be a wee' s'ply of conmeal, lahd, a bit of bacon, a few swee' taters, and some buttermilk. Don' be goin' tru it all cuz dey ain' no mo." She is also carrying two rough blankets, and two changes of clothing for each of them. Without another word, the two deposit what they have carried in, turn and leave.

Both Kumi and Abina stare dumbstruck as to what all this could mean. They haven't understood the details of what has just been explained but are able to understand the basic context as to how these items are to be used.

With the day nearly over, Kumi and Abina are exhausted. Nibling on a few things that can be eaten without preparation, they collapse on the wooden planking, cover themselves with a blanket and give in to a restless sleep.

Once again, Abina has gone to her bed with the sureness that she is pregnant. She has known it since Elmina. The father of this child is the white governor of that facility. As with most mothers, a maternal instinct arrives at some point. She has become aware of this feeling. It frightens her to be alone and away from her mother at this time in her life. To the same degree, she has felt these bad spirits entering her soul so many times since her abduction, she opens herself to the spirits that can lift her soul. When she has practiced this meditation in the past, something occurs within her that allows her to discern a pathway to adapt to an untenable situation.

BLAAAATTTT! BLAAAATTTT! BLAAAATTTT! The sound brings Kumi and Abina shooting out of their blankets like they were on fire. This resonance is beyond animal or human. Never have they heard anything as piercing. Left dumbfounded, they hear the inflections of the white man's language. Making their way to the door, it's pitch black except for a man on a horse with a lantern. By his demeanor and clothing, they recognize their driver Tom. Once more the penetrating sound reverberates across the darkened morning.

"Wake up, Niggas, it be fo-thity. Time tah be up an' in da fiel'!"

Not aware of what is in store, Kumi and Abina wander outside and join the other slaves who are assembling themselves behind Tom's horse. From out of the shadows, a slave woman appears. She is a tall woman similar to Abina. She's wearing white women's clothing. It's apparent she has her eye trained on Abina. Taking her by the arm she pulls Abina away from the assembly.

"Chil', ya'll come wif me. Missy Kilbour' wan' see ya'll in de Big House."

Not understanding the language, Abina nonetheless understands this woman's tone. It possesses an air of authority with assurance. She had observed this same composure many times in her mother. Left with no other options, she follows the woman along a well-worn path. Ahead of them are the bright lights in the windows of the Kilbourn mansion. Even in the dark, the whiteness of the house sketches itself against the blackness of the early morning. This slave woman has brought Abina into a room in the back on the lower level of this magnificent building. The last time a woman brought her to a room as magnificent as this was in Elmina where she was being delivered to the governor. She fully expects something of this sort is in the makings again. She is led to a room that contains a wooden tub with water. There, alongside hang the familiar wash rags, soaps, towel, a petty coat, a white woman's dress, and a head piece to cover her hair.

"These white men sure do like their women clean," thinks Abina. Not to say these baths aren't refreshing, it's what follows that is not heartening. Knowing better than to take too long with this luxury, Abina is aware of the time allotted for the procedure. Finishing with her wash, she looks at the paraphernalia laid out for her with bewilderment. To put all this on her frame appears to be a task that requires more hands than she was born with. In the slave world there is very little to no patience with inefficiency; not knowing something will bring disciple faster than one can learn. In other words, ignorance will always bring a lashing by tongue or the whip. On a plantation, nothing is ever done soon enough, or well enough, to satisfy all the people in charge. This case is not to be the exception. Already a step ahead, entering the room is the tall elderly woman who was assigned to get Abina bathed.

"Da Lo'd sho' ain' shoin' me no mercy tah day. You's niggas comin' off dem ships is dumber dan rocks. Missy puts me in charge ob all you's—wha's a soul tah do?"

She is saying all this as she turns and twists Abina first one way, and then another, all the while pulling underclothes and a petticoat over her head, then following with a dress and a proper head dress to cover Abina's shaved head. Once this task is finished, the tall woman signals Abina to follow her.

Entering another room, Abina feels an overwhelming heat. She finds herself in a place where food is being prepared. She has never in her life seen anything like it. There are several large hearths with huge iron pots cooking over open fires. The tall woman directs her to a stool and a tub of corn still on the cobs. Giving Abina a quick demonstration on how to shuck the kernels from the cob, she continues to jabber despite Abina not understanding a word she is uttering.

"You's gets tah shuckin' dis 'ere coan. Dem fiel' han's gots tah eat in a couple hours. Yo job tah make's sho' dey duz."

Surprised there is no white man coming along to take her off to some secret room in the house, Abina readjusts her thinking to the task at hand.

On another part of the plantation, stumbling along in the dark, Kumi is trying his best to determine what is expected of him. He is paying close attention to those who are seemingly moving along with an air of confidence. By the time they arrive at the field, a bit of daylight is beginning to crack in the east. Some other place in the world this sunrise is promising a better day. This is not to be expected here on this day.

Kumi soon makes out a flaunting figure that needs no explanation. There is a silhouette of a man wearing a broad brimmed hat with his back to the rising sun. He's spraddled atop a wagon with both hands braced against his hips. His right hand grips a coiled instrument that never needs an explanation— the whip. This ominous silhouette belongs to a man to fear even more than the plantation owner—it's The Colonel's overseer. His name is Jack Beauchamp.

These men are generally hired because of their record of efficiency rather than their benevolent tendencies. The idea held by all overseers is, "All niggers need tah be whipped in tah shape." In many cases these are young men whose families have allotted the family plantation to an older brother forcing them to find other means of making a living. Others yet are aspiring to own their own plantation, using an overseer's position as a stepping-stone in that direction. To prevent a revolt from ever taking place is to hold to the belief that slaves must be made to realize they are animals rather than humans—that they have no chance against the superior power of the white man. With these men, ruthlessness always trumps patience in a work situation. The whip is freely used, if for no other reason than to create a sense of total subjugation. All in all, they are to be feared rather than respected.

85

Tom has assigned himself to approach this ominous figure. When Tom returns, he quickly forms several groups, giving each their work assignments. For Kumi's group, he assigns a detail to clear forested land for field expansion. Kumi recalls doing this task for his family's garden plot. It's backbreaking work, but it's work he knows he is capable of performing. His disadvantage lies in the language barrier preventing him from following instructions. At this point he's as vulnerable as a slave can get. The lash is always given first in regard to a negligence of duties. Even at that, a language barrier will be more of a reason to apply the whip by a prejudiced overseer.

"It's bad 'nough havin' tah deal with these domestic niggers without havin' tah deal with them dumbass ship rats they sendin' me," says Jack. "How in hell The Colonel 'spects me tah get his shit done 'roun' here is beyon' me?"

So far, Kumi has avoided the whip. He has an innate ability to see things that need to be done before other things can be accomplished and on first impression is proving himself to be a fast worker and a fast thinker. Jack is taking note of this.

It's ten o'clock. With hours of hard labor already behind them, it's time to have the first meal of the day. Tom blows the same horn to signal a break as he used for morning reveille. Already exhausted, Kumi can't be more grateful. Weeks of inactivity on board the ship have weakened him. Nonetheless, he follows the crowd as they gather in a cluster on the arrival of a wagon laden with a huge iron pot. What surprises him the most is Abina situated on the back of the wagon. Spotting Kumi, she quickly looks about for any white eyes that may be taking note. Satisfied she's inconspicuous, she gives him a slight, knowing nod. Taking note, he returns with a quick nod of his own.

Each slave is given a bowl of boiled corn meal mixed with beans. The rest period lasts for two hours. Many slaves return to their shack for a quick nap.

Others find a place under a tree and stretch out. Not certain where he stands, Kumi remains alert to any unforeseen obligation.

It all comes to an end with blast of the horn signaling a return to work. This period of work continues all afternoon through the heat of the day. Boys no older than ten serve as water carriers; they are obliged to lug heavy pails of tepid water. If they're found to be lollygagging, they are quickly given the cane.

When exhaustion is about to overtake the work crew, Kumi is surprised how quickly a song breaks out. It suddenly makes the work less tedious as the workers synchronize their work to the song.

"O, my Lo'd! Oh, my goo' Lo'd! Kee' me fom sinkin' down. Ah tell you wha' Ah mean tah do.

"Kee' me fom sinkin' down. Ah mean tah go tah hebbin too.

"Kee' me fom sinkin' down. Ah Loo' up yonder an' wha' do ah see? Kee' me fom sinkin' down.

"Ah sees dem angels beckonin' me. Kee' me fom sinkin' down."

Kumi doesn't understand the words, but the tunes have a resemblance to the music he had grown used to in Ghana.

It's well after dark when the day finally comes to an end. Kumi drags himself back to his shack. He's beyond exhaustion. Months of inactivity on board the ship with a near starvation diet have taken their toll on his body, mind, and spirit. He can't see how he can manage to do this for the rest of his life.

Abina's day hasn't proven to be much better. Her day has ended sooner than Kumi's allowing her to get back to the shack and get a meal prepared. Both are exhausted, buried in their own thoughts. It's all been like a nightmare that can't be awoken from.

Chapter 16

Zuchtigen ("Chastisement")

Herr Yunk has taken the rest of the day to confer with the Schultheiss and Ruggerecht (those in charge of maintaining the law in his district.) The topic is to discover to what degree he is legally able to exercise corporal punishment on a runaway indentured servant. The consensus he is left with is he can do anything that does no permanent damage or lead to death. The other sentiment he's left with is if he doesn't apply corporal punishment to an indentured servant's infraction as serious as running away that he runs the risk of having charges rendered against himself for lack of duty as a Meister.

Herr Yunk has left strict orders forbidding Frau Yunk nor Magdalena from having contact with Willie. He is not to be fed nor ministered to. Late in the day, Yunk returns home. His supper is waiting for him. He eats in silence. Neither Yunk's wife nor Magdalena are prepared to confront him regarding his decision as to how he's going to deal with Willie.

Yunk's mind is harking back to his younger years in his father's house. They were Bauer (backward farmers). The title carries with it scorn and ridicule. They were considered churlish and stupid. They were often looked at as animals and of such low caste as they were completely ignored. Herr Yunk feels fortunate in what he has become because of his skill as tradesman. Because of that disposition and his ready willingness to adapt to all the traditions of the village as his own and his family's, he's been granted the respectable status of a Burgher. "I will not jeopardize my family's good name for the sake of

89

sentimentality." Whatever it will take in order to maintain his position in the community is the decision he has settled upon.

After his meal, Yunk remains silent. He knows what has to be done. He takes is no delight in his decision, but that's the German way. It's a duty. And duty always must come before sentiments. His duty is to his God, his family, his village, and his trade. He is a master blacksmith and is a responsible guardian to its proper conservancy. The actions of a bad craftsman only invite a lack of friends and influence. To allow an indentured apprentice to flaunt his disobedience will do his family, his covenant with his village, and his trade a disservice.

Making his way to the forge, he straight away heads for Willie's bed. Willie has come out of his coma. His recollection of events is sketchy, although he does remember Magdalena's voice as he would go in and out of consciousness. He is totally unprepared for the next event. Herr Yunk places his knee on Willie's chest forcing his body nearly through his straw mattress. His next awareness is of his hands being bound. With one powerful arm, Herr Yunk jerks him out of his bunk, with the other arm he throws the end the rope binding his hands up and over a half-plank supporting the top of the building. Pulling on the end of the rope stretches Willie arms in an upward direction in a straight line above his head. Yunk stops stretching him upward only when Willie's toes become the only body parts supporting him. Satisfied with his operation so far, he ties off the end of the rope to a post in the neighboring stable.

Willie is beyond thought. Fear has gripped him beyond his ability to think. "Is he going to kill me?" It's the only thought capable of making its way into his consciousness.

The next sensation Willie is experiencing his pants falling down around his ankles and his shirt pulled up over his head, followed by an excruciating

90

sting. Herr Yunk is using a cane normally reserved for a disruptive horse as a whip across Willies bare backside. Each lash causes Willie to flinch and yell out in pain. After ten hard lashes, Herr Yunk releases Willie's bindings allowing him to fall to the floor. Breaking his silence, Herr Yunk stoops down enough to turn Willie's head upward. "Say your prayers and don't let the fire die." Standing erect, Yunk returns the cane to its proper place, and makes his way to the house. Turning to his wife he says, "Feed the boy."

Willie is sobbing and crying when Frau Yunk brings him his supper. She holds a motherly compassion for him but knows better than to buck her husband's ways. She sets his food where she always sets it and leaves him alone with his misery. He would have liked to have had her sympathy but totally understands why she can't lend it to him. The lashes were not enough to draw blood but have left welts streaking his entire backside. The events of the past few days are leaving an impression that his ways have not been the ways by which his father has raised him. If his father learns of the circumstances surrounding his running away and Herr Yunk's stern reaction, he would, with little thought, add to his beating. It's just the German way. Acceptance of his status is a reality of life. It's a reality powerful enough to stifle any further thoughts of rebelliousness. To further rebel will be to rebel against the entire German order. It's been a stable society for centuries with only a few isolated changes. Reflecting back, Willie's changing thought process is more inclined to foster a new respect for his culture's steadiness than entice him to operate as an outside agent looking to innovate. It isn't the beating that has changed his thinking; rather it is the realization of what he has done to provoke such treatment that has changed his mindset. There is a sense of embarrassment accompanying his recalled behavior. "I am a German. God help me remain a German. Germans don't run away." In Willie's case, he has a requirement as an indentured apprentice to obey his master. He knows running away from one's obligation is not to be tolerated.

91

The misery of his near frozen toes and the welts across his legs and backside prevent him from finding a comfortable position to get some rest. In spite of sleep coming intermittently, he is up before dawn to tend to the forge.

Chapter 17

Confirmation

The days pass as they always do. The impatience of those having endured a long, cold winter can't rush time fast enough into the next season. Staying as close to the kitchen hearth as she can, Magdalena has been unwilling to battle the cold for the chance of going to the village. To occupy herself, she has pondered over her previous year's textbooks, read her Bible, crocheted, mended, and helped with the daily chores of maintaining the household. She is ready for spring. Regardless of human nature's lack of patience, the seasons insist on operating on their own schedule.

The first warm days of spring have appeared at long last. They're holding true to the promise that Mother Nature is about to change her mind and deliver milder weather ahead. These unseasonably balmy days always produce a wonderful sense of well-being in her subjects. But, as in all good things, there is always a downside. The warmth has also thawed the ground, turning the roads into a muddy bog.

Despite this hinderance, Magdalena is willing to overlook the mud in deference to postponing a stroll to the village. She has just returned with a surprise in her hand. While in the village, she stopped by the post office. To her surprise there was a letter addressed to her. She has only received one other mailing in her life and that was an acceptance letter to her school a year ago. Her fingers touch the envelope in a near caress. Her mother hangs near her with a look of bewilderment. With a blade from the kitchen, she slices the end open revealing its contents. Unfolding the creased paper inside reveals a handwritten letter. Her eyes scan across the paper with great anticipation.

"It's from Ida (Ida Meitz is a cousin) in Stralsund. She's inviting me to come to her Confirmation (church rite renewing baptismal vows) next month."

This cousin is the daughter of Herr Yunk's younger sister. They live in the port town of Stralsund in Pomerania on the Baltic sea. Being Evangelische (Lutheran), Confirmation is an important church tradition that commands notice as a rite of passage into a more active role in one's church life; it's where the penitent renews his or her baptismal vow to resist the devil in all his ways and works and with the aid of the Holy Spirit lead a God pleasing life. Since God involves Himself into family life by the church; God and family are the backbone of German life.

It's difficult to miss the excitement in Magdalena's voice as she squeals, "Can I go?"

"You'll have to discuss that with your father," is the nearly instinctive reaction from Frau Yunk.

Magdalena inclination to use any excuse to catch Willie's attention has been observed by the watchful eye of her father. Consequently, she has been forbidden from going to the forge. But now, certain that she has an official reason for violating the order, still bearing her letter, she makes her entrance. Herr Yunk is absorbed with a project. Seeing her in the forge gives him pause. He's wearing a look that says, "this better be good." It's apparent he's weighing his tolerance for her presence after he's forbidden her to be here.

Realizing she has to make her case fast for being on forbidden ground with a questionable purpose, Magdalena practically jams the letter in his face.

"Father, I got a letter today from Ida. She wants me to attend her Confirmation next month. Can I go?" says Magdalena.

Still weighing the possibility of an infraction, Herr Yunk stops with his work. With grime laden hands and a suspicious look, he opens the letter. Quickly reading it, he abruptly hands it back still opened. "We'll discuss it this evening at supper."

Not wanting Herr Yunk to have a reason to reprimand him, Willie makes certain he's still working but finds a reason to replace a tool on the side of the shop where Magdalena is making her exit. Because of her father's ruling, her interactions with Willie have been few and far between. Careful not to overdo a greeting, yet wanting to notice one another but not be noticed, they subtly greet the another with half smile and a slight nod.

Back in her bedroom, laying on her bed, Magdalena rereads her post for the gazillionth time. She has lived in this small village her entire life. Her biggest fear is that she will be caught here like her parents and be forced to live an empty life. Herr Yunk has joined with those who have found meaning and contentment in life, for them the past is not a diminishing memory, but rather a huge savannah on which no bleak winter ever converges.

Unlike her parents, Magdalena has developed a severe case of wanderlust. At home, in the summer there is the garden that needs to be planted and tended to. In the fall it's harvest time, the family is hoping to put away enough to ensure that there will be enough to last through the bleak winter months. In the winter life comes to an abrupt halt in the village. People prefer to sit by their hearth and stare out their window at the endless, sunless landscape. Now that Magdalena is no longer allowed to return to school, the worst of all is the isolation.

She is of this new generation of Germans for whom the old traditions and generations of culture and practices are more of a senseless ritual than a way forward. In view of the world entering into an industrial phase, the old ways are quickly losing their meaning. The new industrial German technology and her generation's awareness of a world beyond their village have put her father's and mother's society under pressure. Unlike her parents, for her to remain in the same village until death has lost its appeal.

When Magdalena had been away at school, she had experienced a life where interests other than the young people's society at church were available. A way of life where people weren't either cutting wood to heat their homes or growing endless rows of vegetables to meet the winter's greedy demands. Rather, they were exploring new innovations in industry and agriculture and politics. By the day, she is growing sick of the village, the garden, the forge, of every Sunday the same hundred people attending church. She doesn't know anything about Stralsund except it's not here.

Another workday comes to an end. Frau Yunk has followed the same routine in supplying her husband with a pan full of hot water, soap, and a fresh towel as she has since they have been married. Herr Yunk soon finishes cleaning himself of a day's worth of soot and dirt and is prepared to seat himself at the same table he has for countless meals. The meal is simple. This time of year, the larder is not quite as well supplied as it is in the fall. Tonight, supper consists of boiled potatoes and pickled herring—and, of course, the ever-present pint of beer.

Not wanting to appear overly anxious, Magdalena has held her tongue. She waits until her father has had several sips from his pint. When he lets out his quintessential belch of contentment, she emboldens herself to bring up her invitation to her cousin's confirmation. Knowing her father's dedication to the church, she chooses her words carefully.

"Father, I hope you have had time to consider my request to attend Ida's Confirmation. I know how important this part of my life was for my own Christian development and I'm certain Ida feels the same. I would so like to share with her, her joy."

There is no question Yunk is moved by his daughter's seeming sincerity to say, "There is nothing in this world more God pleasing than to renounce the devil and all his works one more time through Confirmation. I'm certain my sister will welcome you with open arms."

Not able to contain herself, Magdalena leaps from her chair, throws her arms around her father's neck. "Oh, thank you father, thank you, thank you!"

To say Herr Yunk is not pleased with his daughter's affectionate response would be a lie, but for him to show it, is yet another thing.

Despite the lingering death throes of winter, Magdalena's entire demeanor changes as though the coming spring is a perpetual season. She spends much of the next few weeks planning her trip. A ticket can be procured at the village post office. A coach is unquestionably the best mode of transportation in Germany these days. By coach, it's only a day's journey to Stralsund—by wagon, nearly all of two days requiring a layover. The coach service is fast and efficiently run with its suspension system, it's much more comfortable than a wagon. Improving the coach's suspension system is a reaction to the government's suspicious idea that repairing the roads invites invading armies.

The day of departure finally arrives. Magdalena has barely slept a wink all night. Nonetheless, she is up at the crack of dawn. Her bags are packed awaiting her by the door. With breakfast out of the way, her father has willingly foregone his normal morning routine in favor of seeing Magdalena off in a fatherly way—gathering himself, Frau Yunk, and Magdalena for a period of meditations, imploring God to send his holy angles to watch over Magdalena in her travels.

Willie has the horse and wagon hooked up and waiting. He is standing off to the side hoping to catch a glimpse of Magdalena before she leaves. Soon, the cottage door opens. Herr Yunk and Frau Yunk emerge, each carrying a couple of Magdalena's satchels filled with enough items to start a household. Following them is the person of Willie's concern. The new morning sun drapes her in radiance. She couldn't be prettier. What she is wearing is attractive but her beauty is in her demeanor. He yearns for her companionship, hoping she won't be gone too long. It isn't just her looks, which are assuring an emerging beauty, but something beyond and deeper. It's more her youthful tenacity and zest for life that have him captivated. She's wearing the face of one who has just been set free. Stepping back into the darkness of the forge before Herr Yunk suspects him of voyeurism, he continues to watch from the shadows.

The trip to the village is muddy and rut riven. As usual, Herr Yunk takes these circumstances as he does everything in his life—adapts and overcomes. Never in a hurry, he carefully calculates every ridge and rut in the road, allowing the horse to make the first judgement, correcting it when necessary. As is the case in making correct appraisals, they arrive in the village ahead of the coach. Despite living a mere quarter mile away, Frau Yunk does not get to the village very often. If it weren't so early, she would love to do some visiting. Nonetheless, as it is with the German penchant for timeliness, the coach is on time.

Magdalena is beyond excited. Between the coachman and her father, they manage to get her luggage packed in. At last she is saying her final goodbyes.

"Say your prayers and watch out for Schwarze Verte," teases her mother. ("Schwarze Verte" is a notorious legendary German robber.)

"I will," promises Magdalena. Although the idea of an encounter with famed Schwarze Verte carries a tinge of excitement.

98

The journey is over roads compromised by freezing nights creating frozen ruts and warm days creating mud bogs. It can only be enjoyed by the young who find every new challenge as something to enjoy. Magdalena certainly fits this description. To her, the entire journey is an adventure.

As advertised, within a day—even if it means killing the horses—the coach arrives on time in Stralsund. Magdalena has lost a bit of her enthusiasm due to simple fatigue. She is grateful when she spots her cousin Ida and her Tante ("aunt") Emma and her Onkel ("uncle") Frank. They haven't seen one another since their grandmother's funeral three years ago.

Magdalena's luggage is transferred from coach to wagon and they are on their way. Chattering like a pair of magpies the girls are full of effervescent shrieks and giggles as they reacquaint themselves.

With a full assault on each of her senses, Magdalena spends much of her trip looking up at the massive brick structures. "Where does all this brick come from? You even have brick streets."

Magdalena's city cousins like nothing more than showing off their urban sophistication to their hinter Pomer ("back woodsman") relatives. "Wait until you see St. Mary's church tomorrow," says Ida with an air of urbanity. Magdalena listens with anticipation. So far everything she had hoped to experience has been within her reach.

Within a few minutes, they arrive at the Meitz apartment. It's on the second floor of a five-story Gothic styled brick building. While her uncle Frank returns his horse and wagon to the building's livery stable in the rear of the building, Magdalena, her Tante Emma, and cousin Ida haul her luggage up the flight of stairs to the Meitz apartment. Magdalena can't help but pay attention to the different smells filling the hallways. It's the mingled odors of cooking, tobacco smoke, bad toilets or unwashed baby diapers or both, unwashed humans, and cat urine.

99

Once in the apartment, the ambience changes. The odors from the hallway are left behind, and her aunt's handiwork immediately comes to the forefront. Differing patterns of flowered wallpaper portraying all different color schemes cover the walls of each room, some with full murals of familiar landscapes, also window treatments of handmade draperies adorn each window. Although the floors are inlaid wood with a waxy sheen, her aunt has installed large area carpets to minimize floor wear.

Unlike her own simple home where the kitchen and eating area are all crammed in together, Magdalena's aunt's kitchen is in a separate room off of a dining area. Even the kitchen, with all its conveniences of a pump in the kitchen so water doesn't have to be carried to a hearth that is large enough that four kettles can be hung at one time, is so remote to Magdalena she feels she is in a totally different world. Magdalena is struck beyond comparison. In her entire life, she has ever seen such elegant living—and now within her own family.

Her Onkel Frank owns a fleet of fishing boats and makes a good living from supplying German families with enough herring to insure they won't starve, and her Tante has figured out ways to spend it.

Ida shares some similarities with her cousin in that she also has two older siblings who are grown with families of their own, leaving Ida to be catered to as an only child. Where the differences are striking is in the décor within each of the cousin's bedrooms. The simplistic décor of a straw mattress on a homemade bedframe of Magdalena, hardly compares to the down-filled mattress and beautifully handcrafted bed frame with matching dresser of her cousin.

Just the short time Magdalena has shared in the lifestyle of her city cousin leaves her wondering if they have anything left in the material world that they both share in common.

The next morning is Confirmation Sunday. Ida has a beautifully designed white Confirmation dress to wear. Magdalena is almost too embarrassed to put on her homemade Sunday dress and says so, "Oh, Ida your dress is so pretty compared with mine, I know you will feel embarrassed to have me with you."

Realizing her cousin's feelings, Ida replies, "You look pretty in your dress but if it will make you feel better pick out one of mine you would like."

"Do you really mean that? That is so sweet of you," says Magdalena resulting in her whole demeanor uplifted.

With breakfast over, Onkel Frank has brought out a nicer carriage that he reserves for Sundays and special occasions. Her uncle is also dressed beyond anything her father would have in his simple ward robe. He is wearing a waist coat with trousers that extend just below his ankles, a white shirt, a vest, a necktie, and on his head is poised a black satin top hat.

Magdalena has never in her life felt this elegant. Even though she is not rich, pretending she is, is fun. "Ida, thank you so much for inviting me. You have no idea how much this experience is inspiring me."

"You don't know how happy I am to have you here with me today. I couldn't have chosen anyone better."

Ida has always been drawn to this cousin's effervescent approach to life. She is younger and looks upon her older cousin's tenaciousness with longing.

Only a ten-minute ride from the apartment, they arrive at St. Mary's church. Not thinking about it too much, Magdalena was expecting to see a church much like her own, when she is confronted by a structure that could fit several hundred buildings the size of her own church back in her village inside it. Looking up at the steeple, she marvels at how anyone could have built such a magnificent structure. She is left speechless.

Entering, they are led to their pew by an usher. Never in her life has she ever been in such a magnificent building. Where a large attendance at St. Martin's, her village church, would be a hundred on a good Sunday, there are no less than three thousand people surrounding her on this Sunday. She continues to marvel with every aspect of worship. She has never heard an organ play this beautifully nor a choir sing so magnificently, and the solemnity with which the pastor and his assistants are performing Ida's Confirmation rite brings her near to tears. To her, this is the closest to heaven she has ever felt.

Magdalena had no way of knowing what a heaven experience would be like, she only knows it would not be like her life in her village. To this point, nothing has disappointed her. She is meeting each new sensation as one would while enjoying their own birthday party. And in some strange way, this feels like both a birth and a party to Magdalena.

After church, the day is spent focusing on Ida's Confirmation vows. As a German father, Frank feels it his obligation to be the head of his family not only physically, but morally, and spiritually as well. The church had been satisfied with her taught responses, now he wants to take them to a more thoughtful level. He begins to quiz her on every aspect of her solemn promises—especially those parts vowing to remain true to the church even to the point of death. Magdalena remembers her own Confirmation and her father doing something very similar.

The day ends with everyone preparing themselves to go back to work and Ida going back to school the next day. Even though Magdalena could have had her own bed, she and Ida have chosen to share a bed. They spend the first part of the night talking about anything and everything, and with sleep finally having its way, they succumb to its lure.

Chapter 18

The Market

By the time daylight arrives and Tante Emma is waking Ida for school, Onkel Frank has already left preparing his fleet for a day of fishing. One thing Magdalena had noticed when she arrived on Saturday was the market in the streets. In her own village, the people are suspicious of strangers, so they have passed an ordinance not to allow itinerant peddlers. This has protected the local businesspeople, but has stifled citizens like Magdalena from experiencing people unlike herself. She sees an opportunity of a lifetime now and is prepared to ask permission to visit that market. Concerned that by asking to do something outside the family, she would be disrespecting them, she decides to ask regardless.

"Tante, I have something to ask. I noticed you have a large street market. We don't have anything like it in our village. Would you mind if I visit it sometime today? I promise I'll be careful."

On hearing her cousin's request, Ida appears to be disappointed. She was hoping to take Magdalena to school with her.

Tante Emma weighs the petition for a moment before replying, "I was thinking the same thing, I have some shopping to do and would be happy to have you accompany me."

This isn't what Magdalena had in mind. She would have preferred to experience this new phenomenon her own way, but rather than be disrespectful, she covers her disappointment with a cheery, "Yes. I would love that."

Since the market is within walking distance, they plan to leave so they can have a lunch together at one of the many food vendors. The closer the time approaches to begin their trek, the more the excitement grows in Magdalena. Everything she has experienced so far has been electrifying. Knowing this entirely different lifestyle can be reached in a mere day's journey from her home is heartening.

Nothing in her previous experience has prepared her for the chaos of the street. Her school experience had been carefully structured, always making certain students passed in an orderly pattern. Here there is seemingly no one in charge—it's mayhem—with people jostling one another from every direction. The streets are narrow with as many people squeezing their way in one direction as the other.

Despite the crowded conditions, the first thing Magdalena becomes aware of is there is no mud. The streets are all paved with bricks that have been worn smooth from the centuries of traffic. Within the first block, she has encountered more people than she would in her village in a year. Her senses are being bombarded with not only the colorful sights but the aromas. Considering that Stralsund is a port city, it has willingly or unwillingly made room for a diversity of people of different countries, races, religions, grooming styles, clothing styles, and of course a variety of foods. The narrow streets become even more narrow as they are approaching the market. The vendors in this section have placed their stalls on either side of the street allowing an even finer stream of people forcing their way in both directions.

Suddenly, Magdalena feels an unfamiliar sensation from a chain she wears about neck. Impulsively shooting her gaze in the direction of its seeming

105

cause, she sees the hand of her aunt grasped about the wrist of an unknown would-be pickpocket attempting to snatch her watch. The assailant immediately drops the watch leaving it to dangle by its chain. Jerking his hand loose from her grasp, he simply runs off and loses himself in the crowd. Shaken but not frightened, Magdalena composes herself with a nervous giggle, "Wow, I never saw that coming."

"I should have warned you. These pickpockets run amuck. They have a special sense to recognize new and unguarded prey like yourself," replies Tante Emma.

The thing that bothers Magdalena the most about this encounter is not the violence but that she was so easily spotted as not being sophisticated. Wistfully, reflecting on her happenstance, she contemplates how she can become less of a target. Looking around at others, what is becoming apparent is how hidden behind the eyes of those who seemingly carry an expression of contentment are actually wary eyes, busily watching for suspicious movements from their fellow browsers. She quickly decides this is a valuable exercise and immediately begins to put into practice.

Believing they have recovered their composure enough to move on, the duo of aunt and niece continue to press forward, but not so hurriedly that Magdalena is about to miss anything. The smells continue to mingle—soap with fish and then as quickly changes to perfumes with herbs only to suddenly be confronted by a rack of freshly killed rabbit carcasses with an aroma all their own. Each of these venders is hawking his own goods in accents agreeing with his/her ethnicity. The tobacco merchants tend to be American. The wine merchants are French. Gypsies are selling elixirs guaranteeing cures for everything from growing hair on bald heads to curing gout.

Coming into an open plaza, the atmosphere changes from venders to entertainment. There are puppeteers with small theater venues compressed

106

into areas only large enough to allow a handful of enthusiasts to watch their performances. They generally are brought to Stralsund from itinerant Austrian performers. They catch the imagination of their adherents by the buffoonery of the characters they portray: oftentimes knights and kings, priests and popes of some past age in need of reform. The admission for such performances is the ever-present hat on the ground—suggesting the contribution is a step above a beggar. Magdalena had only caught a glimpse of such a performance in her village before the performers were chased out of the district with threats of fines and imprisonment. A recognizable odor suddenly wafts through a myriad of others, making it straightaway to Magdalena's nostrils. It's the familiar smell of charcoal and burnt metal; it's the smell of her father's forge. This one is not her father's forge of course, but rather it belongs to a young man fashioning cooking ware using a small portable forge. For a moment the young man puts her in mind of Willie.

Moving on to another part of the market square, the sound of music begins to permeate the air. It's coming from the sweet-sounding strings of a violin maestro. While he plays, a craftsman seemingly oblivious to its resonance—lost in his own world—is meticulously placing the finishing touches on another instrument.

In a stall adjacent to the violin maker is a book vendor. This quarter is where Magdalena feels most at home. She has kept all of her textbooks from school. Periodically perusing through them, she is always amazed at the things she had missed in her previous study. If she were alone, she knows she would spend some more time with this vendor.

There is suddenly an uproar from a crowd that seem to be encircling an event. Not certain what may be the source of the ruckus, they decide to scout it out. Cautiously, they begin working their way through the throngs of people pressing tightly together as more and more are forcing their way forward. Tante Emma is more inclined to withhold the effort in discovering its source, where

Magdalena presses forward not willing to miss a single experience. What finally comes into view are two very large, shirtless, men wrestling each other. Their sweat is profuse enough to allow each to slip a hold. Regardless, the crowd goads them on. Not tiring of the bout, but not wanting to miss other events, Magdalena regroups with her aunt, ready to move on to the next chapter.

The next chapter has snuck up on the sensibilities of this Christian aunt. They have suddenly strolled into a section of the marketplace where the women are ostensibly dressed a bit more elaborately than even upper-class women. The telltale evidence that they are something other than high-class women is their skirts are a bit higher, exposing their ankles, and their bustlines are somewhat lower, exposing more than a subtle amount of cleavage. Emma's first concern is with her niece. Taking a quick look at Magdalena's reaction, she is not pleased with her initial response. Magdalena's innocence has not prepared her to be "street smart." She is not seeing beyond what seems to be, instead, she is completely struck with the seeming sophistication of these ladies. Her aunt's concern is how next to move on to some other interest without making a bigger production of the faux pax, which is the duty of this responsible Tante.

"Oh, Magdalena look over here at these circus performers."

Magdalena is hesitant to give her aunt her full attention. She is still enamored with the impressive portrait these ladies are presenting. She has never seen such fancy dresses. To her it looks to be the ultimate in sophistication. Finally adhering to her aunt's beckoning, Magdalena turns her attention in her direction. She is pointing to a group of performers across the way doing daring feats of sword swallowing and fire eating.

The day would not be complete without a German lunch of pretzels and sausage and a glass of beer. Taking their lunch at a small outdoor café further allows Magdalena to watch all sorts of foreigners wearing exotic clothing and talking in languages she has never heard before as they make outlandish hand gestures with their every word. What she has become aware of is how much smaller her circle of world awareness is than she had imagined. She is certain that somewhere in her future, she is going to know more of the world. It's as though she senses a connection with all of God's creation and wants to explore it. Her faith has taught her to look outward toward eternity; now she yearns to look inward to this world's heart.

Chapter 19

A Soul Question

With the arrival of spring, the Yunk forge embarks on the busiest season of the year. The village farmers are beginning to look over damaged equipment that was put away after the previous year's harvest. Being the only forge the village has permitted, Herr Yunk is working long hours to accommodate each of their needs for repairs. The large doors that are kept tightly closed during the cold months now are flung wide open allowing some of the forge's excess heat to escape. It's a welcoming signal that spring has arrived

Enough on the job training has lapsed where Willie is becoming more proficient with his duties. He is beginning to perform his tasks with the satisfaction of doing them well rather than with indifference. His relationship with Herr Yunk has also changed—not that Herr Yunk has softened but Willie is growing to respect his master's superior skills and understand the attitude that correlates with them. Many times a day, he watches the dexterous hands of this seasoned journeyman performing near miracles welding with fire and iron. And as many times, with secret envy, he wonders if he'll ever be as proficient. "How does he know how to do that?" becomes Willie's prevailing question.

The nights are also part of Willie's changing perspective. The time spent dreaming of getting back home has been replaced with an attitude he didn't imagine a few months ago. He wakes anxiousness to resume unfinished projects left over from the previous day. He is also learning that, unlike his

110

father's reactions to praise his labors during his childhood years, Herr Yunk is not praising him for doing a job "well done" where one is merely expected.

Like it or not, he is being thrust full force into Germany's adult world. Options other than an aspiration to become an adult as laid out by the previous generation are doomed to fail in this society. There is very little to no room for individual thinking. Everything has already been carefully thought out and handed to the next generation—not to be critiqued but rather implemented—where family comes first, then the village, then the state. A person's individual status is expressed in limited forms and its precepts—usually buried deep under other concerns—is rarely a consideration. Authority is only questioned when those in authority step out of the role assigned them—either with a violation of a moral tradition or a secular law.

On a more micro setting, a dominant "will," usually prevails. In Willie's case, these are formative years. Adult ideas and reactions are formed by the most significant adult sharing themselves through their values. In Willies circumstances, he is spending all of his waking hours in the presence of Herr Yunk. When a job isn't going smoothly, nearly all Yunk's reactions lack any semblance of eloquence; skirting the edge of forcefulness—just short of violence is the norm: a lot of furled frowns, slamming of tools, kicking things out of his way, and hand gestures that many times reach Willie. This results in a twist to his arm or shoulder redirecting him to another place when words were at a loss for Herr Yunk. When things are going along smoothly, Yunk has a near expressionless gaze. It's his look of contentment.

Willie is picking up some of the bad habits of his Herr Meister. He is careful not to display them when Yunk is around. Herr Yunk has little patience with his own misdeeds much less Willie's. However, when he's absent, Willie frequently finds himself similarly mistreating a tool when something in one of his projects goes awry. When he catches himself acting out like his Meister, he asks God to forgive him.

111

On the other hand, there are attributes of Yunk's to be admired. Willie is finding him to be an honorable man of his word. He has also been appointed to the St. Paul's church council, which, in turn, made him a member of the village Gemeinde ("community rules and regulations commission"). It's part of his responsibility to keep a record of those choosing not to be in church and not taking part in the Sacrament and to report them to the Gemeinde. Herr Yunk takes his responsibility very seriously. Given this sense of community commitment, he is one of the first people to be contacted when the Frieherr (Baron) orders fron ("community service"). The Baron's protocol is to send his magistrate in his place to order the obligation. On this day, a representative appears at the Yunk forge with an order to supply one person from his family to appear the following morning at the Baron's land holdings an hour ride away. It seems the Baron's forests are being overrun with wild boars and he is demanding the obligatory hours owed to him by law for the village to organize a drive to rid his forests of the beasts. As it goes with humans throughout the world, fear will cause individuals to collectively give up their freedom in exchange for safety. In this instance, the village may grumble about the Baron's demands but have exchanged God-given freedoms for protection. There is also a willingness to surrender personal freedoms for the sake of a common interests. By their actions, Germans will willingly surrender freedoms for order. Over a period of many generations, the reason behind the original ideas becomes blurred, and the concept of obedience becomes a matter of mein Phlickt ("my duty").

Duty and order are mainstays in the world of Herr Yunk. There is little question whether to obey the order, it becomes a matter of how. Instead of a member of the Yunk household performing the Baron's community service, the perfect substitute is to hand over their indentured apprentice. Willie has overheard the discussion and has already adjusted his mind to the idea that he will be Herr Yunk's selection. When the day's work is completed, Herr Yunk pulls Willie aside, saying, "Tomorrow morning after your breakfast be prepared to go to the village and make yourself available to the Schultheiss ("village supervisor"). Inform him you are here to represent the Yunk's community service fron for the Frieherr ("Baron"). He'll direct your duties for the day."

Other than church on Sunday, Willie has not been out of the forge in months. Not wanting to appear overjoyed, he puts on his best "Herr Meister's" blank gaze of acceptance. "Yes, Herr Meister. I'll be ready."

By morning, daylight is making its way to the top of the eastern skyline. Willie is up and out in the forge excitedly readying the fire. Frau Yunk has delivered his breakfast. He is visibly eager to get it eaten and begin his day away from the forge. Still chewing, he's out the door, finishing his potato pancake on his trek to the village. There are thirty-five families living within the borders of the village. Most own strips of tillable land surrounding the village proper but still laying within its boundaries. Owning land is what gives its owner the prestige he needs to influence decisions within the village power structure.

Gustave Sieb is the village cobbler. He has lived in this village his entire life. Along with himself, his wife, and two young sons, he has made the Sieb family home above his shoe shop. His father and his father before him raised their families in this same house and worked below in the same shop. They had trained him in the trade the same as he is now training his sons. Considering that he's a tradesman and owns a respectable plot of ground within the village guarantees him the status he enjoys. He's selected himself to represent his family since his sons are busy planting. Waiting with the others in the dawn light, their ages vary but he appears to be one of the older males in the group.

"You up for this, Gus? You look a little tired this morning," asks one of the young men.

"You mind your manners Shnickelfritz or I'll feed you to the pigs," retorts Gustave.

113

Another young man, wanting to get in on the banter says, "Gus, what you got against pigs?"

This lightheartedness is not put on. These men are content with their lot in life. It's a hard life and much is demanded from them, but they have adapted to its rigors. They choose to surrender to this way of life rather than be ostracized into an unfamiliar existence that more often brings death with it. There are stories of generations past who battled against their rulers only to find themselves penniless, destitute, and hunted down until they were caught and punished. Their penalties had proven to be severe—from the rack to quartering—all done in a public setting to serve as an example. Their Baron has learned to balance his high authority to get the most out of his semi-serfs by not demanding more than his subjects can give but always keeping them on edge to remind them what precious rights they do enjoy by remaining complicit.

Demands, like the one the Baron is making today will bring to mind what he expects from each of these peasants. He must continue to keep alive the idea that as defenseless peasants, they are not capable of taking care of themselves and need his fatherly protection. Aside from this, most Germans can live with a spoiled ruling class always making more and more demands on their subjects.

Notably, there is a disaster with wild pigs running amuck, but let it not be said of this nobleman that he can't put a disaster to good use. The Baron has organized a day of hunting involving fellow members of the ruling class. He has the right, according to the contract he has with the villagers, to exercise his privilege to use them so many days a year according to reasons of his own discretion without pay. This is one of those occasions. He and his fellow noblemen will position themselves according to the long-held hunting strategies of legendary huntsmen to shoot as many pigs as the villagers are capable of driving into their sights. This division of labor is purposely designed to remind the various classes of their place in life. The German status strata are layered deep—from indentured servant to emperor—and set nearly in rock. The trap the peasants fall into within their layer is that a sense of duty to unquestioningly obey authorities has replaced personal truth.

Each noble arrives with his own entourage, a variety of hunting apparatus, including an array of shotguns and dogs. The conversations among this group center around each of their beliefs that their enigmatic hunting techniques should become the standard for wild boar hunting. As a group, they are incredibly boring, even to each other.

Willie is one of thirty-five men selected from the village families to provide the Baron with the needed drivers to chase the wild boars through the forest to the waiting guns of this group of hunters. The villagers' sense of duty hardly precludes their sense of irony. The irreverent stories being told by those who have previously been called on to perform other meaningless acts of questionable worth for the Baron begin making their way through their conversations. Only because they are of a singleness of thought toward the flaunting of these over-indulged toads of nobility, dare they share their attitude toward the vain pomposity of this group called "hunters."

Emil Kretchmeir, a local butcher who has been called upon many times to take care of the kill made by these "hunters," can't help but make an observation. "If one of these Arscheige ("ass violin player") had to feed himself with his hunting skills, he'd starve to death."

This bit of frivolity produces an uproar. Rather than looking upon this commitment as an obstacle, the villagers are using it as an opportunity to get together and make a festive day of it.

Many of the group are Willie's age. This opportunity is bringing alive a triviality he has not enjoyed since leaving home. Considering, Herr Yunk is far from being a cheery person, he's pleased to be around a group that is quickly

115

caught up in some innocent banter. Despite all this, by not being a real member of the village, he is content to be more of a listener rather than a donor.

Meanwhile, two wagons arrive to transport the villagers to the Baron's estate. Each wagon can transport half the group. Out of respect to the Burgers (citizens), Willie stands aside permitting each to choose their respective places before being last to find a spot. Regardless of which slot one chooses, the ride remains equally rough in all areas. Nonetheless, one thing Willie had learned while living in his own village is not to assume one is welcomed as a stranger and be content to take an unassuming role.

Once in the wagon, the conversation continues but it has taken a different direction. Albert Krupp begins to recall a past incident involving a wild pig and himself. "I was just doing my job as a driver. My thoughts were on moving forward to keep the pigs out front and on the move. I had scarcely pushed past a group of oak trees when I came upon a herd of pigs. I was as startled of them as they were of me. Some of the smaller ones took to running but one big boar stared me down for a moment and decided, rather than run, he'd charge me. Before I could think, I found myself scurrying up a low branched pine just off to my side. He stood below me grunting and ripping at that tree with those big tusks. All I could see was bark flying in every direction and be happy it wasn't my guts."

While this account gives the listeners pause, it isn't enough to stop any further narratives of past experiences. To continue this vein of personal stories in an attempt to keep it as lighthearted as they had started out, Eldred Hoffmeier points a finger toward Louis Schlaack, asking, "Louis, tell these young guys what they may have to be aware of beside wild boars once we hit the forest."

This is not the first time these two lifelong neighbors have played this game with others. Picking up on the need to play along on the suggestion, Louis turns his face from one of lightheartedness to gloomy, dismal, saying, "You

116

mean that experience with Hackelnberg, the Wilde Jagd ("Wild Hunt") I had in this very forest the last time we were called upon? I wouldn't wish that experience on anybody."

Playing his part perfectly to gain the attention of the younger men, Eldred replies, "Yes, yes, that horrific encounter you experienced. Yes, let these young Hosenscheisser ("one who shits his pants in fear") know what they have to look out for."

As if on cue, Louis's eyes stare off into the distance, they begin to enlarge as if something is possessing his thoughts. Clearing his throat with an apprehensive tone suggesting fear, and hesitating long enough to affect a hard swallow, he quickly takes note of the minds he has gripped. Satisfied he has their attention, he begins, "I became lost and happened to come across ole Hackelnberg's grave. It wasn't where a person would expect to find a grave. It was located in a meadow in among a bunch of wild brush and weeds. The whole area was at least an acre, more oblong in shape. The entire vicinity was completely surrounded by forest, but not a single tree was to be seen in the clearing. One end stretched out toward the east, at the other end, it raised up like it was on a platform. It turned out to be a flat stone—red in color—about eight or so feet long, and maybe five feet or so wide. The stone didn't face the east as a Christian grave stone, rather one end pointed south and the other north. I suddenly took a chill right down my spine to my ankles. It was always said that no one would ever find the grave—not even by chance. What happened next is something I wouldn't wish on anyone. Everything suddenly got real dark, and an awful howling began over my head. I looked up and there was a pack of black growling dogs passing over above me as if they were ghosts lunging at me. It threw me right to the ground in fear. To tell the truth, I've never been that scared of anything in my whole life."

Along with the other men, Willie is more than captivated. This fourth dimensional aspect is not a feature he'd anticipated. He was content just to be

117

out of the forge for a day. He has been raised listening to the accounts of Black Forest episodes. They are all beyond reason, which indicates reason can't deal with these accounts, rather it appeals to feelings and emotions that are a part of the spiritual world. This world is the world of the imagination. Any ability to bring it under the authority of reason is questionable. It seems to have its own life ignoring human reason and wanders unfettered.

The only thing coming to Willie's reckoning at this point is he's dealing with illogical accounts. With no effort, his imagination has little problem moving into full swing to fill the void. These Black Forest episodes have a way of running rampant through people's fancy leaving reason aside as unreasonable. He can't shake Louis's story; it continues to dig its way through his imaginings. The expectation of exhaustion in doing the Baron's bidding is a physical condition that is easily dealt with compared with the condition created by the imagination—this order is a completely different phenomenon.

Willie's immediate considerations are forced to the sidelines as the wagons approach the starting point. It's time to begin the drive. It's a remote forested area of the Baron's holdings. The Baron's Feldherr ("field boss") is quick to begin asserting his authority. Pleased to have an opportunity to demonstrate his importance, he begins by ordering them to remain in a group to hear his instructions. He has in mind a unique zigzag pattern he's ordering them to follow. This method is his assurance to the nobility that the most "productive measures" to complete the drive will be implemented.

It's time to place the drivers in their positions. He has ordered the thirty-five of them to separate themselves one-hundred-fifty feet apart to cover the milewide stretch of forest. Looking to his right and then his left, seeing men in position assures Willie he is not alone and gives him the support he needs to proceed.

Once in position, the field boss sounds the horn to begin the drive. Several miles to the south a horn blast is returned as a signal that all is in place and to begin the drive.

With everything coming together around this event, Willie's excitement has replaced his imagination's misgivings. He's prepared to begin his long trek on a positive note. Ultimately, this day will lead him through thick forest undergrowth, swamp lands, razorback hills cut out by the last glacier to move through the area. These Black Forest hills can run hundreds of feet deep leaving hundreds of feet needed to be traversed to reach the top on the other side— some of these climbs are nearly vertical.

Still conscious of the instructions, Willie begins his march. Gradually, the topography begins to change. At first, he can see both the men on his right and on his left. Still conscious of the zigzag patterns he's expected to follow, he counts his number of steps he needs to take before beginning the Zag part of his Zig. Consequently, having become engrossed in remembering the details of the drive, he has lost sight of the men on either side of him. Confronted with nothing but a vast forest becoming so thick with underbrush that he cannot see beyond twenty feet; a sense isolation is creeping its way over him like an ominous cloud. As Willie is experiencing these conditions, a rebirth of fear produced by the earlier stories is more determined than ever to work its way back into his imagination. Stopping for a moment to reassess his situation only allows the sounds of the forest to have more of him as their audience. The sounds of trees creaking, crows announcing every move of anyone in their territory, the rustle of leaves from a distant squirrel, are all sounds that are foreign to Willie's everyday life. He's suddenly struck with a sense of fear and loneliness. This setting is not his usual element. His life has always revolved around human exchanges, and the forests have always held their own entitlement to do what they do. Forests always take on a life of their own, requiring the inhabitants to obey its rules. The only way man has ever tamed a forest is to cut it down.

Fear may initially drive loneliness, but once Willie finds himself in its grip, it produces even more fear and unrest. Another hour goes by without Willie laying eyes on any of his fellow drivers. This sense of isolation is quickly producing panic. This is not only an emotional phenomenon but is also physical. It's a heaviness settling in the pit of his stomach. It's a sick feeling of emptiness and dislocation. His breathing is becoming more a panting of shallow breaths. All these dislodged emotions tell his legs to run—to where, they don't advise—but run nonetheless. Meanwhile, every bodily fiber is struggling to process all these rampaging emotions. Not certain what to do next, he forces himself to stop for a moment. That moment is proving to be fruitful. In the distance he hears the echoing report of a shotgun blast. The problem he's forced to calculate is, "that sound is behind me." Gathering his thoughts, in disbelief, he concludes, "I've gone in a complete circle." Despite facing this additional problem, Willie sucks in a breath of self-assurance—at the very least, he knows in which direction he needs to return. Another shotgun blast promises him he's making the correct decision. Armed with a new confidence, he turns around and begins his trek once again.

Nonetheless, when it comes to fears, additional trepidations stand ready to battle against Willie's continual dissolving confidence to fend them off. Realizing how nature abhors a vacuum, they hang like invisible gargoyles from every tree ready to pounce on every spiritual weakness. There is an invisible force within him that senses evil before his mind can resolve it. The impending message shoots a chill through his entire body. For Willie—despite the Church's denunciations of ill meaning spirits hanging around the Black Forest as "merely folklore"—the hair standing upright on his arms and neck alert him to their realness. As these interloping thoughts find their way into his mind, Willie finds himself facing the merciless possibility of every forest clearing becoming the portrayal of "ole Hackelnberg's crypt" just as Louis had described it. He finds this diversion more thought-provoking than chasing pigs but also more disconcerting. More alone with himself than makes him comfortable, Willie's fears are much more prepared to dominate his forest trek than the joy of the hunt. The fallen and rotting trees, tangled underbrush, along with the undulating nature of the terrain prevent any semblance of straight-line travel. This phenomenon has placed him at the mercy of the forest and the fears it's producing. Willie is as close to a panic attack as he has been in his life. He's unable to get a grip on his emotions, they have hooked his thoughts as one would a dray animal and are leading him into an emotional breakdown. Every creaking tree, every rustle of the overhead trees left by frolicking squirrels produce within him a shortness of breath. As he gasps for his next gulp of air, his body begins to shake with anxiety. His bug-like eyes shoot from one forest disruption to another causing his head to snap as though it is tethered to the disturbance.

Willie's legs have gone from a measured stride to an erratic run resultant in a stumbling trudge. His mind and body have become one—but not in a constructive sense. Their energies have combined into what can only be described as a full-blown panic attack. With ensuing illusions, he is already experiencing Louis's demon hounds racing overhead in an unstoppable pursuit, hellbent to carry him off to some godless torment. His reaction only allows his voice to make unintelligible, guttural sounds—intelligible only to his animal persona. It's an amalgamation of whimpering and heaving gasps of despair. All in all, it's much more exhausting than merely a physical exercise. This powerful invisible enemy attempting to possess Willie's body, mind, and soul is suddenly interrupted by the clear sound of gunshots. BAM. BAM, BAM, BAM! The shots are resounding. Each shot is followed by an echo only to further demonstrate the earthly aspect of its origin. Willie is acquainted with this sound and is clearly connecting with it. It is the world Willie knows best and he welcomes the interruption with a lighthearted laugh. With a sigh of relief, he gladly faces what could easily become his death as buckshot rips through the foliage surrounding him. Unlike his fourth dimensional experience, this physical danger can be dealt with by simply hitting the ground. This is a welcome exercise compared with the mysterious, invisible elements his imagination has concocted.

As each guest continues to indiscriminately shoot, seemingly unconcerned with the possibility of striking one of these "lower-class" subjects of their host, Willie is content to stay flat on his belly. As dangerous as it is, it's a welcome change compared to his previous hallucinations. Clearly back to an earthly reality, Willie's eyes search the locations these shots may be coming from.

BAM! BAM! Another round flies through the trees. This permits him to zero in on the location of the shooter. What he perceives is an overweight middle-aged man wearing plaid knickers with knee socks, a plaid shirt, and a dark cape draped around his rotund body hoping to serve as camouflage. He's perched on a wooden platform some ten feet above the ground, permitting him a broad visual scope. He's not alone, he has several other shotguns, all propped along the platform's waist-high barrier.

This man is the quintessential bourgeois lout of the day, taking full advantage of his social position to aggressively remind ordinary citizens of their low-class status. With the exception of a few troublemaking tenants, this class division is accepted as one of life's fundamentals. Despite the violence of ricocheting gunshots, Willie is typically resigned to this class division.

After facing the challenge of making his way to a safe cover behind these shooters, Willie continues to belly crawl his way to protection. Once accomplished, he's met, along with his compatriots, with the duty to gather the slaughtered hogs and hang them on a viewing pole. This provides each participant bragging rights for the biggest hog and an opportunity to provide a full verbal portrayal of each of his kills.

The Baron expects each of his subordinates to remain as much out of view as possible—to be seen only as it benefits his guest's comfort. This necessitates Willie and his compatriots to expect a day of preparing the hogs for smoking, pickling, and roasting—all without getting caught sampling any of their efforts—although for a job well done, they are eventually provided with the less desirable cuts for their own pleasure.

Despite the careful protocol maintaining the strict differences between the upper and lower class, Willie and his group have successfully fulfilled their work obligation as well as cementing their own personal relationships with one another. The day ends with each participant exhausted from its endeavors.

Willie's day has been an experience in learning. Much has had to do with what is required to be an adult male in his world. It's been one of watching his fellow citizens display a nearly servile role in their relations with the Baron and his quests. There has been something about their obsequious behavior that isn't setting well with him, although he did find a few taking great delight in getting away with some infraction of certain entitled services owed to their rulers—but it ended there. Their final behavior is one of obedience. Willie's protestant upbringing has always emphasized obedience to God and those He has placed over him, but there is something about these rulers' arrogance and how they attempt to depersonalize him that rubs him the wrong way. Despite it not setting well with him, it nonetheless brings with it a sense of guilt.

After all he thinks, "Aren't these rulers placed here by God? I know my responsibility to them, but don't they have responsibility to me? If I'm created in God's image, why do my rulers feel the need to diminish me? It leaves me feeling ashamed of God's creation in me."

The thought surrounding this seeming dysfunctional relationship lingers deep in his soul.

Chapter 20

The Whip

In answer to Tom's ubiquitous horn announcing a new day, Kumi falls in line to return to the fields. So far, his keen perception has kept him from the whip, but along with the workload, it is an exhausting exercise to not know the language and attempt to second guess every order. Toward the end of the day, he finds himself beginning to fall behind the rest of the crew. Suddenly, cutting through his work shirt, Kumi feels a shocking sensation across his back. The cracking sound the whip makes as it meets flesh results in Kumi recoiling around to find its source. What he meets are the fierce eyes of his tormentor. Without warning, Jack has laid a stripe of fresh blood across Kumi's back. There is no reason for Jack to say a word—the whip says it all. Kumi, in turn, doesn't need an explanation—he has quickly discovered the boundaries revealing him as an errant slave. This corporal punishment leaves him with mixed emotions. On one hand, it has labeled him as a wayward slave who doesn't know his place and needs to be dealt with. (There is a concept very real to slaves--that if one slave falls back on work, the overseer will take it out on the rest. This produces a culture among slaves whose focus is to become and remain a "good slave" or suffer the wrath of the slave community. This is all the work of the slaver to bring about a reification of slavery as an accepted form of human existence.) But, on the other hand, there remains something deep inside Kumi that finds this horribly insulting. Unless he wants to feel the sting of the whip again, Kumi quickly sets aside his inner debate for another time and hustles back to work.

124

Considering this is only her second morning on the Kilbourn Plantation, Abina, nonetheless has compelled herself to trudge to the Big House; she is forcing herself to adjust to her unsolicited role as a domestic slave.

Arriving at the slave entrance, Abina is met once again by the tall women who on her first morning introduced her to her new duties as a house slave. The rest of the domestics refer to her as Mammy Ceceilia. This woman, although a slave herself, readily makes it obvious that she is not an ordinary run-of-the-mill house slave. It immediately becomes clear to all that she is the overseer of the domestic slaves. It's her responsibility to organize the household tasks. This is not her only passion. She also possesses a fervor for "de Lawd." If there is anything Mammy Ceceilia dislikes more than a "lazy nigger" it is a pagan "dat doan knows de Lawd."

This morning Mammy Ceceilia is giving Abina more than a casual look. In this otherwise quiet, contemplative young woman, Mammy suspects a pagan may be lurking in her midst. She's been heard to say, "Dey is some born ta pray, some is born tah dance an' sing. I's born ta cast de devil out de Lawd's chilin."

Mammy is quietly contemplative as she continues to stare intensely into Abina's eyes. It's the kind of unblinking gaze someone uses when they are attempting to find the soul in another. Not comprehending a word in English, Abina doesn't understand the words Mammy is using, but Mammy's hard look transcends language. It's the same kind of entrancing gaze her mother would use in her dealings. It's captivating. Nonetheless, Abina can feel the power from Mammy's hard stare absorbing into her soul. Not surprisingly, it doesn't make Abina feel intimidated or uncomfortable—rather it is giving her a warm sense of trust toward Mammy. Mammy in turn, is also perceiving a strange union with this young woman that she finds genuinely engaging.

Tapping Abina's chest, Mammy says, "Chil', you gots someting in der—I sees it deep in you—sho nuff I sees it."

125

Moving on to another apparent concern, Mammy points to Abina's growing belly. Condescending to Abina's ignorance of the English language, Mammy reduces herself to using simple sign language. Holding up nine fingers, she motions as to how many months Abina has been pregnant. Abina's eyes look off across the room for a moment as she processes Mammy's seeming question. Indicating she understands the question, Abina grasps three of Mammy's fingers Abina lowers her eyes, nodding.

Abina's pregnancy lays heavy on her mind. Her demeanor is meant to show that she is reluctantly preparing herself for the inevitable day she will be bringing this new life into a world. As her own life has been tragically altered, she is becoming more and more aware how totally different the world will be for this child than the world she grew up in.

Nonetheless, within this simple exchange is a new connection. Each has understood that something intriguing is happening that is growing between them. It gives each of them a renewed purpose within their different roles. Mammy has several children of her own. Some have been sold off, others have been absorbed into the work-a-day life of the plantation. In spite of her waning role as a caregiver to her own adult children, she feels an inner compulsion to nurture—Abina has become the focus of this demand.

On the other hand, remaining cautious, not certain what this forthcoming relationship with this somewhat overbearing overseer is going to produce, Abina warily withdraws back within herself. In turn, Mammy is surprised at how the overwhelming desire to mother this young immigrant has overtaken her. Somewhat embarrassed by her softening tone, Mammy catches herself, quickly retrieving her overseer tone.

Pointing to Abina's stomach, "Dis here don' mean you ain' gonna have chores, cuz you sho nuff is," snaps Mammy resuming her assertive role. With this interchange behind them and realizing that they have reached an unspoken

126

awareness between their souls, they go about getting the day's activities started.

Today, Abina is paired with another pregnant domestic. This woman is slightly older and already the mother of four children. She is called Vel, although her real name is Veliane. Along with her normal chores, Vel is to teach as much English as she can to Abina.

Considering herself a quick learner, Abina is very receptive to Vel's efforts. She finds she can retain much of what she is being shown and taught. The day goes by rapidly with all the new duties she is expected to complete. Today being laundry day at the Big House, on her way back to the quarters, she finds herself repeating English words she learned: "Hang de close. Dis here be da soap. Marssa. Missa."

Quite pleased with her accomplishments, Abina can hardly wait to show off her English proficiency to Kumi. She needn't wait too long. It's dusk and she is nearly at the door of their shack when she sees the shadowy, but still discernable form of Kumi making his way up the path from the fields. He's walking much slower tonight than he has in the past. Abina hurries into the cabin to get a lantern lit before Kumi comes in. So far, their relationship has been platonic—more like cousins than housemates who are expected to procreate for their master.

Entering the door just as the light from the lantern flashes across his forlorn countenance, Kumi slumps to the floor. Abina has never seen her friend so disconsolate. It's only now that she sees the torn shirt and the red blood sticking the ripped edges to Kumi's open wound. Forgetting her new English words, Abina gasps, reverting to the only language that will allow her to display her alarm.

"Kumi, you're bleeding. What happened to you?"

127

Kumi, barely able to form the words he needs to answer Abina, replies "I got the whip."

No more need be said. Both are fully aware they are trapped in a life that will never offer escape. They are at the mercy of an unfamiliar power they don't comprehend. Not even the Arabs are known to mistreat their slaves as brutally as these Americans. Abina immediately prepares a pan of water and a rag. Soaking the rag with enough water to loosen Kumi's shirt from the bloody gashes, she begins the gruesome task. The cool water feels remarkably good to Kumi allowing Abina to calmly execute her task.

There are no words that either Kumi or Abina can offer to explain the distress they feel toward their situation. They have been chained, starved, and left to survive as best they could on a grueling Atlantic voyage, but this is the first time a physical whipping has been used against one of them. While applying a small amount of whale oil used in their lamp to the wound, Abina can't help but shudder at the thought of herself suffering the same fate at the hands of this remarkably dissimilar breed of humans.

A barely audible knock at the door interrupts Abina's nursing action. Simultaneously, Kumi and Abina snap their heads in the direction of this interruption. A second knock brings them to their feet. Both look at the other as though the other will have an explanation. Fear of further trouble is the first emotion both must deal with. Both think, "Who can this possibly be?" A second thought comes to Abina quickly. It's more pragmatic. "Maybe it's a neighbor coming to visit." With this thought in mind, Abina carefully cracks the door open enough to see a tall black man standing at the door. The shack's lamp casts a soft light crossed the man's face giving his skin an unusual glow. Along with this are unsmiling pensive eyes. It's a man Kumi has been working with clearing a wooded area. He's known as Able. His left hand is clearly empty—it's the hand he used to knock on the door. However, the other hand is clinched shut. It's obviously holding something. The man begins to speak.

128

"Us knows you 'all don' unerstan' a word I be sayin' cuz you 'all don' speak no English but us knows dey be some conjuremans dat wans mess wit' you 'all. He be all bou' placin' a spell. Dem conjuremans sho bad. My Mammy make up a jack fo' you 'all ta put in a pocket."

With this said, Able opens his hand revealing a piece of red cloth tied together with a string. In spite of not understanding a word being spoken, Able has both Kumi's and Abina's attention. Carefully untying the string, he reveals it's sorted contents. Lying as though it were on a bed is the remains of a dried frog. Alongside the frog is a piece of nutmeg.

"Dis here go in de pocket ta keep from gettin' conjured." With an air of authority Able demonstrates by pulling his own jack out of a side pocket.

"See dis here," Able further adds, "Dis here got da power ob ten conjure man."

Kumi as well as Abina know from their own village what power this gift is predicted to bring. With both hands clasped together as one would in accepting a precious gift, Kumi takes Able's offering. The heartfelt emotion Kumi has for this deed can't be missed. Despite the pain he's feeling across his back, he's truly grateful for Able's unsolicited friendship.

With Able taking his leave, Abina and Kumi are truly uplifted by the friendly gesture of their concerned friend. With all the horrific experiences they've undergone over the past months, the connection with their home village is fading. The desire to have companions is strong in them. For the first time since they arrived, they feel like they can make a community with these people.

Chapter 21

Hauntings and Church

The days turn into weeks, the weeks turn into months. Part out of necessity and part out of attrition, Kumi and Abina have improved their English skills tremendously. It's far from "King's English"—more in line with the way black slaves have developed an explicit vernacular among themselves. Nonetheless, it's reached the point where, without noticing it, they have abandoned their native tongue more and more and begun to supplement English except when making a specific point between themselves. They have also begun to form stronger community ties with the other slaves. Many of these are already the chattel prodigy of several past generations of slaves. Because they have come from all regions of North America and various regions of Africa, they have a conglomeration of traditions that have developed into a new American experience. This certainly is setting them apart from the slave experience in other places of the world; it's truly taking on a matchless tradition that proves to be unique from the slave communities of many other countries.

By tradition and a need for reason, Saturday has become a short workday. The intension is to allow the slaves to clean up for the "Lord's Day" on Sunday when there is no work. But, as things go, time will be used according to the impulse of the community. The Kilbourn plantation has included other traditions into their free time. Saturday night is for "jollification" as it's aptly put. This involves a mixture of events, including a period of prayer meetings, singing, and dancing. Although there is a mixture of ethnic groups within the slave community, many of the original cultural focal points have been blended with other ethnic groups. What is held in common despite their differences is how their point of convergence adapts into a shared ritual with physical gestures like swaying bodies or in a dance step and hand clapping. They are much more devoted to the patterns of ritual than the intellectual memories behind them. Nonetheless, music appears to be the mediator between their spiritual and sensual life.

Another favorite of all of them is in relating stories involving mimicking the humorous habits of their "Mistis an' Marse." This latter event always brings a roar of laughter. It's a subtle way these folks have of maintaining their sense of dignity while fending off the degradation of slavery. This is also a time when hunting and fishing skills are traded, ailments and their cures are discussed along with a variety of other relative topics. There are always several sure-cure remedies from people harking back to an ancient "cure" a mother or grandmother had sworn by. This is also a time when wary parents discuss with the children how to get along with the "Mistis" and the "Marse," all the while attempting to give themselves a life's purpose. This results in many of these multigenerational slave parents teaching their children how to be good slaves. This often differs from first generational slave children still being taught to watch for an area of escape, as the latter's parents still possess a remembrance of being free.

It's not unusual to have outside white people offer rewards to slaves enticing them to steal certain arranged contents belonging to the plantation. The slave-trading gospel preachers made a point of telling slaves to stay out of the master's hen house, nor steal his livestock, but they refrained from reproaching the poor white people who encouraged this behavior.

A Saturday night is not complete without relating an unusual ha'nt ("haunt") tale. A slave named Mo'es, who has just been bought begins to relate an account of a "ha'nt" he had experienced on a previous plantation.

"Dey was 'bout a couple hunert niggers on ole Marse Roy's plantation. De trouble come our way wid one mighty bad oberseer who beat on niggers so bad he near kilt 'em. One day he was alone at de creek cleanin' hiself up when he got kilt hiself. Dey fine' his mean ole body floatin' face down snagged up on tree limb dat was in de creek. Dey never did 'scover who done kilt 'em, but ole Marse Roy figured it were de field hands who done it.

"'Fore dat us niggers useter go der an' wash up, but a'ter de oberseer got hissef drown' us nebber go der no mo',' us jes' leave off dat washin,' 'cause some of 'em, sho' nuf, seed dat overseer's ha'nt floatin aroun' 'bove dem waters."

With the attention of everyone in a near spellbound frame of mind, and not to waste a good moment, another old man named Wellington begins to unravel another "ha'ntin.'"

"'Fore any of you was here, dey was a big nigger dey calt Bill. He weren' good fo' nothin.' Couldn't get him tah work like da res.' He always givin' De Colonel trouble. De Colonel has 'em whipped good one day. ole Bill, he done never forget dat whippin.' He had it in his mind tah get even wid De Colonel, so one day, he comes at 'em wid a hoe handle. De Colonel pull out his pistol an' shoot po' ole Bill dead in his tracks still grippin' dat hoe handle. Well, dat killin' start at da skirt of my garden patch what I gats my vege'ables. So, us an' my boy wen' down to dat patch ta do some hoin' 'roun' da termator plants. My boy, he hoin' close by an I hear da clankin' ob his hoe. Den I hear da clankin ob anobber hoe 'tween us. Dey ain't nobody else wid us, jes me an' him. It don' stop, it jes keep on aclankin' an' da ground is turnin' over wid every clank. De hair is standin' up 'roun' me. Lookin' at my boy, I draps da hoe aside an' tellin'

132

him a' do da same an' t'ketch up wid me effen he can. Den, I high tails it lickety split outta dat ha'nt.

"Us was near outten breath by da time we comes on De Colonel setten on his porch. He look at us 'tho we jes done somepen trouble.

"'What you niggers runnin' from? You up ta somethin' you got no business?' he say to us.

"No sir," us tells him. Den us tells him all 'bout de hap'nin,' How 'asides us, dey wuz somebody else a'hoin' 'long side.

"He look at me wid a big grin. Den he say, 'Dat was ole Bill. Dat where I kilt him. Jes give him a termator once a' while cuz 'ats what he likes.'

"At dat time on my part you coulda heerd a pin hittin' de groun.' I ain't been back at dat patch since," says Wellington recreating the same look of alarm he held during his encounter.

When Sunday morning arrives, the slaves are expected to harness as many mules as it takes and as many wagons as are needed to haul every slave on the plantation who's not been given a pass to stay away from services; they're all required to attend The Colonel's church, and those who have not been baptized are expected to undergo the initiation as soon as the preacher says they're ready.

These Sunday morning excursions are outings that are looked forward to. It's one of the only opportunities to get away from the work-a-day routine of the plantation, a chance to get to know one another; much visiting is done between wagons rambling along the three-mile route. There is singing, calling one another, and making and renewing old friendships. Once at church, they go directly to their own section where they are expected to sit and be attentive. For the most part, this type of structure is preferred to The Colonel's "high-falutin'" church building. It's also here where slavery is reinforced by pointing out in the Bible where slavery came about as a result of "Ole Ham's" sin, and how it was their duty to mind their masters as they continue to pay the price for "Ole Ham's" shortcomings. The preacher never misses an opportunity to remind these slaves of their duty as slaves to obey their masters.

He doesn't stop here, but continues, "It's like God was making man, He chose the purest, whitest clay to make the white man, the same that is used to make the purest china. The devil was watching all this time and thought he could do the same, so he chose some black mud and created a black man and called him nigger."

As if this were not enough, the preacher goes on to remind them of how fortunate they are.

"Nevertheless, the Lord in His mercy saw fit to be merciful to all of you. For your salvation did He not pull you out of a country that was destitute of Bible light, worshiping idols of sticks and stones, barbarously murdering each other. God put it in the head of these good slaveholders to risk their lives to cross the ocean to snatch you out of the burning fires of hell into a world of God's making. Here you have been selected. Oh, niggers how happy you are that your eyes have been opened to view the heavenly light. Many niggers have yearned for what you have and have died with never having their eyes opened. Many times, I have envied your place because God's blessings seem to be ever over you. It's as though you have been especially chosen by the Lord, for how much happier could your position be if you were a free man who if he falls sick must pay for his doctor's bill, or if hungry must buy his food and drink? Here, your master has all this within his care for you. He supplies your daily wants, your meat and drink. When you are sick, doesn't he provide you with the best skills to bring you back to health. And above all when you die, if you have been good niggers and obedient to your master your black faces will shine around the throne of God like polished black ebony."

134

Back on the plantation, Col. Kilbourn has allowed for what he refers to as "my niggers brush church." The Colonel has provided an outdoor brush pavilion for their Sunday night "hootenanny" as he prefers to regard their style of devotion. It's a pole structure with a roof consisting of pine boughs. This is graciously provided for their own church services on Sunday evening. It gives a sense of freedom without the constraints of walls. This is all allowed providing they follow prescribed Baptist teaching. This is just another example in which a white society controls and censors a black one. That compliance is attempted, but rarely ever happens. Mammy Ceceilia is the song leader while "Bro'r Joe" leads the worship part. He's a rather puny man—not fit for field work, rather, he's been trained to be "Missa Kilbourn's" driver.

Mammy Ceceilia is in her glory as she brings to life old familiar African tunes all along encouraged by banjo playing, accompanied by abundant hand clapping, and foot and body movements to the African rhythms. The "ring shout dancin,'" as it's become known, brings with it both praise and hope, pain and sorrow. To watch these people sing and dance is to see the heart and essence of a life struggling to stay alive. The pure, unadulterated, African dance expression would have been much more ritualistic and ended in a frenzy like highpoint. These dances tend to have become more "Negro" rather than "African" and promote restrained movements. This comes to light because the white system in which they live tends to repress just those gestures not permitted in everyday life, which further indicates the African meaning of these dances has been lost and now lies not in the dances themselves, but in the attitudes toward them.

To merely introduce Christianity alone is to introduce a subtle form of cultural genocide. For these people have discovered how Christianity is able to complement their traditional beliefs by bringing to life just the right measure of regard for evil spirits—which they consider as influencing all the evil stuff going on all around them—along with an internalized set of values to live life by. In this vein, in spite of his diminished size, Bro'r Joe is able to hold spellbound his

135

adherents with just the right amount of Bible teachings, all offset with a fitting compliment of voodoo. He carries himself in much the same way the white preachers carry on with changing voice intonations and hand gestures to bring his adherents to a near fever pitch of holy devotion.

Chapter 22

Tom

Abina and Kumi are at a time where much of the subtler remembrances of their former village is becoming more of a distant reality. Much of the forgetting has to do with the pain of realizing that village life is a permanent loss. Nonetheless, while the memory gradually fades, it is being replaced. The community they are forming on The Colonel's plantation has all the ingredients of a small town. As often happens, humans entering a new community often resist until the community begins to appeal, until it begins to meet their needs, and until they begin to be a part of other people's lives and allow others to become part of their lives. Abina and Kumi are finding themselves readily becoming participants of this developing community.

An example of this connection is with Mammy Ceceilia's constant vigilance. Abina is fast reaching the due date of her unborn child.

"Chil' you lookin' mighty po'ly. But it ain' nothin' a good dose a'castor oil cain' make better."

Mammy has access to many of the Big House remedies such as castor oil, dogwood tea, and jimson root and is making certain Abina is getting all she needs to stay healthy. Even though nearly a year has passed since Abina has seen her mother, she feels a desolation as her due date approaches. Pregnancy is not a legitimate reason for not working in the world of slavery; Abina's duties at the Big House continue. Along with many of the old people who are too old for field work, Abina has been assigned to look after the children of slaves still able to work in the fields. Part of their duties as caretakers is to be certain these young black children learn their status in the world in which they are placed. Abina finds this difficult to do. After all, she had not been born into slavery and well remembers her days of freedom and privilege as a chief's daughter. Watching the attitudes and actions of others who are second- and third-generation slaves toward their circumstances is a disconnect with her. There is an assent on the part on the slaves to prepare the next generation to become "good slaves." This is not to say Abina is hostile toward her apparent titleholders, but, through her own experience, she does possess a different thought process regarding the idea of slavery. In spite of her tightlipped struggle, she realizes she is outnumbered by the obsequious and servile decedents of onetime free men and women. They have accepted their lot.

"Accordin' t'what been issued out in de Bible, de be a time for slavery—peoples needn t'be punish' fo' der sins. We's still bein' punish' I 'spose," says an old black man named Charlie.

Nonetheless, considering that her child will be of mixed race, Abina is curious as to how this will affect the life of this yet unborn offspring. Privately, she has paid particular attention to the treatment of other mulatto progeny. The most obvious is a slave named Jim who is one of The Colonel's overseers, who resembles him in both facial and body image but is nonetheless not pure white. Still, according to the one drop law, he's considered as a black man and despite this man's half-white linage, his remaining blackness will allow him to have only a marginal advantage over the rest. The Colonel has never claimed him, but everyone knows the story.

Back in Africa, slavery is a reality—to the victor go the spoils—this includes conquered humans. This tradition is an accepted reality throughout the region. Although in Africa, as opposed to America, a slave is treated as a fellow human alongside his captor. The worst that would happen is that a captive

138

would be moved to a place his captors found he or she could serve him best, then after a number of years as a captive he or she could earn his or her freedom.

Unlike other places where slavery is practiced, in America, race has become part of the slave picture. For different reasons, Kumi has become more agitated over this situation than Abina. He has not resigned himself to being a slave. Nonetheless, for the sake of avoiding a beating, he has given his body over to his tormentors. He physically agrees to the station he's been assigned. Regardless of this decision, his memory of his life as a free man lingers in his psyche—his mind and spirit have not been altered. Without warning, his mind will drift to some occurrence he recalls from his days as a young man fostering hopes and dreams. In retrospect, Kumi is further able to analyze why his village was chosen to be attacked by a neighboring village. In doing so, he realizes how vulnerable the people in his village had become. Not blaming Abina for the actions of her father, Kumi holds her father responsible for the failure to protect the village. In Kumi's opinion, Abina's father was much more concerned with the importance of his position as chief than he was with keeping his village resistant to an attack.

Like most communities, the plantation population is comprised of various kinds of individuals with different physical, mental, and spiritual temperaments displayed through different personalities and dispositions. When placed all together it will determine their collective character. Most slaves are compliant to the wishes of The Colonel. Mostly this compliance is based on the need for systemic order within a community—things work more smoothly for everyone if a sense of compliance is observed. Although enslaved, they are encouraged to become good, obedient slaves. Obedient slaves are rarely whipped. In exchange for this compliance, they are provided food, shelter, and a strong sense of purpose in becoming a better slave.

139

Kumi has not become one of these. But what he has come to learn is to keep his thoughts to himself. He has observed the methods The Colonel uses to keep his slaves intimidated. It's not an unusual occurrence to find an old-time slave, along with others of his disposition, come down hard on a slave who may not be carrying his weight. The reason this method is effective is, if this laggard isn't corrected by his peers, The Colonel will punish everyone for the laggard's noncompliance. There is a predetermined standard of decency composed by the slave owner; the hope is it will end with a collective identity. It is not in a slave owner's mindset to observe "noblesse oblige," in other words accommodating those of lesser privilege. The Colonel, in most cases, believes he has set his policies according to biblical principles. It is expected the slaves will take on this standard as their own. If they all play their cards right, they will be taken care of from cradle to grave. The endgame in the slave world is to be the best slave to the master one can be, thereby, giving living a purpose and keeping one's life as trouble free as possible. It's a collective identity at its best.

Not ready to fit the mold of "best slave," Kumi's deep sense of self is his predominant emotion. Since his arrival, he has learned of the fate of only one slave who had attempted running away. In his role as master, The Colonel believes in what he is doing. He honestly believes to be a good master requires him to keep order in the slave community by any means that works. The Colonel is not known to renege on the importance in asserting dominance over his slaves. In the case of runaways, he will go to any length to dishonor their disobedience by having them branded, shackled, mutilated by amputations, and hung if the slave can't be reoriented to the proper life he's held to. Consequently, Kumi is forever keeping his eyes and ears open, always calculating the risk of an escape.

With the mindset of an escapee, Kumi has only physically joined the plantation's slave community—but then, only to the degree that it serves him. He enjoys the singing and dancing because it reminds him of the good times experienced in his village. There is a clear individualistic strain in Kumi. He finds

140

he must make autonomous choices while working within a system. He finds the collective identity too restrictive. For reasons he can't explain, Kumi has always felt his essence is to become more than someone's slave. He doesn't mind the work; except that it's mandated and overseen by Jack Beauchamp.

Lately, Jack has taken a dislike to Kumi. It's more that he recognizes a level of independence in Kumi that is not demonstrated by the ordinary slave. It's not a physical noncompliance that is getting Jack's attention, rather it's in an attitude—it's held within that hesitancy to respond to a direct order followed by a look Jack reads as rebellious. It's this part of a slave Jack fears. Out in the field he has particularly taken note of Kumi's pensive and evaluating nature. It is deeper and more analytical than the others. By giving him a lash occasionally, Jack satisfies his need to dominate not only the bodies of these captives but also their minds and spirits. Consequently, Kumi has become Jack's whipping boy of late. This is in contradiction to The Colonel's policy of maintaining a healthy usefulness within his slaves. Kumi's physical usefulness has been at risk several times as a result of Jack overreaching his assignment with the whip.

Jack has his own private quarters behind the livestock outbuildings. It's a well-built cabin with logs coming from the plantation's ample supply of pine forests. He, at will, picks himself one of the female slaves to be his housekeeper. Other than the fact Abina is nearly full term, Kumi has noticed how Jack looks at her. Kumi has never had relations with Abina despite sharing the same quarters. There exists a code in Ghana that men don't have relations with a woman while she's pregnant. Kumi's sense tells him he needs to find a way of ridding his and Abina's life of Jack. These are dangerous thoughts. Once they are formulated, lest they fall from unguarded lips, they must be dispensed with an extremely careful design. Other than sharing with Abina, Kumi has kept his thoughts regarding Jack to himself.

It's the end of another day of nonending work. Kumi has received another of Jack's degrading lashes. Jack is careful to hurt Kumi only enough to where they both understand who is in authority, but not enough to bring the injury to the attention of The Colonel.

Speaking in their native tongue while Abina once more attends his open wound, Kumi laments, "I cannot live like this for another day. I must do what I can to protect myself from this demon."

Abina can detect in his tone a mixture of what she determines is either reckless foolhardiness or a calculated determination. Unable to read what his intentions entail, Abina attempts to make her question more poignant, asking, "What do you imagine you can do?" Undertones of doubt are clearly detected in her question.

Kumi is quiet. He recalls the account told by the new man about the drowning demise of the overseer on his previous plantation. The question poses the difficulty that continues to plague him. Short of getting caught up in brooding over the impenetrable aspects of his situation, he forces himself to consider Abina's question in a more pragmatic way.

"I think I can at least do something that will cause him to have second thoughts." Kumi pauses for a moment as he recalls how war was carried on in Ghana. The ambush was perfected to the point that an enemy was never seen coming until they were on their victim. As he considers the circumstances his own ruin, he further adds, "I'm not the only person he's singled out, there are several others."

"Are they people you trust?" queries Abina displaying her concern as she continues applying her special balm to Kumi's wound.

Kumi mulls over her question for a moment. "I'm not certain," he adds.

Even though there is a community on the plantation made up of slaves, and within this community are even smaller communities based on things like seniority, age, sex, house slaves, and field slaves, he has never detected an underground escape group. Despite the fact Kumi has attended every Saturday and Sunday get together with nearly every captive on the plantation, he contemplates the certainty of who is trustworthy. Admittedly, Kumi has not found anyone whose company he enjoys well enough to say he can place a confidence in them. "After all," he thinks, "they may be snitchers." So far, he has been content in remaining aloof from the community at large. But this is one time he could use an ally. In retrospect, he wishes he had been more diligent in bringing people into his world.

At this moment there is a knock at the door. Puzzled as to what this could mean, Abina carefully answers the knock. There in the doorway stands Tom, the driver, also the slave in charge of carrying out Jack's work detail.

"Sorry 'bout callin' late like dis," says Tom looking around Abina to get a look at Kumi. He sees Kumi with his back is all salved up with Abina's ointment. This gives him his open. "Us wan' you know you don' 'serve dat kine a'lashin.' De Colonel don' knows how Jack been treatin' his niggas. If he knows 'bout how bad you lookin,' he hab his hide."

Kumi is reticent to say anything as he knows Tom can give him grief if he would choose to do so.

Tom looks hard at Kumi indicating he has more to say and is choosing his words. Jack isn't the only one who has recognized this kind of grit rarely found in slaves, Tom also sees it. Unlike Jack, who fears any display of fortitude, Tom admires Kumi's seeming poise despite Jack's attempts to degrade him.

"I'm a fearin' fer you, Kumi. Jack, he sho nuf got it in fer you. I reckon he ain't gonna lighten up 'til you daid," continues Tom.

Kumi listens without response. He's more than willing to let Tom do all the talking.

"Us s'posen you wonderin' what in tarnation us be doin comin' 'roun yer quarters. Well, us be here tah let you know iffen us can hep you in some way you gots tah let us know."

Kumi is taken back by this unexpected overture. It's an offer he didn't expect coming from Tom. After all, Tom is more often regarded as Jack's messenger boy. He's often seen in a position that is not in the best interest of his fellow slaves. On the other hand, this also places him in a position which supplies him with information not generally available to other slaves.

Kumi is daily struggling with understanding English spoken by white people as well as that spoken by the slave population. Considering how his interaction in the fields has eased his interactions with slaves, he has progressed rather quickly in that capacity.

In understanding Tom very well, Kumi wastes no time in forming a rejoinder. Able to use the English dialogue of his fellow slaves, Kumi says, "Why you do dis for me?" The reply becomes his straightforward question to what he suspects to be more of Tom's deception. Afterall, Tom hasn't gone out of his way to protect Jack from unnecessarily whipping him—why should Kumi consider him to be a friend?

Taken aback at this distrust but at the same time understanding where it is coming from, Tom pauses for a moment to process Kumi's abrupt attitude. Although he finds Kumi's gruff attitude unwarranted, he is hoping with his upcoming explanation that Kumi will have a new perspective. For the present, Tom chooses to ignore Kumi's immediate attitude. Forming another thought, Tom continues, "I knows you got whuppins you din' have a-comin, but iffen I drap down on ole Jack whilst he whuppin' on you, he fo sho whip me near ta death. I gots ta keep 'im understandin' he can trus' ole Tom."

Kumi is caught off guard with Tom's explanation. He had hoped his curt attitude would be enough to cause Tom to leave his quarters as well as get out of his life. But he can't help but hear a tone in Tom's voice he has not heard before. Still not certain he's doing the right thing, Kumi hesitates long enough to indicate to Jack he's willing to listen.

Tom seizes the opportunity to pick up where he had left off. Pointing to an outbuilding, Tom continues, "Iffen De Colonel know'd ole Jack was whuppin' his niggas de way he doin,' he'd hab ole Jack's ass tacked up on dat shed."

Tom continues to watch Kumi. Pleasantly pleased with the way Kumi is picking up on what he's saying.

At this point Kumi breaks his silence. "You figgurin' you gwinter gib ole Jack a whuppin'?"

"Us gwinter do more den dat. Us gwinter sen' 'im ass a'packin,'" says Tom with a look of dead seriousness.

"Jes how you plan on doin' dat? Dat man gots more eyes an ears den a ghos,'" laments Kumi.

"Oh, don' worry, us gots hund'eds aways ta come on his life wid some misery," says Tom with a reassuring grin. "But what bringin' us here tonight is t'ask you t'join in wid us to hep bring ole Jack some bad luck."

Still sitting with Abina attending his wounds, Kumi further contemplates, "What you wan' me for? I ain't got no misery skills."

Tom is ready with an answer. "I lernt a heap ob de misery skills from niggas been molden in de grave long time now. I 'member em good an' gib a bunch anew niggas a heap a learnin.'"

Abina sets Kumi free as she finishes dressing his wound. With this personal project completed, Kumi's able to meet Tom face to face. "What you think you can learn this nigga? I been dreamin' up hoodoo stuff a'hopin' I can hab Abina hex him wid it—she wan' no part ob it."

Tom is carefully watching all of Kumi's demeanor—his words, his angry tone including his body language—satisfied that Kumi's frustration is ripe enough, he begins to draw him into the conversation that has brought him to Kumi's door.

"You belieb you been done bad by ole Jack, don' 'ya? Without waiting for an answer, Tom continues, "Us knows you does. Der be ways ob drawin' up on ole Jack's blind side wid out him know from where his misery 'risin.'"

Satisfied with Kumi's reaction, Tom's reassured to win over Kumi's confidence. "You throw in wid us an' we hep bring ole Jack his comin's." Just for good measure Tom adds, "Fo sho, ole Jack, 'im gwinter have no idea where de misery 'risin.'"

Kumi is stunned at what he's hearing from a man with whom his everyday involvement has been less than enjoyable. It's taking him a minute to process what he's hearing.

"How us knows you ain't leadin' us out fo' another whuppin'?" asks Kumi with all the earnestness he can muster.

Tom never flinches as though he anticipated Kumi's question. With the determination of a man that knows exactly what he's talking about, Tom continues, "Cuz us gots niggas dat brought misery to de las' oberseer an De Colonel t'row his ass off."

Still not convinced that Tom has his best interest in mind, Kumi asks another question, "What kind ob misery you gwinter rough 'im wid where you ain't ketched?"

146

At this point, Tom senses he's made some inroads into Kumi's inner person. He feels that he can now advance to his next step. "Us gwinter hit 'im good. Us ain't gwinter hit 'im wid no hoodoo. Us gwinter hit 'im where it hurt 'im de mos'—in de purse."

Kumi is spinning all that Tom is saying around and round inside his head. Seeking vengeance is a tactic Kumi is very much aware of. Back in Africa, each village kept a close tally on the conduct of other surrounding villages. It was a matter of honor to seek retribution from any neighboring tribe or village that may have caused a slight. Many times, the slight had been enough to initiate a war between villages—as had happened in Kumi's village. Something familiar is striking Kumi. He's experiencing a sensation he has not had since he left his African village. A shot of adrenalin is plowing its way through his body. It's the most empowering sensation Kumi has had since his incarceration. Now, Tom has his total attention.

Kumi is nearly on his toes. "Wha' kien misery yo got agowien? Us sho'lly don wan' be lef' outten de terr'bles, "declares Kumi with the self-assurance one has when a conviction is ready to become an action.

Tom is satisfied he has Kumi's allegiance. "You get 'long wid us t'night. Us gwinter meet in da bush church bye an' bye. Dey be some niggas dat knows some miseryian trickeries," declares Tom. His enthusiasm has quickened in direct proportion to Kumi's.

Kumi is silent during his supper. His thoughts have become bolder as he contemplates that there are more than just him alone struggling with Jack; he realizes there are others willing to come together to deal with this seemingly no-win situation. This is the first time since arriving that he is experiencing a feeling that offers hope. It's optimism that holds a promise that after nearly losing hope of better days that hope has taken a new course.

147

Chapter 23

The Plot

     As the evening progresses, he's finding it compelling to follow through with his clandestine meeting. With his supper finished, Kumi finds it's time to go. The evening has turned into night with an overcast sky making it exceptionally dark. Kumi has a great respect for the nighttime. He knows this is the realm of spirits. Some are good and some are not so good. Tonight, he has another task to take care of and doesn't feel inclined to deal with either kind.

     "I hope dey ain't no gos' out here tonight. I sho don' wan' be dealin' wif none of dey kind right now," is his thought as he makes his way along the path to the bush church.

     The path is well beaten with summer grasses and various weeds lining each side. With his eyes adjusting to the dark, this vegetation provides enough of a border to guide him. Soon he arrives to the sounds of muffled talk and the distinct smell of tobacco smoke. Entering under the canopy, Kumi is met with the silhouette of at least a half-dozen men. Tom welcomes him with a typical West African handshake where the middle fingers are crossed and snapped against the palm. He is then introduced to each of the other compatriots from right to left with the same handshakes. This sense of tradition is drawing Kumi into a oneness with the others that he has not experienced since leaving Africa. The brush church is very dark and the only time he gets a clear vision of these men is when a tobacco pipe needs to be relit. He knows them all from the field but has never imagined that relationship would be organized into this

148

clandestine meeting. Kumi immediately recognizes one of the men he splits rail with by the name of Nate, another is a man named Rue who had handled the horses he had helped pull stumps with. Tom is the leading voice in the group.

"Us comin' t'getter here t'get a handle on how us gwainter put some misery on ole Jack," says Tom in a strained whisper.

Tom has been on the plantation nearly his entire life. When it comes to witnessing slaves getting unwarranted beatings, he's had to deal with getting rid of other overseers who overreached their assignments. For Tom, getting rid of Jack is going to be a rather routine task—providing everything goes according to plan. Slaves have no legal recourse, nonetheless, over time they have developed their own ways of dealing with unruly overseers.

"Iffen De Colonel knowed how bad dis oberseer treatin' 'im slaves, he'd be a'kickin' ole Jack's ass up 'roun 'im neck an' den kick 'im head off," Tom continues to the nodding head agreement of each of these men.

The next hour is spent with Tom laying out a plot. His strategy is to hit Jack with enough distress that it catches the attention of The Colonel. The Colonel has had enough experience with his slaves to know what trouble a rebellion can cost; with as many as he has it would be next to impossible to quell a rebellion without a serious financial loss of slaves. Tom has been around long enough to know how to hit both in the pocketbook to garner good results. After an hour discussion, each man has a clear idea of what his role is going to be.

As usual, the next morning comes without fanfare. Tom is about his familiar routine of gathering all of his crew to one place to wait for Jack. Jack's daily custom is to use this occasion to inform Tom of the day's work schedule. Within a few minutes, Jack arrives on horseback in his customary regal grandeur—it's become his expected style. Today he has chosen a large white mount freckled with dark speckles of black. Over the years, he has proudly mustered a stable of prize horses—some he has bred, and some he has purchased. Although not an exceptionally large man, mounted on this stud, Jack perceives himself as larger than he is, even though when contrasting his size against the size of the horse, he looks rather puny.

Around his shoulder is a coiled whip ready to be detached at a moment's notice. Hooked on one side of his saddle horn is a feed bag of oats that he prefers his horse feed on rather than merely pasture grass. He has employed a small shed he had built to store some of his personal items he will require throughout the day. It's here where he also stores his horse's feed bag.

Once Jack has concluded dispatching his work routine, he leaves Tom in charge as he makes his way over to an adjoining field where a group of women are tending tobacco plants. It isn't that the women need his guidance as they have an older slave woman that tends to their scheduling, and it isn't because he has become so interested in tobacco plants. But it does have to do with women. He is drawn to this side by a much baser inducement—his own lustful desires. Jack is not the type of male who courts a woman. He is more of the opportunistic kind who finds it easier to take what he wants from among the slave women.

Tom has paid special attention to Jack's routine this morning. He has placed a lookout to signal if Jack is seen returning. A slave named Ed, whose woman is a house slave, has supplied him with needles from a Yew tree found at the Big House. He is preparing them to be mixed with the oats in the horses feed bag. The yew's needles are highly poisonous to horses.

Meanwhile, the preparation has been handed to Kumi. He has been given the task to get the ground up needles into the feedbag and mixed in with the oats. It's a nerve-racking task, but Kumi knows it must be done. With the small bag securely hidden in a pant pocket, he guardedly makes his way to Jack's small shed. This area is unquestionably forbidden to slaves to the point that any infraction is dealt with by the whip. Kumi feels the tension building in his mind which is wasting no time to make it to his body. He's beginning to shake so hard that the simple task of opening the shed door is difficult. Every illegal move that he makes is causing the stress within him to increase. Looking around, he doesn't see the feedbag. He frantically begins to paw through everything. "Where you at? Where you at?" is his panicked chant. The primordial, unnerved urge to throw things around to quickly find it is in place, but his second thought kicks in. It strongly suggests he calm down and use his brain. Now, carefully scanning the shed's interior, he spots the feed bag hanging on a hook behind an article of clothing. His body and mind are once again working together. With the dexterity of a surgeon, Kumi has the small bag of ground yew needles readily mixed in with the oats. In another flash, he has turned toward the open doorway, quickly makes his way out, careful to leave the door exactly the way he had found it.

The timing couldn't have been closer. Just as Kumi has made his way free of the building, Jack rides back to resume his tasks.

Things go as normally as can be expected with the heightened anticipation of the several men awaiting the finality of their efforts. As usual, Jack spends the morning intimidating everyone that he can to work harder. Avoiding the whip is always the incentive to obey. The slaves grudgingly submit, doing whatever it takes to circumvent its sting.

At last, the noon break arrives. As much as possible, everyone goes about their business. Through the bush telegraph they're aware something is up. There is a tension in the air that places each of these men in a relationship with the whole; being a cohesive group, they mysteriously share a similar soul that connects them to one another. Although it's only the seven men who are privy to all the details pertaining to fulfilling this exploit, the rest await the aftermath.

At the noon break, it's the usual habit of these men to make their way back to their quarters to take their rest. Today there is a lagging—a waiting. Rumors have spread throughout the work crew that a life-changing event is in the making.

Jack is going about his routine involving taking inventory of all the slaves who were on task and those who weren't. He also has returned to his shed. Kumi and the other six involved in the plot are watching Jack go from one thing after another with his duties. It seems to them as though he is never going to feed that horse. They steal nervous glances at one another hoping not to display any behavior out of the ordinary. At last he appears from the shed carrying the long-anticipated feedbag. Hoping not to be noticed as he watches Jack's every move, Kumi feels a different kind of sweat running down his side than his work sweat—it's a nervous sweat.

As Jack fastens the feedbag over the horse's head, Tom is quietly going about his own duties, but he is also paying close attention to what will become of Jack's unforeseen misfortune. The horse wastes little time in sating its appetite. Satisfied that they have met their objective, Tom gives a knowing glance to the others involved. They knowingly nod and quietly go about their own routine. Those who are only on the periphery of this affair also recognize by the change in the atmosphere that something has been done. Not yet aware of its changing circumstances, they content themselves to wait and watch.

Not to arouse any suspicions Tom, Kumi, and the rest of the holdovers prepare to go off to their allocated quarters to rest. None of the seven say a word to each other as they place themselves on Tom's wagon for the ride back to their housing. Everyone is holding to the idiom "the less said is the best choice." When Kumi enters the shack, Abina also holds her thoughts to herself. She can tell by the look on Kumi's face that he carried out his mission. Neither are certain what can come from this action. Regardless, it holds a place in each of their minds with the certainty it may not be good.

152

Kumi's rest period has been fraught with anxiety. Tom's blast on the horn announcing the rest period is over brings with it the reality of facing an overseer who is dealing with a prize horse that is either dead or dying. The trip back to the workplace is as somber as the trip leaving a couple hours earlier.

The picture Kumi has been entertaining in his mind is exactly the picture he is viewing as they come on the scene. Jack along with several of the other white overseers are standing over the carcass of a large white and black speckled horse. As Tom's wagon loaded with slaves draws closer, the group of white men all turn with a silent eye in their direction. Aware of the white men's conspicuous hard glowered gaze in their direction, the reaction of each slave is to go about their business as though unnoticed. After Tom brings his wagon to a halt allowing the slaves to unload themselves, he continues his traditional obsequious behavior in making himself available for Jack's further orders designed for the rest of the day. The silent eyes from the gathering of white men maintain their steady gaze directly at Tom as he continues his approach. He doesn't have to worry about a prolonged wait on Jack's part. Jack is already taking steps forward to meet Tom. His furrowed eyebrows prepare Tom for an angry harangue. "What you an' the rest of your nigger's know about this?"

Tom feigning a silent concern, looks first at Jack then back at the horse laying prone on the ground in front of him. With years of shielding himself against the ensnarement of working with suspicious white men, Tom has perfected his contrived allegiance to their concerns. "Wha' in de name ob de Lawd goin' on wid dis po' hoss?" is Tom's affected reaction.

Jack's frustration over his loss has predictably turned to anger. "You and the rest of yer nigger's gonna pay fer this. I know damn well they had a hand in this. I'm leavin' it up to you to get to the bottom of this today or I'll make every damn one of you wish you had!" This becomes Jack's final rant as he turns and walks back to rejoin his white sympathizers.

153

This is what Tom expected. From his past personal encounters with abusive overseers, he is of the opinion one needs to strike while the iron is hot. While Jack is still talking, Tom is formulating the next attack that needs to follow this episode. For the rest of the day Jack is absent busily disposing of his deceased horse. This leaves Tom in charge. He takes little time before he speaks with his selected crew. With Jack gone, he pulls them under the shade of a big oak tree.

"Yaassaa, us hot on 'im now. Us gwinter use ole Jack up pretty rough, 'im ain't seed nottin' 'til 'im see what comin' down da road t'night.

The discussion continues until Tom becomes certain everyone knows exactly what his designated task is to be. The agreement is to meet at the brush church after the supper hour and lay down their final plan. Even among slaves there is a measure of mistreatment they can bear and remain alive—this is beyond the given fact that slavery is singularly a mistreatment. In this case, they are being mistreated and driven to the edge of their endurance by a tyrannical slave driver named Jack Beauchamp.

By the time supper is finished, Abina is busy putting together a gris-gris bag of red flannel with several good-luck charms for Kumi to wear to keep him safe. With darkness well on its way, things around the quarters are settling down; at the same time seven men are creeping out of their quarters as silent and inconspicuous as possible. Each is aware of the consequences should he be caught. Being out without a pass is considered a violation punishable by a severe whipping. Nonetheless, each man reveres the mission they are on as a righteous undertaking. Tom has arrived early, prepared to meet each man as they entered the darkened church pavilion. Satisfied he has his quorum, Tom once more quizzes each man of his duties for the upcoming feat, categorically going through a list with each man to insure they have the interconnected cache of materials needed to complete their next campaign.

154

"Rue, sho you gots plenty what you needs?"

Producing a bag, Rue says, "Sho nuf, us gots a'plenty."

Assured all parties are ready, Tom leads the group in a single file down a darkened path. The sound of dogs barking in concert at nighttime shadows is prevalent on all corners of the plantation. Singularly, these men would be moving with unimaginable fear. Since they have all worked together and are familiar with each other's individual strengths and weaknesses, as a team, they share their anxiety together. Mysteriously, the dread of a misstep is reduced. Tom is secure in his picks for both physical skills as well as mental acuity.

This nighttime path eventually brings these men to their destination. It's the cabin of Jack Beauchamp. For the present, the troupe is happy to stand back in the cover of a thicket surrounding the structure. They are studying what they are able to see of Jack's place at this juncture. There is the glow of a light in the window, a certainty Jack is inside—right where they want him. They also know Jack keeps a hound he describes as his "nigger catcher." In his own callous way, he has made it known, "If any you niggers think you can outrun ole Blue, I challenge you tah give 'er a try."

In this case, Tom has also provided a way to entertain this hound should they have an encounter. One of the men named Bert, has been given the assignment on how to deal with the dog should it become necessary. They don't have to wait long when the all too familiar growl of an angry hound is heard. All eyes are on the beast as it makes its way toward their hideout. Bert is hesitant for a second, as though he were making the decision to either flee or fight. Tom has already made the decision for him by pushing him into action. With his hand in a bag, Bert tosses a biscuit in the direction of the interloper. The hound stops for a second to smell the seeming gift. In the next second, he gobbles the whole thing in one bite. The waiting avengers watch as the hound is suddenly going through some unusual incantations usually reserved for an animal in distress.

155

They have given the unsuspecting animal a biscuit soaked in bacon grease and laced with the same deadly yew needles they had given the horse. In less than five minutes the hound is lying dead on the ground. The quiet that follows is almost ghostly as all of the other hounds on the plantation have ceased their incessant howling—it's as if all of nature has become aware of one of its own having left this world to enter a different realm.

Now, with the hound out of the way, Kumi creeps to the window. What he sees is Jack sitting at a table with a bottle of what appears to be whiskey. The bottle is half empty and Jack appears to be drunk. Considering Jack's condition, to wait for him to extinguish the light may be to wait for it to burn itself out. Reporting back to Tom and the others, the decision is to wait for Jack to pass out and then make their move.

With this step of the mission accomplished, they wait for Jack's head to hit the table. The waiting silence these daring men are left with is a new phenomenon for each of them. To be true, the courage this group is displaying for the sake of others is remarkably significant. Most others don't possess this level of bravery. Rather, they spend their time grumbling and suffering without taking the necessary action needed to change their circumstances. Without realizing how unique it is to be doing what they are preparing to do, the seven men ready themselves to make their next move. Within another fifteen minutes, they check on Jack's condition. The decision is to make certain Jack is given enough time to fall into a good, hard drunken stupor. With the satisfaction that he has reached the limits of sobriety, they spring into action.

Making their way to the south side of the building where it faces the sun, where it is considered to be the driest, Rue produces his bag of dry tinder, methodically piling it under the building in that space between the floor and the ground. Another of the men, going by the name of Zeke, produces a vile of whale oil. He follows behind Rue to pour its contents throughout the tinder. This is followed with Kumi striking together a piece of flint and a piece of iron pyrite.

156

The result is a hot, sturdy spark flying into the tinder producing an immediate flame. The men stand for only a moment watching the flames begin to leap under the floor and up the outside wall. Convinced they have completed their mission, Tom wastes little time signaling to make a hasty retreat.

With little or no sympathy for Jack as to whether he survives the flames, the troupe of avengers return to their quarters. As agreed, Tom remains alone. He has one more assignment to finish. BLAAATTT! BLAAATTT! He is on his horn sounding the fire alarm. This performance is more to serve as a cover for his and the rest of the retaliators' whereabouts. Within a few minutes there are a few dozen men assembled. Tom quickly opens the supply barn and supplies the men with pails and torches.

With his finest show of concern, Tom shouts out, "Faller us. Looks tah it be de oberseers house a'fire!"

The men stumble to form a line to wait for Tom's next command. In a flash of proficiency, Tom orders a man named Ed, "Get on t'de Big House an 'lert De Colonel. De res' you niggas, get on dat fire fo' it burn de whole plantation." Once on site, Tom makes a hasty assessment. He immediately sees a familiar form standing helplessly off to the side of the clearing. Recognizing it as no other than Jack, he wastes no time in leading the men in a rag tag attempt to mount a fire brigade to pass buckets of water from a well. It's obvious the dwelling is a complete loss. Jack is standing as though in a trance. He has suffered the loss of a prize horse and is watching his house with all his belongings burn to the ground—all in one day. It's having a sobering effect on him. It's a new experience for him to be on the receiving end of a blow like this. There is a sense of powerlessness that is trying very hard to overtake him. His anger is quickly replacing his moment of disbelief.

"You ain't got but a minute t'come up with which of yer niggers is responsible for this or I'll whip the hide off the whole bunch of ya," bellows Jack still wearing the results of the bottle he drank earlier. This is said just as The Colonel has arrived riding in his carriage. He's in time to overhear Jack's harangue. Certainly not about to have his property left in the hands of a man seeking revenge, The Colonel takes immediate command.

"You ain't whippin none o' my nigger 'less I say so," says The Colonel. His presence catches Jack on his blind side.

"Yes, sir, Colonel. I ain't about to do nothin but get the truth out these lyin' heathen," exclaims Jack in a much more controlled voice. "They kilt my best horse; now, they burnt my house to the ground."

Over the years, The Colonel has dealt with a various number of overseers—some better or worse than others. He's come to readily recognize the bad ones. When humans are mistreated—and that includes slaves—they will find ways to mistreat their mistreater. While listening to Jack, Colonel Kilbourn's suspicions arise that things are getting out of hand. When slaves go to the length to kill an overseer's horse and then burn his house down with him still inside, that says that they are willing to risk their own lives to rid themselves of this kind of oppressor. The Colonel is noticeably deep in thought as he weighs these elements of decision. The sum of these parts can only weigh against one of the two parties—the slaves or Jack Beauchamp, the overseer. He has watched his expensive slaves becoming progressively less productive coinciding with a harshness growing within his overseer; he has heard it in Jack's voice and seen it in his demeanor during his monthly report. The Colonel is of the opinion that when his slaves are content, they produce more with less overseeing. Still, processing his decision, he decides to sleep on it and make a decision going forward in the morning.

With the dawn of a new morning, the plantation awaits the consequences of the previous evening's disruption. The first thing every slave becomes aware of is that there is no morning reveille. Tom is absent because he has been summoned to the Big House. On arrival what he views is not surprising. He is watching Jack leading what's left of his horses down the road as he exits the plantation. It doesn't take a fortuneteller to explain to Tom what has just transpired.

Tom is at the servant's entrance where he is greeted by Ceceilia. Tom never feels he is being greeted by Ceceilia—it's more of a scrutinization. Her hands are gripping the sides of her hips, her chin is in the air, her face is wearing a wary look of suspicion, and her voice bears a challenge.

"What you wan'?" barks Ceceilia.

With hat in hand, Tom is as obsequies with Ceceilia as he is with white people. Within the slave pecking order, house slaves are on a higher order. Ceceilia wastes no time in letting Tom know he's only a lowly field slave.

"De Colonel, him say dat he wan' us at de Big House," declares Tom.

With her chin still in the air, Ceceilia drops her eyes pausing only long enough to inspect him from head to toe.

"Humph," is her singular word for a moment. "I'll let De Colonel know you out here an 'waitin'—an don' be a'puttin' dem dirty boots on any ob dees spankin' fresh floos," she adds with a definite tone of annoyance.

In a few minutes, Mammy Ceceilia is back. "De Colonel, 'im say dat you go in der now."

Without a further word, Tom leaves the kitchen. Watching him walk precariously across the room, Mammy can't help herself. She has to get in the last word. "An' don' be putin' dem fithy boots on anything in dis house."

Tom is dead set against getting in any kind of dispute with Ceceilia. He realizes that, while she is still a slave, she has become an essential fixture in

159

this house for nearly as many years as he has been alive. It's become nearly as much hers as it is her white owners. He is not about to challenge her place in this household.

As Tom enters a large anteroom, he can smell the familiar odor of cigars. Two more steps place him before a huge set of closed double doors. These doors were made from the lumber Tom and his crew had milled years ago. He glances at them remembering a long-deceased slave they called "Pappy" who built these magnificent doors. Tom has been in the Big House several times and always looks forward to seeing these grand portals. With a light nonintrusive knock, he hears the unmistakable voice of The Colonel, "Come on in, Tom."

With hat still in hand, Tom slowly makes his way into the room all the while servilely bobbing his head in a show of impotence in the presence of his master. The Colonel is seated behind a very well made, ornate desk. Tom also remembers ole Pappy spending many hours tweaking and retweaking every detail needed to perfect this piece of furniture. The Colonel suddenly swings his chair around to confront Tom. Firmly chomped between his teeth is his familiar cigar. In a voice Tom has come to await, The Colonel begins:

"Listen, nigga, ahm a patient man, but ah have had all ahm a 'gonna do with yer shenanigans. Ah reckons Jack wasn't doin' right by yo nigga standards, but there ain't a 'gonna be no more burnin' er poisenin' on this plantation. You unnerstand, boy?"

Tom swallows hard, all the while still obsequiously bobbing his head saying, "Yessah Marse, us 'stands. Yessah Marse, ole Tom 'stands."

Since The Colonel has Tom's full attention, he continues with another thought, "If I have a nigga that oughta be whipped, ahm a 'gonna get rid of him for he taints the rest—like one bad tater in a bag gonna spoil the rest."

Tom has heard this diatribe many times before and is aware of the certainty The Colonel has in keeping his word. He knows this conversation is The Colonel's way of letting him know that if he can't keep his charges in line, The Colonel will. On the other hand, Tom understands how well The Colonel recalls in times past when he had a similar overseer causing the slaves to sabotage machinery, slow down work, and in some cases burn crops.

Satisfied he has won a round; Tom returns with the welcomed news of Jack's dismissal. It's as if the reign of terror has come to an end if only temporarily.

Chapter 24

Exodus

Several thousand miles across the ocean in a forge in Germany is another young man who no longer has the freedom to make his own decisions. The tradeoff in this instance is to set aside his freedom to have himself indentured to a master blacksmith in order to learn the blacksmith trade.

While last tracked, Willie had just returned from performing community service his master owed to the Baron of this region. Although he had looked forward to having a day away from the humdrum of everyday life in the forge, the experience had proven to be more stressful than he had expected. Happy to return to the familiar smells of the forge and an accustomed routine of work, he is finding a new purpose behind his labor. What had previously been regarded as tedious toil is now being examined with different eyes. He is learning the value of becoming a good servant/slave. His life may in many ways may be miserable; it nonetheless has a degree of predictability surrounding it. Without holding the words to describe his newfound contentment, he is discovering a satisfaction that comes with compliance; he is accepting this world thrust upon him with all its rules designed to restrict his freedom. He is aware that he has accepted a new outlook toward obedience as a desirable behavior in more and more of his daily proceedings. The transition that began with a youthful rebellion against a system that is hell-bent on taking his God-given identity only to force as much of his person as possible into an identity killing cultural peg-hole is prepared to reach yet another stage where it is felt that whatever God failed to rectify, the state is confident it will succeed with its own remedy.

On the other hand, Magdalena is not only realizing her innate dignity but is ready to expand on these birthrights; she is undergoing a yearning to experience more of the world than her family, village, church, or state is capable of delivering. The simple occasion to attend her cousin's Confirmation has proven to be only an appetizer. She is experiencing what the Germans have described as wanderlust.

With seven years passing, the year is 1814. In this period a distance has grown between Magdalena and her parents. Her resentment against her father for stopping her education has contributed to this gulf. She, nonetheless, has turned into an outspoken twenty-two-year-old woman. The values her parents have prescribed for her are respected only when she is in their presence, otherwise her thoughts are imagining ways she can leave the levied constraints the village, her church, and her parents have laid on her. She remains just short of tormenting her father with a loathing for all that he holds dear. He in turn, seeing his twenty-two-year-old still unmarried, has taken it upon himself to instigate different men in the village to call on Magdalena with the possibility it may turn into a marriage. This has resulted in even more reason for Magdalena to want to escape.

Willie has only a few months before his indentured contract to her father is completed. With this short period of time remaining, Magdalena continues to envision Willie as an active player in her plan to escape the confines of her seemingly hapless life. Over the years, her relationship with Willie has gathered momentum despite her father's efforts to quell it. Her mother has been well aware of Magdalena's sly visits to the forge after she and Herr Yunk have retired for the night. She is also fully aware of her husband's lack of support for such an arrangement, but, in her own heart, she is more inclined to endorse her daughter's preference.

163

Of late, it's become another of these nighttime liaisons. Magdalena taking her usual spot next to Willie on his roughhewn bed of straw and horse blanket coverings is unusually quiet. She seems distant and thoughtful.

"I can't wait until you are finished with my father so we can get away from this awful, boring life," bemoans Magdalena.

Willie's arm cradles her head against his chest as he silently listens to the laments of his paramour. His thoughts are as anxious as hers, but for different reasons. He has the anxiety of having to go before a panel of master blacksmiths to be tested. He knows he must do well to receive his journeyman certificate. In this scenario, he cannot afford to alienate Herr Meister Yunk as he needs him to provide a good report. Having his master's daughter share his bed is not the best way to foster this kind of rapport.

Despite German men's penchant for keeping emotions under a cloak of self-possession, the tension in the forge is apparent as Willie's days of obligation begin to come to a close. Herr Yunk is also anxious about Willie's move from apprentice to journeyman for his own reasons. He has had the advantage of a trained tradesman for a number of years at little to no cost. As many times as Herr Yunk has worked his way through this procedure, he remains frustrated in having to begin again with a new, untrained fresh-faced adolescent.

The day finally arrives for Willie's testing. By late afternoon it has been completed. Having finalized his most troublesome chapter in dealing with the guild, they come to their basic conclusion: Willie has successfully impressed the guild with his expertise and is granted his journeyman certificate.

In another venue, as with all things on earth subject to chronological time, the day comes when Herr Yunk has to deal with the loss of Willie; his two thousand five hundred fifty-five days of indentured obligation are over. Yunk would like nothing more than to keep him on, but now he's obliged to give him his freedom. His legal claim to Willie's body, mind, and soul has expired.

The reality of this day is quickly become apparent to Willie. Realizing that he will not be here tomorrow, he slowly looks about the forge with a sense of loss. Every tool in this shop has his hand prints on it. Many of them connect him with memories of failure and success as his skills varied; there is nothing here that hasn't been a part of his life for the past seven years. But it's too soon to miss them. With the clothes on his back, a few small personally handcrafted hand tools, and the same satchel he carried when he was brought here by his father, Willie prepares to walk away from the only life he has had for the past seven years—food, shelter, rudimentary clothing; all in exchange for labor and obedience. The only object that belongs to Herr Yunk that he will be leaving with is his youngest daughter.

Within the past few weeks, Magdalena has made it quite clear that she and Willie will be leaving together for Stralsund and that marriage will be when Willie completes his journeyman obligation. Once there, she will be living and working with her Tante and Onkel Meitz. Her Onkel Frank owns a fishing fleet and with this enterprise there are daily needs that only a skilled blacksmith can meet. Onkel Frank is willing to take on Willie as a journeyman to keep his fleet's needs met. Her Tante Emma made it clear that she has enough contacts to assure Magdalena to have plenty of work as a domestic servant.

Avoiding a face-to-face confrontation with her father, Magdalena has used her mother to be the buffer between them. Frau Yunk has been bridging this difficulty without Herr Yunk having a physical conversation with his daughter. All that is left for him to do is watch his daughter packing her belongings in conjunction with Willie preparing for his departure. The days where Yunk could provide Willie with a good whipping for this kind of underhanded behavior are long gone.

Magdalena is not only handily packing the items she will need on a day-to-day basis; she is also leaving behind all the mementoes she gathered as she grew up. Little items that had interested her at her different growth levels now leave her emotionless. At this time, much of her bits and pieces have more meaning for her mother than they do for her. Remembering her confirmation and first communion as stifling; Magdalena haphazardly tosses the certificates in a pile along with her baptism record. It's all to be left behind, only to be revered by her mother.

Frau Yunk, to be of help to her last child to leave home, finds herself fondly going over these items recalling many of the growing up steps Magdalena had passed through to arrive at today's moment. She is spending much of this time in tears. Along with her mindless discard of her past, Magdalena simultaneously watches her mother trace her fingers over the different objects that she had crafted for her over the years with one hand while her other dabs her apron across her wet nose and tear-filled eyes. Magdalena is of such a mindset at this point that leaving her past behind is not a concern; all she is focused on is her departure. She is so certain that she is prepared to burn all the bridges connecting her to her past—including her connection to this room.

Willie has undoubtedly become a product of his master—like it or not. He has been opinionated only where he can achieve it without fear of Herr Yunk, the village, the church, the state, the Baron, and in many cases Magdalena—he has become a typical German adult male who will do nearly anything to prevent disorder from entering his life. Compliance with every higher earthly authority, though fawning, is considered godly.

Magdalena has taken notice of Willie over the years and how he has taken on a similar persona as that of her father; after all, Herr Yunk has been the only dominant male in Willie's life. In an odd way she finds this comfortable—maybe because it's predictable. Also, she has observed how her mother has been able to calm the "beast" in her father. She has been practicing her mother's techniques on Willie since his arrival seven years ago. She feels confident she and Willie will make a suitable pair.

All that's left undone for these two young people is to make their way to the village and wait for their coach. With an uncomfortable approach and an attempt to elevate their relationship to a more professional level, Herr Yunk has stopped working long enough to say his good-by. Wiping his dirty hands on a rag, he reaches into his pocket and retrieves a sum of money dutifully allotted to Willie. It consists of a small sum traditionally provided by a master to buy a coach ticket to the next town. Upon receiving this stipend, Willie is just as uncomfortable with this new arrangement as Herr Yunk is. Extending his hand, he self-consciously receives the token. Magdalena and her mother have provided for herself out of savings they have together managed to scrounge together.

Willie has looked forward to this day but now that he has come face to face with its reality, his demeanor has visibly turned to one of fear. His every physical need has been met by Herr Yunk since he was fourteen, now he's twenty-one and expected to make life decisions on his own. He would have been just as content to continue to work for Herr Yunk. After all, in the forge there are very few loose ends, order is always the endgame; everything is tangled together to correspond to everything else; every motion a blacksmith makes is in relation to the whole of his project. As much as Magdalena has yearned to leave her home, Willie has grown accustomed to it; it's been the only home he's known as a young man.

Now, thrown onto another course, Willie finds the way of the blacksmith guild less sympathetic with his wishes, providing a designated path for him to meet their demands. They have set the course of action for journeyman to journey from one forge to another to gain experience. To say the least, he meets this new day full of apprehension.

Magdalena, on the other hand is full of excitement. She barely slept last night. This is the day she has been dreaming of as far back as she can remember. For much of her life, she has been fortunate enough to place the correct causes to work in her life to get a worthy effect; she is one of those people who can nearly see her future unfold before it reaches her. In this case, she has spent the last month advocating for both herself and Willie with her Tante and Onkel in Stralsund. It has been Magdalena who negotiated Willie's position with her Onkel Frank and lined up domestic work for herself. When a task interests her or challenges her, Magdalena can nearly make a festival of it; what could be considered by most as drudge work is quickly converted into a triumph.

While waiting for the coach to arrive, the reality of this expedition is beginning to hit Willie. For the past seven years his life had been programed from the time he woke in the morning until he fell asleep at night. Since he has never experienced anything remotely like this, he is like a small child left to fend for itself. For the moment, he is totally dependent on Magdalena to deal with their schedule. Fear and self-doubt grip him as though they were his new masters. As if this isn't enough, there is another kind of fear overtaking Willie— it's a fear of strangers. His entire world had been in Herr Yunk's forge with the exception of Sunday church. He was never obligated to deal with the clientele coming to the forge since that was Herr Yunk's specialty. Consequently, his wariness of people has caused him to retrieve a hammer from his satchel and place it in the inside pocket of his coat. Magdalena, on the other hand is bubbly and quick to give all people passing through their village a polite nod and smile. For the moment, the strategic hiding place of the hammer is the only security giving him some solace.

The coach finally arrives. Even though it is exactly on time, for Magdalena it can't be soon enough. Turning to an already stressed-out Willie because of the arrival of the coach, she laments, "These coaches never run on time!"

168

Willie is at a complete loss as to what to do. In every way, he is still finding himself wishing he could reach back to the most recent time when his life was in place; when he knew what his place was and what needed to be done. This freedom that's been restored is an enigma. It's such a new concept that he has no idea what requirements he is to adhere to and even less what his rights or responsibilities consist of. He has that wide-eyed look men have when they don't know what is happening: they sit insecurely with hunched backs, grasp their hands in their lap and fuss with their thumbs. His trips outside of the forge other than church have been far and few between. Magdalena senses his trepidation and is more than organized to grab his hand and direct him to a seat in the coach. Once there, he remains frozen as if to stir could cause the world to collapse around him.

In typical German obsession for timing and order, the coach's driver sits alone above and in front of the coach under an awning of sorts attached to keep the worst of the weather at bay. In one hand he holds his passenger manifold, in the other is a watch. With a tone of voice that could have come from some celestial command center, the driver announces for those still lingering to reembark. Even the horses are jittery as though they too have acquired a similar inclination toward punctuality.

Without further warning and without a hint of hysteresis, the horses and coach lurch forward in perfect unison. Their destination has a well-rehearsed given end point. The trail they travel has become the corridor by which man and beast can pass between points having physical boundaries called villages, towns, or cities. Willie is looking out a side vent as one-by-one, they begin to pass by all the village's fixed points: bier garten, tannery, livery stable, farmhouses—all to be left behind as the coach dismisses each of them. Soon, they pass by the cemetery along with a familiar church building. His mind suddenly has a recollection. It's of a task he had never been relieved of for the entire duration of his apprenticeship. "Many a Sunday I have spent cranking that organ. Goodbye, organ." It's a singular thought that quickly leaves as the coach

169

continues its mindless journey. The whole of Willie's world is soon left behind and decidedly the coach is rushing into a world that he knows nothing of. The only thing Willie is certain of at this juncture is that he is uncertain about this entire venture.

Other than himself and Magdalena, there are several other men journeying with them. Traveling is not the typical situation in which German people let their guard down. Suspicion of anyone with a different dialect is the natural inclination of most people. And, heaven forbid in this region that a fellow traveler could turn out to be a Catholic. These are part of the reasons why villagers are reluctant to leave their burg. Magdalena's ready smile is, nonetheless, capable of crossing over all dialects and beliefs; the men on board become immediately more at ease with the two of them despite Willie's lack of interaction.

Although the driver is skilled, doing the best he can, the German roads leave much to be desired. The occupants are tossed to and fro more often than they are able to adjust. To make things worse, the road has led them into a forested area. Many people are suspicious of forested areas and are relieved to find a way through quickly. Many a story has been told of misadventures with wolves, bears, and robbers occurring in the timberlands of Germany. The foliage is heavy this time of year making it difficult for daylight to make its way through. No one on board is willing to let on how nervous they are about being in this terrain but each is indicating it by how frequently they peer out the side vents as to check on their surroundings.

Without warning, the coach suddenly comes to a halt. The driver is seen falling past the side vents. There remains a moment of freezing as each of the coach's occupants attempt to process what has just happened. In the next second, the coach door is jerked open, a scruffy man appears wearing a scarf across his face. Very noticeably in his hand he's brandishing a scabbard.

"ALL OUT!" he orders as he uses his free hand to dislodge those that he perceives to be laggards. Still not quite certain what is transpiring, the occupants stumble out of the coach. It soon becomes apparent they are being accosted by an armed marauder. Conspicuously, another scarfed assailant armed with a similar blade is perched on the top side of the coach. It's obvious he's serving as an accomplice. The man on the ground makes it certain that each person is expected to empty their pockets and purses into a passing bag. One by one, the frightened passengers fidget with their belongings. Within minutes they are nervously filling the bag. Everything has happened so quickly, leaving Willie as stunned by this twist of events as everyone. Standing speechless, not able to put a good defense together and with the bandit suddenly standing precisely in front of him, Willie suddenly finds himself staring directly into the eyes of his perpetrator. What he sees looking back is fear. This changes things abruptly. At this juncture, the thief has already plundered everyone except Willie and Magdalena. Still locking eyes with the marauder, Willie takes a hurried assessment of his situation. With the awareness that the other accomplice is still stationed on top of the coach and is also armed, he makes his move. In a flash, he reaches inside his coat followed with his hand intently gripping the familiar handle of his hammer. Instantaneously, still gripping the hammer, his hand is out of his pocket. In a blaze, he sinks its anvil face into the forehead of the unsuspecting invader. The only sound is a dull CRACK. The man drops as though he has been poleaxed. In another sweeping motion, Willie scoops up the fallen man's scabbard. Now armed with a hammer in one hand and the scabbard in the other, he turns his attention to the man aloft on the coach roof. The man is wide-eyed—obviously astonished as he sorts out what has changed. With it well-defined that he is at a strong disadvantage, he immediately scurries to the far side of the roof, leaps to the ground, and flees as a man fleeing for his life. In seconds, he has disappeared in the underbrush of the forest floor.

Reluctant to pursue him into an unknown terrain and with the danger past, Willie's attention immediately turns to Magdalena. Although, she is still

171

standing, her face has turned to an ashen grey. She is visibly shaken to the point she cannot muster a word. The frenzy has come to an end as quickly as it started. Magdalena has remained frozen with fear during this entire ordeal. With the danger compromised, she rushes into Willie's arms. All that remains is her trembling body pressing against his. The others are in various stages of recovery. After hitting the ground, the worst the driver has suffered is having the wind knocked out of him. Where fear among them reigned only moments before, it is as quickly replaced by a sigh of relief. It isn't long before each begins a search through the thief's bag to recover their lost items.

With the singular perpetrator still lying senseless on the ground, the driver busies himself rummaging through a compartment under his seat. With his hand in the air, "Ahhh!" is his exclamation of satisfaction as he finds what he's looking for; he produces a rope. With help from all the other men, they lift the motionless body of the hapless highwayman and manage to lash him to the roof of the coach.

It's not long before the driver returns to his obsession with the time he has lost, fearing his coach will not be punctual. He is mumbling to himself as he examines and reexamines his time piece. With conditions back to normal, he gives his official loud decree that those still not aboard need to return to their seat.

Magdalena is still silent. She has not fully recovered as she sits with her arm locked through Willie's. She can't seem to get close enough. Willie on the other hand, has taken on a much bolder demeanor. During this event he has abandoned his fearful character and met the challenge. This kind of event is just what he needed to emotionally leave the secure environment of the Yunk forge. The look of stress is gone. It's replaced with the same self-confidence he had developed over the years with his growing competences in the forge.

Chapter 25

Stralsund

It's late in the evening when the coach finally arrives in Stralsund. The station is nearly empty but for the quiet, tired people waiting rather impatiently for the overdue coach; Onkel Frank being one of them. One by one the sleepy, exhausted passengers disembark. The authorities are on site to deal with the conscious but disordered perpetrator. They take a report from each of the passengers as well as the driver and dismiss them. At the end of their query, the authority in charge turns his attention to Willie, saying, "Thank you for your bravery. The Kaiser is grateful for brave men such as yourself." Willie is ill at ease with the attention directed his way, but is able to muster up a, Danke schoen, mein Her" ("Thank you very much sir.") The last that's seen of the culprit is him being led off stumbling to a waiting wagon installed with a cage.

Onkel Frank greets Magdalena and Willie as enthusiastically as one can after a long, hard workday. With the two travelers' meager baggage loaded onto the carriage, Onkel Frank begins the ten-minute ride back to the family apartment. Tante Emma is waiting up for them. After a few platitudes they all agree, they will discuss more in the morning. Tante Emma leads Magdalena to Ida's bedroom. It's been vacant for several years since Ida has married and started her own family. It's been years since Magdalena had shared this room with cousin Ida but it remains as beautiful as she remembered it. Many of Ida's school awards that have followed her life from kindergarten to her graduation still hang on the walls. Others are carefully packed in her empty dresser drawers. Magdalena sits on the edge of the bed remembering the first time she was in this room. "It seems so long ago," she ruminates, "Now, we are starting a new life." Dismissing the memories, she prepares herself for sleep.

Next, Willie is led to a guest bedroom that is nice but a bit more spartan. It has a bed—which is in itself a very large upgrade compared to his rough straw bed at the stable.

As the house quiets down with everyone retiring to their bedrooms, Magdalena quietly creeps out of her room down the hallway to take a moment to regroup with Willie. She finds him sitting on his bed with a lit candle throwing an eerie shadow of him on the wall. Sitting down next to him, she loops her arm through his, pulling them closer together. She remains quiet for a moment as though attempting to say something.

"Willie, you have no idea how wonderful I know you to be. The way in which you handled that horrible situation we found ourselves in today, there can be no doubt in my mind how capable you are."

Willie listens as he continues to mull over the experience. The feeling of satisfaction in foiling the robbery that he experienced is fleeting. There is a confusion of mind and body that has not reconciled itself into an identifiable emotion. On one hand, when he had been frightened, that quickly turned into an anger. Not wishing to labor over its incomprehension, he merely responds with a commonplace banality saying, "Thank you, Magdalena."

She takes a moment to kiss him on his cheek, releases her arm from his and brusquely makes her way back to her own quarters.

Willie is left alone to lay in his bed assessing his day. With absolutely no way of knowing what the world has in store for him, he falls back into his fears. The relief that his day is over is surpassed by the realization that he would gladly trade his freedom for the security of Yunk's forge. His overwhelming reckoning is life had been easier, predictable, simpler, straightforward, and less stressful in spite of his lack of freedom. "God, why do you punish me so. You took my freedom years ago and allowed me to become content in obedience to my master. Now, I have been granted an independence that has become my chastisement. I am lost. Please don't abandon me!"

Back in her room, Magdalena is similarly measuring her day. "God, I thank you for the protection you granted me in the person of Willie." With that comforting thought, she continues with the simple nighttime prayer she learned as a child, "Now I lay me down to sleep. I pray the Lord my soul to keep. If I should die before I wake, I pray the Lord my soul to take."

As the colorless light of dawn seeps through a crack in the heavily curtained bedroom, Willie awakens to find the environment enveloped in a heavy fog. The rising sun is finding this eerie development as a formidable foe. There is no question which will win over the other but, in the meantime, it requires an abstract mental adjustment. It's not unusual this time of the year for the sea to share more of itself in the air as the temperatures drop.

Willie slept well enough to awaken at his usual time. This is the first morning in years that he has not had a forge to bring back to life. Lost again, not only in his thoughts but also in his body and spirit, he makes his way to the only widow in his room. Between the fog and the lack of sunlight, and no task upon which to focus, he feels very isolated. Not certain what is in store for him today, he lays back on his bed. This is the first real bed with a real mattress he has slept on in seven years. He hears the stirrings of someone else as well. Along with it, there is a light tap on his door. With no time to answer or get out of bed, he hears the door open and a very familiar blithe figure bounces onto the edge of his bed, bending her head to meet his lips, kissing him heartily.

"Can you believe it Willie? we have made our escape!"

Willie continues to distress over his troublesome perception that this outside world has no discipline—only limitless boundaries that grow out of

175

personal wants. His life had been as whole as he had wanted it while at her father's forge—miserable at times, but predictable, nonetheless. All in all, it had provided him with a sense of community. Now, he finds himself thrown out of his safe, immediate, straightforward world into a world of peril and jeopardy with no guide. He loves Magdalena but he also sees her as the force behind his loss. But on the other hand, without thinking, he discovers that he is looking more to her for support in areas of his social fear; trusting in her display of worldliness to guide him in socially disturbing situations.

Already feeling a sense of displacement and not wanting to display more of his insecurities, Willie musters up as hearty an agreement as possible with Magdalena's perception of making an "escape."

"Yes," is his immediate answer. His next response comes as a surprise to even himself. "This is the beginning of our lives together."

Magdalena is so certain of her decision to leave her parent's home that she can't imagine Willie not being on the same page as herself. Snuggling close to him, she wanders off into her own private world. "Yes, this is just the beginning."

This little liaison is short-lived as there comes a knock at the door announcing breakfast. "Thank you, I'll be there in a minute," responds Willie. With this announcement, Magdalena waits for the coast to clear before she slips out to discreetly make her way back to her own room.

With his feet on the floor, Willie dresses himself in his work clothes as he has for the past seven years and makes his way to the kitchen. There he is met by Onkel Frank who also is preparing to begin his workday. He's well-coiffed and superbly dressed in a uniform that informs his laborers that he is their boss.

Meanwhile, Tante Emma has prepared a breakfast of potato pancakes and sausage. Willie is famished. All he's had to eat is the cheese and bread Magdalena had packed for their coach trip the day before. But now he finds himself perplexed at all of this. His thoughts stumble over themselves. He's digging back into a past time when it was commonplace for him to sit at a table such as this. Now, merely taking a seat is daunting. What comes to mind is that the last time he'd sat down to a real table was the morning that he left for his indenture. All the time he was with the Yunks, he was never invited into their living quarters, much less to share a meal. He always ate his meals alone, always in the forge, usually alongside a project he was behind on. In this breakfast instance, there is a mixture of anxiety over struggling with recalling the proper table protocol and speculating what other unknown duties his day will require.

Onkel Frank studies Willie for a moment. "Please, Willie, have a seat," he offers.

Within the hour Onkel Frank is introducing Willie to well-muscled man in a leather apron with forge grime well worked into every crevice in his face and neck. He's Onkel Frank's master blacksmith. His name is Maximillian Albert Hendricks. Other than his mother, everyone refers to him as Max. He's been alerted by Frank that he would be taking on a young journeyman and to show him his duties. In a long-established German division of labor tradition, this master blacksmith is readily prepared to establish the difference in his forge as to who is in control. Before long, Max has Willie involved in a project that will determine his skill level.

Meanwhile, back at the Meitz apartment, Tante Emma is quizzing Magdalena about wedding plans for herself and Willie. It's obvious that she is not comfortable with the situation the way things presently are. Tante Emma glances at the window, sighing something between a worry and a concern.

177

"Magdalena, your father, the church, and the city officials will hold us responsible for sheltering you and Willie as an unmarried couple under the same roof. Maybe we should place you and Willie apart until we can get your paperwork finished."

Magdalena shot a sidelong glance. Her blue eyes glistening with a defensive gaze. For a moment, she seems to be weighing her options.

"Willie and I have discussed our intentions between us but the problem lies with guild directions prohibiting a journeyman blacksmith from marrying until his three to four-year stint as a Journeyman is completed."

Tante Emma listens without interruption but her thoughts are on how she is going to make the adjustment in the meantime. Pausing for only a moment, she considers this enough discussion for the present time and as abruptly as the conversation had begun, she changes the subject.

"Frau Mueller has been desperate to meet you and to try you with a few household tasks," confirms Tante Emma with the same clarity with which she holds all of her discussions.

As a glimmer of sunlight makes its way through the fog giving objects a silvery tone, Magdalena, happy the conversation has changed, is giving her Tante her full attention.

"I'm ready to meet whoever you have brought about for me," replies Magdalena, "I'm prepared to go to work."

Back at the forge, Willie is all ears as Max introduces him to a technology he has only heard of from rumors. "This is the future," explains Max as he points with pride to a boat which has only recently been added to the fleet. Willie is full of awe as he is given an opportunity to study its function. The exterior of the boat is similar to the rest of the fleet but the interior is unique compared to anything he has ever seen. It has a boiler fed by coal that drives a piston that turns a propellor. The Yunk forge resisted this kind of modernization. Herr Yunk was aware of steam innovation but only gave it a mild glance.

"These contrivances are not what runs this forge. We have no call for its nonsense," declared Yunk with the exactness of an expert.

Unlike his former master, to say that Willie's attention is not taken by this wonderful contraption would be an understatement. His entire demeanor of doubt and fear has transformed to one of anticipation and courage.

"Sir, I thank you from the bottom of my heart for introducing me to this magnificent machine," are the only words Willie can find for the moment. Max is surprised at Willie's overwhelming enthusiasm for this revolutionary boat. Running his fingers over each transport pipe, each gauge, each valve, Willie is captivated with everything he sees. This is proving to be a component of his journeyman training he had never expected. "I hope Max will put me on this detail."

Although the seeds of a definitive change in technology are not coming from Germany—they are introduced from without—Frank is a visionary and he has given Max unrestricted freedom on this assignment in the hopes it will revolutionize his fishing fleet. Max has caught his employer's enthusiasm to fit this new innovative technology to his use. Now, Max is seeing within Willie a kindred spirit to share their fervor. It's so new a technology that, as of yet, no guild has claimed it as its own. It's still looked at as a step outside of traditional blacksmithing. This nether land category affords them an unlimited opportunity to innovate without oversight.

Chapter 26

Growing Inclinations

Because of a possible scandal with an unmarried couple cohabitating under the same roof, Tante Emma has appropriately decided with her husband to find Willie sleeping quarters somewhere other than where Magdalena is living.

This plan is to place Willie in the cabin of a fishing boat held in reserve until needed during the peak season. This arrangement brings a sober approval to Tante Emma as well as fitting well with Willie, allowing him a proximity to his new assignment. Max has answered his prayers by involving him in retrofitting another boat with a steam engine.

Frank fancies himself an engineer of sorts. He's never had any formal training but has taken it upon himself to stay current with the technologies that relate to the fishing industry. Max on the other hand, achieved his master blacksmith under various blacksmiths who were progressive enough in their trade to dabble with producing parts for different innovative pieces of machinery. This has given him a working understanding of how steam can be harnessed for many different uses.

Over the following weeks, Willie has taken every lead presented him during his workday as well as his off hours to learn more of the different uses for steam power. This break is a welcome diversion from the ordinary hands-on sort of blacksmithing that requires hammer and anvil. This introduction to this technology asks for molds durable enough to shape liquid metal to be created in sand or clay. The end product must meet metallurgical standards strong enough to withstand high steam pressures. There have already been several blacksmiths who have either been seriously injured or killed resulting from their parts not being capable of withstanding high steam pressure.

With only a finished product created by a foreign forge available, Max has made the transition from the quintessential blacksmith shop to a machine shop. Frank is rightly concerned with the quality of the reproductions Max is putting together. With only a serious interest as to how this steam machine has been manufactured, Frank and Max often collaborate nearly all day on a design or on the quality of the metal. Much of this has to do with advancing beyond ordinary iron products to manufacturing steel with superior strength needed to meet their demands.

Since Willie has moved to the boat cabin, the time he could be spending with Magdalena is being consumed with his obsession with his new responsibilities. Max has taken advantage of Willie's obsession and made certain that he is going to get his money's worth from Willie. By the light of a whale oil lantern, deep into the night, Willie pores over every detail of a piece he has forged. His project is to use the imported design to construct a valve that is substantial enough to supply steam in a more efficient manner. Certain that Max will approve, he turns the lamp off and lays down on a makeshift bed in the shop.

Magdalena is not happy with these arrangements, but for now, she is willing to accept what her aunt has deemed appropriate. She is willing to accept this adjustment is because she has assured herself that this obstacle is only temporary. Magdalena is certain that better things will replace the inconvenience of the moment. In the meantime, she has taken the position offered to her from Frau Mueller to become a domestic servant and nanny to her children.

Frau Mueller has a sweet disposition, but she can also be disagreeable—especially when her rheumatism flares up. Lately, she has had to rely much more on her cane in order to move about. Because her physical condition grows weaker doesn't mean her mind is following. She attempts to make her physical condition into an abstraction—like it was no more than a mere figment of her mind. Her function as chief domestic engineer is still in place and she's ready to display that authority to anyone daring to challenge her role. Nonetheless, her husband, much to her consternation has provided a budget for extra household help. Even with this in place, she spends a considerable amount of her day in making lists for Magdalena to accomplish—things that not that long ago, she had accomplished with dexterity.

Frau Mueller also has two children—an eight-year-old boy named Emil and a ten-year-old girl named Frieda. The children have become accustomed to their mother's disability as much as one would expect of children their age. They have had a number of nannies and on first impression, they are curious about Magdalena. As children so many times do with a new teacher or, in this case a nanny, they put her to the test.

Herr Mueller is a brewer spending much of his time tending to his business. The way the laws are designed in Germany, he must have documents exclusively authorizing him to brew and sell beer within his region. It's here that he holds the prestigious title of Brew Meister. His family have held these documents for over a hundred years. The governmental authorities not allowing competition has made Herr Mueller a wealthy man. The opulent home the Muellers have designed reflects the traditional position in which he has carried his family name forward.

Magdalena has a feeling of inferiority when Herr Mueller is present. It's a demeaning reaction she holds within herself that she can't quite explain. It's a sensation she resents. The more she feels it, the more her life shrinks, and the more resentment she has for having been trapped in her small out-of-the-way village for her entire life. To expand her shrinking feeling, she encourages herself, saying "When Willie and I get to America, I'll have a house such as this." Although, it's always been her dream to go to America, these intuitions of actually going there are occupying her mind more often. She hasn't shared much of her sixth senses with Willie; realizing that he is inclined to dismiss much of it. Regardless, her feelings toward making it a reality are growing stronger and stronger with or without his participation.

After Magdalena tasks with the Mueller family are completed, and before she returns to her aunt's and uncle's apartment, it's become Magdalena's routine to visit Willie's quarters at the boat launch. Willie's living conditions are rudimentary at best. It's an older model boat serving as an auxiliary to the Meitz fleet. It doesn't take much to notice that it is seldom used or maintained. The boat is secured to a dock that if it could speak, it would readily admit that it is an embarrassment to have such a rickety vessel attached to it. Willie could care less. These quarters are no different than what he has grown accustomed to back at Magdalena's father's forge. For the most part, Magdalena is more interested in Willie than she is in his primitive living conditions but on this instance her contempt for the backward ways of Willie are front and center.

"I don't understand why you don't speak up for yourself to my Onkel. This is disgraceful the way he makes you live."

Surprised to catch a glimpse of Magdalena's sudden change in attitude, Willie is noticeably flustered. Taking note of her concern, he gives the makeshift living area a once-over survey. Seeing a few things laying around, he attempts to quickly tidy up the small cramped quarters.

"I didn't realize you were going to be here this early or I would have made it tidier," says Willie. It's become Willie's way to more often agree to acquiesce to Magdalena's wishes in words than have it become an action.

183

"I'm not concerned with your sloppiness as I am with the conditions of this tub your forced to live in," laments Magdalena.

"I can adapt to this. It makes me appreciate anything greater than this even if it is insignificant to those with much more," maintains Willie.

With so many of Willie's notions, Magdalena is left with bewilderment. It's incomprehensible to her why Willie seems to lack the upward drive she deems as a necessary component to a satisfying life. With a pause to consider Willie's reaction, she finds the words her thoughts have produced.

"Willie, don't let yourself fall into a rut. You have a huge imagination; I see your potential to be successful in life as enormous."

Willie finds that he agrees, but his confidence isn't found in the nuances of Magdalena's world of gaining material things but in the passion of ideas put into action by creating things. This opportunity to become part of Germany's revolution into a new technological age is more than compelling to him, it's what is giving meaning to his otherwise mundane existence.

"Don't worry about me, Magdalena. I could live under this boat for the opportunity your uncle is giving me," states Willie with an accompanying smile Magdalena has not witnessed in some time.

Realizing they both have ambitions, but in different capacities, Magdalena turns her attention to their relationship.

"Willie, it is so unfair. Your guild is living in the dark ages. We love each other, yet they refuse to give you permission to marry until your journeyman years are over. We could both be dead by then," whines Magdalena.

This conversation is not a new phenomenon to Willie. It has become a portion of their interaction. Willie always finds himself falling back into his pragmatic ways much to the frustration of Magdalena.

"I realize it doesn't fit your agenda, my Mädchen, but we have to decide what is going to give each of us what we want in life and what we are willing to exchange for it. In our case, without my journeyman documentation we will have neither of our wishes."

Realizing, they are stuck for a while and that together they must stick to the priority set by the guild, and realizing this is their only option to bring about their desires, they agree to continue to work through it. In the meantime, they settle for the moment to enjoy each other as things are.

Chapter 27

Confrontation

Willie is deeply embroiled in his project with Max to redesign a steam engine to retrofit into the Meitz fleet when he is suddenly and very unexpectantly met with two men wearing the familiar uniform of his guild's inspectors. He couldn't be caught more off guard.

"Herr Beinecke, it's been three months since your registration. We are here to inspect your roster of projects you've completed."

Willie confidently presents his roster all signed and approved by Max. flipping through the roster, they seem to be looking for something in particular.

"Herr Beinecke, you don't seem to have registered much of your time on the anvil and made note of those projects you've achieved," says one of the men with the tone of one who is condescending to Willie and seemingly enjoying his pain.

"I understand, Mein Herr, but I've been working with a crew here that has taken on a steam engine project, and I've been a major part of the project," explains Willie.

Upon hearing this, the two guild authorities take a moment to conspire. Coming back, they are ready to make a statement.

186

"Herr Beinecke, none of these steam projects are noticed as a part of your journeyman internship. We cannot include the time spent on this diversion as time attributed to your training period. We therefore recommend that you stay focused on the blacksmith projects that will benefit your placement," states one of the men carrying the most weight of authority.

Willie is listening to this decree as though a judge had just given him a threatening sentence. It's leaving him absolutely speechless. This is not anything akin to what he had expected from these individuals. As if this were not enough, then comes personal and detailed instructions. These men begin to give orders to Willie as though they are regimental commanders.

"You get back in the forge and begin to refine your obligations relating to your craft. We strongly suggest you pay more attention to your anvil and forge than you do with these diversions. Steam will always remain a fanciful solution to man's difficulties and cannot be considered as part of our order. We cannot recommend you to remain in our guild if you refuse to follow the prescribed journeyman protocol."

Willie has not said a word to rebut this unexpected development. Max is standing off to the side hoping to remain as anonymous as possible. He's listening, but is fully aware as to how this guild functions. He knows beyond a shadow of a doubt that he is being scrutinized for ignoring his responsibility regarding the regimented prescription that encompasses Willie's training. Max is aware that if he doesn't reconcile with these Herren ("gentlemen") quickly, it could cost Herr Meitz his journeyman placement credentials. Realizing the nature of this confrontation, Max readily acquiesces to the guild's mandates. He realizes the pervasive conservatism these age-old guilds hold. Many of these ancient guilds have been responsible for holding the delicate balance of small villages together, but in the progressive cities, the guild remains blind to losing their traditional purpose, only to remain naively true to its outward form.

To attempt to debate these men is pointlessness. From experience, Max know it's an effort born out of futility. Radical departures from traditional, safe ways of doing things are not introduced without long, bitter debates. For either side of this dispute to lose will be deleterious to their cause. In this world, it's all or nothing. The threat of losing is not just for the individuals involved but for an entire cause. It makes the gamble too great to even begin the debate; therefore, in the mind of the guild, innovations are to remain unused.

The men soon leave, satisfied the heady smell of innovation has been crushed. Without further word, Max has retreated to some enclave of his own for a breather. Willie is left with a feeling of abandonment. He can't recall a time in his life when he has experienced this much despondency: it's a vacantness, an emptiness that's overtaken his entire being. Sounds around him have become distant as the vacuum within him is pulling in the forceful rages of frustration and disappointment. Without an established blueprint as to how to respond to this unexpected development, he finds himself distractedly wandering the streets of Stralsund. If it were not for the full attention of those around him, he would have been run down by any number of carriages—even causing one man to grab him by his coat in time to save his life to say, "What in hell is the matter with you, man—are you drunk?"

So, consumed by his own despondency, Willie stumbles to his feet, without a word, he continues his reckless quest.

"Why, God? Why are You doing this to me?" is all his mind will shout.

Already drunk on his emotions, not aware of how he got to where he is, he realizes he is in a beer garden with a pint of beer in his hand. This one leads to another, then another, and another, and another.

The disappointment, the disenchantment, the disillusionment that Willie is undergoing is not being soothed by the alcohol, instead the alcohol is fueling his growing anger. With a snoot full of booze and a what is being processed as

188

a righteous cause that cannot be attended still torturing his person, Willie stumbles out of the beer garden into the street only to have a loose paving brick catch his attention. Without as much as a hesitancy in thought, he snatches up the brick and in one frustrated, convulsive heave, the brick sails through the air, through the glass front of the beer garden, striking a man sitting at the window table.

Despite his deteriorating condition, he is struck with a moment of regret. Struggling beneath all this exterior behavior is a well-brought-up man who suddenly realizes the gravity of his action. Regardless, at this point, the struggle has pointed him in another direction; the thought of fleeing overtakes all other considerations. Running quickly becoming his mode of departure. Panic-stricken, he finds himself tearing through the streets like a madman; the rage Willie had only moments before is replaced by an overwhelming sense of guilt, thinking "What in God's name have I done?"

Each piercing remembrance of the wince the struck man exhibited before falling from his chair to the floor is leaving him with devastating pangs of remorse; his sense of integrity is nearly irretrievable.

Someway, between the alcohol and his want of a rational mind, Willie has stumbled back to the boat. Collapsing on his bed, he has a momentary sense of relief. It's a reprieve short-lived as the woe of guilt and remorse, interspersed with doses of contempt, continue their unruly desire to overtake him. With his face buried in his mattress, employing both fists, Willie pounds round after round into its padding, shouting, "I hate this world."

Without notice, Magdalena appears. She had gotten word that the guild had come down hard on Max and Willie. She is not so much worried about Max's reaction as she is about Willie's. Discovering Willie in the condition he has brought on himself is a jolt—it hits her like a thunderbolt. Here is the man who singlehandedly had brought an armed robber to his knees, now, whimpering like a baby girl.

"I feel like they have taken my arms and legs leaving me to crawl about and go nowhere," whimpers Willie.

Pausing for a moment, she chooses an option. One of these options is sit and let Willie come out of this performance at his own leisure, another is to run from the situation, another is to grab him by his shirt collar and to shake him until he comes to his senses. In a moment, she is undeniably drawn to the latter of her choices. With both hands gripping his collar, with all the strength she can garner, she has lifted him from his bed with her face in his, and is yelling, "WE'RE NOT GIVING UP THIS EASY; WE ARE GOING TO AMERICA WHERE WE CAN GROW!"

Chapter 28

A Gate Closes

This pronouncement by Magdalena flies in the face of everything that has shaped Willie. Disasters are the things that remind a journeyman like him that he knows his status. Even though the callousness of these encumbrances restrains him and he is surely suffering under their weight by nearly destroying his spirit, revolt or escape are not the things his dreams are made of. All Willie has ever wished for is to have a life free of struggling.

At this point much of the alcohol has made its way from his brain out through his bladder. If nothing else, Magdalena has brought a sobering thought to his fuming mind.

"Magdalena, what are you saying—are you losing your mind? Everything I've worked for is here. We can't just abandon our life for some pie in the sky change like that—it's crazy. I've heard about people who have gone to America—it's a land full of savages and slaves."

Magdalena is listening but not hearing. While half-listening to Willie, she is planning her own delivery. Since she was a small girl, she has had the wanderlust equivalent of ten women. She has dreamed of going to America for as long as she can remember. Not in the least dissuaded by Willie's mindset, she is ready with her own opinion.

"Willie, you have told me with your own mouth how you yearn for the freedom to create without the guild's restraints. You will never be free to become

191

the producer God created you to be as long as you're controlled by the ignorance of useless traditions."

Willie is always in awe of Magdalena's line of reasoning. She seems to have an uncanny ability to zero in on his strongest argument and weaken it to where he often agrees to abandon his entire evaluation.

"Magdalena, you've confused me enough for one day, let me work through this without distractions."

She agrees to leave because it's been her experience that he has said these same words before and it means he knows his case is becoming weaker, but when she opens the door, she is confronted with a new predicament. It's a uniformed police officer. In a very official tone without details, the officer asks her one question.

"Is this the residence of Willie Beinecke?

Before she can answer, Willie makes an appearance.

Yawohl, Mein Herr. Das ist mich. ("Yes, sir. This is me.")

Without a second question, the officer produces a set of iron handcuffs, places Willie with his hands behind him, and secures them to his wrists.

"You're under arrest for attempted murder."

Magdalena is left standing with her mouth agape. She has absolutely no idea what could possibly be behind this. She has no other option than to make her way to her Tante's and Onkel's apartment. When she arrives, she notices her Onkel motioning her into his study.

"Magdalena, I have a crisis. The authorities contacted me today about Willie. They're bringing charges against him for attempted murder. They're basing it on an incident in a local beer garden."

Magdalena, not wanting to reveal the fact that she is already aware of Willie's arrest but unaware of the circumstances, decides to allow her Onkel to disclose as much information as has been given him. With true concern, she asks the pertinent question.

"What in heaven's name happened?"

He reveals to her all he knows of the incident. Then in his typical business attitude, Frank switches to a matter-of-fact tone he uses when issuing guidelines to employees.

"The blacksmiths' guild will certainly be contacting me. I will have no other choice but to follow their protocol. There is no question that they will remove Willie from their register. When this transpires, they will demand I remove him from my employ as an undesirable."

Magdalena sits frozen to her chair. She is reviewing the different times Willie had shown this type of aggression in both a responsible and irresponsible fashion. She is recalling the times her father had disciplined him for his various behaviors, but then also how his aggression in his work put him a notch above the ordinary apprentice.

"I have known Willie for seven years—you might say we grew up together. In different ways, but yet together, my parents raised both of us. Neither of us were allowed to get away with bizarre behavior—especially Willie."

Her Onkel is listening halfheartedly. It's apparent by his manner that he has other things on his mind. He begins to speak as though in part he knows

193

what his actions are to be, yet in other parts, unknown measures will be taken as required.

"I will bail Willie from jail; although, because of the seriousness of the charges against him, his future in Germany is drastically dimmed."

Hearing the horrific fallout of Willie's behavior sends a hot flash of fear throughout Magdalena. To the same degree the consequences of Willie's behavior have settled in with all their force, she begins to sob.

"What are we to do?"

Similar to most successful business persons who have lived their lives directing others, her Onkel is quick with an option.

"I have acquired fishing rights across the straights in Denmark. I can settle you there in the hopes of giving you a new start. I can put Willie to work in the fish market while you work as a domestic."

Magdalena is listening to her uncle with mixed emotion. Her thoughts are swirling. "This may be a godsend toward the next step we need to get us to America." Ever since she has had the ability to reason, Magdalena has been providential and she has always been able to find a pony in a pile of horse manure.

Tante Emma has been listening at the door. There is an issue on her mind that has been festering since Magdalena and Willie arrived.

"Now that Willie is no longer bound by guild laws concerning marriage, you are free to marry," declares Tante Emma with the assurance of a Vatican lawyer.

Magdalena's face brightens for the first time since she became embroiled in all the hoopla.

194

"Oh, Tante! Are you sure?"

"Oh yes. As soon as we can contact the church, I'm certain they will agree once they understand there are no outside restraints preventing your lawful union."

"Oh, Tante! What would I do without you?" replies Magdalena.

With all this settled, the only thing left to do is to bail Willie out of detention.

In his orderly German fashion, Onkel Frank is on a mission to get his carriage prepared to get on with the duties of the day. It's less than an hour when all the legal work is worked through to gain Willie's release. Willie is unusually quiet as the full thrust of his actions are falling on him like chickens coming home to roost. To make the results of his actions even more clear, Onkel Frank takes the carriage by the beer garden allowing Willie to see the realities of his actions. He can't help but react to the boarded window where hours before had been a clean sheet of glass. Not able to restrain himself, Willie throws both his hands across his face, dropping his head in shame. It's almost more than he can bear.

Instead of returning Willie to his boat residence, Frank takes an alternative route directly to his apartment. The ride has been uncomfortably quiet noting Willie's interspersed sobs as his mind continues to rewind back to all the happenings—each torturing him more intensely with each rewind.

Onkel Frank wastes no time in bringing Willie into his study and updating him on all that he and Magdalena had earlier discussed. Willie is in not in a condition to argue with any of the proposals. He willingly agrees with all its parts, much as Magdalena had agreed to.

195

Tante Emma wastes no time in preparing herself, along with Magdalena and Willie to meet with the pastor.

Talking directly to them both, she purports, "Since there is a two-week period between the time you announce your intensions and the time you can marry, the sooner we get on with it the better. Within the hour, the three of them are seated in the church office talking with the pastor. With all things worked out and agreed upon, they dismiss themselves. Within the next hour, Willie has been returned to his boat abode and Magdalena is resting in her bedroom at the Meitz's apartment.

Over the next two weeks, Willie has taken time to reflect on his actions. It's left him miserable realizing he can't fulfill his ambitions in Germany. Magdalena is doing her best to keep both their heads up. She can sympathize with Willie but refuses to enter the victim trap he's been laying out for himself.

"Willie, you can be miserable or see this as an opportunity, it's your choice. We can't go back and undo the past, but if we work together, we can make certain our future has a good ending."

"I know what you're saying Magdalena, I thought I knew how to live but everything has turned upside down. Right now, I feel as though I'm accomplishing nothing.

Chapter 29

Growing Roses in Hell

It is the day after Willie and Magdalena are married. Onkel Frank has arranged to have a boat transport them across the straights to Denmark. As usual, Magdalena is excited. She views this change of events much the same way she views nearly every change in her life. To her, they are all a sign of good things to come. On the other hand, Willie views these as disruptions and as bad omens meant to magnify his sense of loss.

During their day trip across the channel from Germany to Denmark, Magdalena's thoughts wander to what it would be like on a much longer trip. This the first time in her life she has been on the water. This is a mere six-hour, one-hundred-thirty-kilometer voyage compared to the six to eight weeks, six-thousand-kilometer crossing of the Atlantic.

There is a brisk westerly breeze that's caught the sails, driving the schooner forward at a heady nine knots. With this short voyage as her only reference, she imagines herself standing on the deck of an ocean vessel basking in a warm breeze the same as she is on this beautiful fall day. As could be expected, Magdalena finds the voyage exhilarating.

"Isn't this great, Willie? We are actually starting a new life together in a new place."

Willie is far from enthused considering he is spending a goodly portion of his time with his head in a bucket, gladly supplied by a crew member in lieu

197

of him barfing on his deck. Despite Willie's physical condition, Magdalena's enthusiasm remains high even after bearing in mind that it's indirectly proportional to Willie's misery—he couldn't be sicker, and she couldn't be happier—she loves change—he loathes change. What some may consider as a blithe attitude toward Willie, she is certain she'll be vindicated as soon as Willie finds himself. Afterall, he'll have lost his misery—even though at the present moment, he's convinced that happiness will continue to elude him.

"Magdalena, how can you remain so happy when we have the entire universe against us?" complains Willie.

Magdalena doesn't pause for as much as a second. Her answer flows as easily and as soothing as hot wax on an open wound.

"We must believe that life is worth living and I just know it will happen. I feel it in my soul."

Willie has to admit that there is an aroma around her actions that sweetens the air. Considering the caution of his nature when left to himself to make his own life-altering decisions, his life would be a solitary path of mistakes and further withdrawal, resulting in keeping himself aloof from those who otherwise may have become great companions.

"I hope you're right," says Willie still firmly grasping his bucket between his knees.

A familiar look makes its way across Magdalena's face. This is the determined look Willie saw when she first taught him how to make charcoal. In a strange way, he is as much attracted to her determination now as then.

"Our goals may appear distant but we are on our way Willie, we're going to have a great life, just you wait and see. We are just scratching the surface of what God can do for us."

Magdalena continues her watch on deck. She's become mesmerized by the ease with which the schooner is single-mindedly cutting its way through the small swells fulfilling a sense of purpose. At the moment it's keeping its pledge with the universe to accomplish its vocation. Without the necessity of words, there is always something about nature that shares itself with the human spirit.

The ship's destination is Denmark's Island of Falster, the city of Nykobing. Frank Meitz has made arrangements for Magdalena and Willie to begin a life there. There is a lively German community in Nykobing dedicated to the fishing industry. This is perfect for this community of foreign Germans. The Danes have always looked at this community of aliens through a jaundiced eye, deeming the accents of their cousins to be viewed with suspicion and are happy enough not to have to deal with them in their own neighborhoods. Setting aside the nuisances foreigners have as guests, Onkel Frank has assured Willie that he will have a job at a local fishery where he holds a Danish license, and Magdalena will work as a domestic for the wife of its manager.

The manager and his family are placed in a large living space adjacent to the fishery. Willie and Magdalena are housed above the fishery but not with such a desirable accommodation as that of the manager. It's a small, two-room apartment that's been used as a storage area and hastily cleaned out to accommodate living needs. At first, the smell of fish saturating everything had been overwhelming to the point of making both physically sick. But, after a short period of living with the never-ending aroma, they no longer can distinguish it as an odor.

With this obstacle neutralized, it doesn't take Magdalena long begin to visualize a home out of these otherwise spartan conditions. Willie has not adapted to the work in the fishery without feeling a devastating sense of loss. In Magdalena's typical approach to life of seeing beyond what seems to be, she addresses Willie's difficulty.

199

"Well, at least you're discovering what it is in life you don't want to pursue."

In Magdalena's response meant to offer her husband comfort, it can't help but remind him that without her positive mindset, he would never consider this menial work as an opportunity. It continues to amaze him how this "innovative" wife doesn't lose faith and continues to find her way around in the dark.

In contrast, the enigma behind Willie's character is that his lofty and abstracted ambition remains too often in a very narrow zone; how to further the acceptance of steam power throughout the region has become his night and day preoccupation. For him, the contributions steam power can make to the world are now being thwarted by powers beyond his control. The medieval remainders of control over the guilds and the church's control over mankind's spiritual lives have so far had a devastating effect on Willie's aspirations.

Even though he's settled in with his fishery job, it doesn't take him long to see where the fish plant could benefit from steam innovations. The frustrating part is there is no one here like Max who shares his enthusiasm. Rather, most are content with the way things are providing they have a few extra kroner left over on payday for a few pints of beer.

There is time following supper and before bed time to discuss those concerns with Magdalena. She has proven to be a good listener.

"I know that I haven't been born to live an undistinguished life. Magdalena, you have showed me by your encouragement that my desires can be turned into hope. Now, my hope is that hope can be turned into certainty."

Magdalena listens with the delight of a coach who has just brought a "wow" moment to a lingering trainee. She remains heart warmed and silent with the anticipation of Willie erupting with another of his new "insights." True to her intuition, Willie isn't finished.

I'm beginning to see more possibilities," says Willie. This rare moment of discernment brings with it a slight smile of determination, in turn, forcing a further explanation.

"I hope I can find a place to bring my dreams for steam power into a reality. As cheap as it is to produce, I know beyond a shadow of a doubt that it can become something that can make the entire world an easier place for both rich and poor to live comparable to one another."

Willie pauses for a moment as if waiting for further clarity; it's as if something in his statement may have been overlooked.

"More often now than in my past, I'm beginning to understand how ignorant people can be more dangerous than wild beasts."

Magdalena listens intently, but with a different set of ears than Willie. While Willie is frustrated over not being able to get the attention of his fellow Germans for his augmentations, she still holds the same eye turned toward America as a final opportunity that she has held since her school days. Knowing her husband's reluctance to geographical change, Magdalena chooses to keep that desire silent for a more opportune time, "I know it has to be Willie's idea or he will never agree to leaving Europe."

Now, seeing the moment, she says, "Willie, there has never been a doubt in my mind that given the opportunity, you can change history."

Willie is not surprised at his bride's optimism.

"My darling wife, I believe you could grow roses in hell. What would I ever do without you?"

201

Chapter 30

Change of Mind

It's a peculiar reality that people who share hardships but have differing interests will form an understood, but often unspoken, bond between them. It's not through thoughtlessness or recklessness that the armed forces of a country will draw people from every background of race, color, and creed, and by forcing them, together, pushing them beyond their individual limits to achieve an unprecedented measure of durability. This exercise has been developed by every Army in every country in the world since the beginning of time to coagulate a team that has no other interest than that of dying, if necessary, to protect one another—even if they are united by no other interest than a common hatred for a common enemy. In these cases, the process is utmost. It isn't always necessary to be so extreme.

In the case of these newlyweds, as different as their personalities may be, the struggle they are both experiencing in a country other than the country they were raised in, is enough to huddle them together at the end of their workday to discuss their struggles. The angry encounters Willie experiences with others primarily originate out of a resentment he holds with the journeyman guild back in Germany—it remains with him as a festering adversarial encounter and taints all of his relations.

Neither is Magdalena free from unpleasantries. In her responsibilities involving the plant manager's family, they can be very demanding and tend to overburden her with menial tasks. Because of the restraints of a day only lasting so long, she is not able to complete all of them to their satisfaction. This, in turn, leaves her frustrated.

The span of similar experiences between Magdalena and Willie is vast, but they are able to bridge the gap. There is simply no escaping the fact that they are the only ones supporting the other. They are two Germans in the land of the Danes. Unlike their other German brethren who have found themselves a safe conclave with other likeminded countrymen, both Willie and Magdalena have lofty ideas that are only valued between the two of them. Their yearnings stretch from Willie's inability to resume his experimenting with steam power to Magdalena's failure to find a good enough reason to convince Willie that they need to go to America.

Nearly a year has passed without any satisfactory answer for either of them. They have done nothing to improve their outside relationships during this time, resulting in becoming even more isolated from the other Germans. This has resulted in the couple being treated by their neighbors as an annoyance to be tolerated only as result of the direct orders from Frank Meitz to regard them as a part of his family.

Apart from Magdalena, the only other social outlet Willie has is an occasional visit to local beer garden. It's amazing how quickly men from different backgrounds, ages, and status can find common ground and bond together in their complaints about the weather, the government, how horrible the transportation system runs, and anything else that may be wrong.

On this particular occasion a large man speaking German with an American accent, dressed in the distinct fashion of a ship's officer has appeared with a passenger manifest. It seems he's attempting to fill it to sail a ship to America. Willie has had enough beer to attempt to present his well-rehearsed diatribe that he frequently uses in defense of himself against Magdalena. His strategy is the same; his challenge is to outtalk this purveyor of optimism by shouting over him, the same as he does with Magdalena.

"Why would anyone want to leave the civilized hub of the world for an outpost filled with savages and slaves? There's nothing but chaos and killings in America."

The difference is there are enough men here in the beer garden who are willing to hear what this agent has to say. After several of Willie's interruptions, more than a few are ready to throw him out or shut his mouth for him. In spite of the beer clouding his reason, Willie is smart enough to realize that he is in the minority and succumbs.

Realizing that with Willie out of the way, the agent has the additional support he needs to make a convincing demonstration. He says to his remaining listeners,

"Could anything be worse for you and your families? Do you recall how no matter, or in what way you were prudent that you could not build a reserve to absorb the shock of crop failure? Do you remember when you looked to your larders only to find them empty and no savings were enough to prevent your roots from rotting in the ground? Is it disaster that's chained you to your present situation; is calamity so familiar that you are willing to let it immobilize you?

"Many of you watched your older brother given the last scrap of land able to sustain a family while you were expected to find a living in a foreign land, or you have all been driven out of your native land by the everchanging greed of your native landlords, a pack of thieves willing to continue to consolidate their land holdings only to leave you to suffer."

The large man is aware he has said the words these peasants have only thought. It's true they have not had the adeptness to put them into words or in other cases because of their long habit, the seeming changelessness of

205

their society has stifled their impulse to improve or even rebel. Regardless of their individual situations, he is aware he has enough of their attention to create a new direction for many of them. With that settled, he continues his discourse.

"You can only thrive if you own land. The reason you're all in the situation you're in is that economic growth has stopped in Europe; the land has been consolidated to only improve the lives of the landholders—there is no land left. In America, rich farm land is so available that it is not unusual to own forty acres of prime ground.

"I have also been made aware that tradesmen are needed. America is building a new city nearly every day. You can easily bring your skills to a people who are able and willing to pay you for your services without the stifling of an overbearing guild."

Willie had been unmoved by all this man's talk about land. He hasn't been on a farm since he was a young boy. But now that the man has switched his tenor from the land to the trades, his interest has picked up.

Emboldened by his beer, Willie raises his hand to be heard. Knowing that he has the upper hand with the crowd, the agent is more than willing to let Willie speak; the agent is fully ready to put to rest any adverse retorts this prior troublemaker can fabricate.

"How much steam power are Americans using?" Willie asks with a noticeable degree earnestness replacing his former hostility.

Surprised by Willie's sudden change, the agent speaks up with the same authoritative tone he had used with those seeking land.

"America is leading the world in all sorts of innovations, all unburdened by the repressive guilds hindering progress as they are known to do in Europe."

Taking particular note of Willie's newfound interest and the potential for a convert, the agent continues, "On my last arrival, my ship was led into the harbor by a steam powered tugboat. They are constantly being improved and in need of skilled mechanics."

Willie is riveted on this fresh depiction of America. With the possibility that all he has heard is true, all his resentments toward the guild, all his angers toward the church in their repressive actions are suddenly being liberated. He can hardly contain the feeling of deliverance this beacon of hope, this purveyor of independence is giving him. In conclusion, the agent now directing his attention on Willie, says, "A man much smarter than the two of us combined once said, 'When it's obvious that the goals can't be reached, don't adjust the goals, adjust the action steps.'"

This last sentence was to have a permanent effect on Willie. His next thoughts are on how he is going to reveal to Magdalena his change of heart toward America without the need to eat crow.

The nights he spends in the beer garden are times where Magdalena writes letters to her parents, previous classmates, her cousin Ida, and her Tante and Onkel. In her classic way of making silk purses out of sow's ears, she has found ways to be content in their less than desirable existence. Startled by the door flying open, her head snaps to discover its cause. She is obliged to look up from her writing long enough to focus on the demeanor of a man she has not experienced in some time. It's Willie coming through the entry. He's home earlier than usual on these beer drinking nights. His energy is fresh despite a long day in the fishery.

"You'll never guess what I just discovered."

He stands across the room with the broadest grin, all the while displaying an uncharacteristic patience awaiting her reply.

Poignantly puzzled, she exclaims with the only response coming to mind, "What?"

"America needs steam!" is his overtly excited response.

Listening to something that she has pointed out forever is like an echo resounding across the twelve-foot chasm between them. She has pointed this fact out in many of their discussions. Having a second thought, Magdalena wisely decerns what she has always said, "If we ever go to America, it will have been Willie's idea."

Still, certain discernment is needed, Magdalena decides to remain naïve. Her only reply is, "Where in the world did you ever hear such a thing?"

"An agent for a shipping company came into the beer garden and told how America needs mechanics to keep their steam powered industries working. I'm tired of breaking my back on alien soil for no meaningful return. We need to put our roots down somewhere other than Denmark."

Still not certain what response she should offer, Magdalena opts to let Willie go further to explain the road he has been exploring. In spite of the fact many more are also making the same decision; the decision is made by each person alone—each one leaves as an individual; more often than not, desperation has driven the decision.

Magdalena, our world is falling apart. I can't go back to Germany without going to prison, we can't stay in Denmark and prosper. We are left with no choice other than to make our way to the new world," pronounces Willie with an air of decision. "What do you think Magdalena, should we make the leap?"

No longer able to disguise her delight, Magdalena is off her chair, bolting across the floor, colliding with her husband, nearly knocking him back through the open door. She can't stop kissing him.

208

"The only way you'll get me to say no is if you can drag America to our shores."

Chapter 31

Unfixed Times

Emigration is truly the end of life in post feudal Europe, but it's also the promise of a new life in a young country named America. What must be kept in mind is that this is just the beginning. Just the physical gap alone between the two continents is overwhelming. If anyone expects to stay true to their desire to make the six- to eight-week crossing and being, most likely, a novice to seafaring, the only thing to save them is not to dwell on the expanse for any length of time.

What is proving to be beneficial is that Willie and Magdalena are both ready to move forward without knowing what forward will prove to bring with it. They both know where their roots are, where they were born, what their native language is, where most things remain rigid with a historical purpose for existing. But for many, these traditions no longer hold the value they once provided. For the foreseeable future they are resolved to downgrade themselves to become nomads wandering wherever the future places them. Day by day with fewer and fewer alternatives remaining, the day arrives where the only option left is to leave. Those whose desire to make the change, depart. The rest are left to talk about what they could have done, or should have done; they eventually die unfulfilled.

There is little problem with packing, since their possessions are few. This past year their savings have been sufficient to imagine this kind of undertaking is within their limit.

Free of the money worries, their thoughts turn to packing. Concerning his tools, Willie realizes the difficulty with transporting his heavy anvil, and a few other of his heavy iron tools. He, therefore negotiates a price with a local blacksmith—the extra money is welcomed. The next step is to make their way to the port and look up the agent whom he had met in the beer garden.

When Willie and Magdalena made their decision to leave behind the only life they have known, they hardly were aware of the countless number of others making the same decision. It hits them directly after they have made their way to the docks where the heavy oceangoing ships are berthed. The herds of people with sullen looks of desperation brought on by having been dislodged from the miserable fallout of the economic failure of the entire European region are flocking here like so many sheep without a shepherd. The idea that the post feudal system would leave them near starvation, riddled with an unpayable debt to where they have indentured themselves for the price of a ticket, would be unimaginable were it not for their desperation.

Willie and Magdalena pick their way through the multitude of people, guarding as best they can their individual supply of sacks, bags, satchels, trunks, all enclosing their small number of belongings. Many carry their religious icons (crucifixes, pictures of saints, religious statues) close to their hearts as though these symbols embodied the aid of a Divine Presence they need to make the journey. The meagerness of these possessions tells how distressed many have become.

With little to go other than a handwritten note with the name Gleason B. Fredrick, pier #18, Salisbury shipping, scribbled across its face, Willie and Magdalena press on. Finally, they look up to see a weather-beaten sign with faded letters spelling out the words SALISBURY SHIPPERS. Relieved they have achieved their goal; they enter a small building with rough sawn planks covering its exterior. They are met by the same affable man Willie had met in the beer garden a few days prior.

211

Not remembering Willie immediately, he greets them in Danish through his American accent. Willie returns the greeting in German giving his host a heads up. Catching on, the man returns the gesture by switching to German. It's obvious that he's versatile in several languages. Willie reminds the man that they had met in the beer garden days before. The man suddenly broadens his smile a bit wider followed with the comment, "Oh yes, I remember you, you were my little troublemaker that day."

Willie feels his face reddening with embarrassment as he recalls his intoxicated conduct.

"I hope you can forgive me; I've had a change of heart since then," confesses Willie. "Are you Herr Fredrick?" he continues.

"Consider it done and yes, I'm Fredrick, what can I do for you?" says Fredrick still as amiable.

"We need to get to America. You said you have a ship that that will be leaving soon, is it still available and if so, how much is the fare?"

"You are in luck; I have a berth for two left in steerage at thirty rigsdaler (Danish currency) apiece."

Recalling his many years of observing how Meister Yunk always started at a high charge all the while knowing he would be haggled down to a more reasonable price, Willie clasps his face between his open palms exclaiming, "We could never pay such an exorbitant amount, I can give you fifteen rigsdaler apiece and not a rigsdaler more."

Fredrick barely wastes a moment before he counters, "I can go twenty-five rigsdaler and that's my lowest price."

"Make it twenty and you got a deal," returns Willie.

Extending his hand to meet Willie's already extended hand they shake, consummating the deal.

With this part of the ordeal finished, and with tickets in hand stating they are privy to a berth in the steerage compartment of one ship named New York, they also are supplied with a minimum amount of oatmeal, molasses, bread, sugar, rice, a small amount of pork, a few ounces of tea, and twenty gallons of fresh water per person. They also must supply their own bedding other than the straw provided in each berth. All that's left to do is to wait at the pier for the ship to sail.

What soon becomes apparent is that the ship is far from ready to sail as its cargo hold is not filled. It appears that it will be several days before this aspect becomes a reality. They are obliged to be available at a moment's notice to access their placement. Returning to their former apartment, because its distance is too far away to be practical, is not an option. The problem confronting them is where to sleep and eat for the interim period. Their choices revolve around staying outside on the pier or staying in Gleason Fredrick's rooming house for nearly the cost per person per night of a half-weeks rent in town. Willie and Magdalena hold a discussion on what they believe to be the better choice. Willie is quite adamant on his preference.

"I practically lived outside for seven years in your father's forge; I can do this. I prefer you sleep inside and I'll stay out here with our possessions."

Magdalena is happy about this arrangement. Sleeping outside has never been something she has felt a need to do to complete herself. To say that what she faces as the evening calls for sleep preparation is something that she had prepared for is definitely an understatement. The sleeping quarters are in a ramshackle building with lines of makeshift platforms with dirty straw filled mattresses. In hushed tones of foreign languages, several families with overly tired crying children attempt to quiet them. It's been long days for all who find

213

themselves at these crossroads. Tensions stemming from unfamiliar activities along with the grueling physical demands of keeping possessions intact create a strange kind of exhaustion. Not seeing this as a place to build lasting relationships with strangers, most are content to keep to themselves; making the best of a bad situation.

Willie is one among many others who have opted to bear the outdoor mix of night, sea, and ship aspects with all their never before encountered sounds and smells. Large ships with planking, heavier than observed anywhere, creak along with the squeals produced when these huge behemoths respond to the sea's power in small undulations, that force them against the pilings. Ropes straining against freeing these massive captives, twang with the night dampness and changing temperatures.

With years of pounding surf, the pier flooring is a wood decking worn hard and smooth by its ever-increasing abuse. Among mountains of cargo, Willie finds himself sharing deck space with a pile of iron ingots. He's very familiar with the product. It's very similar to the iron he used in the forge. In the midst of all the lingering tensions produced by these anxious migrants swirling about, just the familiar smell of these memorable pieces of ferrous metal gives Willie a momentary sense of well-being.

Other considerations include immigrants being accosted by every kind of peddler able to make his way to the piers. They are skilled in homing in on the neurotic fears these poor people endure of not being adequately prepared. They have everything to sell from cooking ware to clothing heralded as just the thing each of these wayfarers will need to avert their fear of starving or the catastrophic weather during the voyage.

To the delight of lingering passengers, the shipping company has provided an overhead canopy to ward off a rain assault. Although this has been a godsend protecting passengers stranded till boarding time, this has been put

214

in place as more of a consideration to protect goods waiting to be loaded than as a safety measure or courtesy to the hordes of journeyers.

Exhausted, not only physically, but also emotionally, Willie takes a break. He feels a connection with this group of seeming likeminded people. Nonetheless, he has cautiously placed his hammer inside his coat as a means of defense. In his attempt to fortress their possessions from others, he drapes his arms and legs across as much of their possessions as possible. His body is weary, but his mind is wandering, refusing to rest; it can't resolve the unknowns like, "When will we board, what kind of accommodations will we find, will our food provisions last, what will the weather conditions prove to be, can we survive this ordeal?"

There is nothing he is viewing that looks familiar, sounds familiar, or smells familiar; it's all unknown, untried, and in so many ways foreboding. All this is adding up to give him a moment of fear. Up until now, this entire episode has been more planned than acted on. It is suddenly occurring to Willie that today, the planning stage is completed and has switched to the action phase— and he can't predict its outcome. Closing his eyes for a moment, he reflects back on his faith. He finds himself humbler than he has been in some time. His own strength has waned to where he turns to The One Who Has All Power, praying, "God, be with us." This acknowledgement becomes the center of his thoughts. Even though his body and mind are exhausted, he feels a sudden resurgence deep in his soul—a lifting of his spirit. In a moment he drifts off to sleep.

What wakes him is the feeling of something shifting beneath his leg. It takes him a moment to decern where he is. Once it's clear, he realizes the sack containing a portion of their belongings is sliding from under him. The only source of light is from an oil streetlamp many yards away, its dim glimmer is hardly enough to identify the root of the problem. In response, Willie's hand reflexively grabs the still moving bag, while the other hand has retrieved his hammer. In a flash the hammer's head has met an object, still unseen, but firm. It's a solid blow. Whatever the hammer's recipient may be, having a human voice attached to it, it lets out a yelp. As the shadowy figure makes its escape, it's stumbles through the throngs of dozing journeyers, producing still more protests.

This ordeal has added another dimension to Willie's ongoing dilemma. Not only is there very real physical danger to himself and Magdalena at sea but he must also be on the lookout of being dispossessed while still on land. Opportunistic, petty thieves roam the streets and byways of urban centers like their wild predator cousins roam the forests. What better prey than unsuspecting, honest, hardworking people forced out of their element? First, the incident in the forest with thieves, and now experiencing a repeat encounter in the city, Willie is learning that there is much more to life than he could have possibly speculated confined to a small village forge for the last third of his life.

With morning arriving, while waiting for Magdalena to appear and not willing to leave their possessions unattended, Willie contents himself to gnaw on a potato he had sequestered inside a coat pocket. He soon spots Magdalena standing in a line. She is standing along a row of small outbuildings attached to both sides of a narrow pier with people coming and going. This facility has been provided with a series of holes cut in the floor allowing for toilet needs. The waste drops through the openings directly into the sea.

These conditions are less than those Magdalena has become accustomed to but in typical Magdalena fashion, she adapts and overcomes. The secret to her character is a high and abstract ambition. She has always been entranced with life's surprises and is willing to overlook the unsettledness it often brings with it; for her happiness doesn't mean everything is perfect, it means that she's decided to look beyond the imperfections.

After making her way to Willie, she finds him agitated. The pressures that come with freedom are overwhelming him. In spite of the closeness they held growing up in the same location, they have experienced much different outcomes. Magdalena, despite her father's objection to her wanderlust ways, and her unremitting craving for more than he was willing or able to offer, has determined her strength comes from within. Willie, on the other hand, had found security in the permanence of his craft. Now, to find himself in the most unfixed time of his life, he feels the over powering insecurity that often accompanies displacement.

"I feel my life to be one bitter trial after another. I don't know what I have done to deserve this," he laments out loud.

Magdalena has grown accustomed to Willie's penchant for pessimism but has never let it go unchallenged. Her faith that God will prevail in directing their path prevails.

"We are going to get through this, Willie. This is just one of those storms of life God has designed for us to draw near to Him for our strength."

Willie listens half-trusting her words. A part of him would like to agree with Magdalena but another part—a pragmatic part—prefers things to be tangible. Harking back on his days at her father's forge when life was predictable, he sensed his life's purpose.

"My life was fine. I don't need storms."

The tenor of Willie's resentment is apparent.

"Willie Beinecke, I don't believe you just said that. How do you expect to grow if you're never challenged?"

Magdalena is looking directly at him with a look Willie's seeing more often nowadays—her look is one of displeasure.

"God didn't give you your talent to be wasted in my father's forge. He has given you a great gift to make a big difference in people's lives—you need to keep that in mind. What would your life amount to if you don't have the courage to attempt something outstanding?"

These are the words of encouragement Willie needs to take stock of himself and his abilities. It renews his purpose to reengage his commitment to further the development of steam power. Once more, Magdalena has spoken the very words he needs to hear to move on.

Chapter 32

The Boarding

The ship with NEW YORK carved in bold letters across the stern awaits a final inspection of the cargo that's laid in her hold. It's a small barque style sailing ship with square sails, designated as a merchant ship; suitable for cargo or passenger. She measures 145 feet (long) from stem to sternpost by 39 feet (wide) in the beam. Willie and Magdalena, along with hundreds of other passengers from all walks and stations in life, await boarding instructions. Each has set aside a small section of the pier deck for themselves along with their possessions. The wealthier sit on well-made trunks of wood and leather while the poor sit among sacks and battered trunks bound with ropes, all holding the most precious of their belongings. With little left to do but wait, they nervously adjust and readjust the pattern of their arrangement as if the previous layout was faulty. The only sounds are coming from children noisily playing with other children. These are chance meetings but what remains true with children is their introductions are brief. Within minutes they find enough interest in one another to begin to play.

In a little while, a ship's officer announces boarding protocol. What had a moment before been quiet reflection suddenly bursts into deafened chaos. The realization of the need to board has awakened their apprehension. Shoving begins along with parents attempting to keep sight of their children. With agonized faces, last goodbyes are made between weeping loved ones who likely will never see each other again. Some of the young single men, reluctant to wait their turn, begin to board by climbing ropes and riggings used to secure the ship to the pilings. Others, accompanied with worried faces, begin to wrestle with their belongings. Acknowledging the privilege that accompanies wealth, the first-class passengers are boarded first, assisted by crew members carrying their belongings. Some belongings are to accompany them to their cabin, others will be laid in stowage. These passengers will occupy the calmer, first-class accommodations located in the aft section of the ship. The rest of the passengers are in steerage located in the stern section where the motion is more violent. When it comes to luggage, this group is left to fend for themselves. Husbands and fathers grapple with barrels and chests as they jostle their way up the gangplank.

This latter group includes Willie and Magdalena. Struggling with their meager possessions, they make their way up on to the ship. Once there, they are met by the steerage steward who directs them to the steerage section located two decks below and one deck above the cargo section. Steerage aboard the New York can best be described as a barn for people. Barely visible in the variable light, their eyes discover a middle aisle barely five feet wide. It takes a while before they can make out the other structures within the compartment. Once their eyes accustom themselves to the darkness, they see the aisle itself is framed by two rows of bunks that press against the sides of the ship. Not only is it dark and not ventilated down here below deck, the lingering smell is horrid. With the crew member turning up a lantern hung on a protruding mast post, the light casts ominous shadows about this watery vault designated to be their home for the next six to eight weeks. The length of their passage to America is uncertain, for the ship is at the mercy of the winds and currents, of the navigational skills of the captain, and the witlessness of a scarcely experienced crew.

It's apparent that this compartment has barely been cleaned since the last group made a crossing. The sleeping areas are platforms supplied with dirty canvas mattresses filled with straw. It's too dark to perceive what the scurrying sounds are but it's the familiar commotions a rat makes as it attempts to avoid discovery. The crew member in charge checks each of their tickets to ensure it correlates with the assigned bunk. With each bunk is assigned a food manifest to retrieve each person's share of rations from the ship's larder. Located at the far end toward the stern is a small galley functioning as the kitchen to service the entire steerage population. It consists of two cooking stoves and a couple small tables serving as preparation counters. Beyond this is the common toilet for the women to share, while men and crew share a toilet on deck. Magdalena looks at this convenience with a wary eye. "How is everyone going to use this—it's too small?" is her first thought. This is the first time during this entire period since she has left the well-being of her parent's home that she has experienced this stark of a reality. This bleak environment is not something anyone could appreciate unless they had been homeless for a period and are offered these conditions as an alternative.

Among the scraping noises wooden trunks on wooden planks make, there is an unsettling quiet about everyone as each is introduced to the disturbing reality of their conditions. If the lantern light were brighter, it would reveal a look of desperation on each of their faces; they're dealing with conditions which could conceivably turn into a longer time period than they are prepared to endure. Obliged to provide their own bedding, women are pulling bedding from various bags trying to make as much of a home out of these disconcerting conditions as possible. This space is where they will sleep, eat, socialize, and in some cases—die.

It's not long before these small compartments are jammed with new occupants, each attempting to protect their narrowed down borders from a neighbor's encroachment; everyone has more stuff than there is room to store, giving rise to neighbor intruding on neighbor.

Following suit, Magdalena prepares as best she can the space allotted for herself and Willie. It's a three foot high, boxed-in, six by five foot floor level,

221

corner cubicle with the straw filled mattress, with room enough for her and Willie to lie in place with some of their belongings stashed outside on the floor.

Above deck, the ropes connecting the ship to the pilings have been loosened. Before the ship begins to recklessly drift, there is a well-rehearsed method required to setting the correct rigging to move the ship in the direction the captain desires. The crew has taken up their stations awaiting a signal from the first mate to set the sails. The signal is given. Suddenly, the ship tilts delivering a slight jerk as the wind catches the jib sail. After a kneejerk reaction to grip the nearest thing to them and a fear of an unknown, Willie and Magdalena anxiously make their way to the deck. With open mouths they fixate themselves on the strange activities. With a singleness of purpose, each member of the crew methodically preforms a sole function that is related to the whole process; with the captain shouting orders from the bridge, the crew, like a well-oiled cog, flawlessly meets the demands of the wind and masts. All the while the land dwellers are left to humbly watch, realizing their total dependance on this bawdy, vulgar, unrefined, rough-edged crew and a ship stressed to its maximum. For many of the haughty, it's a sobering experience. Despite the truth of this well-deserved portrayal, these sojourners quickly develop a new respect for their crew's skills and the capability of the ship.

With the obvious reckoning that the ship is underway, many of the passengers linger on deck for a moment. There is a concentration, (or more succinctly, a complexity) of energies surrounding this event. As the land behind the ship grows smaller, the promise of anything substantial out front, other than the mass of water, is uncertain. There is an altogether new awareness that they are leaving the only life they have known for something mysterious. With differing mindsets, everyone is caught up in their own private expectations.

Some, including Willie, remain apprehensive of what the future holds. Clutching skepticism, he nonetheless reveres the noblest aspects of his past, but is not forgetting the ruthless circumstances that led to these new wild events.

222

His inability to manage these overwhelming circumstances has brought him to this unfamiliar spot where he finds himself a stranger.

Others, including Magdalena, refuse to allow their uncertainties to overtake their lives—the future is something to behold rather than fear—and a yearning desire for a better opportunity is transformed into hope; hope, long relished, has become like a certainty which tosses its light onward while not yet having it in hand.

There is nothing aboard this manmade vessel that will give them the security each of them craves; there is nothing on this ship to remind them of home—not rope, not riggings, not heavy canvas sails, or an unstable wooden structure struggling to remain afloat. The solid land that once stood beneath them has been replaced by the uneasy motion of liquid. If nothing else, this phenomenon reminds them that they have committed to a new destiny.

What arises from the deep recesses of each traveler is a spontaneous flow of emotion amid the certainties that the ship will disregard all their concerns—its only function is to float. If they expect to complete this journey, they must find a way to adapt themselves to the ship and its foibles rather than expecting the ship to adapt itself to the individual.

In the journey of life, the healthier the spirit, the healthier the mind and body; all three together enables a satisfactory end. Achieving this calls for a power greater than themselves to fill the problematic voids between them. Regardless of their past relationships with divine providence, each of the travelers bears the ominous circumstances their weaknesses are mired in and confronts their own need of a spiritual renewal if they hope to draw near themselves any available heavenly consolations.

Among the scores of souls aboard journeying as immigrants, their nationalities vary. They're made up of Americans, Germans, Russians, Bohemians, Finns, Norwegians, Swedes, French, Irish, Scotch, Welch, and

English. Many of these German pilgrims are pietistic Lutherans with an objective to Christianize America's savage indigenous people. In mass, they are certain they possess enough of God's true and pure word to enable them to survive this trip and reach their objective. Many of these men have answered the call to enter the missionary field. All are being swept along together, yet each moves alone. The act of uprooting remains individual, and their response is also individual. They are leaving the place of their birth. Like it or not, they are now wanderers.

Chapter 33

The Journey

Ultimately, the only thing real about this journey is how one reacts to the moment. That's all that can be done. The ship's master has reserved the top deck for the working crew, although during good weather passengers are allowed access in small groups. How this is determined is left to the crew and those representatives the passengers have elected to speak in their behalf. The passenger representatives have been selected by each language/ethnic group to arrange with the deck crew as to when these visitations are feasible.

Because the men's toilet is located on the top deck, Willie has a limited but more frequent access to fresh air. Magdalena, on the other hand, is sequestered tin the confines of this lower deck environment. As usual, she is making the best of the situation. Because of her affable personality, she has been selected to organize the kitchen schedule for the German-speaking group. There is never a time, day or night, that it is quiet or not crowded. The air is filled with different tongues, foreign for some and familiar for others. Whenever there appears to be a break in an aisle someone quickly fills it. Tempers are quick to surface over commonplace issues. These disputes must be resolved just as quickly or risk a physical conflict.

The first few days of the voyage the weather is amicable, not too many are complaining about the change from land to sea. But this is to be short-lived. Soon it has become the plight of these land dwellers to encounter a threatening gale. At first, passengers are allowed access to the deck. Once there, each

225

one's fascination is held as the foaming sea crashes against the hull. It is a magnificent yet daunting sight that the most seasoned seaman never tires of. With the intensity of the wind increasing, the ship is beginning to plunge into the fearful trough between the waves. The sense of awe and exhilaration originally experienced is quickly being replaced by fear. It soon becomes apparent that the storm is threatening not only the welfare of the ship but also the lives of the passengers. The hatches are quickly battened to prevent seawater from overtaking the ship and all oil lanterns must be extinguished to prevent an accidental fire. Consequently, the steerage section becomes a dark, dank abyss tossed about at the pleasure of the sea. With a few exceptions, seasickness is soon running rampant through the entire passenger population.

Magdalena is one of the first to feel the effects of seasickness. Willie is doing as much as he can to minister to her, but unfortunately, it's a malady there is little another can do to relieve its misery. It not long before he too is overcome with the same problem. So great a suffering is it that, for some, their recovery is questionable. As much as can be done, others try and minister to those they can. As much as everyone tries no remedy proves effective. For anyone to cope with the added problem of vomit spilling everywhere is to invite further problems with other diseases.

With the storm moving into its third day, some are suffering more than others; by its conclusion, it will have taken the lives of several of the elderly. With little opportunity to perform a proper Christian funeral—the Lutheran clergy are reluctant to officiate for any funeral for anyone other than one of their own in fear the deceased may have been Catholic— amongst the bitter tears of those left to continue the journey without them, the captain says a few words before committing their bodies to the ocean.

Since precious drinking water is never used for bathing, after a week of several hundred unbathed bodies crammed in spaces designed for a tenth the number, along with toilets that are never vacant long enough to clean, the stench is overwhelming. The only ventilation is through the hatches during good weather. During the past bad weather, the hatches had been battened down for days. With this contained environment, sickness is also beginning to rear its head. Temperatures on the ocean can vary from day to day from stifling hot to inclement cold accompanied with a sharp wind. Add to this the continual attempt to keep drinking water from contaminating, the ship's cook continues to add vinegar. The well-meaning attempt at disinfecting only exploits maladies such a yellow fever, cholera, dysentery, measles, and what the ship's doctor—who is also the ship's barber—refers to as "ship fever." To further add to already sordid conditions, rats run free in all the filth. As a matter of course, the ship's master expects death to take up to ten percent of his human cargo including part of his own crew.

From the harshness of the trip there is no effective relief, misery only compounds. As time lapses, the Lutheran missionaries, with all their previous ecclesiastical haughtiness, and Catholics holding their Catholicism as a barrier to non-Catholics, are becoming tenderized by their common plight and are finding common ground in their powerlessness to invoke God together; what had been held as inflexible reasons as to why they could not approach God together has lost its supremacy and been replaced with a common desperateness and a need for God to save them all.

Separated from the rest of the ship, steerage becomes a world unto itself. A most noticeable thing about sea life in this seeming underworld is how quickly some can throw off the encumbrance of civilization. Finding themselves in a strange unpredictable environment where they are no longer under the influence of home, country, or religion, unrestrained by convention, unbounded from the opinion of family elders, fellow villagers or church rules, they let themselves go, giving in to their baser nature. If conditions are not boding well for good behavior, this change may begin with small incremental changes in a person's reaction to pressures they had not had to deal with on land and find themselves reverting to a brazen uncivilized behavior.

227

No sooner has the danger of the storm left them where they had taken solace in a common prayer for deliverance than they begin to snarl and growl at one another over the slightest provocations. They're language is lewd and quarrelsome. Fights break out with the ascendancy of brute strength shamelessly reigning as righteous conduct. Men and women alike fall into filthy habits of staying in their berths for days without the changing their clothing. They eat, sleep, and those with dysentery often vomit and discharge their bowels where they lay—all without the benefit of soap and water. The sea seems to utterly dishearten them.

The most prevalent group on board are males, mostly made up of single men in their thirties. The next prevalent group are married couples and their children. A good share of these are nervous men with worried, anxious temperaments. They weren't born this way; it has come on them as a result of previous failures. Their hope is to start anew in the America. Most of these have no relatives waiting to help them when they arrive. In one way or another they're on their own. This is the source of much of their nervousness. A good percentage of these men are bound for rural areas where they can farm. They have heard from others how a man can possess as much land as he can till. This hardy group are primarily made up of Germans and Scandinavians. But by far the larger part of the immigrant population are made up of young men bound for the cities. These are mostly from the British Isles. They have a penchant for causing quarrels among themselves as well as others—a brotherhood of troublemakers.

Although confined within their five by six-foot compartment, Willie and Magdalena have spent nearly every waking as well as their sleeping hours together, but they have had little privacy to show for it. To carry out as much as a simple conversation amid the constant din of voices, the constant movement of shuffling bodies feeling their way through crowded aisles, and crying children resonating their wailing through the entire hold, is a challenge. Due to an unfortunate experience while on deck (a crew member accosted Magdalena),

228

Magdalena has become more guarded, finding herself staying in her bunk with Willie despite the lack of privacy.

The voyage is well into the third week. The voyage had begun with an orderly arrangement of passenger concerns being sent to the ship's master through chosen representatives. Two of these representatives have already succumbed to deadly disease leaving the dysfunctional steerage population to deal with their ever-growing problem individually. In the rapidly changing milieu, mayhem is quick to replace order. Adding to this increasing problem, the horrific environment in the steerage compartment is leading to disease with nothing to stop it; it is raging its way through unabated. The decking in this abysm of disease is in a constant flux of fresh layers of vomit and excrement left from those suffering the ravages of dysentery.

The tediousness of the trip is increasingly reflected in the faces of what had been hopeful expressions just a week ago turned now to a dour near doomed expression. The death toll is mounting daily with nothing to challenge it.

Magdalena's usual effervescence has flattened in reaction to her increasing swings between terror and boredom. This is in direct proportion to finding minimal solace in her compartment during storms and nearly unbearable monotony during calm seas. She is finding that not only are her physical capacities weakened but even her mental and spiritual capacity to organize an elementary prayer is reduced to three simple words, "God, help me."

Willie is not in any better condition. Sensing the reality of his own mortality in this seeming abysmal coffin, he too is finding his prayers to be simple prayers of surrender. The words of St. Steven as he was being stoned to death come clear in his mind, "Into Your hands, Oh Lord, I commend my spirit." As much as he loves Magdalena, barely able to meet his own needs, any concept of taking care of her is buried in his own lack of power, either physically, mentally, or spiritually.

To make matters worse, the division by gender is blurred. What may have been respect and protection of unmarried young women weeks ago has eroded into a near state of promiscuity. Regardless of the state of well-being a woman is in, healthy or sick, married or single, old or young, there are male passengers as well as male crew members who will, if given the opportunity, beguile every woman crossing their path for sexual favors.

For everyone, this trip cannot be over soon enough.

Chapter 34

'Scapin'

From the middle of the Atlantic Ocean to the Kilbourn Plantation in central Georgia is over a thousand miles. It's four o'clock in the morning. Mammy Ceceilia has been awakened and she is making her way to Abina's and Kumi's quarters. Trotting along behind her long-legged strides is another younger woman. The reason for this exceptional visit at this time of the mourning is in answer to Kumi's desperate plead.

"Mammy gots come quick to da quarters. Abina laborin' mighty hard wid da chil.'"

By the time Ceceilia has reached their shack, Abina is outdoors squatting on the ground over a freshly dug hole. She had assisted her mother with more than a few deliveries back in Ghana and is familiar with all its preparations. It's important in Ghanaian tradition to bear a child on the ground as it has religious overtones—it indicates the fertility of the earth and the mother's contact with it. Despite the pain, Abina is adamant not to overlook this important ritual with her own delivery and has made her way to the outside at a prepared location.

After examining Abina's condition, Ceceilia shoos Kumi away. In her world, men are not allowed at a childbirth. Kumi readily obliges. This is an event he is more than willing to skip. Abina is relieved to have Mammy Ceceilia and her assistant with her but is longing for her mother more than she has since her

231

abduction. Surrounding this epoch event, her Ghanaian tradition would have provided her with all available female relatives encircling her—some acting as midwives.

The birth pains of Abina are met with soothing words and a continual back rub. The combined efforts of herself and her two alternating coaches are soon brought to fruition. With Ceceilia drilling her over and over to "PUSH!" Abina finally succeeds in dropping a small human body covered in afterbirth. Due to the absence of Abina's mother, Ceceilia cuts the umbilical cord, also taking it upon herself to bath the infant. During this process, Abina dutifully pushes the placenta and umbilical into the hole and covers it with dirt. Since infertility is regarded as a great tragedy, this procedure assures that she will remain fertile.

Few words are needed since the delivery. Ceceilia has returned the screaming infant to Abina's waiting arms without a spot of afterbirth. This new arrival has resulted in a noticeably light skinned boy with startling blue eyes, tight curly blond hair, and a strong voice. This strange new pedigree confirms her suspicions that this boy's father is none other than the Dutch governor from her days at Elmina. Still surveying the child's physical departure from any child that she has been acquainted with, she wonders what is going to become of him. It's been the practice for slave owners to pay little attention to keeping families intact if it's economically beneficial to sell them off individually. Abina has witnessed the heartrending tears mothers have shed over children lost to the slave traders. The thought of it happening to her brings about a tinge of dreaded reality. Nonetheless, Abina does what all mothers have done since Eve, she counts all the child's fingers and toes. Satisfied things are as they should be, at Ceceilia's superintendence, Abina begins to breastfeed the disgruntled infant.

232

Ceceilia is biding her time before she takes leave for her regular routine at the Big House. There is one more thing she is contemplating. Her thoughts shift for the moment as they always do for a newborn.

"De Colonel goan' wan' dis chil' baptiz' as ta be a Christian. Him say dey ain't goan' be no heathen on dis plantation."

Abina listens without comment. Her thoughts are taken up with the immediate needs of her infant. It's all that she is willing to sort out for the moment.

By now Tom's morning reveille is announcing the dawn of another day. Kumi's thoughts are also milling around these impeding circumstances. He recalls, while still in Africa, how his uncle had assumed the role of mentor toward him and whether he'll be called on to do the same for this boy. But like all slaves, regardless of their circumstances, the day doesn't stop for them. They are still required to fulfil the duties assigned for the day. The only difference for Abina is she will be carrying the child in a different place than she has for the past nine months—and because Ceceilia likes her, she'll be given light duty for a few days.

With no expectation of anything other than another tedious day in the fields, Kumi has resumed his regular assignment for the day. There is one difference that has arisen. With Jack Beauchamp fired and not replaced, Tom has been given temporary duty as overseer. While the work assignments are being allocated, Tom makes a point to draw Kumi aside.

"Us wan' see you at noon break," says Tom in a low enough tone that only Kumi hears it.

Not certain what this statement could pertain to, Kumi gives a slight nod that he understands. Kumi is given his assignment as a stump-piker (digging stumps) for the morning shift. With noon arriving, Tom is busy fulfilling both

233

duties as field manager and overseer. This business is quickly concluded with his attention turning to their rendezvous.

"Us gettin' ready ta carry a load ah logs fo' De Colonel to de mill ober in de nex' county. Him always have us take 'nodder nigger 'long ta hep wid de burden. Us thinkin' you be de nigger dat goes 'long ta hep."

Kumi is more than delighted to have an opportunity to get a break from the daily drudge of the plantation, readily agrees to the invitation.

But Tom isn't finished. Being the offspring of slaves, Tom has spent his entire thirty-five years in the service of The Colonel. The Colonel has promised Tom his freedom, but recently managed to change the terms when the conditions were met. As a result, Tom has come to a point of despair. He is entertaining another option. What had merely been a faraway thought is turning into more of a nearby thought—to become a runaway. He had met a Quaker man in town a while back who entertained him with the idea of escaping.

"Us knows you hab a great hankerin' for bein' a freeman, comin' from Africa and all. Ole Tom gots de same hankerin.' Dey be a right Christian man in de nex county who say 'im can refugee a nigger tah freedom. Him be ober by de mill."

Tom pauses for a moment as though he's struggling with a thought, then adds, "Yous say yous gettin' 'long 'bout goin' dat far, after dat, us goin ta keep on trackin.'"

Kumi is struck dumb for a moment as he processes what Tom is telling him. Looking about to see who may be overhearing their conversation, Kumi musters up a cautious reply.

"Yous sayin' yous planin' a 'scapin'?

"Dat wha' us sayin.' Us gwainter Canadee where da niggers is free," replies Tom in a nearly inaudible voice.

The very marrow in Kumi's bones shivers at the prospect of freedom being spoken by such a man as Tom.

"Us ready ta 'scape wid yous effin yous hab us," declares Kumi in an excited voice.

Tom is nearly as excited about the prospect as Kumi has become. Still attempting to hold the excitement in his voice down, Tom remains forthright.

"Wunt hab it no way den yous refugeen 'long wid us," declares Tom.

Kumi's soul leaps within him. Being that Tom is twice Kumi's age, he's come to look upon him as a mentor. But pulsing just beneath his heart and soul is a loud voice insisting, "I will be a free man or die tryin.'"

Kumi once again takes a pause. It's as though he's having a second thought. His mind is going to a place he has come to commit a lot of himself into over the past year. It's a nascent sense of obligation to Abina—and her child.

"Us 'gree ta 'scape effen we take Abina an de chil 'long."

The look on Tom's face says this is not what he had in mind.

"Us gots ta min' on dis fo' 'while," says Tom hesitantly. With that said, they both return to finish their afternoon obligations.

The kind of people who engage in escape activity are generally people who kneejerk and runaway after an altercation with their owner, or those who plan and try and reduce the chance of encountering the "pattyrollers," slave patrols looking for escaped slaves. Those who are successful are generally those who are able to reduce their chances of being caught. This demands a good mix of preparation along with an intelligence that recognizes the value of motivation, patience, courage, resolve, nerve, impudence, confidence, all bunched in with a bit of lucky naivete that refuses to overthink a decision.

Not able to add one more minute to the day, it ends as it does for all people—slave or free—with the need for rest. Kumi, unable to shut his mind off, has arrived back in his quarters. He finds Abina busy with her effort to put together a meal. He can't help but look at her without recalling all the struggles they have encountered together over the past year. There is something very powerful in the recognition of this unified effort. To leave without her is out of the question. He is usually more animated around their regrouping but tonight he is uncommonly quiet. The conversation he and Tom had cut short earlier in the day is still banging unresolved against the sides of his mind. Other than the noises babies produce when content and the occasional clang of one of Abina's cooking utensils, there is no other sounds—even the shack has quietly settled for the day with only a flickering glow coming from an oil lamp. Abina, with one eye on her duties and the other on Kumi, notices his unusual behavior. When there is just the two of them, still preferring to speak in their native tongue, Abina prepares to confront him. But before she can open her mouth, she is interrupted by a soft knock at the door. Not certain what it can mean, both their heads snap in the direction of the interrupter. Reverting to English, Kumi in turn offers a challenge.

"Who der?"

"Jes ole Tom," is the return answer.

Tom turning out like this resurges a hopeful encouragement in Kumi that he bears good news. Kumi is immediately up on his feet, racing to the door, and swinging it open with the excitement of one who has the delight of freedom dancing in his mind, body, and soul, he meets the hard stare of Tom. It's as

236

though they had just finished the conversation that had come about at noon and Tom is bringing it back in his first sentence.

"Us gwinter tell de truth. It ain't gwinter be no place fer de woman an de chil.' If dem pattyrollers runs up on us, it hunert-fitty lashes."

By now, Abina is finding herself drawn to the conversation.

With one hand is on her hip and the other with a wooden spoon directly in his face, Abina says, "Wha' kine talk you makin' Marssa Tom 'bout a woman with a chil'?"

"Us talkin' 'bout 'scapin. It ain't no place fer a woman dat totin' a chil," says Tom with a tone of authority.

Abina is moving a step closer to Tom, still wagging her spoon directly under his nose.

"You don' know nothin 'bout what a woman wid a chil' can do when she haf to. Us sees woman wid chilin chain up bein' driven like dey a herd ah horses by slave drivers 'cross Africa. Den us sees de same woman and de chilin in de belly ob a ship fo weeks."

Tom is stunned by Abina's forceful defense. Kumi is taken aback by Abina's outspokenness. In all the time he has spent with her, he has never seen her display a face such as this.

This stops the conversation until the two men can digest what has just happened. Kumi is definitely leaning toward backing up Abina's diatribe, while Tom is wondering if he can make a defining argument against her inclusion while keeping her quiet enough not to alert the entire countryside.

Within an hour of discussion, both Tom and Kumi realize they are outnumbered and Abina and her child will be part of the escape. The next step is to arrange how this is to come about. Tom takes charge from this point to lay out his strategy.

Facing Abina directly, Tom spells out a major problem. "Ain't no problem ta gets a pass fo ole Tom an Kumi but us needs do sumpin 'bout yous. De Colonel ain't gwinter make no pass out fo no nigger woman an' a chil leavin de plantation wid us."

Abina listens to this concern with little worry. Mammy Ceceilia has given her special freedom since she has had her son, allowing her to take time off when he has shown sickness.

"Us gwinter ax de woman next door, who work wid me at de Big House to get word 'round ta Mammy Ceceilia dat my chil' gots de fever. Den us ready fo refugeen."

Tom listens with a wary ear. He had a wife years back but she died in childbirth along with his only child. He has had little to do with the what he refers to as "woman fussin" since and prefers it that way. Realizing his freedom has become his obsession, and he needs Kumi's help in his ruse to carry the load of logs to the mill, he reluctantly is willing to put up with the inevitable that Abina and the child must be worked into the strategy.

Within the hour they have discussed the finer details of the ploy to place Abina and the child inside a large wooden toolbox behind the wagon seat. All that's left now is to get a few hours of sleep if possible and be ready to meet the challenges of a new day.

The morning begins as normal with Tom's horn announcing reveille. On the surface, everything remains routine. As is customary, Tom gets the men to the fields. From here a new overseer is prepared to supervise the work crews. This allows Tom to cut short his need to see the men start their morning tasks and begin his own task that hopefully initiates a new chapter in his life. The

Colonel has given Tom the assignment to prepare a wagon load of logs to haul to the mill some eighteen miles away along with a pass stating that he and Kumi have permission to be on the road. Everything is readied—Abina and the child are placed in the toolbox, with just enough logs covering their hideout to discourage any thought to unload them. Tom is still uneasy with having a child aboard whose disposition is to cry at inopportune times. Abina feels the tension she is under but is certain she can keep her baby fed enough to keep him quiet for this leg of the journey.

She has lined the bottom of the box with what meager belongings she has—an extra dress and a blanket. Over the period of Tom's life, he has managed to save two hundred dollars with which he had hoped to buy his freedom. Concerning Kumi and Abina, they have nearly five dollars between them. This money came by way of Abina practicing some African medicine her mother had handed down to her and Kumi having sold various vegetables he had grown. They clearly have less than adequate funds to make such a bold journey and are going to have to rely on Tom's generosity as well as the benevolent kindness of strangers.

With this appearing to be nothing more than just another occurrence among many others that are playing out on the plantation at the same time, the journey has begun—hardly noticed and without incident.

Confined to a tight space in the dark and unable to roll over, Abina recalls the last time she had experienced this kind of restrictive movement—it was in the dungeons of Elmina and then again on the ship. This time is different. These previous incidents ushered in the beginning of her slavery where today could be the beginning of her liberation. What she is presently holding close to her bosom ten months after having several sexual encounters with the Dutch governor at Elmina, is a child that at a whim could be taken from her at any moment. Although this boy is born in slavery, her hope is he will grow up free.

His name is Rife—a name picked by Abina to correlate with what she considers to be his Dutch heritage.

Tom and Kumi are well on their way when seemingly out of nowhere a patrol of white men on horseback pull alongside.

"What you niggers up to?" is the question of a fortyish, red faced, heavyset man riding a small mount that one can only pity. Since Tom is driving the team and without waiting for an answer, he immediately directs another question at Tom, "Where you passes, boy?"

"Righ' here, suh, yessuh, us gots 'em righ' here," says Tom sweeping the papers across the gulf separating them.

While the heavyset man reads over the passes a scrawny man in a long trench coat examines the load. Tapping on an exposed end of the toolbox as though listening for a sound to return, he asks Tom,

"What you got in 'at toolbox, nigger? Don' lie ta me, you got any niggers in 'at box?"

"No suh, us ain't gots nothin' but tools in dah box," declares Tom with the conviction of a choir boy.

The man is watching and listening intently to how Tom is reacting. With the quickness of a serpent, he turns his attention to Kumi.

"How 'bout you, nigger; got any niggers hidin' in the box?"

Realizing the man is addressing him, Kumi begins to speak in Ghanaian.

"Dis boy jes come off de boat. He ain't lernt no 'glish yet," says Tom quickly catching Kumi's ploy.

240

Still looking hard on Kumi, the man bites down hard on the stub of cigar he's chewing on. An unexpected smile appears. Speaking to Tom, he says, "So, you got yerself, yer own personal nigger here." Without waiting for an answer, the man slaps his thigh. "If that don' beat all, a nigger got himself a nigger."

By this time the man reviewing the passes is seemingly content with what it clarifies. Handing the papers back to Tom without a word, he turns his horse and with a head gesture, he signals to the others that they are finished with this and they head out for further patrolling.

Just as this patrol is out of range a muffled baby screech erupts from the box. Tom takes no time to deliberate on what disaster this would have caused seconds before, instead, he considers this to be an incident—though close—that didn't happen. With no time to dwell on the consequences had they been discovered; Tom snaps the reins across the horse's buttocks causing the wagon to jerk forward. Once again, they are on their way.

Chapter 35

Quaker Friends

The original plan was to deliver the logs to the mill, then make their way to the Quaker residence, but with the unpredictable nature of the baby, Tom has decided it would be safer to hide Abina along with the baby in the woods before they get to the mill. He and Kumi will then proceed alone to finish their business. Afterward, they will return to retrieve her and the child. Abina is not happy in the least with this alteration but is happy to be out of the toolbox and, after assuring her it will be safer, she relents.

Tom and Kumi make their way to the mill. A man by the name of Byron Keeting has run this mill for years and has done business with Tom many times. The routine follows the same procedure with a cash payment placed in a strongbox with a wax seal and given to Tom to deliver to The Colonel.

"De Colonel puts trusts in ole Tom to git de money fo de logs, den us brings it back. Us been doin' it atter way fo' years. But dis time ole Tom gwinter keep 'at cash fo' de refugeen."

With the logs delivered and the payment secured in the strongbox, Tom and Kumi retrace their steps to where they left Abina. She is relieved to see them appear without incident. After a short discussion it's agreed to abandon the wagon and proceed on foot. It's only a few miles as the crow flies. After releasing the horses, they abandon the "big road" not wanting to risk another confrontation with the pattyrollers and take to the forests and the fields. Both Tom and Kumi

242

have done enough work in the forest to feel a sense of unity with it. More for the protection of her child, Abina also feels more comfortable off the big road where their chances of detection are optimal.

Within an hour, the Quaker settlement is in sight. It's a group of log buildings with what appears to be a good-sized meeting house made of unpainted clapboards. Although Tom assures the duo that this is the right settlement, they remain hesitant. There remains a systemic fear of white people—even those whose intentions appear to be righteous.

"Marsa Tom, yous been 'round de white folk a heap more den us. Yous sho' dey no' gwinter turn us obber to de pattyrollers?" asks Kumi in all seriousness.

"Iffen dat was on my mind, us wouldn't brung yous dis way," retorts Tom with an assuring tone.

Abina has her own opinion and isn't hesitant to share it. "Dem white folks, deys be angels one day an' debbils de nex.' Us don' trus' none ob 'em. Us jes gwinter stay back here stayin' ready fo' de scatterment."

Being inclined to dismiss Abina's disagreements, Tom begins his lone trip across the field, leaving Abina to bicker to herself. Kumi and Abina remain content to remain hidden in the brush, as they watch Tom boldly walk across the opening right up to the front door of a log house. Soon, they watch a white man open the door and shake Tom's hand. Tom quickly disappears inside the house. Not wishing to be caught napping, Abina, with one eye on her baby and the other on any troubling circumstances takes advantage of the break to nurse Rife. Not long after, Tom reappears signaling them to move forward to the house. Still hesitant, with cautious eyes diverting in every direction watching for some suspicious development, not completely satisfied with the choices left them, they make the decision and make their way at a full tilt to the awaiting open door. Once there, they are met by a kindly appearing white couple. The man is very pleasant looking and his wife, being what is referred to as "pleasingly plump," compliments their genteel impression. The man's name is Jacob Hirschman and his wife's name is Anita. They are Quakers and secret members of an abolitionist group.

After the four of his newly acquired guests are safely in the house, Jacob continues a cautious vigilance by apprehensively going from window to window. In doing so, he hopes to ensure that all remains undisturbed. It's become widely known that Quakers will come under close scrutiny of the slave patrols if they are suspected of any abolitionist activity. It's been Jacob's experience that one can never assume safety no matter how safe things appear to be.

Relatively satisfied with their security for the moment, he moves to his next undertaking. Pulling the two men aside, Jacob begins to give them an overview of the situation.

"From what thou have informed me of, Mister Tom, thou art about to be in a heap of trouble (Quakers have maintained the lower class use of thee and thou as a way of not showing superiority to anyone)."

Tom is listening intently with absolute confidence that this benefactor is trustworthy. Kumi is also listening but remains cautious. Everyone is paying attention as Hirschman continues.

"We are in a bind. Thee must agree to move very quickly. Those who wish to keep thee as slaves will have the pattyrollers with their hounds hunting thee down before sundown. Hiding by day and running at night will be thy life 'till thou reach Canada where thou will be free."

Meanwhile, Mrs. Hirschman is busy arranging some fresh water, bean soup, and pig's feet for her guest's present needs. Her infectious smile renders the common language of all humans. It gives the three refugees a breath of ease. When this task is finished, she rushes off to another outbuilding leaving them to renourish themselves. In just a few minutes she returns carrying a bundle of clothing.

"It's necessary that thee get out of thy slave clothes and dress properly, so thee don't stand out as runaway slaves," she says all the while busying herself with sorting through them for the size for each. Abina is watching with more than a little interest. She has her eye trained on a dark shear cotton with straight sleeves and hooks from waist to neck, the likes of which she could only hope to have. It is far removed from her colorful African attire and way beyond her slave wear. Nonetheless, she has seen proper ladies wear this style, and though it is plain by design, it has something noble about it that draws her to it. Despite the difficulty this style with its button hooks presents in nursing her child, she is willing to pay the price. Along with this dress is a simple bonnet of the same color and material. Never in her life has she felt as refined as she does in this simple Quaker attire.

Kumi is also being outfitted in a pair of cotton trousers and a farmer style sack coat along with a button-down shirt and boots. The purpose of this is to make them appear as free despite being legal slaves.

Hirschman has one more deception to help cover them in the event they should be overtaken by pattyrollers. He is presenting them with forged documents with fake names declaring them as free persons of color.

Looking at Tom, he presents the document, declaring, "Thy new name is Henry Rogers. Thee are from the state of Michigan and are visiting in Georgia. These are thy papers to prove thy status as a free man of color."

Turning his attention to Kumi and Abina, he also has documents that declare them as free persons with the names of Edward and Maude Phelps.

245

"Tonight, thee will be met here to begin thy trek to freedom by a guide who is sympathetic to our cause. He will take you to the nearest waterway to travel by the cloak of darkness and to avoid the traffic on the big roads."

The three slaves have never had this much attention shown to them by white people whose mission is to treat them as equals. Reviewing their experience with white people involved with their lives, it has been to ensure their enslavement. This change in attitude can't help but make them feel suspicious.

Tom has had a lifetime of enslavement by this same ethnic majority that is now volunteering to risk their own freedom to lead him to freedom. He has what could be considered by most slaves as a naïve trust in people he knows very little of.

Kumi, on the other hand, has lived his formative years as a free man. His dignity still lies within the truth that he is unjustly enslaved. He considers it the duty of other free men to champion his cause regardless of color. Thus, he feels confident the right thing will be done by these white people.

Abina is more frightened than her male counterparts. This is due more to her fear for her child and the anxiety caused by actions outside her control. She also has spent her formative years as a privileged female in a culture that awards women of her stature benefits not given to everyone. In that old culture, her anxious moments were few. Understanding that kind of privilege is in her past, never to be found in this American culture, she nonetheless yearns to regain the dignity once again that came with that tradition.

Thus far, everything has seemingly been forthright. Without conditions, they have placed themselves in the hands of these white benefactors. Considering they have don't have a surplus of options at this point, they remain guarded. None of the three have ever experienced this kind of humane treatment from a single white person. At best, the respect that's been laid upon to them by most white people has been condescending. It celebrates how

246

they've been good slaves and good niggers to their white superiors. Because of Tom's lifelong conditioning, he is more inclined to consider this as proper conduct. His only complaint has been The Colonel's reluctance to accept his payment for his freedom. He's held a resentment for a long time and has finally decided to act on it rather than fume over it for his remaining years.

On the other hand, Kumi and Abina were born free and this slave development came on them much more violently than with Tom. Neither of them has been able to understand the position many white people have who view them as less than human and are inclined to treat them badly.

What is becoming more important than all their past individual offenses is their common need to join together and make a success of their future. Presently, what had been unseen is now in full view. It's in the form of a wagon that has appeared from the shadows with a white Quaker driver whose objective is to aid with his very life the bid for freedom these black African slaves yearn for.

Kumi, Abina, and Tom are in foreign waters. From this point on, they are to depend on the expertise of others who hold their interests as vitally as they do their own—and in some cases more so. To say they have no fear is not a proper assessment, but to say they are willing to fight their fear by not giving it any more of their lives is to create courage. At this point, there is not a yesterday, not a tomorrow, only the present contained in a passion for freedom.

"Us ain't ever goin' to 'complish dis refugeen if us don' move out," says Tom with a new layer of enthusiasm.

What could easily have been turned into a terrifying experience has been replaced with hope. With the source of their behavior flowing from desire, they feel awash with a new sense of bravery. With this additional layer of white people assisting them, they feel as though the entire universe is helping them.

247

At the same time, there is a sense of unworthiness coming over them as a they review their dependence on white people.

Picking up the small pieces of luggage that hold their meager needs they boldly make their way to the waiting wagon. Once aboard, their bodies are given a rest but their minds are alert to every occurrence. Tom and Kumi are accustomed to relying on the dark of night to conceal many of their previous activities while on the plantation. But they are also alert to what Tom refers to as "conjurin'" that goes on under a cloak darkness.

This kind of thinking is not new to Abina. Rather than seeing the evening darkness as being an unwelcome guest, it is to become a constant companion for the duration of their escape. Above the sounds the wagon and the iron horseshoes produce as they strike a steady cadence, Abina eyes and ears are attentive to the forest's night sounds. In Africa, it's during this time the spirits roam the forests. There is no reason for her to imagine this phenomenon is different here. Despite Abina's extrasensory perception to their presence, she also prefers not to deal with them. On the other hand, a quieting affect comes over her as she recalls how her mother had taught her to pay homage to spirits in hopes of special favors. This remembrance brings with it an enduring sense of contentment, uniting itself with her breathing which, in turn, leads to a stabilizing effect on her body. Abina finds herself in a near meditative state for much of the of the journey. As this new chapter of her life unrolls before her, between breaths, she's finding a new path to herself.

Chapter 36

Subterfuge

With dawn appearing, it's time to find a daytime hiding spot. They have managed to put twenty miles between themselves and the Kilbourn plantation. This time of morning is well into the time frame where they will be missed. Awareness of this fact reminds them that their window of opportunity is narrowing. The Colonel, with certainty, will have alerted the pattyrollers to be on the lookout for the three escapees. The Quaker driver who prefers to remain anonymous other than being referred to as "Friend" is pulling the wagon outside an outbuilding displaying a lit lantern shining out from a dusty window. It is learned this is a signal of a safe house.

Beyond this occurrence and out of the corner of their eye, the three refugees catch a glimpse of another unexpected panorama. This is the furthest from the plantation any of them have been since their arrival, they have no idea where they have found themselves. What they are viewing is the first morning light reflecting itself from a surface of water. It turns out to be a river—but where remains a mystery.

The Quaker driver is met by another man coming from the building. With a guarded voice, this stranger greets the driver and with another gesture directs the man's attention to his cargo of humans.

250

"Thee needs to hurry inside before daylight. This road gets used by early rising fishermen and slave patrols. If we are discovered, the slave patrollers will have thee and me hung together."

Without a word, the three refugees scamper off the wagon and into the barn. They are quickly led to an inner room where there is a stove that's been moved to the side, which reveals that under it is a trap door. Once opened, it reveals a ladder leading to an underground chamber equipped with an oil lamp, a few blankets, and benches surrounding the walls. Reluctantly looking through the opening into the cavern below, the three are simultaneously struck with the same misgiving.

"Us knows yous a 'ligious man but wha' kin' trickery yous playin' on us wantin' us go down dis hole?" says Tom to the stranger.

"Believe me when I say we wish thee no harm. The slave patrollers are aware of runaway slaves making their way north and are in the habit of patrolling these back roads from time to time. They often stop under the guise of needing a drink of water and will ask questions hoping to find information on our activities. It's best thou are not visible."

This explanation provides the ease the three need. Just as they are about to make their way to the bunker, little Rife lets out one of his disgruntled screams. It's obvious there is something he's not happy with. This brings a high alert to their benefactor. In turn, he stops them from entering, taking a few steps toward a closed door, he opens it even as he calls out, "Rose, can thee come in for a moment?" Entering the room is a young wife carrying a baby. "Bernie, did I hear thee call for me?"

Pointing to Abina, Bernie declares in an authoritative voice, "Yes. Rose, we need thee to care for this child."

Abina is looking on this turn of events with an objecting eye. She has seen this happen in the past where slave mothers have been separated from their children. Considering this prospect brings with it an anxiety she has not had to deal with until this moment.

"Missus, please don' take my chil.' Us can keep 'im still."

Rose understands the ensuing terror appearing in Abina's face—it gives her pause. She has a baby of her own and can't fathom anyone taking her child. She takes a pause long enough to consider her resulting course of action.

"I have no intentions to take thy child from thee but for the moment if the slave patrol comes as they usually do, there is a chance they will hear thy child's cry and discover thy hide-a-way. They know that I have a child and if thine cries, it will be thought of as mine and not become a concern and I can nurse him as he needs."

Abina listens intently for any deception in Rose's voice. Finding none, she removes her feeding breast from little Rife and reluctantly hands him to her.

Together, the three refugees begin their daylong concealment. Each is left to themselves as they adjust to the dimness of the small oil lamp. The fatigue of the previous twenty-four hours is catching up to them. Each in their own way contemplates the risk they are taking against a new kind of freedom they have never experienced. Each has become enamored with the concept of freedom without knowing what its framework involves. Regardless, there is something systemic in the word "free" that gives them the courage to set their doubts aside and push through their fears.

Against the odds they have been warned would not be in their favor, they have managed to remain at large longer than even they have imagined was possible. The daylight has soon given way to darkness. The stove has been

252

removed; the trap door is opened to release its weary occupants. Abina is joyfully reunited with little Rife and once again, the refugees find their quest for freedom in the hands of others.

Unbeknownst to any of them, they soon discover that their challenge tonight is a boat ride on the river. Trying his best to make light of a fearful situation, Tom nervously remarks, "Us don' know nothin' 'bout swimmin' 'til a gator 'pels us tah learn." Abina fails to see any humor in Tom's attempt at wit.

"In dat case, if pushin' come to shovin,' you gwinter be da fust man overboard," she rejoins.

What they find waiting for them is a pole driven river boat with one white man and two African men preparing to carry them north. The conveyance is designed with an enclosure centered in such a way to allow cargo to be out of sight. Abina and her child are quickly tucked inside the enclosure leaving Tom and Kumi to aid in poling the conveyance against the current. The white man's name is Reverend Ed Higgins, a barrel-chested man with an intimidating demeanor. Behind this outward appearance is a kindhearted abolitionist Baptist preacher with dozens of successful missions into slave territory. In the event they would be challenged by pattyrollers, his purpose is to portray himself as the typical austere overseer of the Africans on board.

What is soon discovered is these African men are free and are dedicating their lives to freeing other Africans. Considering there is absolutely nothing to protect them, they routinely risk their freedom by coming into slave territories to aid those seeking refuge in the northern free states. As a matter of fact, if either of them was to be caught doing this work, they would also find themselves on the auction block.

The two African men are similar in dedication but physically on opposite ends of the spectrum. One, named Dan, is dark skinned and tall. The other, named Louis, is lighter skinned and short. What becomes apparent is how equally efficient they are at managing the raft. Within minutes they have employed Tom and Kumi, providing them with hickory poles long enough to reach the bottom of the river and still provide them with enough length left to grip and propel the raft forward.

For security reasons, they are prepared to navigate without a lantern. The darkness would be a hinderance for less qualified men, but this experienced group is prepared to employ every glimmer of light the stars provide against the water as their guide.

Tucked away inside the enclosure among gunny sacks of pecans and barrels of sugar, Abina, happy not to be separated from little Rife on this leg of their trip, attempts to prepare the two of them for what the night may bring. Explaining an African woman with a newborn aboard a work boat would prove to be more than difficult; therefore, it's important she remain hidden. In the silence of her abode, Abina can make out only the muffled voices of the men getting to know one another as they work the boat forward. They have worked out an arrangement that at supposing an encounter with pattyrollers, she should expect to listen for a sharp slap on her roof warning her to keep silent. Not certain what she could do to remain hidden upon an inspection, she feels about in the darkened quarters. It's leaving her with options yet to be discovered.

The night wanes on without incident until, at the break of dawn, a mile down river from their destination, appears the faint lantern of a sailing skiff. Aboard are a group of men whose intention suddenly focuses on the darkened pole driven boat coming at them from downstream. It's become obvious they aren't going to ignore the encounter, instead, they drop their sail and slide alongside the darkened boat.

"Ahoy, there! Where be your light?" comes the angry voice from the skiff.

"With the crack of dawn around the corner, I shut 'er off," rejoins Higgins with a boisterous voice matching his intractable persona.

Not finished with this explanation, the voice from the skiff further questions, "What might you behavin' on board?"

"What makes it your concern what I may behavin' on board?" replies Higgins using his most defiant tone.

"Ya ain't got any runaway niggers on board, have ya?" comes back the man with a much more poignant disposition.

"Who in the devil you think you are asking me questions?" returns Higgins.

"We sworn agents of the state regulated tah return rightful property to its citizens," blurts out the man.

By this time the skiff is alongside the pole boat. The skiff crew are exercising their assumed right to search the boat as they lash ropes with a hook to the side of Higgins's craft. Higgins stands with legs apart and both hands on his hips, shouting back, "You'll board this boat over my dead body."

"That can be arranged if you don't step aside," says the man as he produces a pistol aimed directly at Higgins.

Seeing how the odds are not in his favor, Higgins steps aside as the man from the skiff boards his boat while the skiff's remaining crew stand with guns drawn on alert.

Refusing to be intimidated by Higgins's overwhelming stature, the slave patroller makes another demand.

"You got papers on these niggers?"

Higgins rises to his full stature, a full head over his challenger. "These niggers are my property same as this boat is my property, an' yer trespassin.' Now I'm only gonna say it once, you get yer ass back on yer skiff an' quit herrasin' folks 'for I throw yer sorry ass overboard."

As soon as these words leave his lips, Higgins hears the clicking sounds guns make as they're hammers are pulled back.

Not to be intimidated, the man pushes Higgins aside as he makes his way to the enclosure. This action brings a surge of fear through each of the boat's occupants. Having no good options, the Higgins crew stand down to wait for the obvious conclusion. They are able to hear the sounds of the cargo being slid around inside the enclosure, bringing with each sound the inevitable engendering of a black women with a child to the opening. At last, the man makes his exit—alone. Without a word, he makes his way to the skiff, gives the order to cut the boat loose and makes his way on down the river.

The Higgins crew wait until the skiff has disappeared around the bend before they rush to the enclosure. It takes but a minute to discover a wooden lid over a barrel moving its way upward with an ensuing human head and shoulders following suit. It proves to be no other than Abina and little Rife. A spontaneous cheer suddenly fills the enclosure. During this heartfelt joyful relief felt by all, Abina explains how early into the trip she had discovered this empty barrel and decided this would be her ultimate hiding place if needed. Reverend Ed Higgins gladly resumes his desired role as a man of God with a heartfelt prayer of thanks.

"Lord our God, You are mighty in Your works of mercy with which You indulge Your children. It's in these moments of Your loving decisions that our destinies are shaped. We thank and praise You for Your loving kindness. Amen."

With new energy, the crew make the last mile before they sight the solitary lantern indicating a welcome safe haven.

Chapter 37

Arrival

Meanwhile, another safe haven is welcomed in another part of the country. Despite their weakened condition, many of the passengers still able to get to the top deck of the barque New York are seeing land for the first time in well over six weeks. Even though they are yet to touch it, tears of joyful relief flow from nearly every eye. This experience touches every aspect of the human condition—physical, mental, and spiritual. Men, women, and children break out in spontaneous cheers, others begin to sing songs of celebration in their native tongues, still others prefer a thoughtful prayer thanking God for his deliverance. All in all, it's a cacophonic expression of human relief.

Willie and Magdalena are among these on the deck. Magdalena's arms are squeezing Willie's neck so vigorously, he is forced to loosen her grip before he passes out.

"Willie, we are in America! We made it! We made it!"

Now that the reality of surviving the voyage is over, his thoughts swing to a new crisis. In contrast to Magdalena's exuberance, Willie's attention has already shifted gears. His mind—in a whirl—has transported itself to the mainland, "What do we do now, where do we go?"

For a young German man who is trained to have order in his life—this juncture is proving to be disconcerting.

They have been alerted to gather their belongings and prepare to disembark. The port is none other than the much talked about New York harbor. The waterfront is jammed with ships—many of them are Naval vessels. (America has been at war with Great Britain). Their ship has opted to anchor some two-hundred yards from the endless line of wharfs lining the waterfront and portage their cargo of immigrants ashore by "jolly boats." These boats are generally eighteen to thirty feet long and powered by oars. There is only one lashed to the stern on this ship. The Captain has let it be known that after he has been taken to shore, it will be available for those willing to wait their turn. Otherwise, there are boats provided by various young, strong male entrepreneurs willing to carry these refugees to shore for a fee. To get off this ship at this time the quickest way possible is the intention of everyone regardless of price. The negotiations are going on in various languages shouted from the array of boats surrounding the ship. Those who recognize their own native tongue make their arrangements as quickly as possible. These then tend to gather in a line forming to that boat.

With their few belongings in tow, Willie and Magdalena are assisted by a crew member providing a rope ladder hung off the side of the ship to aid their disembarkation. Finding themselves packed in with as many as the jolly boat can find room for, they begin the last leg of their journey to the new world. Willie's eyes as well as Magdalena's are scanning as much of the scene as possible. Suddenly, Willie's attention is focused on a phenomenon he has not seen since leaving Germany. His heart nearly skips a beat.

"Look, Magdalena," he nearly screams pointing to a floating conveyance.

Magdalena's head twists in the direction expecting to see a golden building of note. Instead, there in the harbor is a ship unlike the rest. In the place of a network of masts and yards, there is a smokestack belching coal smoke.

259

Willie could not be more intrigued. This is the most optimistic sight he has had in months. The rest of this short voyage is filled with a promising expectation.

Their German-speaking jolly boat captain provides his passengers with addresses for lodging in the German district. Once again, they are on their own. It isn't but a moment before another young man speaking German approaches them with the offer to carry them by wagon to an address—for a fee of course. Anxious to find lodging in this strange environment, they agree on a price and begin the first leg of their land journey. Even with the pressure to find lodging, Willie cannot get that big steamship out of his mind. It's not long before they reach their destination. Finding themselves standing with bags in hand in front of a sign saying DAS WOHNGEBAUDE EINES INTERNATS ("Boarding House"), they timidly stand for a moment staring at the building. It's far from the sturdy buildings of German cities stationed along cobbled streets. What they are viewing is an unpainted building made of lumbered wood on a dirt carriageway. The only thing compelling about this structure is the aroma of pork and sauerkraut wafting into the street. This is enough to set aside any misgivings as they make their way to a side entrance with the painted words spelling OFFICE across the door's window. Behind a desk is a thin, pipe smoking elderly man with a drooping moustache. He's attentive enough as he asks in German, "What can I do for you?"

With limited funds left over from expenses incurred thus far, they are hardly prepared to rent for a long period. Nonetheless, tired, filthy, and hungry, once they discover meals are included, they reach an agreement. After nearly six weeks in the cramped, filthy hold of a ship, this spartan room with only a bed, a small table, and two chairs may as well be in a palace. Spending their first night in America in a house with good food, a bath, and clean bedding is more than they could have imagined.

Continuing into the next day, they leave their bed only for food, drink, and toilet needs. More refreshed the second day, Willie's mind drifts back to the magnificent ship he had observed in the harbor. His excitement quickens as he recalls its details. Determined to discover its secrets, he gathers himself together to make the trip back to the harbor and see for himself what he could only dream of developing in Germany. He also remembers the ship's name boldly painted on her hull, CLERMONT. To his dismay, the ship is nowhere to be seen. With virtually no skills in speaking English, Willie is getting nowhere in discovering its whereabouts. Finally coming across a man who speaks German, he gets his answer. What he hears is that this ship makes routine trips from the New York harbor to a harbor north named Albany. With a little more investigation, he comes across a German blacksmith. The man is twice his age with a similar background. Having learned his trade in Germany as an indentured apprentice, he immigrated to America years before, sharing many of the same complaints as Willie.

"Here in America, I am free to work without the guild restricting how I do things," reports the tradesman.

More interested in the workings of the Clermont and who produces her parts, Willie presses him for further information. He soon learns that the internal parts of this ship are forged by a forge owned by the Fulton shipping company. With this information, he is able to put together a plan to make himself available to the right people for a job on the Clermont. He is willing to consider any kind of labor to get himself aboard the ship. With this networking mission finished, he is satisfied that he has not left a stone unturned. Soon, returning to the rooming house, he learns that Magdalena is considering working as a teacher in a German Lutheran school. It seems the pastor serving the people who own the rooming house paid them a visit and discovered Magdalena's educational background and immediately offered her a position teaching kindergarten.

Through the course of discussion concerning Willie's and Magdalena's new American experiences throughout their day, they are overwhelmed and excited with the opportunities they are either being made aware of, or, as in Magdalena's case, opportunity offered.

"We are going to have to work on our English, if we are going to share in all this country has to offer," says Willie speaking to himself as well as to Magdalena as a factual matter.

"I'm happy," says Magdalena in agreement. This is the first time in several month's this word has been considered in either of their vocabulary.

Not quite ready to declare he is happy, Willie is willing to admit that, at the very least, "I am hopeful."

They have agreed to stall making a commitment on Magdalena's offer until Willie makes contact with the Fulton shipping people.

"I have a list of the people in the company that I need to see who speak German who can advise me on how to move forward to get a job," says Willie. Magdalena hears the less than optimistic tone in Willie's voice and is nonetheless hopeful things will work out for them.

Remaining confident, Magdalena reminds Willie how she had already informed him months before that America would answer his prayers enabling him to further his work in the steam industry.

"Must I remind you, my dear wife, that as of this day, I'm not working in any industry," says Willie warily.

"Oh, but you will Willie, you will," says Magdalena without a hint of doubt in her prediction.

Deprived of this optimism, Willie's mind drifts back to his days in Germany, where his life had a sense of security and purpose surrounding it. "After all, all that was asked of me was compliance to those God had placed over me. In turn, I was given food, clothing, and lodging. What more could a man ask for?"

After serving as a near slave in his formative years, these warped thoughts come with no effort or no warning. When they arrive, they have an uncanny ability of giving themselves a priority they don't deserve. Like many indentured apprentices, he had built a sense of identity with his condition in life and had surrendered to it.

Morning has once again arrived with its challenges pushing themselves into Willie's itinerary. With the schedule of the Clermont in hand, he knows when she will return to the harbor. Furthermore, he has a list of people who may be able to help him. Nonetheless, he is still less than optimistic toward his chances of fulfilling his dreams.

Making certain he has a lunch; Magdalena kisses him with the certainty things will work out in his favor. He has made his way to the address of one Rudolph Heinig. This man is in charge of placements within the Fulton enterprises. Willie is met with a lobby filled with waiting men hoping to gain an interview. He is soon handed a paper that he is expected to fill out explaining his work abilities. While looking at it a cold chill suddenly comes over him—It's in English! Now the chill has left, and he's beginning to break out in a sweat. Looking forlorn, he is debating on whether to get up and leave or take a chance the person handing out the forms may speak German. Once again, he finds himself struggling against his handicap in not speaking English.

Approaching her desk, his words are nearly inaudible, "Madam, do you speak German?"

"Yes, I do," returns the secretary.

Lifting his paper in hand, Willie, with an embarrassed tone, says, "I can't read English."

263

"Do you speak it," she further asks.

"I can't speak it either," admits Willie with a sinking feeling.

Searching through her stacks of applications, she suddenly announces, "Here is one in German."

Relieved on the one hand but further embarrassed at his failure, Willie politely accepts the substitute application. Making his way back to his seat, he finishes his task in a timely fashion. Once again making his way to her desk, he meekly returns the paper. Smiling, she accepts the copy as a matter of course. She is accustomed to immigrants and their struggles and holds a soft spot in her heart as she remembers her own family's struggles when they first arrived years before.

One by one the men in front of Willie receive their interview. At last, Willie receives his turn. Sufficiently tenderized, he meekly makes his way through the same door he has observed man after man enter and leave. Behind a plain desk of yellow oak sits a balding man. He's a portly gentleman, but not fat, with sleeves rolled up baring strong arms with telltale burn scars that can only come from a forge.

Never looking up from the paper in hand, he automatically motions for Willie to take a seat on the only chair in the room. Soon finishing his overview of Willie's application, he looks directly at him with a blank stare that could be one of fatigue or one of contentment with his duties. Speaking in German, he says, "So, you're a blacksmith. You got any proof of that?"

Reaching inside his coat, Willie produces a folded document.

"Yes sir, I do," he says as he hands the paperwork across the desk.

Heinig unfolds the documents, studying them as he goes.

"Why did you leave Germany?" he asks with the same artless tone that his demeanor demonstrates.

This question catches Willie off guard. Not wanting to enter into the details of his drunken escapade he nervously clears his throat, giving himself the extra moments that he needs to conjure up a suitable explanation.

"I want to further my experience with steam. My guild prohibited my desire to do that, saying it didn't fit the guild's guidelines for a blacksmith. So, my wife and I decided I could further my desires if we came to America."

Heinig listens without comment, still not looking up from his review of Willie's application. At last, looking directly at Willie with the same blank expression. He asks,

"So, you don't speak English?"

Certain this is going to be his Achilles heel; he takes a breath only to sigh. "No sir," says Willie with the hopeless tone of a lost, defeated man, never feeling as lost and as alone as he does this moment.

In his abrupt straightforward manner, Heinig hands the papers back across his desk.

"Until you learn English, I'm willing to put you on the Clermont as a fireman passing coal."

Still not finished, Heinig says, "Report to the Clermont this morning and give them this." Taking a few more minutes, he scribbles some words on a sheet of paper and passes this on to Willie.

Not certain where this places him in his hope of being more in an engineering position, he thanks Heinig and leaves his office to report to the Clermont. He is told to present his paperwork to a man named Hugh Pardee.

Pardee, Willie learns, is the first mate onboard the Clermont. He's wearing a well-worn blue uniform that indicates he is far from being the polished do-nothing officer many in his position would like to portray. Presenting his papers, Willie is led to a part of the ship that has the least engineering thought behind it. What he is facing is a pile of black coal and a man covered in its soot making him nearly as black as the coal itself. It's obvious no one in this community is able or willing to speak German. This places Willie in a position where he must adapt and overcome or give up and return to Germany. Something inside him would like to give up—but he knows Magdalena would never agree. With a sigh, he picks up the shovel he's presented and follows the lead of the other man he's to work with. "At least, I know something about regulating a fire," Willie thinks to himself. The smell of the coal smoke brings with it a sense of comfort he'd longed for. He hasn't realized until now how much he missed working with fire; it takes him back to his early apprenticeship days when he became the master of the forge's soul—the fire.

As the day wears on, Willie nervously attempts to follow orders spoken in a language he doesn't understand. What he has found is he needs the man next to him who understands English to take the lead in an action that the engineer wishes performed.

For today, the ship has remained in port while preparing for tomorrow when they will be bound for Albany with a cargo of passengers and fruit from southern growers wanting to get their produce as far up into the northern regions as possible.

By the end of the shift, Willie is nearly unrecognizable with black coal dust sticking to every inch of exposed skin, not to mention the condition of his clothing. He has done more physical labor on this day than he has since he left Germany. Nearly exhausted to the point of falling asleep, he stumbles his way back to his rooming house. Magdalena meets him with a plate of food she has kept warm for him. Within an hour, he has eaten and, in trying to get the grime

266

out of his pores, he's fallen asleep in the tin bath tub. Magdalen gently wakens him and helps walk his exhausted body into bed. After all, he needs his rest to prepare himself to make it back to the ship by 6:00 AM.

The fatigue that he suffered from the exhausting trip across the Atlantic is totally different from the healthy tiredness he is left with today.

By morning, Willie has a resurgence in both energy and purpose. He is up and prepared to meet his day by 4:00 AM. He discovers that he is not alone. There are also several other men (also new immigrants) ready to report to their waiting employments. Already, Frau Schmiege has breakfast prepared and readied packed lunches for these newcomers. The bigger picture is that this work ethic is good for America, but for the individual, it makes the difference between prosperity or poverty—eating or starving.

To arrive at his work station on time is paramount for Willie. His years of training at Herr Yunk's forge has left an indelible mark within his attitude toward the obligation he owes his master. In Willie's case, it is no longer obligatory by law but has become an integral part of his thinking to reverence his duty to his work.

Even though his work is not considered as anything more than manual labor, Willie is already gaining an understanding how to bank the fire for optimal steam power without wasting fuel. Within a few minutes, he and his English-speaking partner have brought life back into the Clermont and have her prepared to make the northern jaunt to Albany.

This is one of the few times since his arrival in America that he has felt this confident. As simple as it may seem, it's the assurance he needs to survive the day. As simple and lowly as passing coal may be, Willie's beyond enthralled to be playing a part in this innovative technology.

267

Once out of the harbor and into the river, the Clermont announces her departure with a blast from her steam driven horn. The sun is just coming up over the horizon and every craft on the river is visible. Though the Clermont holds a government monopoly for complete dominance of steamship usage within this waterway, nonetheless, commercial sailing sloops are everywhere. It's obvious the shipping industry is meeting the challenge demonstrating waterways to be swift and worthy of improving.

Willie is in the lower level of the ship where the coal fed into the furnace transforms the boiler water into enough steam energy to turn two large paddlewheels. It's the job of the engineer to pay close attention to all the gauges and moving parts that make this ship push forward. Willie's curiosity for all of these wonderful components is hopelessly starving as he tosses another shovel of coal into the open mouth of the furnace. Despite the importance this job holds, he would rather be asking the engineer countless questions concerning every moving part that causes this engine to function.

Chapter 38

Higgins

Twelve-hundred miles to the south is another group of displaced persons. They are a group of black refugees fleeing north in a desperate endeavor to free themselves from the grip of slavery. Despite their fatigue from twelve hours of traveling in the dark, their eyes strain for the promised shelter. Finally, they spot the steady glimmer of a lantern placed in the window by another kindhearted person. Its warm glow bids them come in for refuge. It's a long-deserted wilderness outpost some 800 feet up a small knoll. It's a trapper's cabin left over from this region's frontier days. Now, it's repurposed as a secluded respite building that offers sanctuary to runaway slaves. After examining the compound and recalling the close call they had with the slave patrol on the river, they are skittish about anything that doesn't have a plan "B" offering an escape route. In this location there is a horse trail that is rarely used but still marked as a trail. Dan and Louis have been down this route many times in their slave freeing missions. They have a plan "B" in mind that can easily be orchestrated. In an emergency effort to escape their pursuers, it involves stretching a line across a dark section of the trail that leads from their skiff to their building. The line is placed neck high and will unhorse anyone attempting a charge through it. With these chores finished, they concentrate on getting a fire started in an old open hearth used for cooking and as a source of heat. Soon, they share a meal of corn meal and smoked pork.

After Higgins has retired, the blacks continue their talk. As usual, it focuses on sharing their own personal struggles with being a slave.

269

"Us barely 'members my mama," says Tom, "She was sol' off when us 'bout twelve. What us 'members is how she takes us an kneels down in front de bed an' pray dat de Lawd gwinter get us all free."

At this time in Tom's life these prayers are expectant.

"Us knows dat da prayers sent up to de Lawd fo' freedom been heerd, but now us have tah get up off our knees an' take it fo' uselves."

Men like Tom have already determined that these prayers can only be answered when they stand up and begin the process. The time for meeting in secret to plan an escape is in the past. The meetings held today are operational. What remains the same today as yesterday and continues to drive them on is the great soul hunger for freedom.

"If us gwinter be free, us cain't wait fo' de white folks ta do dis an' dat fo' us. Us gwinter have tah do mos' fo' uselves," says Dan the taller of the two free blacks.

Louis is a cousin to Dan. By nature, he's a quieter and more pensive than his cousin. With a thoughtful expression, Louis articulates, "It been regular in da family tah have a place fo' runaway niggers ta hide an' res' an' gets some food when dey runnin' away from dey mean massa," adds Louis, "Where us come from, dey been operatin' like dis since us been chillen."

With another thought, Dan reiterates something he's been observing, "Dem pattyrollers gettin' real bol' lately. Dey jumpin' out in a swarm everywhere. Us gots tah be on de alert every minute."

Turning to Abina, Dan breaks out in a smile.

"Girl, you done real good hidin' in dat barrel." Breaking out in laughter, he continues, "You sho' snooker dem pattyrollers good."

With a laugh of relief, and gladness, they all join Dan in congratulating Abina on her quick thinking.

As with all of these meetings that blacks share with one another, it would be remiss if the relationship between slave and slave owner didn't arise as a principal topic of conversations. The conversation has gotten around to regarding how slave owners maintain their slaves love them and don't want their freedom. Tom is nearly outspoken in this concern.

"Us knows dey talks up wit dese tings, but dey all lies. ole Massa can talk like dis 'til da cows come in; but one ting's fo' sho'—dey don' dare try us. Jess put da whips in our hands an' we sho you not only us knows how tah whip, but who needs da whippin.' Us say de truff, De Colonel wouldn't be wuff a snuff if us was doin' da whippin.'"

Louis is listening with open ears. "I been free all my life but us knows dat if us had a master dat do whippins, when he lay down at night, he doin it 'cause he all mangled up an' bleedin' from da whippin' us give 'im. Den, when morning come, an de cousins see what he done, dey whip 'im some mo.'"

This image is far from the myth that slaves were faithful to death for their masters.

"Oh, dat ain't tah say dat dey ain't dem niggers dat happy tah jess be gettin' along way tings a goin,' but dey gettin' tah be plenty sparse," admits Tom.

Soon, they are arranging to get the sleep they all need so badly, each finding a place where they can stretch out comfortably. With each person having a varying sleep schedule so as to take a turn as a lookout, the day wears on but not without each hour claiming another hour of freedom for each of these courageous refugees.

271

Suddenly without the slightest warning, the door bursts open. Two men armed with pistols and whips stand in the doorway. They are immediately recognized as two of the slave patrollers that they had encountered earlier that morning. One of the men shouts out in his loudest voice, "We got warrants on all you niggers, so show yourselves and line up outdoors." With that he grabs Dan to his feet while the other grabs Abina who is nursing her baby and shoves her toward the door.

While pushing his weight around, one of the men pointing to the fireplace speaks out again with the confidence of a conqueror, "Just like a bunch of dumb niggers to light a fire an' send out a smoke signal."

Kumi, seeing what is happening is already on his feet looking for an opportunity to reshape the present. Not able to choose his circumstances, he is quickly able to choose how to respond to them. In a flash, he grabs a shovel resting against the wall of the hearth. In another flash, he has scooped up a full shovel full of burning coals, flinging them on both intruders. They scream in horror as the room immediately fills with smoke and the smell of burnt clothing and seared flesh. Seeing the opportunity, Higgins shouts, "Everyone out! Out!" With that said, every person is on their feet on a full run heading toward the open door. The waiting skiff is still a few hundred feet out front as they look back to see the two men recovered enough to mount their horses. Straddled on their saddles, the men turn their steeds in the direction of the fleeing evacuees. With the reflexes of mountain lions, their horses charge forward. Within seconds plan "B" has been executed. Suddenly, two riderless horses overtake the fleeing refugees, run past and out of sight. Looking back, there appears to be two unconscious men laying perfectly still on the ground.

Higgins realizes the temporariness of their condition and doesn't hesitate to speak.

"We gotta take care of these guys before they come to."

272

Not knowing exactly what Higgins means by his choice of words, "take care of them;" lacking a ground plan, each of the others look to one another for an answer. Staring down at two unconscious men with burns and possibly crushed larynxes, Higgins is quick to respond. Realizing that he already has them at a disadvantage and with their horses running off, he shouts, "Dan, get those weapons off 'em an' help me strip 'em down 'for they come to."

Not only does Dan respond but so does everyone else. Short of killing them, all look for the next thing that has to be done to ensure their antagonists are as compromised as they can make them. Tom has pulled down the line that had caught their necks and dismounted them. Along with Louis and Kumi, they come up with a novel idea to place the two naked detainees face-to-face, tie their arms around each other securing them tightly together with their lips pressing against each other's. Realizing the remoteness of the region, and with a little luck, these two will not be accounted for, for days giving the refugees a good head start.

Short of bursting into laughter at the sight of the two hapless men lying on the ground in such a compromising position, they leave them lingering in their agony and quickly return to gather up the baggage which they had left behind in their haste. Still aware that they are a long way from Canada, they hastily make their way back to their waiting skiff.

Chapter 39

Willie's Maiden Voyage

273

The Clermont is a fine-looking steamship. She's 142 feet long, 18 feet wide and capable of employing its nineteen-horse steam engine to push it against a current at five miles an hour. It is capable of overtaking nearly every schooner on the river only to leave them wanting. The 150-mile trip takes a mere thirty-two hours as compared to the forty-eight hours by a wind driven schooner. There had been a time when this ship was jeered at and referred to as "Fulton's Folly," but no longer. It has proven many times over that steam energy is the path leading the future.

Today is Willie's maiden voyage on the Clermont. He has worked a twelve-hour shift, dropping from near exhaustion. He drops into a berth he shares with another fireman who has replaced him for another twelve-hour shift. It's on Willie's shift that the Clermont has finally berthed itself in Albany, a city in upstate New York. There is to be a layover only long enough to unload and reload the ship of its passenger ledger and its commercial cargo and to take on a supply of coal.

Willie takes advantage of this period to get a pass to leave the ship. Wandering around the wharf, he overhears some men speaking in German. He wastes no time in introducing himself. He quickly learns they are part of a group of Palatine Germans and have been here for years and are fairly well versed in English but choose to speak in their mother tongue when among other Germans. Taking advantage of this, Willie questions them about everything and anything he can think of. It's here that he learns of a river connection that leads from this location into the waterways that circle around the Great Lakes. It's also in this conversation that he gathers information about the need for steam engineers on the channels between a Michigan city named Detroit and a Canadian city named Windsor. Although this information is to remain only something to think on until he raises enough money to make such a trip and also possesses a command of the English language. Presently, both of these necessary cogs are missing, but the incentive to bring both to fruition is strong.

Meanwhile, back in New York, Magdalena has taken the German Lutheran school offer to teach kindergarten. Der Pfarrer ("the Pastor") of the Lutheran parish of St. Peter is named Pfarrer Florian Wurtz. He's a kindly man with a superb understanding of human behavior matched with an uncanny sense of humor. He spends much of his time visiting with his parishioners always listening and looking for ways to fill their spiritual nooks and crannies. He's been known to linger longer when a glass of beer is on the table to accompany his tireless pipe smoking.

He's very much aware of Willie's position with the Fulton company and the amount of time he's required to spend on the job. Since he is obliged to pastor a new flock of immigrants each time a boat arrives, he is very much in tune with their feelings of being strangers in the midst of this new world. These feeling are often accompanied by a sense of dismay and loneliness. He especially takes extra pains with these new arrivals, realizing that they are much like a stray pet needing a friendly, reassuring caress.

Pfarrer Wurtz makes a point to visit Magdalena this afternoon. Despite Magdalena's upbeat personality, Pfarrer Wurtz senses Magdalena's hesitant steps around uncertain dangers unknown in the relative safety of her European village. She has just completed her teaching responsibilities. Pfarrer Wurtz, in his caring manner, reminds her that he is here for her and Willie.

"I have big shoulders—I invite you and your husband to lean on them. What God has given me can only remain with me if I share it."

In a strange new way, Magdalena is reassured by Pfarrer Wurtz's unexpected, but nonetheless, welcomed, concern. Since she and Willie have arrived, Magdalena has had mixed feeling regarding her place in the new world. The Old World had its miseries, but they were predictable—as bad as they could be, there was always a sense of community with them—here in this new world, there are many seeming risks that aren't as foreseeable. Even in this small German community, the social patterns are not like in the Old-World villages—in many ways, her old ways are hostile to these crowded neighborhoods. These changes are giving her an uncomfortable pause. Even though this rooming house spontaneously fosters connections with others through common language, bathrooms, and dining spaces, these associations are established through unconventional behaviors. The crowded conditions in her ship's steerage compartment were similarly unconventional but were looked at as being temporary, but now a comparable situation has arisen within a crowded tenement that could prove not to be so temporary.

Despite these concerns, Magdalena hangs on to the certainty of her life with Willie within this new culture. With Willie's job keeping him away overnight, during the past night, she had reached over to the space next to her where he should be resting only to find him missing. The empty bed feels desolate. Even when she was so violently ill on the voyage across the Atlantic, he always rested so close to her, always reassuring her that all would be okay. Now, she finds it disturbing that she is spending a night alone. She feels an overwhelming yearning for his body next to hers. For a moment her thoughts take on spoken words. "Where are you Willie? You belong here with me." The certainty of this American experience she had dreamed of all her life is becoming uncomfortably tenuous. Turning on her side, she pulls Willie's pillow close to her hoping it can give her the comfort she craves. Speaking out loud once again in an attempt to recover her strong enthusiastic vision, she closes her eyes, saying, "Don't be such a little girl, you are a strong woman, go to sleep now, things will be better in the morning. With that settled, Magdalena, still clasping Willie's pillow to her bosom, turns her head back to her own pillow. Soon, she is fast asleep.

This feeling of separation she is undergoing from the land of her birth—and now from Willie—is more thorough than she had presumed. She recalls how hazardous her father supposed the universe to be, and how he would often make the sign of the cross before entering an unknown area. In her homeland, she never experienced fear like she is undergoing at the present. Uncharacteristic of her, Magdalena has found a trust in Pfarrer Wurtz that she never needed with her village clergy. She finds herself confiding things in him as she shamelessly forms the words directly from her thoughts.

"All has changed since we began this trip. I don't know why I was so confident in the beginning, but now it seems we are left alone in a world we know little of—it's as though all else has passed away since we left our village. After our marriage, had we stayed, we would have had some status, but since we have arrived here, now we are all alone."

Pfarrer Wurtz is very attentive as he listens occasionally taking a long draw from his pipe. He says nothing. He has found that many times, if given the opportunity to talk, his flock has the capacity to find their own answers. Content just knowing she has his full attention, Magdalena takes a deep breath, letting it out slowly, she continues,

"I am confident that in holy matrimony where I made Willie my husband and he made me his wife that together we will not change that. This we will hold intact. We will, indeed, make a good life here."

Smiling with a smile of confidence in the words he has just heard, Pfarrer Wurtz taps the ashes from the bowl of his pipe. His thoughts drift to the many broken dreams many of these new arrivals experience. He hears the same expression of anguish over and over from those bemoaning how they can't financially escape the cities and gain that piece of farmland that had eluded them in the Old Country only to find it is still eluding them in the new world. He sees a different kind of strength prevailing in Magdalena that's not readily found in most immigrants. She seems to be capable of finding her place in the universe despite her circumstances.

"I have no doubt that God has given you many gifts. We discover them in many different places, under many different circumstances. Keep aware and you will discover more—even in the darkest places. After such discoveries your gift to God is to use them wisely."

Magdalena feels much better after speaking with Pfarrer Wurtz. With her spirits lifted, she rediscovers the personality with which most people in her life have been acquainted. A smile has replaced the strained demeanor that had, uninvited, crept its way across her countenance.

Willie is also having his own difficulties. While shoveling coal into the fire box, his memories, authentic, true, and real, begin to bring back the only way of life he has known. The majority of his formative years was spent learning to understand that his place in the universe was to be a servant to those powers God had placed over him. This was so ordered to discipline him in such a way that his behavior would please his masters above his own needs and wants. In doing so, he never formed a sense of himself and consequently he became a part of Herr Yunk's forge—body, mind, and spirit—his life, his sweat was mixed with everything in that enterprise. Without a rehearsal, his mind could immediately bring to life every smell, every feel, every sound from that environment. It had given him a sense of belonging. The new world estrangement from this memory is creating feelings, until now, he has never had to deal with.

Willie is suddenly jolted back to the present by a pair of foreign hands jerking the shovel out of his hand. It's the hands of the ship's engineer and he's yelling in a language Willie doesn't comprehend but from the tone, he understands it as a reprimand.

"What in tarnation are you doin'? Yer overheatin' the boiler!"

With his thoughts a thousand of miles away while entertaining a way of life that will be forever in the past, Willie had fed much more coal into this boiler than it

278

was engineered to endure. It doesn't require the reproach of the engineer to make Willie realize his faux pax. He's had enough experience with fire to understand the gravity of his mistake. With the only choice he possesses, Willie returns the obvious scolding with an apology in a language that the engineer doesn't understand.

This failure has shamed him beyond that which his sense of worthiness will grant him. The crisis he feels is a horrid sense of failure, guilt, and remorse overtaking his entire person. It's an odd shock bringing with it a familiar numbness he had regularly endured under Herr Yunk when being reprimanded for a failing. It's at this point he must recall his training to use critical thinking and get back on track.

As with other incidents such as this, it takes a while to process all that it brings with it. For Willie, the obsession to look backwards overtakes him. He finds himself, once again pondering his past life with its ties to his work, the village, his obligations, his duties, even his privileges (scant as they were), connections, and how each had their special unique flavor in giving his life value and meaning. Willie has not replaced the comforting embrace of these previous meanings in his life with the isolating freedoms that America is granting him. For the moment, Willie finds shoveling coal is a good cathartic against dealing with the unquestionable contradictions between the Old World and this new world. Willie's mind drifts back over the past again. He recalls how being endowed with the special skills of the blacksmith trade made him a specialist worthy of honor. All his services were meant to bring salt, tea, and other valuable returns to the Yunk forge—even if at times, they were used to barter for poultry, horses, or other livestock. Life was hard, but ties were deep and predictable. Here in America, ties are shallow and without roots. This makes it even more imperative to hang on dearly to what little bit is left. Willie's thoughts continue to plague him. Grasping convulsively at the familiar supports he's dragged along, the traditional bulwarks of his security slip out from under him. Nothing he has learned as a German is any longer bearing the weight of his needs. "I am made to feel like an outsider. Nothing is predictable. Everything is constantly changing—even the mainsprings of the economy—all with different agendas. I feel like a wanderer and can't help but yearn for the stability I left behind." Willie knows deep inside that by leaving his homeland he has cut himself off from where he was born and knows he will never return. But by reaching into his past, he can still belong—he can still have a connection to something that he can call his homeland. Nonetheless, the discipline he acquired in Herr Yunk's forge is irreplaceable when it comes to seeing each shovel full of coal as working toward the moment that he can fulfill his dream of becoming an innovator in America's steam power world.

One thing he has become aware of is how goods from the Old World make their way to the interior of America by way of the waterways. Commodities are exchanged in intricate trading venues along the water routes. Yet, even under all his adverse conditions, with all of his vulnerabilities still close at hand, Willie nonetheless keeps his eye on how he may apply his knowledge of steam energy to play a bigger role in this growing phenomenon.

Chapter 40

On the River

Another phenomenon is playing itself out in another part of the country. After their close call with the slave patrol, the refugees are back on the river once again. Realizing it will only be a matter of time before they will be back in the sights of another group, they are hellbent on placing as much distance as possible between themselves and any future unseen nemeses.

The darkness, with all of its strange lurking's, has become their ablest ally. Higgins, being genuinely shaken by the white-knuckle, hairbreadth escape, has recovered well enough to carry on with the escape plan. Kumi is also gathering himself together. His thoughts have turned to Abina. For nearly a year, they have become accustomed to being with one another every day. As a result of the disorder of the past few days, they've made the best of not having that routine. Opening the door leading into the skiff's small cabin, he finds Abina nursing her child among the bags of bogus cargo piled in the compartment. The moonlight shining through the open door is the only light provided to distinguish her shape from merely another bag. Looking on her moonlit face, seemingly content with her role as a mother to this light skinned infant, brings with it a type of strength Kumi recalls seeing in his own mother. Sitting down beside Abina with both her arms cradling her nursing son, he places his arm over her shoulders.

Speaking in their native tongue as is their custom when alone, Kumi asks her, "How are you doing?"

She's quiet for a moment as if she either doesn't care to answer or she is gathering her thoughts. Kumi has grown accustomed to her idiosyncrasies and, not to seem impatient, he allows her time to respond. Turning her head toward him as though she were prepared to respond, she stops again and continues to remain speechless. Kumi, still willing to wait but with a growing concern notices the moonlight glistening off a tear on her cheek. Seeing this, he decides to ask another question.

"Abina, are you okay?"

Having gathered up what she needs to respond, she answers,

"I don't know what I am right now. During our sleep time earlier today, I had a dream that I was back in our homeland. The sky was so blue, and the sun so bright that our river glittered like jewels. I saw my mother floating through our village as though she was a spirit. I was shocked and overjoyed at the same time. I could hear my heart beating. At first, I thought she was alone until I saw another spirit come closer and closer finally floating alongside her. The closer she came, I began to realized that it was my grandmother even though she appeared to be much younger.

"My mother looked directly at me, and even though her voice was in a whisper, but then again, it seemed to be carried by the wind, I could clearly hear her words as though she were speaking only to me. I could plainly hear everything she said. There were others who were familiar from our village there also, but they didn't seem to see either my mother or grandmother or to hear my mother's voice. Her face also appeared to be much younger than I remember it. Also, her smile was much warmer. She kept saying the same words over and over, 'Your spirit is free, your spirit is free, your spirit is free.' I was awakened by a sense of peacefulness that I hadn't had since before our captivity—that was until those fools broke in on us!"

282

Kumi has learned that Abina has a special sensitivity to spirits that he neither possesses nor understands. Because this gift often leaves her feeling desolate, it means that she needs the warm, physical touch that he is learning they both need. If they were still in Africa, their culture would have placed Abina under the care of her family—the society's matrilineal lines follow the mother—and she and Rife would be nurtured more by Abina's brothers. Kumi, on the other hand—if he were Rife's father—would be nothing more than a companion to his son. Since they are not in Africa, little of the old culture fits their present condition. Kumi has taken Abina to be his wife as prescribed by The Colonel, but has adhered to the African tradition of not having sexual relations with a pregnant woman so as not to have a puny or stunted prodigy. Wrapping both his arms around her, Kumi draws both Abina and little Rife close to himself. Removed from their old cultural restraints and realizing they have only each other gives them both a way to begin a different life together. Abina responds by snuggling closer. The sound of their heavy breathing and the hickory river poles striking the sides of the skiff as it moves them slowly toward freedom is all they can hear for the moment. In lieu of the lack of turmoil, the excitement as well as peace this occasion has brought with it is enough for now.

Kumi is more aware than he has ever been that he is on the threshold of manhood. This is an amazingly important turn in his life. Understanding that his present position is based on injustice, Kumi has a longing to cast aside the chains of slavery, not only because they chafe his skin, but because it vexes his spirit. Even if this desperate group is successful in reaching Canada, Willie realizes he has only a dim perception of the responsibilities of a free adult man in this strange, new culture. For now, he can only relate to freedom as he experienced it in Ghana. If he were there now, his experience as a maturing adult male would be defined much differently than in this oppressive American culture. For the present, he still has a strong desire to return home to what he remembers to be true about a free life. This thought is good enough for the present to keep his eye fixed on the prize—to be out from under the white master's heel and become free again.

283

The mixture of a constant threat of being caught and returned to the plantation and the feats the group has victoriously lived through has added wings to their heels. Kumi is beginning to realize more wholly the magnificence of his growing position as a free man.

The fact that he's willing to share so much with Abina in itself tells how divorced he's become from the roles young men and women assume in Ghana. Maybe it's because they are like two unlikely people attempting to thrive on a deserted island and discover through their common roots that together they can survive if they set aside upbringings that prevent their supporting each other's needs.

With a significantly heightened consideration for one another established, they continue to converse in their native tongue. Abina is an independent individual in her own right, but since both have undergone the identical degradation of slavery, she is also more readily open to Kumi's attentions than she would have been if both were still in their village. Despite their class difference in the village, their mutual experiences have placed them on a level playing field where they can battle this anathema together.

Since this unprecedented flight has lent little time to assess where they each stand, Kumi asks a direct question, "Abina, how do you explain your experience of free life?"

Abina lets a sizable, unchained laugh flow, before saying,

"When compared to my plantation existence, nothing could be greater. I am no longer under the suspicious eye of an overseer or the leering eye of The Colonel—I never liked the way either of them looked at me. How about you, Kumi?"

"The demands these white men want of us are not unlike the blunt sounds of a lead musket ball hitting its target. In our case, Abina it's our souls

284

they want, these blows are only meant to deaden and destroy us. I've had a difficult time understanding how they could turn their own souls so dark in trying to kill ours."

After a moment of reflection, Kumi continues, "My need to be free gives me the motivation of a speeding gazelle escaping the jaws of a lion. I was always watching for bright rays of light through the cracks and ridges of their cruelty like I used to in the jungle when the sun would finally make its way through the trees—seeing those rays of light is called hope."

The night continues undisturbed. By morning, they have tied the skiff off the riverbank in a small channel hidden by overhanging brush. In their view, down the waterway is a cottage. It's a small farmhouse built of logs in a clearing on the edge of the channel, along with what appears to be an outbuilding containing a chicken coop. The crew is anxiously watching for what can only be described as an awkward signal. The lady of this house is described as a kindly, white abolitionist. The slave "telegraph" system has managed to get word to her to expect a cargo of freedom seeking slaves at her door requiring refuge. Although her husband doesn't share her sentiments and has forbidden her to be involved, she has tactfully kept herself enmeshed in the network of support helping escaping slaves move north, to freedom. The purpose of the wait is to keep their eyes on a clothes line. When she hangs out a towel, it indicates that her husband has left for his job at a tannery some miles away and it's safe to come forward. With daylight anxiously creeping through the darkness, the signal can't come soon enough. Through the haze of a dim morning, Ben is the first to notice the woman of the house is at the clothes line. "Us bes' be gittin' 'long now, da lady done hang da towel." With the towel in place and a wary eye, the ragtag group makes their way to the door. Once there, they are greeted by an amiable matronly white woman. Her pleasant disposition is a sharp contrast to the nervous disposition of the Quaker couple that had initially gotten them on their trail to freedom.

285

"Please, come in," she says, holding the door wide open. Her name is Priscilla Logan. She became involved with the abolitionist movement when she was a young woman on her father's plantation. Her closest playmate and companion had been a black slave girl who became more like a sister than just another of her father's chattels. When her father sold her dearest friend and companion, Priscilla was heartbroken. From that time on, she swore to do all she could to remove the scourge of slavery from the country.

The invitation is taken eagerly as, one after the other make their way, until all six of them are inside the building. The cabin is efficiently furnished and suitable to give each person a small space to call their own. It is comprised of two rooms, one is the sleeping room, the other is a kitchen—a living area and an eating area combined with a table made of logs with milled planks used to form the benches. This is not the first time this table has been full. Mrs. Logan has surreptitiously performed these acts of lawless behavior for many years. Her children used to help, but they are grown and have left home. This fact alone, and her husband's disapproval, have not dissuaded her. She is still ready and willing to suffer any and all reproaches that challenge her convictions. They all soon find themselves sharing eggs, dumplings, and boiled chicken.

Her good-natured disposition should never be mistaken for weakness. At one point, a pair of slave patrollers showed up at her cottage with a caged wagon demanding entrance on the suspicion that she was illegally harboring runaway slaves. Instead, she refused them entry and ordered them off her property. When they hesitated, she proceeded to smash a lit oil lantern onto their wagon and watched them fall into a panic as they drive off hysterically with it still ablaze.

Particularly partial to Abina, Mrs. Logan shows her to a room supplied with some fresh water allowing her to clean up. Abina readily accepts this. The men have from time to time dipped themselves in the river. They were never in the least ready to remove their clothing during this impromptu process. As Tom aptly put it, "Us gwinter wash de clos' right 'long wid de body." This did not fit Abina's notion of a bath enough to follow their lead.

Meanwhile, Mrs. Logan is quite drawn to little Rife. She readily conveys the same kind of simple affection to these rescued slave children as if they were her own. Conversation soon settles down as each person is overcome with sleep. With the afternoon waning toward evening, they soon awaken. Anxious to get back on their quest, they bid their charming host goodbye. Before boarding the boat, Higgins leads them in prayer, thanking God for another opportunity to bring their hopes of freedom to fruition. Rising from their knees, they quickly board the skiff and prepare to launch into another night of travel. For men like Higgins, Ben, and Louis, who lead their secret lives in the dark of night, where glory prefers to remain anonymous, this is where their sacrifices are appreciated—it's all the reward they require.

Chapter 41

An Interior Move

With Willie fully recovered, the days change into weeks. He has made several trips with the Clermont—hauling everything from oranges to barrels of herring—all from New York harbor to Albany. From here, freight is transferred to another of Fulton's ships intended to make its way through the river waterways into the Great Lakes to the faraway destination of Detroit.

There is not a part of this ship that Willie has not scrutinized to the last screw and pin. For him, it is no longer an inanimate object; rather, it is a living, pulsating organism throbbing beneath his feet. Its powerful engine is the very heartbeat of America. The sound of each turn of the paddle wheel bears a song of progress. This innovative method of travel has also caught the attention of the business community. It has a steadiness that the sailing schooners lack. "This ship acts like it walks across the water." This is just one of the many satisfied comments being made by previous cynics. The early suspicions surrounding such a mode of travel had expected it to fail miserably. These have been overwhelmingly replaced by good reviews coming from satisfied travelers. The convenient cabin spaces are supplied with a bunk, toilet amenities, a desk, and a chair for undertaking paperwork while traveling. The sight of people lounging about on the deck adds to the impression of luxury. Accordingly, this is quickly becoming the preferred method of travel for the business world. The ship is also supplied with a cook and a galley, which provides meals for the paying travelers as well as the crew. The negative side has to do with the smoke belching from the stack depositing itself as soot wherever it chooses to set

288

down; depending on the inclinations of the wind, it often touches down on passengers' clothing and in the cabins.

It's been barely a month since Willie and Magdalena have arrived in New York. In spite of their attempts to plan, of the many episodes that they have faced since leaving the old world, most have been left to Providence. This evening, their conversation reflects the concerns that seemingly are inside their control. They have shared the evening meal with the rest of the house, as is their usual practice, and have retired to a common sitting room for conversation and fellowship.

On this particular evening, Magdalena is listening with different ears. It isn't the mixture of broken English and various German dialects that is catching her attention; rather it's the despair she is hearing in their conversation.

All along, Magdalena, has held a different view of America than the other Europeans—even more so than Willie. Against those who have viewed America as unstable and lacking the orderly elements of a stable community, she is inclined to see this new land developing. Most of these immigrants are inclined to be older and had been more settled in their villages than Magdalena and Willie. Unlike her, where her father was a successful tradesman in Stralsund, many of these people have come from barely subsistence farms and had lost enough to force them to consider this kind of change in their lives. Unfortunately, they are finding that poverty has followed them into the new world. The farms they dreamed of have been replaced by a daily struggle to find food enough to feed the family. This continues to trap them in their unfortunate circumstances. All but a few, who either had the means before landing in America or had saved enough to buy the land they need, are released from the life the squalid tenement misfortune creates. Magdalena and Willie, on the other hand, are young, and have never owned anything to lose and have everything to gain.

Considering the lingering post feudal system in Europe, these new arrivals are surprised at the lack of concern the American government has for regulating them. This new world's laisse-faire attitude toward their behavior is a condition they have only heard about. In contrast, the European model is to provide protection for the peasants against many of life's hazards. It's the duty of the Bergermeister to provide for many of the peasants' needs, providing they give up their freedom. Consequently, the thought of being out from under the Bergermeisters' insatiable appetite for more of their goods and services has a fascination surrounding it, but in turn, they have no idea what it would be like to experience freedom where they are the primary source of most of their lives' needs. Never having lived entirely free nor having ever had a clear understanding what it means to be free, the result is a culture shock when they hit America's shores. The old saying "Be careful what you wish for" has a stringent attachment to it for those expecting someone would be here to see them settled in.

There are those who yearn for freedom, but those who yearn to be taken care of often outnumber those yearning for freedom. Many of this latter group never get beyond the ghetto of the city where they've arrived. But, for those who have prepared themselves to comprehend what true freedom is allowing them, they take full advantage of the many avenues offered to advance themselves. This is the group that more often moves forward. When sayings like "Do with what you have where you are" and "What would life be like if we had no courage to attempt anything?" are internalized, they bring about life-changing results. America is quickly found by those inclined to move ahead not to stifle talent as is done in much of Europe. With a noninterfering government, much of what had been Europe's raw talent is adding to the wealth of America.

With the conversations still lingering, Willie and Magdalena have returned to their room. Still struggling to use the English they have learned; Magdalena is the first to bring up some of her concerns. Unable to express what she wants to say in English, she reverts to using German.

"Willie, do you realize that we have been here now nearly a month?"

"Yes, I know. It feels as though it were just yesterday that we arrived here. Time is flying by so fast."

"That is what concerns me. Did you hear the conversation at supper tonight?"

Not waiting for Willie to respond, Magdalena continues with the point she is making.

"Some of the immigrants here in this building were discussing how it seems like yesterday they arrived here and it's been two years and they are still here. I'm certain that was not their plan when they got off the boat."

Willie is listening with a puzzled look wondering what point his wife is trying to make.

She continues, "I'm saying we need to look at what plan we have to keep our sights on what we came here to do and not become one of these who lose their vision and get stuck here. We have saved enough money to make a move. What we need to do is to focus our vision on where your dream of making our living in steam is to be."

With barely a second thought, Willie says, "I have to say, I agree." The spirit of Magdalena has always been infectious. Unfortunately, his years of indenture to Herr Yunk has not prepared him to have opinions of his own.

Magdalena has found some fulfillment in what she is doing with the little ones she has in her kindergarten class, but she is aware that because of the financial strain placed on these poverty-stricken immigrants, many of them have had to put their children to work in the textile mills in order to keep the family from starving. In some cases, the entire family is working in order to meet the

291

needs of a bare subsistence. She also realizes that Willie has been disappointed with his job on the Clermont. He has been passed over for a promotion and is left to continue to pass coal. Consequently, she is feeling an urgency that her husband is conveying to pack up and leave for another unknown destiny.

With a questioning expression, Magdalena asks, "Where can we go, Willie?"

Willie is disappointed in the way his work is going but lacks an American mindset to deal with the way his work is functioning. Magdalena possesses the yearning for freedom in many more areas of her life—more so than Willie. Willie, on the other hand, still does not fully understand what freedom is and that it belongs to him. Much as he did in Europe, he grumbles against the system that seems to keep him from utilizing those ideas he has proven to be revolutionary in the development of the new technology in steam power, but his tendency, nonetheless, is to remain true to the company that has employed him in the hopes that they will recognize his additional abilities.

Through the grapevine, he is learning of the areas of the country that are growing faster than others. It's a new concept for him to imagine leaving a job for another. With a tone of hesitancy, Willie expresses a thought.

"I've learned that Detroit is the next place for steam."

He lets out a sigh, "If we stay here, I'll be shoveling coal for the rest of my life. If I don't want to remain a fireman, I'm going to have to move beyond menial labor."

Still hesitant to express his disappointment with the Fulton company, nevertheless, he expresses a novel thought, "I've learned from some German guys at work that the best opportunity will be found in the Great Lakes area."

292

This discussion continues until they come to a common decision to look into what such a move will entail.

"Up river, there is a community of Palatine Germans. I have talked with a number of them. They have a blacksmith shop that I am led to understand needs help. If we can get out of New York, I know it will be a move forward.

Willie's and Magdalena's decision to pack up and move separates them from those still struggling with the question of where they belong. Most still prefer to remain in tight communities of likeminded people. Others, like Willie and Magdalena, who have laid hands on enough money to take the risk to move out of the relative safety of the tenement are distinct.

Taking into consideration Willie's many years of indentured service and despite their mutual decision to make the move, Willie is more inclined to let his insecurities color his outlook. The day of their departure is not an exception. Magdalena has taken special note of his quietness which she knows is really disguised agitation. Confronting him, she asks, "Willie are you going to be okay?"

Not ready to answer, Willie continues to feed his uncertainties. He has quit his job with the Clermont and is feeling beleaguered. When he becomes overwhelmed, he closes down, allowing his thoughts to drift back to Yunk's forge where his existence had a certainty and a purpose. "Why did life have to change? Why is everything so difficult?"

Aware that Willie is not responding, Magdalena repeats her question loud enough to guarantee a response, "Willie, are you okay?"

Her earnestness catches his attention causing his head to jerk in her direction. Aware of his woolgathering, he barks, "I'm okay, I'm okay!"

Not eager to entertain his hesitance with a wordy conversation, she reminds him, "You realize we have to be on board and ready to sail in an hour and we still have to get to the boarding dock."

Without Magdalena in his life, Willie would find himself living in the "I'm gonna do this or that" world, only to eventually discover he's entered the, "I shoulda done this or that" world; he only envisages his dreams. What Magdalena has to offer is the push that shoves the dream into action.

To Willie's credit, despite his lack of confidence in this strange American culture, he has persisted in his attention to details. Whatever elements of "order" that persists in this disorderly system come with likeminded workers in conjunction with Willie. The German way of being organized in this unfamiliar land is either slipshod or nonexistent. There is little to no pride taken by many in the labor force in doing a good job that ultimately contributes to the well-being of the nation. His insistence on everything being ordered before he makes a move ensures that many jobs come to a halt at his station and will forever remain frozen if he remains dissatisfied with other workers' performance. To reassure himself that doing things in his familiar way is the right way, he readily criticizes those workers who approach their work haphazardly. This attitude alone has been a detriment to Willie. This more often creates ill feelings between himself and his fellow workers. Many of them come from different European countries with different work ethics and different languages. The common mindset among many of these immigrants is to view low paying work more as intermittent and transitory; they don't view their job as earthshaking in its importance as Willie views each job being an important part of a whole. In his view, every job is essential for a successful outcome. Rather, at the end of a temporary menial job many of these workers grow weaker and older with little chance of moving out of their rut. They're left with little options other than stifling their rage at their growing impotence. Being hired for a short season, a day here and a day there, many feel that this is not a proper way of life befitting a man's potential, not a dependable way to meet the needs of life. With every ship entering the New York port it guarantees another boatload of unskilled peasant labor. Unfortunately for these new arrivals, the older American industries disdain the foreign worker; consequently, unskilled janitorial jobs are what they are generally assigned, but there are some new innovative industries on the horizon that can sort out the foreign talent they can utilize. Willie is hoping this will be the case when he is able to reach Detroit.

Even though Willie has been a crewman on the Clermont, he isn't entitled to a discount. With the fare beyond his budget, they have booked passage on a sailing schooner. Happy to be getting out of the city, Magdalena has placed her own judgement on these circumstances, saying, "It may move slowly and take longer to reach our destination, but we're still moving forward."

With Magdalena's proficiency, and Willie's penchant for order, they arrive on time to get aboard. Much to their consternation, they discover they have a berth in steerage. Neither of them is prepared for what this experience is bringing back to mind. This is bringing with it ripples of remembrances of their voyage a month earlier. Even though neither of them has had anything less than a difficult life since leaving Europe, this is an unwelcomed condition. Hesitating at the familiar looking ladder prepared to assist them to their quarters, they drop their belongings and continue to stare at one another. Willie is in the same mode of uselessness as he has been with every move they've made since leaving the forge. Once again, he looks to Magdalena for support. Not one to shirk from this kind of mental conflict, she takes a deep breath and says, "Willie, we've done this before and survived—we'll survive again." With that, she picks up a share of their belongings and makes her way to the darkened hole below. Blinking is what Willie does when he is left with decisions he doesn't care to make. Still blinking, not wanting to be left alone, he picks up the remainder of their belongings and follows suit.

The conditions remain crude at best and impart the dank air they remember from their weeks at sea but without rendering the filthy odor of filthy

295

bodies and the unforgettable smell of human waste. There is only one other family sharing the space with them. They are immigrants from Bulgaria. With the little English they speak and the little English Willie and Magdalena speak, they manage to get by.

Chapter 42

An Invasion

So far, Kumi and Abina along with their angels, Ben and Louis, have successfully made their escape into the free state of Ohio. Reverend Higgins, who has unselfishly given himself to the abolitionist cause, has honorably dropped out of the mission since his role in getting them to a free state is complete.

Once over the border into a free state, a feeling of relief and a renewed sense of independence overtakes them. Being emboldened by the assumptions of arriving in a free state, they boldly enter a small village to rest. It's not long before they become aware of a group of white men watching their activity. With a wary eye one of these men interrupts their doings.

"What you up to?" he asks.

Not indicating to which of these new arrivals he's addressing his question, Ben takes it; returning one of his own, "Not much, what you up to?"

Not willing to let the conversation end here, the man makes an additional challenge.

"Where you heading?" he asks.

"North," is Ben's short reply.

"Little late for that kind of travel, isn't it?" questions the man. There is an edge to his question that indicates he has more than a passing interest in their affairs.

"No later den you," Ben returns.

"Your business must be of some importance," declares the stranger.

"It is. Now if you got some 'fair tah be 'tendin, you need be 'tended to it an' stop botherin' folks on da road," states Ben with an air of indignation.

Unnoticed, another of these men has been rifling through a stack of papers. Suddenly his demeanor changes to one of astonishment. Waving a paper in one hand and shouting out to his partner, he announces, "Them's the niggers they lookin' fer. Got their description dead ta rights, right here."

As it turns out, the description couldn't be more accurate, "even tells about the woman havin' a picaninnie with light hair and blue eyes." Furthermore, these men are kidnappers who make their living capturing runaway slaves and returning them for a fee or reselling them for a price.

The stranger has been emboldened by the look of fear coming over the faces of Kumi, Abina, and Tom.

Taking one step forward, the man places his hand on Abina's wrist. With one quick stroke, Kumi strikes the arm of the purposed kidnapper with a wooden staff he's been carrying for just such an occasion. The man lets out a yelp as his arm goes limp to his side; it's obvious it's been broken. The other man rushes forward only to receive a blow to the side of his head from the same deterrent. This causes him to slump in a heap on the ground. Seeing what has just transpired, the other men take to their heels with Kumi hot on their trail. Unable to catch up to them, he finally rejoins the others.

298

This whole affair has drawn enough unwanted attention to reconsider resting here any longer and to move beyond the village for the night. Ben and Louis are acquainted enough with the area to get off the main road and take a trail leading back into the woods.

Tom is unusually quiet. For him to be this removed, Kumi can tell that something noteworthy is on his mind. Using his best efforts at speaking English, Kumi asks him, "Tom, wha' you moanin' 'bout?"

Hearing the abruptness in Kumi's voice catches Tom by surprise. He's reluctant to answer; instead, his remoteness continues. Kumi continues to patiently give Tom the time to work out an explanation. Realizing Kumi is not backing a way, finally with a sigh, Tom agrees to answer. "De Colonel, him ain't never whipped me. Us feelin' po'ly cuz we rund away."

"Us rund away cuz we don' wan' be slaves no mo'—wid or wid out de whippin,'" chimes Kumi. "Good many ob dem niggers gots plenty tah eat, a place tah live, de used tah slavin' an don' wan' leave de plantation, but for us jes bein' a slave is reason nuff tah run off." Looking at Abina, Kumi adds, "Us born free, an us gwinter die free."

Listening intently to the conversation, Louis feels he has to interject a point. "Us been in de business of freein' niggers from all kind plantations; some folks gots mean Marses other gots good Marses; but mos' think dey wan' be free niggers. Problem is dat mos' niggers don' know how tah act free. Dey still act like dey 'holdin' ta der white Marse."

Their conversation is suddenly cut short by a surprise. A mile or so into this back country there's a group of log cabins spread out over a few acres. Ben holds up his hand as a gesture to stop for a moment. With what appears to be a signal, he then gives out a yelp. This has the effect of bringing a man to his doorway holding a rifle. In the dusk of evening the man appears to be a black man. With the man stepping out from under his overhang, it becomes apparent

299

to those in the group unacquainted with the situation that he is indeed of a man color. He and Ben greet each other with an embrace. It soon becomes apparent that this enclave is a group of free negro farmers raising blueberries, strawberries, sweet corn, chestnuts, and soybeans. The farmer's name is Able Strong. Ben and Louis have become acquainted with him as well as a dozen others in the same family as a result of their endeavors as abolitionists. It doesn't take long before the rest of the clan come gathering around to greet the runaways. The grandparents of this family had escaped into this region years ago and they have been friends of all escapees who have made it to their door. This is to be no exception.

Able, along with his wife Nina, welcomes these latest guests into the cabin with nothing short of treating them as celebrities.

"Tain't only here an' der us gets to 'tend to guests sech as yous," says Nina pulling a large smoked ham from a larder. Within an hour they have all had their fill. Next, Able and several others produce several musical instruments. Soon, everyone is clapping, dancing, and singing. There are no song books, but it seems many of the songs are familiar. One went like this.

"My knee bones am achin,'

My body's rackin' with pain,

I 'lieve I'm a chile of God,

An' dis ain't my home,

'Cause heaven's my aim."

Hardly able to grasp the joy they had experienced during the evening with these free colored folks, Kumi and Tom are given lodging in a stable while Abina and the baby are lodged in a small tool shed supplied with a cot and a pitcher of water. The night is suddenly interrupted by the sound of a female screaming. Kumi immediately recognizes it as the Abina. Jumping to his feet, he bolts outdoors in time to see a group of horses riding off with what appears to be a screaming woman in the grips of a male rider. Louis is the next person to make an appearance. "Dem sho' nuff kidnappers. Dey sho' nuff up to no good."

Kumi is beside himself when he discovers little Rife has been left behind without a mother. A sense of the old slave helplessness over takes him. It wants to linger and destroy him as it has countless others.

Able is the next to sound the alarm. He quickly selects one of his grandsons to get on the trail of the interlopers. Explaining his selection, he states, "Dat boy gots da lung of a horse, he run like da win.'" Within a short time, a group of men have mounted up and are prepared to pursue the abductors. Kumi insists he be allowed to accompany the men, but because of his lack of horse skills, he is obliged to wait. Ben and Louis are capable riders and are allowed to saddle up and accompany the posse.

It was assumed that the kidnappers would not be under any pressure to curtail their getaway. Able believes he has an idea where they are heading and takes the lead. It isn't long before the sun is beginning to rise. This allows the pursuers to track the riders much better. Off in the east appears a lone person running back to join the main group. It soon proves to be Able's grandson. The thought has been they would be heading for the Ohio/Kentucky border. This has proved to be true. The boy is reporting that they are camping no more than a mile ahead in a valley between two hills known as Turkey Gulch. It's surrounded by heavy brush and forest. Able knows the area well and is issuing orders for half the group to dismount in a forested area on the north side and surreptitiously make their way on foot to where these culprits are located. He and the rest of the crew will make their way to the south and do the same. The idea is to be in a position to surround the kidnappers. Able, along with Ben

301

and Louis and a few others, soon has the culprits in sight. They have also detected Abina in their midst tethered around her wrists. It's obvious by their lack of caution that these men have little fear of being challenged. Spotting the north side group, Able gives the predetermined war whoop as a signal. Within seconds they descend and surround the group of white men. Seeing they are surrounded and outnumbered, a portly man with a rough appearing beard and disheveled oily hair attempts to take command.

"I don't know what you niggers think you're doing, but you best wise up and get out of here before you get a whippin."

With that said, he uncoils a whip and snaps it as if to fulfill his threat. Just as he does this, another man in his group grabs Abina by the hair, pulling her to her feet with a pistol to her head, all the while saying, "And then I'm gonna blow this nigger wench's brains out along with the lot of you."

As if this man's actions were at once connected to three of Able's men standing behind him, they have him on the ground in a second. The reaction from their brazen actions has resulted the man being overpowered. Realizing they have been caught holding a bad poker hand, the rest of this group begin to run. Able's group of hardy volunteers immediately overtake them and begin to thrash the life out of them. Before the melee is over, two lay on the ground near death, several others are suffering with their bodies being severely battered. Only one of Able's men suffered any kind of wound, and that consisted of a sprained hand resulting from overly pounding on one of these invaders.

A tearful Abina is immediately unbound, and her gratitude is immeasurable. Even amid all the fracas, her motherly instincts can't be restrained as she asks to be taken back to her child.

After running their horses off, leaving these wounded men to fend for themselves as best they're able comes with no effort. Their only interest in is getting Abina out of the clutches of these invaders.

Chapter 43

German Flatts

A few hundred miles to the east on the Mohawk River trail another couple—refugees of a similar but yet different circumstances are also making their way to a destiny of unknown circumstances. Willie and Magdalena have successfully left the City of New York and are in the process of making their way to their final destination, Detroit, Michigan. The majestic appearance of mountains, the lush valleys overflowing with advanced agriculture suddenly take the place of the city's bareness. Even the air has a fresh pine fragrance as a further demonstration of the region's incessant bounty.

Today, they have arrived in the village of German Flatts. Happy to be off the boat, but aware of having no immediate place to lay their heads, Willie leaves Magdalena with their few belongings at the wharf while he makes his way through the village in search of the blacksmith shop. It isn't long before he hears the familiar clang of a hammer striking an iron anvil. It's music to his ears. Until this moment, he hasn't realized how far he'd drifted away from that commonplace, everyday sound. Following the sound around a corner, there is posted a sign above an opening in a barn saying, WEISER FORGE. Willie stands watching as a short man, wearing a leather apron with bare arms and possessing the dexterity of a musical conductor, moves his arms in perfect tempo with his task at hand; tongs gripping red-hot forged steel to the anvil with the left hand and hammer blows from the right hand rendering the red-hot glow to his will. Willie continues to stand mesmerized at the sight. Realizing that this procedure is at a critical juncture and is not to be disturbed, Willie waits until an

304

opportune time to approach the man. Within a few minutes there arises a point where a pause is required. With hat in hand, he takes the opportunity to nervously stammer his way through an introduction. The blacksmith gives Willie a suspicious look—the kind of challenging look an expert gives to one yet unproven. Since Willie spoke to him in German, the smithy returns his reply in the same tongue.

"So, you're telling me you're a blacksmith?" he says. Without hesitancy, he adds, "Let's see what you can do."

He tosses Willie a leather apron similar to the cover he's wearing. Caught off guard by the abrupt gesture, Willie clumsily catches it. The smithy stands with his thick arms folded across his broad chest, staring hard at Willie. Pointing to a tethered horse in a nearby stanchion, he states, "You are going to make a fifteen-centimeter shoe for this horse's rear hoof and you have fifteen minutes to get it done."

Quickly slipping into his apron, Willie takes a moment to look around. He finds the shop arrangement similar to the German guild's way of spacing the work area. Within minutes, he is well into his assignment; the steel is forged, hammered, and bent on the anvil, meticulously listening to his will. With nothing more than a knowing nod, he signals his evaluator where it requires an extra pair of hands. Well within the allotted time, Willie confidently presents his shoe.

With a discerning eye, the smithy quickly examines the finished product. Looking back at Willie with the same deadpan gaze he's had through this entire interview, he says, "I can take you on for a few weeks until I get caught up, but can't promise anything beyond. I'll pay four dollars a week and give you room and board."

Willie hasn't mentioned he also has a wife. Until now, it didn't seem to be pertinent.

"I also have a wife, Mein Herr," says Willie.

"If she can do kitchen work, bring her along," he says, "my wife can always use extra help."

The deal is made. By the time Willie has returned to Magdalena, he finds her shouting epithets at a couple of young boys. It seems a few of the deckhands roaming around the docks felt a woman, seemingly traveling alone, was fair game. "They wanted to know where my husband was and what was in my bags!" she blurts out.

Feeling responsible for leaving her alone and having to undergo such an outrageous debacle, Willie asks, "Did they lay a hand on you?"

"I told them if they touched me or my belongings that I would bite their noses off and gouge their eyes out," pronounces Magdalena with a defiant set to her head and a frightening force to her voice.

Never surprised at the tenacity of his young wife, Willie senses in her the thrill of the fight she had made. It's evident in this case these boys had come across a formidable foe and felt there to be easier prey elsewhere and readily moved on. Nonetheless, he is relieved to have her safe and no longer traumatized. More than once, it has been beyond just convenient that she has taken his side; at times, years back with her father, she had successfully sheltered him when her father had intentions of beating him.

With this situation resolved, he quickly moves on to the good news he's bursting to share. Hardly able to get his words out, he gives Magdalena a blow-by-blow description of his interview with Herr Weiser. And, not to disappoint Magdalena because he was certain it would be on her mind, he informed her, "They are Lutheran." To say the least, she has heard that many of the Germans in this area belong to the "dark Calvinist church" whereas the Lutherans are the people of "sunshine and hope." Happy that she did not have to make acquaintance with Catholics or Calvinists, she is more relaxed. What she soon encounters is a robust family of fiercely independent Americans of German descent who fear God and are highly industrious. Herr Weiser is the son of original German Palatinate immigrants. His wife, also a Palatine German, whose maiden name is Herkimer, is also a first generation American. Together, they had two sons, Paul and John, who lost their lives three years ago in the 1812 war with Britain, and eight daughters and many grandchildren.

Despite both Herr and Frau Weiser being born in America and their families having fought against the French and Indians, then against the British during the American Revolution, then again, a few years ago in 1812, and identify themselves as Americans, they have nevertheless retained German as their first language. This may have more to do with the church stubbornly presenting only German as the appropriate language for worship, thus keeping language as a defining factor in what it means to be a Christian.

This initial meeting is giving Willie a sharp contrast in how these free Germans have developed themselves apart from the servile Germans in the Old Country. Willie has a difficult time viewing himself as a free man apart from his master—or for that matter as a man. These Germans have been free enough to discover their true selves. This genuineness gives Willie and Magdalena the reality that their own young lives are no longer developing in Germany, rather the fire that is growing within them is now in America.

As soon as the living quarters are established and a few domestic questions are attended to, Frau Weiser and Magdalena retire to the kitchen for a cup of tea while Willie, under the tutelage of Herr Weiser, begins his work in the forge. Herr Weiser has a Naval contract he's gotten behind with and is grateful to have a tradesman such as Willie to lend a hand to finish it.

The first week has had no shortages of cultural surprises. The local Indian tribes have discovered the that steel blades make superior skinning knives, and steel headed axes and tomahawks are much preferred over other natural materials. These needs bring them into the forge very often. The cultural trading habits of these indigenous people are not so different than most Europeans have practiced in their villages. Since European peasants are ignorant of hunting, if it hadn't been for the willingness of these natives to barter fresh game for knives and axes and to share their hunting skills with these newcomers, many more would not have survived the period between one harvest and another.

Listening to the English language bartering skill of a half clad, near barbarian wearing skins, fur, and feathers, impresses Willie. In spite of the language barrier, Willie is held nearly spellbound as Herr Weiser barters a steel spear point for a number of fresh fish. Seeing this negotiation, Willie becomes very much aware of his inadequate English language skills and a need for them to compete in this ever-expanding and diverse American economy. It has been a constant worry—and becoming more so—as to how he is going to overcome his inadequacy.

Chapter 44

Ruth

It's been nearly a year since Kumi and Abina have been cut off from a continuous past to an unrelated present. In their home land, the African village presented the universe as it needed be seen—it had been clearly defined with roles and purpose. Now, slavery has transformed the entire world within which they had formerly lived.

With the hopes that slavery is behind them, they struggle daily with new situations, new activities and particularly, new meanings that force them to abandon all their African past as immaterial for their new roles in white America. In the process, in their eyes, they are becoming less worthy to be called humans. There is a continuous sense of degradation that has forced itself upon them. This feeling comes in the quiet of the night when sleep is in flight, "Why had this happened? Why can't I be the man I am?"

Most troubling, the change is not confined to slavery alone. The attitude white Americans have toward free black Africans is problematic. The framework between the two races has narrowed to reveal only distorted fragments of a culture, hardly reminiscent of their function; there is a disconnection with not only skin color but religious traditions, food, marriage traditions, everything.

Tom has been a slave all his life. To say he's ignorant is a fact. To say he's stupid is a misnomer. The purpose of keeping slaves ignorant is because their potential to demand freedom is too great if they are allowed an education.

"Dey knows us gets 'splorin' 'bout who we is, dey gwinter hab some mighty troublins, so dey 'specked on keepin' dey niggers dumbsided," reckons Tom, "Us say it been a hard case all de way."

One of the differences Tom may have with the others, is that the institution of slavery is not questioned as much as how he may have been treated within its parameters.

They are well into Ohio, still traveling on the rivers as much as they can. There is plenty of time to have conversation and it's constantly being taken advantage of.

Kumi has had the potential to be an obstinate slave. He never has bent his head and looks the world straight in the eye. His manly language and determined spirit against slavery has given Kumi the capability to take for granted the true gifts of others. After all, he's been fed, clothed, and sheltered by good-hearted abolitionists on the way to freedom, he should not neglect to say thanks. But he realizes the need to remind himself that freedom requires making one's own way as much as possible. Always remembering how he was not born a slave and how he was by nature as well as nurture a free person, he sees things through different eyes than those who have a generational legacy of slavery. Using his English skills, as awkward as they may seem to those better educated, he states a remarkable insight of his own.

"De Colonel, him don' like if a nigger smarter den he is. Da smarter da nigger, da mo' De Colonel jealous him, an' da mo' he gwinter whip dat smartness out 'im. Us 'member 'im say dat dem Ab'lishonist ain't ta be dealt wid 'cause de trickin' us. Him say dat dey gets us up north, den dey gwinter sell us. Us knowed dat was a lie. Dey ain't nothin' 'bout slavin' dat ain't a lie, but us gots ta be right smart like us pay 'tention."

Louis is much more a free spirit than Ben. After listening to Kumi talking about paying attention, Louis has a quip of his own. "Us niggers don' pay 'tention cuz we to po' ta pay anything." This brings an expected roar of laughter in agreement.

Ben is a different kind of man. His tendency is to deliberate deeper than many. By now the group depends on him to have the last word. Tonight, is not to be an exception. He is fully aware what the responsibilities of freedom demand.

"You niggers gots lots ta learn, dat fo' sho.' Yous cain't let dem yesterday's take up too much ob yo' time. De fact yous had dem slave days ain't gwinter change but yo cain start today to make yo end days change."

To bring his point home, he pauses for a moment; continuing, he says, pointing to the boat's planking, "Yous gots ta learn tah go as straight as dat crack in da flo,' cuz yous cain't be traffickin' in thievin' like yo was still on de plantation, or yo be havin' mo trouble den yo wants. Us know us equal to da white folks, de doin' us mighty wrong, dat fo' sho,' but dat don' mean us goes ta thievin ta get even. Yo on da highroad tah liberty—yo done broke da bonds. From here on yo gwinter get paid fo yo labor. At de same time, yo gots ta be holdin' a vigilance cuz dey is still folks dat be 'nappers willin' ta send yo back for da price of it."

Not to be left out of the conversation, Abina makes her own revelation known, "When I hear some colored folks say dey happy wid bein' a slave, I jes knows dey 'fraid. Dey don' want no mo' 'sponsibility den what dey massar want give over 'em. Us knows what goes on in de house. Us gots tah please not jes De Colonel but all dem white chillen, an' all dem aunts an' uncles an' dem cousins and all dem relations dat white. Ain't nobody happy wid dat—'specially me!"

Since arriving in Ohio—a free state—traveling by day has been the preferred choice. Without warning, the sky darkens, pouring a torrent of rain over the river and making it so dark that it's impossible to travel any further. Along with this phenomenon, the temperature is dropping rapidly, reflecting the nature of the climate in the northern states this time of year. With no chance of reaching their predetermined safe house, they make the decision to get off the river before they have a disaster. With all of them soaked to the skin, except for Abina and little Rife sheltered in the cabin, they make for a collision landing on shore. Unable to avoid oncoming hypothermia, Ben opts to take a risk and approach a farm house in the distance with the hopes of getting assistance. Even though this is the north, a group of black people asking for interaction of any kind with white folks is viewed with a suspicious eye. In this instance they feel their circumstances are dire enough to take the risk.

With nothing but a guess to go on, Ben begins his trek. It's taking him across a swampy area that is turning out to lend insult to injury as he is covered with mud to his knees and nearly frozen. What at first appeared to be a single

311

house is the end house of a small village. The first house refuses to come to the door despite it being apparent from the sounds inside that there is an occupant. The next house found fault with him for bothering them and slammed the door. Not to be daunted and after being turned away at several more homes, Ben comes across an elderly white lady who appears to be living alone. After telling her a snippet of their plight—especially the part about the young mother with a baby—she offers her help. Ben can't get back to the boat quick enough to rescue his crew. After telling them the good news, they make their way through the storm across the swamp. By the time they reach the settlement, each of the crew is covered in mud.

The elderly woman is very receptive to their dilemma. All Ben has revealed is that they are merely traveling to Michigan's Detroit and have been caught in a weather crisis. Once she is able to see firsthand their bone-chilling circumstance, she is hauling out men's clothing and blankets. It turns out, her husband had died three years earlier. She had stored all his clothing in a large trunk and for sentimental reasons has been reluctant to see them being worn by villagers. This is the perfect dispersal opportunity for Mrs. Ruth Eddy. Within an hour they are all in dry clothing and their bodies are no longer shivering wildly. Not willing to leave anything of value in their boat, they have brought their larder of food and are soon cooking a meal of cornmeal and bacon. Ruth is overjoyed at the opportunity to have company and to be feeling useful. She and her husband have never given in to the bullying of the community. Her willingness to take in this ragtag conglomeration is a testament to this. Elsewhere in the village, prying eyes have taken up the spaces behind vacant windows in the hopes of garnering gossip.

The rain has let up and the crew is preparing to resume their quest. What had originally been the hope of enough time to dry out has turned into a day and a night. Ruth Eddy has made a point of introducing herself as Ruth. Despite this protocol relaxation, Abina, Kumi, and Tom have a difficult time not placing "missy" in front of her name. Patiently, Ruth invites them once again to drop the slave talk as they line up to thank her for her unflagging kindness. She accepts this gesture of gratitude genuinely, not as one who is a wolf wearing sheep's clothing—her heart honestly goes out to them and their quest for a new life. Along with her heartfelt concern for their well-being, she embraces each of them with the promise she will enter them in her prayers.

The sun has returned with a fresh presentation of life gleaming down at them from its vast loft. Along with a life-changing experience with a white woman whose heartfelt love for them is marking the beginning of an uplift that has the ability to draw them out of the pit into which they were falling—one of anxiety, doubt, and enumerable fears that avoid a detectable name. They understand, now, how genuine care and concern for each other can have such a powerful impact on their spirit. Unnumbered times, each of them has had their spirits thrown into the pit of despair by the culpability of white people.

Chapter 45

Canada

Everyone in the crew with the exception of Abina is dripping with sweat (her fulltime work is keeping little Rife entertained). The big push is to get to Fort Sandusky, Ohio. This is where the Sandusky River empties into Lake Erie. This also marks the end of the river route for this exhausted crew of refugees. The rest of the journey from here to the Detroit/Windsor area is going to have to be accomplished via a larger launch than the river boat they have resolutely pushed for several weeks.

They are aware, in a limited way, that they are in a free state, which means slaves are not owned; but having the same rights as whites is another matter. It's important they keep their eye to Windsor, Canada, for the time being because when it comes to rights, there is a more even playing field with the British than with the Americans. The Americans often turn a blind eye toward southern plantation people attempting to recover what is perceived to be their property. Canada, on the other hand refuses the plantation owners plea to give up an escaped slave.

This Fort Sandusky port has ships leaving on nearly a weekly basis to trading ports around the Great Lakes. In the past, Ben and Louis have maneuvered this certain impasse for runaway slaves ignorant of the ways of travel. There are ship captains known for their sympathies toward the

314

abolitionist movement and they will willingly make passage for those escaped slaves making their way to freedom. Before saying their goodbyes, Ben takes a share of the remaining money and purchases tickets from an abolitionist captain who assures them that he will do all in his power to get them to Windsor. Ben also gives them a name and an address to seek refuge when they arrive.

Before the day is half over, they are on board a commercial schooner destined to make its way into the fur trading Great Lakes region. This ragtag band of slaves' encounters with water travel are very different. Tom has never experienced traveling on anything other than a small river launch. He is both excited and apprehensive to board a ship as large as a Great Lakes schooner— especially when he can't see the opposite shoreline. For Abina and Kumi, the experience has a different component. Soon, finding themselves in the ship's steerage is like peeling the scab from an old wound. Like many survivors who entered America, they have had their share of physical and emotional trauma caused by death surrounding them and the inescapable threatening behavior of the crew and the captain. They don't need to share words, the very looks on their faces tells it all. It forms like the sudden storm cloud on an otherwise sunny day that they are, once again, facing this daunting experience. With no need for an explanation, rather than stay below, they opt to spend as much time on deck as they can. They both silently confirm that their passion for life exceeds their earlier experience with their passage to America. They both look at the other with the silent agreement to continue to hang on to the same hope that has never abandoned them and to trust in their dreams of being free once again. Life can change very quickly into a positive if it's not hindered. They are training themselves well.

Kumi and Abina are aware that they cannot bring the social patterns of their old village back to life; they realize the impossibility of imposing these social norms on the new world. Everything they are encountering is hostile to their African village ways, whether it be a social pecking order, or religion, or even something as everyday as the foods they eat. The forms their lives are

315

beginning to take are the products of American conditions. They are more and more aware of the here and now of the steps they are taking to achieve their goal because that's all there is.

Another fact they are discovering in this world of new physical realities is that the weather patterns are changing drastically from a warm to a cold. They all remember their masters warning them of the eternal frigid temperatures of the north. It is beginning to look as though it's heading in that direction. Hardly dressed for the frigid air on Lake Erie, they are forced back into the steerage compartment.

Abina struggles to busy herself with little Rife as best she can. Nevertheless, this steerage compartment reintroduces memories that Abina has not confronted in nearly a year—the darkness, the dank smells, the filthy sleeping compartments. Without permission, the tears begin to well up in her eyes as she recalls the horrendous degradation of her earlier passage. Kumi has sensed a change in her the moment they boarded. As he suspects, her demeanor begins to deteriorate. He also is feeling an identical trauma but is more concerned with Abina's reaction than he is worrying about his own. He puts his arm around her and rests her head on his shoulder. There are no words that need to be exchanged. The starkness of this experience brings with it an array of emotions and thoughts. Through it, they are reminded of how much of themselves has been left behind in their village and how much of themselves has been reconditioned by this American experience.

Tom is still on the top deck. This is the first time since his escape that the reality of the experience is making its way into his consciousness. He's standing at the ship's rail looking at the immense body of water surrounding their ship. The ship no longer looks as large and forbidding as it did while in port. He feels the same confinement he imagines he would feel if marooned on an island the size of the ship. Other fears are beginning to plague him as well—

316

fears wearing many faces he's never had to deal with. The reality of the need for food, clothing, and shelter strikes him like nothing else has.

"What ole Tom gwinter do now?" he laments staring off into an abyss of emptiness. Until today, the loss of these basic needs has not been a conscious part of his thinking, as they have all been provided by his master. Now his future well-being belongs to himself. It will be by his own hand that his basic needs will be provided. This is a completely new concept—and a fearful one at that.

But beneath this undercurrent of fear runs the realization that he has come this far and is holding freedom in his own hands. Following this perception, Tom begins to sing,

"Wade in da water

Wade in da water

Wade in da water chilin

God gonna trouble dis water

My Lawd deliver ole Dan'l well

Dan'l well, Dan'l well

Din' my Lawd deliver Dan'l well

Den why not er'y man?"

317

Still humming the tune, Tom's lips respond with an oddly reassuring smile that tells him the tension he's been under. He gives himself a sigh of relief, saying to himself, "De Lawd 'ready gots dis one all reckoned out." With this unexpected gift of consolation, he returns to his steerage quarters prepared to take a nap.

Reluctant to sleep, Abina lays alongside an already sleeping Rife and Kumi. Not until she is stretched out listening to the familiar creaking of the ship does she realize how exhausted she has become. What wakes her six hours later is the hungry protestations of Rife.

Kumi and Tom have already wakened and made their way to the top deck. They are busy watching the crew readjust the sails. Tom realizes there is something poetic about what he is seeing. Grabbing Kumi's arm, he points toward the sails, saying, "You know what us been considerin', Kumi?"

Kumi is surprised at Tom's unseemly exuberance. He responds by gazing in the direction of Tom's outstretched finger unable to see the point of his question.

"What you thinkin', Tom?" is all he can manage to say.

Continuing to gaze, Tom says, "Us been considerin' dat us can't 'termin' which way da wind gwinter blow, but us can 'just da sails ta reach da destination us headed to." It's as if it was hope that had abandoned him and in an instant it flew into his face again.

Kumi feels the force behind Tom's calculation. He gives him a little knowing smile—a little look of wonder. The energy that accompanies a fresh hope flows through them like nothing has before. They are coming to terms with the bond that has been created between them over the past few weeks. It's a bond by which brotherhood is determined; it's built on trust and cooperation.

318

By the middle of the afternoon, their schooner has arrived in the Windsor port. There, anchored in the bay is a ship appearing to be on fire as smoke billows out of what appears to be a short mast situated in its center deck. This phenomenon is like nothing any of them have ever witnessed. Setting this phenomenon aside for now in favor of a more pressing concern, for the first time since their initial escape, Tom, Kumi, and Abina find themselves stranded on a foreign wharf without the aid of anyone other than themselves. Frustrated, Tom grasps the parcel of paper given him by Ben days ago. Unable to read, Tom unfolds and refolds the script hoping that in between folding, some miracle will allow him to understand the meaning of its words. He knows it's an address directing them to a house in a nearby town named Sandwich but that's as far as his understanding will take him. His attitude remains hopeful as he approaches a white man working on the wharf.

"You able ta direct us to dis place?"

The man is friendly enough. After examining the address, he takes the time to direct him block by block and house by house. With the needed information in hand, they quit talking and begin doing as they head off by foot into this strange new community. To say they have no fear would be a falsehood, nonetheless, together they begin their trek with nothing more than hope—hope for a new free life.

The address leads them to a well-built colonial style house, much different than the others in the neighborhood. It is a three-story, built of red brick rather than those nearby clapboard dwellings. It has a rather imposing rounded and bracketed cupula centered on the top of its roof, making it stand out as the most remarkable home in town.

The three of them, looking no better than vagabonds, stand on the road staring at the front of the building. It definitely is an imposing sight. Remembering Ben's instruction to make their way to the rear of the building and

319

wait to be introduced, they follow suit. With hats in hands the three are met by a gracious appearing lady who is unmistakably colored. With the latest in fashion, she is remarkably well-dressed from head to toe. They have never seen anything like this woman. They stand in awe of such a well-dressed servant. Leading them in through a rear entrance, up a flight of stairs through a kitchen and dining area, to a set of large double doors, the lady stands before them, knocking politely before opening. Here they are met by another surprise. It is the figure of a well-dressed man smoking a cigar sitting behind a hand-carved oak desk—he is definitely not white.

"Come in, come in," he insists, all the while arising and leading them to a grouping of leather-bound furniture—the likes of which they have never sat on before.

The lady is making a fuss over Rife and inquiring about his name and age. To say that Abina is not nervous over this unlikely scenario would be an understatement. What is becoming obvious is that these people before them are the gentleman and lady who occupy this house. Never in their wildest dreams could they ever have imagined seeing anything like this anywhere in America.

In the course of the next hour, it's discovered that the odd-looking ship in the harbor appearing to be on fire is a new innovative ship referred to as a steamship, and it is the property of this middle-aged negro man whose name is Garret Steensma along with his stunning wife Harriet. Both are former slaves who have purchased their freedom and made their way to Canada. Steensma, had been enslaved in Massachusetts by a Dutch ship owner named Steensma where he learned the ins and outs of the shipping industry. Through hard work and shipping shrewdness, he was able to buy his own schooner. From here he became interested in the new steam technology and has become the owner of the only ship capable of towing others through the everchanging channels connecting the Great Lakes.

Within this same hour, Tom and Kumi are offered jobs aboard Steensma's steamship, the Sunrise, and housing owned by the company. This is much more than they had ever expected.

Chapter 46

Last Chapter

On the eastern end of the Great Lakes, is another immigrant couple of a different but in many ways with similar circumstances. They are making their way along the river channels that eventually empty into the Great Lakes.

Willie and Magdalena have spent a month in German Flatts with Willie working for wages in a forge making iron pins for the navy which make use these monsters to tether a ship to shore. Now with enough money to continue their journey to Detroit, they are trudging the Niagara trail around the falls with the intention getting back in the river that connects Lake Ontario and Lake Erie. The expectation is that soon they will be in Lake Erie, hopefully on the last leg of their journey. Danger and insecurity have become other words for freedom and opportunity as they faced the physical, mental, and spiritual hostilities along the way. As Germans, they miss the order, the support of a community, the assurance of a ranking. Many of these values and customs had been nearly innate in that they are so ingrained that speaking of them was unnecessary. These are all things that in spite of their simplicity defined the arrangement of life. All have become unrepeatable memories.

One of the advantages of working in German Flatts, despite its name, is that English had been the business language spoken there. In their time there, Willie and Magdalena had been forced to use English and have gotten a good start in grasping a command of the language.

There is an old saying about travel, stating that no matter how slow travel may be, providing it's moving forward, a destination will be reached. This is proving to be true with navigating the Niagara River, which is unnavigable in many places and requires traveling by trail. But as the old saying holds true, thanks to an Indian guide, they soon arrive at the outlet of the Niagara River finding themselves at the trading community of Buffalo, New York.

It isn't long before they have secured passage on a vessel bound for Detroit, Michigan. They find that they are sharing steerage with some very dark-skinned people. These folks seem to be agitated and disconnected. Despite their close steerage quarters, they view Willie and Magdalena with suspicion. On the other hand, Willie and Magdalena come from villages that view all strangers with suspicion; neighborliness, obedience, respect, and status were values only shared with fellow villagers. This behavior became valueless as the crossing reversed all these friendly roles. In turn, each person who wished to have space pushed in and took care of their own needs. This behavior is considered judicious by all involved until proven otherwise.

Perhaps, the most luminous lesson for each of these passengers is that a totally new way of life lay ahead for each of them. What each of these individuals are undergoing is an uprootedness from communities that were predictable—miserable for certain—but predictable. Now they are uprooted, finding themselves in an inexhaustible state of crisis—crisis in the sense that their roots are left to helplessly dangle—praying for a place to settle. It's been weeks and months to have been left to exist day by day, hour by hour in suspense as to what is going to constitute a permanence. Every adjustment to date has been temporary and bears the seeds of maladjustment, for the circumstances that are presently met are found to be strange and ever changing.

After a night of sailing, the vessel finally arrives at its destination. For this ship, the drop-off point for its passengers is on the Canadian side of the river at Windsor. The first vessel that Willie sets his eyes on is a steamship belching smoke from its stack. It has distinct lettering claiming the name

SUNRISE pained across her stern. Willie is hardly able to believe his eyes that the very object that has drawn him to this frontier is sitting before him. He is overjoyed at the opportunity it promises. By midmorning, their vessel is moored and waiting for its cargo to be unloaded. Willie is so overtaken by the possibilities this new part of the world is presenting that he can hardly wait to disembark. His next move is to get a closer examination of this behemoth dominating the harbor. His hopes are soon brought to fruition as he discovers this steamer is the Detroit River's way of connecting Detroit and Windsor. After purchasing tickets, all that's left is to board her and make the last leg to reach their destination. The ship is soon underway to make the short voyage across the river. Once more leaving Magdalena to fend for herself, Willie begins an inspection tour of the ship. What he first notices is how many "Nigerians" are working on the ship. From what he can observe of the engine room, he finds much of it needs updating, especially the lack of automatic pressure gauges. He also notices that his previous coal passing job on the Clermont is being performed by two black men. Another thing he becomes aware of is the lack of an engineer in the boiler room. This causes him some concern as he watches the firemen adding shovel after shovel of coal into the firebox. He also is aware from the glass tube connected to the boiler how dangerously low the water level is above the firebox. If this is left unattended, it will cause a fire and burn the ship. This dilemma is causing Willie great concern—enough concern that he feels he needs to make someone aware of the dangerous situation. Quickly making his way to the wheel house, and mustering up the best English words he can produce, Willie attempts to explain the situation to the wheelman. Not able to make himself clear, the first mate orders him out as if his were the blathering of a common drunk. Because of Willie's predisposition of obeying those in authority in spite of the circumstances, he succumbs. Yet, not able dismiss the danger that he had perceived, he returns to monitor the situation. Still not seeing an engineer to warn, he is visualizing the boiler blowing up and the ship being destroyed along with passengers and crew.

Not able to successfully warn those in charge, something else deep inside him begins to rise to the surface. It's replacing his normal obsequious character with that of a man with a definite purpose. It is the same man who arose months earlier to fend off a vicious bandit. Willie is well aware of what has to be done and his experience is telling what to do, but his lack of confidence is not allowing him to do it—a limit on what his will is telling him needs to be done is putting a limit on what he can do. He suddenly has a picture of Magdalena struggling in the water. Before he realizes how his body is reacting, his mind has already put it into action. In a second he has transported himself into the engine room, pulled the shovels out of the hands of the firemen, released water into the chamber above the firebox, and released a dangerous excess of steam using the hand operated valve. All this activity has left the shocked fireman surprised and motionless. It has also brought the ship's paddles to a halt, leaving the vessel to helplessly drift.

Within seconds, the captain along with the first mate are in the engine room demanding to know who is responsible for the engine failure. The first thing they are aware of is a stranger systematically throwing open the firebox, checking gauges, nearly oblivious to their intrusion. He's finally curtailed by the strong hand of the captain demanding an explanation.

"What the Sam Hill do you think you are doing?" shouts the captain with a firm grip on the back of Willie's jacket.

Willie is having difficulty forming the words in English but manages to blurt out a mix of German and English, "Pressure zu high. No wasser em dem tank. Burn de sheep zu hell!"

Meanwhile, the first mate has located a passed-out drunken engineer. This information is brought to the captain's attention. In the time it takes to reassess the situation, the captain loosens his grip on Willie. He's just beginning to get a sense of what this gatecrasher may have averted.

Facing Willie with a frustrated look, the captain asks the million-dollar question, "How'd you know about all this?"

Quickly reverting back to the obsequious demeanor of an indentured servant, Willie is still not ready to become anything other than servile in answering the captain's question.

"Ich vas engineer in Deutschland?" he says in a meek tone.

The captain remains silent for a moment recalling the incapacitated condition of his drunken engineer. Still staring hard at Willie, he blurts out another question, "Can you get this ship running again?"

Willie is blinking incessantly at the question, but is firm and honest in his answer, "Ya, mein Herr, ve can do zat."

"Then get busy," says the captain as he turns to resume the responsibility of getting an anchor down to keep his craft from drifting aground.

Within twenty minutes, Willie has managed to get the ship back in action.

Not able to find Willie in all the commotion, Magdalena soon becomes aware of Willie's part in creating it. She is not surprised when she learns the details surrounding the incident. She is hearing people thanking God for men like Willie. She has learned not to be surprised at her husband's responses in emergency situations as she also has experienced it.

As a result of this chance meeting and having to work together to get this ship moving again, Willie finds himself working with two black men. Between his lack of ability in using the English language and their creolizing it, he learns their names are Tom and Kumi. The surprising result is that they all are able to communicate well enough to get this boat back underway.

The captain has kept his eye on how this outsider is treating his ship. He's more than impressed with the attention Willie is paying to details. By the time they reach Detroit, the captain has fired his drunken engineer and hired Willie. Willie is absolutely elated over this chance encounter supplying him with the very opportunity that led him to the new world a few months ago.

Within hours of landing in Detroit, Willie and Magdalena have found adequate housing. With full-time employment, Willie leaves Magdalena with the chore of finding likeminded Pomeranian Lutherans to worship with. What she discovers is a group who are holding their Lutheran mass in an Episcopal church on Sunday afternoon. This tolerance toward other Christian denominations in America is unprecedented. This is definitely not something that would have ever occurred in Germany.

Willie is also discovering another tolerance that would never have occurred in the Old Country—a tolerance for those races other than Caucasian. Half of the Sunrise crew are Negro—including the Captain. What Willie is discovering is that, like his situation, these men all had masters at one time, but also like him, they are free men now.

Kumi and Tom have been assigned the job of fireman. As engineer, it is Willie's responsibility to manage their work. The work is intense and, at times nerve racking, but there are times when the ship is idle. These times have become periods where interaction between the crew takes place. These are times not afforded in less-structured atmospheres. It's at times like this that these immigrants, despite their cultural differences, sort out an understanding of their coworkers as free men and in a growing sense as their equals. The workplace attitude toward people of differing religions or races tends to reduce the effect of narrowmindedness by placing an emphasis on seeing each person as a member of mankind rather than through the narrow outlook of belonging to a particular race.

A major insight for Willie has been how much in common he has with these former slaves; his experience as an indentured worker is shared with the experiences of being mere chattel to a master as were these fellow workers. A slave mentality remains in all those who's formative years were developed as chattel—this includes Willie. The only member of this group who holds a different mindset is Kumi. His formative years were developed with a much stronger sense of independence than his counterparts; he is much more inclined to question his superiors than the rest or to act independently with a task. This characteristic displays itself in specific circumstances. Willie being his superior doesn't prevent Kumi from questioning certain procedures.

There is something about Kumi's tenacity that Willie finds appealing as healthy but he can't find a way of incorporating it as a value into his own character. The biblical imperative that slaves should obey their masters is seared into Willie's consciousness as much it is into the minds of those born into slavery. In a conversation that Willie is having with Kumi, he is questioning Kumi's unusual individual outlook toward authority. As a rule, Kumi wastes little time with these conversations, but in this situation, he feels compelled to confront Willie's continual obsession with his needlessly obsequious behavior.

"Da way us sees yo' pro'lem is dat yous don' know yous is free a freeman, an if yous do, yous don' know what tah do wif it, cuz yous actin' like yous still a damn slave."

This observation stuns Willie. He has heard this from Magdalena at times, but this time he is hearing it from one who has also been under the bootheel of another human. Over the next year, through the many trying circumstances that life provides, Willie, as well as Tom, and many others joining their crew who have desired freedom but have been ignorant as to its prescription are learning what it entails—particularly in how to make it on their own.

328

May this story provoke you to question your own concept of freedom and remedy your own lack of understanding and want of the full use of this God-ordained right. Good luck.